THE SORCERERS GLEN

Lucinda Hare

Book One of the Fifth Dimension Chronicles

For Sandra Jensen for being there time & time again

lucinda@dragonsdome.co.uk
http://www.dragonsdome.co.uk/
http://thedragonwhispererdiaries.blogspot.co.uk/

Published by Thistleburr Publishing

The Sorcerers Glen
Thistleburr Publishing, ISBN: 978-0-9574718-2-5

Also by Lucinda Hare

The Dragonsdome Chronicles

The Dragon Whisperer
Flight to Dragon Isle
Dragon Lords Rising
The Stealth Dragon Services

In memory of my beloved soul-mate, blind Smudge
Killed on Christmas Eve 2014

Can I survive now you are gone?
Can I survive the silence of your song?
Can my heart beat while yours is still?
Can my love wait long years until
I am with you again?

So winter turns to spring
and the days are growing long
and still I search the silence
for an echo of your song
and though I yet survive
my world is torn apart
my soul is crushed and broken
as is my beating heart

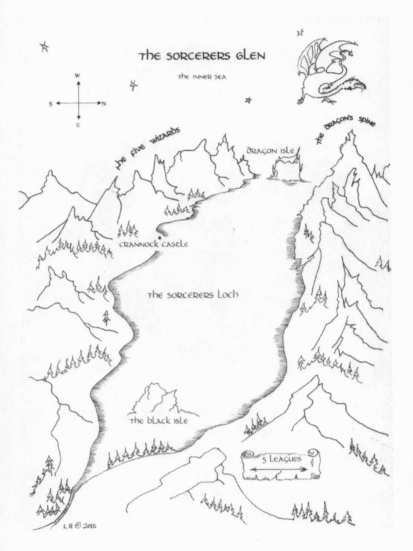

The Fifth Dimension

PROLOGUE: THE LEGEND

In the never ending Books of Creation, deep down in the molten vaults of the Earth, fifteen billion years have passed since our Universe and others like it exploded into being, scattering the cold vacuum of space with countless galaxies, stars and worlds. Fifteen billion years since the Immortals first spoke the eternal words 'Once upon a time...' so beloved in children's stories. And in these ancient volumes where creation fashioned life out of chaos and molten worlds were moulded from meteor strikes, there is a Book of the Living Earth: a Chapter on the emergence of life in the ocean deeps, a section on the dinosaurs as the Triassic, Jurassic and Cretaceous eras came and went, and a paragraph written as the woolly mammoth grazed the plains and the sabre toothed tiger stalked its prey. But mankind? Mankind is merely a footnote so far, and there are those in the Fifth Dimension who believe he should remain so...

But there is a legend. When danger threatens there is always a legend. Generally it involves a magical sword and heroic deeds by the bucket load. A lost heir to the throne and wizards are mandatory. Dragons are an optional extra. Generally.... But times have changed and so must legends, else they be forgotten and vanish like Excalibur and Avalon into the mists of the Fifth Dimension. No, today it is no longer enough to be able to ride a white stallion well. The best you could hope for is Horse of the Year Show. Nor is it enough to have blue blood flowing in your veins. After all, the world is full of deposed monarchs seeking alternative employment.

Today's hero or heroine has a totally new job specification, and danger lurks down different corridors. This is the global age of quantum technology and the world-wide-web, where boundaries of all kinds are irrelevant. A world where money can buy you anything – even a tourist trip to the International Space Station – and where knowledge is power.

Perhaps one thing hasn't changed. The playing field for this contest remains our world, only it is not mere crowns or paltry principalities that are at stake. Today the prize is the Earth itself. Its riches and wealth. But ... there is hope. Contrary to public opinion, Magic is alive and well, and kicking hard if you have the imagination to see it. And Lucy Pemberton most certainly does. So, open your mind to infinite possibilities and picture if you will a storm, somewhere in the Highlands of Scotland. But not just any old storm ...and not just any old night...

All Hallow's Eve. The moon had long since been banished behind churning dark clouds. The night was as black and wet as a hippo's backside. The crack of thunder hammered onto the mountaintops and ricocheted through the glens like a vengeful bullet seeking a victim. In the roiling gloom the percussion pulsed and thundered, overlaid by a rising descant of shrieking wind that whipped the waters of the Sorcerers Loch into a frothing fury. Pounding rain fed the raging torrents of the normally sedate Adder Burn, causing it to burst its banks. In the gloom, few noticed the strange light emanating from the derelict old grange in the Wychs Wood, nor the spectacular lightning strike which seared through the storm, splitting the central stone arch of the Necromancer's Ring into ragged shards, leaving it a smoking ruin.

A nightmare, unleashed by the storm and given free reign, raced across the sky and vanished with the first hint of dawn. Giant hailstones hammered on roofs and windows like the thunder of hooves over the moor; a whisper, and the ghost of a laugh, cold and hard, as the chink of shattering ice faded with the howling wind. Across the burgh of Thistleburr, dogs barked and cats hissed. Children awoke from their sleep, crying and folk started, glancing fearfully upwards and then smiling at their own foolishness. Nightmares were only bad dreams after all, weren't they? They didn't belong in the digital world of the third millennium.

As the dawn unfolded the storm rolled and crashed into the mountains, gathered itself one last time, and reeled drunkenly into the glens below before collapsing, exhausted, in gusts of rain over the sodden moors. In the rapidly fading darkness someone smiled at a task well done.

Far, far away and away, away afar in another world, a young woman lay dying, her pale face glazed with sweat and pain. Shrouded grey eyes looked up to the distraught man standing over her.

'Peace,' she whispered. 'I knew the price and now give it willingly.' She looked at the squalling baby struggling in the midwife's arms. 'Take her,' she was struggling to breathe now. 'And keep her safe ...teach her as you taught

me. *All is not yet lost.'*

'*Lady,*' the midwife nodded her head in assent. '*I shall raise her with my own child. I swear by the One Earth.*'

Death was coming for her now, her life ebbing as relentlessly as a rip-tide in spring. Taking her cold hand in his, the Sorcerer Lord described the cardinal elements of earth, wind, fire and water above her brow, drawing them together into the One Earth, symbol of life, death and rebirth since time itself began.

As her rasping breath grew more ragged, he cradled his daughter's head in his arms and wept.

CHAPTER ONE

A Party Invitation

A fresh breeze was blowing in from the sea. Dawn was but a distant splash on the horizon. The Sorcerers Glen still lay in darkness. A longboat under full sail was cresting the headlands below the Virtual University, heading for the already crowded City harbours of the Black Isle. Down beyond the University jetty where skiffs and boats dipped on the swell, there was the faintest of sounds as the wind hissed over the sand dunes and rustled through the long grass. To the unpractised eye, the old timber quayside appeared deserted.

'My tights are too tight!'

'Too many chicken dinners in jelly, that's what it is,' said a second, deeper voice unhelpfully. 'And full fat milk. You eat too much.'

'No I don't!' protested the first voice without much conviction, its owner squirming uncomfortably. 'It's not my fault if I'm her favourite.'

'Are not!' contested the second voice automatically.

'Am!'

'Not!'

'Am!'

'Not!'

This was a well-rehearsed argument and continued along in the same vein until, predictably, the owner of the second voice threw a temper tantrum and stalked off to sit on a rocky outcrop. Then there was a hot uncomfortable silence while the wind continued to hum through the grass.

'He's late,' muttered the first voice, nervously.

'Sorcerers are always late.'

'Have you heard the rumours?'

'Ignore them. There are always rumours.'

There was a faint stamping, as the owner of the tight tights tried to pull her tights up, interrupted by a rending sound accompanied by a squeal of dismay.

'Well,' said the second voice, gleefully. 'That's torn it, hasn't it?'

Across the breadth and length of the Highland burgh of Thistleburr, eagerly awaited invitations were dropping through letterboxes. Bright red envelopes gaily decorated with pumpkins and pointy hats were grabbed by little hands or over-enthusiastic dogs, and rushed to the adults of the household or the dog basket, depending on who got there first.

Despite the early morning chill, Mr McFeeley, the village postman (and policeman and traffic warden), paused halfway up the hill to catch his breath and mop his brow before peddling precariously on his way. With so many sacks of invitations to deliver, his plump little legs were already working overtime, and having an equally rotund cat named Haggis in the front bicycle basket wasn't helping.

As the sun crested the frosted peaks of the Five Wizards, he took a deep breath of tangy sea air and looked out across the ancient royal burgh. Narrow streets led his eyes downwards from where he stood to the village green, flanked on one side by small shops and guesthouses, and on the other by The Guddlers Arms pub and the Red Letter Box – the village Post Office. He followed the boisterous course of the Adder Burn, wending its way between houses and shops to the Sorcerers Loch, with its brightly painted waterfront hotel and cafés.

There in the harbour, protected by a stone breakwater, fishing boats and small yachts bobbed on the early morning tide. Overturned hulls and lobster creels lay beached on the pebbly shore that wound for miles and miles around the gentle curves of the loch, before reaching the wild Atlantic beyond the distant headlands. To either side, reflected in the mirror-still water, lay the prospect of lush, rolling grassland slopes, dotted with sheep and the autumnal russet of bracken. Beyond, rising gently at first, the scree slopes climbed wild and sheer to the ragged slate crags and the forbidding snow-capped peaks of the Sorcerers Glen. And rising from the loch lay the midge infested Black Isle, one time stronghold of the McFeeley clan.

Turning back to the task in hand, Mr McFeeley momentarily considered evicting the big grey cat and leaving him to find his own way home. But then the idea was instantly doused by a vision of an outraged Mrs McFeeley. A large and kindly woman, the sheer volume of her was rather overwhelming at the best of times. And she doted on 'dahling little pushkins' in just the same way as he doted on his over-bearing wife. The unfamiliar spark of rebellion flared, then fizzled out like a match in a gale.

Mr McFeeley glared at the smug tabby, sighed in defeat, and having completely lost his momentum as well as his breath, started to push the protesting bicycle up the hill.

It was early autumn, and the Pembertons were having a Hallowe'en party!

'The girl nears her fourteenth year. Her *power* must be growing. Do any suspect?'

The slimmer of the two gnomes considered the question, resisting an overwhelming urge to groom. Fortunately his foot could no longer scratch behind his small pointed ears, and he certainly couldn't and wouldn't wish to reach those particular places that only a cat could – at least not in public. The gnome coughed loudly into his grey beard to cover his embarrassment, and looked up at the wizened sorcerer who wore the distinctive hat of the Most Ancient Order of Apothecaries above his scholar's robes.

'Nay, Lord. She has been well guarded ... and well taught. None suspect, and in truth, why should they? To all she is but one of a family of two children from the far south, no different to any other. They are poor, they pass unnoticed.'

The scholar nodded. It was true; the poor were always invisible. They had chosen well.

'And the migraines. Do they also continue?' He rummaged in his satchel amongst brass weights and measures, his breath condensing in the chilly air.

The rotund gnome in the loud clothing and ladder-ripped tights took the pouch from the apothecary's shaking, blue-veined hand, and stowed it carefully in her purse. It smelt of loamy earth and bark.

'Yes, Lord. The pain exhausts herrr,' she purred, pink tongue darting out to lick her lips.

'And the frequency?'

'Once every moon.'

The apothecary smacked his toothless gums. Rheumy eyes watered and blinked in the poor light. 'Then it is well past time she came to us. This preparation is powerful, but will only dampen and mask her abilities for two or three moons.' The old man drew in a deep breath. 'Convey my good wishes to Mistress Pemberton. Bid her send me word.'

The gnomes bowed their heads and remained unmoving till the Sorcerer shuffled out of sight, leaning heavily on his staff. Moments later, they too were gone, leaving the wind to hiss undisturbed over the sand dunes.

An hour later the postman was down to his last bag of mail and his last gasp. Looking forward to a now overdue recuperative cup of tea and a sustaining cucumber sandwich at The Manse with the Minister, he decided to take a shortcut down Gorse Hill Lane. Why not ride down? He always used to in his younger days. It didn't look so bad, did it?

Mr McFeeley had forgotten how much he hated going down hills. Especially steep hills. Especially steep and cobbled hills. And, wouldn't you know it – with a name like Gorse Hill Lane – a steep and cobbled hill with prickly gorse bushes at every turn, just waiting to welcome the unwary traveller! A recent shower of rain didn't help either. The cobbles had about as much grip as an ice rink.

The wobbling bike and oscillating postman gathered speed at an alarming rate. An already overstrained uniform decided to give up on an uneven battle. Silver buttons showered in all directions. Bounced around like a dice in a cup, an irate Haggis realised that this was one bike that wasn't going to stop until it got to the bottom. Scenting disaster, the tomcat prepared to exit at the earliest opportunity. The opportunity in question was at that very moment conveniently arriving in the village green below.

By now the Thistleburrgers were well into their Saturday morning routines. Small cafés stood tooth-by-jowl with a jewellers, hairdresser and ironmongers. But by far the busiest shop this early in the morning was The Chocolate Cauldron, an old-fashioned sweet shop that conjured up confectionary of every imaginable shape, size and description. The sale of special Hallowe'en themed chocolates had been eagerly anticipated for weeks.

By the time Lucy and Oliver Pemberton arrived to shop, the queue was already snaking out the door and down past Thistleburr School gates to Goose Green.

'Two scoops of white chocolate cauldrons, three witch's hats – the ones with the Smarties *not* the fruit pastels – and four toffee wands. Remember I've only got four pounds fifty, so check how much they cost.'

Olive rolled his eyes with exasperation. 'I *know*!' He declared, indignantly pushing his glasses firmly up to the bridge of his nose and drawing himself up to his full height so that he almost looked his taller sister in the eye. 'You've only told me a hundred times!'

'And if they-'

'And if they don't have any wands left, I'm to get two liquorice broomsticks or one white chocolate cat...'

Moments later, soaking several villagers waiting at the bus stop, an armoured Cadillac with darkened windows drew up outside Ratchet & Hatchet WS (Est. 1702): the village solicitors. Old Mr Hatchet, in his best suit and absolutely worst tie, hovered anxiously outside. He knew he shouldn't have had that last calming cup of camomile tea, but then he had never dreamed of welcoming an international billionaire to his office.

The driver's door opened and a huge man eased himself out and stood up, and up. Muscles rippled under a dark suit; square jaw, no neck, only a double helping of shoulders and dazzling white teeth. Military haircut. A mini in-ear receiver. Straight out of a Bruce Willis action movie. Diverted from their Saturday shopping, curious villagers began to congregate.

'Is-is it President Obama?' Old Granny MacDonald asked, peering myopically through her glasses.

'Wow...' breathed Oliver, brushing tousled dark hair from his eyes. Leaving his place in the queue he shouted after his sister. 'Lucy, Lucy.'

Lucy ran over from the newspaper shop, tangled hair hiding her face behind an unruly mane of russet. Unlikely as it seemed, two cats danced around her feet.

One was black-and-white and very plump, waddling hastily to keep up, its whiskers tinged with cream; the other was slim and wolf grey, clearly a pedigree and more careful of its rightful feline status in the natural order of things, and it followed at a more dignified pace. The local dogs knew well to keep their distance.

A small gawping group had gathered curiously around the car as Lucy joined her brother. On the other side of the Cadillac, dark glasses carefully surveyed them before Man Mountain opened the rear kerbside door.

'M'Lady?'

An elegant stockinged foot emerged, clad in an impossibly high heel. Draped in silver furs and dripping jewellery and prejudice, Thoralda DeSnowe, allowed herself to be helped onto the pavement. She wrinkled her nose in ill-concealed disdain.

'What a *ghastly* little place. Are you sure we are in the right village, Chesterton?'

There was a collective intake of breath amongst villagers who had been close enough to hear. Indignation rippled outwards.

'Well! ... Did you hear that!? ... Who does she think she is? ...'

Sweeping past a now bowing and scraping Mr Hatchet, who appeared glued to the spot, 'she' turned at the edge of the pavement to wait for her husband: Warwick DeSnowe, international armaments and media magnate, emerged from the car.

He was neither tall nor short, and it was hard to tell his age. Indeed some villagers thought him an old man, frail and slightly stooped as old men are; and yet others swore they had seen a young man or remembered only the compelling eyes and a powerful predatory face. Lucy's acute senses saw both and many more, as if the billionaire's features were as fluid and fleeting as sunlight on a windswept hill. *Like a chameleon*, she thought with sudden insight, *skilled in the art of deception.* And beneath that carefully constructed calm she also sensed threads of great *power* woven like a cocoon around a chrysalis, hiding the true nature of the creature within. Intrigued, she studied him more carefully.

Warwick DeSnowe moved suddenly with the predatory swiftness and economy of a shark, causing many in the parting crowd to glance uneasily towards the open door where they thought he still sat. The multi-billionaire was dressed in black. Black, and yet not black. Like a raven's wing the subtle colour seemed to change its mind as the billionaire moved, or as the light caught it. Night to Thoralda DeSnowe's day: a shadow in the sunlight. Or, had anyone cared to notice, no shadow in the sunlight.

'No!' Oliver breathed in as he recognised the Black Raven logo on the car door. 'It can't be!'

'What?'

'He's the owner of NeXus, the largest gaming company in the world!'

'No, it can't be,' Lucy doubted him. 'Why would he be here?'

Thoralda DeSnowe, pausing at her husband's elbow and surveying the now openly ogling villagers disdainfully, had exactly the same question on her lips. It was quite beyond her why Warwick wanted to buy a property in this parochial village in the middle of nowhere, when they had half a dozen homes from Monaco to New York. Something to do with his ancestral village and the recent Homecoming events – but really!

Verging on panic and driven by pain, Mr Hatchet frantically tried to prise his foot loose from under the front wheel of the parked armoured car where his toe cap was very firmly stuck. '*Such* an honour, Mr DeSnowe...' he attempted through gritted teeth. Finally cottoning on to the old man's dilemma, the solicitor's young assistant rushed to assist, along with several of the crowd.

'A..A.A...R.R.R...aarrrGGG...GGGHHHH!!!!'

Heads turned towards the new sound rapidly approaching from the direction of Gorse Hill Lane.

Argh? Villagers looked at each other in puzzlement. *Argh?*

'Hey, it's Mr McFeeley!' shouted Oliver, spotting the flash of post-office-red descending towards them. 'He's going awfully fast,' he added, clearly impressed by the postman's BMX skills as he hit a bump and took off over a gorse bush. Not even Oliver's friend Kealan could go down that fast, and Kealan was the best in the burgh! Admiration turned to consternation as it became clear that George McFeeley's new-found sporting prowess stopped short of being able to brake. The crowd scattered. Everyone except the DeSnowes, that is. Chesterton moved swiftly to avert danger.

Thoralda DeWinter finally noticed that she was no

longer the centre of attention. 'Where does that *ghastly* little man think -?' She got no further, because at that very moment the ghastly Mr McFeeley and Haggis arrived and pandemonium broke loose.

Flying through the air, Mr McFeeley closed his eyes and prayed for a soft landing. He opened one eye for a peek. Someone or something huge was moving to block his path. Looked vaguely like a person, only no one was *that* big.

'Offfh!' Stopped in his tracks by the unexpected road-block, the postman soared overhead, his momentum carrying him directly into the already wet queue at the bus stop, which went down like dominoes. The letter bag followed a few seconds later, just to catch out anyone who had managed to duck as the flying postie went overhead, and who might have been congratulating themselves on a lucky escape. Having been rudely catapulted from his basket, Haggis, with a cat's unerring instinct for survival, landed on something soft.

Hands over mouths, the riveted crowd had watched as the drama unfolded. This was serious entertainment in their normally quiet burgh and they gave it their undivided attention.

Click... click... click...The local Thistleburr press had arrived. The camera shutter was a blur. The photographer couldn't believe his luck. Reuters would pay handsomely for these photographs of the world's wealthiest recluse and his newly wedded third wife. Once one of the highest paid models in the world, Thoralda DeSnowe sat disbelievingly on the puddled pavement: expensive hairdo ruined, grey furs bedraggled. Her lips trembled with rage. Letters drifted gently down like snow. There was a moment's fascinated silence. Everyone watched a ladder relentlessly unravelling from a hole in the knee down to the elegant point of a very expensive stockinged shoe; now muddy and minus its high heel. The silence was broken as a pale string of pearls let go and rattled down the drain in quick succession.

'Oh look, that's Haggis,' whispered Lucy to Oliver with ill-concealed delight. 'Look where he's landed.' She giggled mischievously. *Odious woman. She deserves what's coming.* 'Fur,' Lucy frequently declared to anyone who might listen, 'belongs to its original owner, and to no one else.'

Confused, Oliver looked around. He could see the local scout-group leader fussing over the prone postman, thrilled at finding an inert victim to practise his first-aid skills on. Several others, including Fergus McGantry from his class at Thistleburr Secondary, were getting helped to their feet; but for the life of him, Oliver couldn't see the big grey tabby.

The huge bodyguard shrugged off the mangled remains of the bicycle and bent down to retrieve his mistress. Her fur stole twitched its tail angrily and hissed. Thoralda DeSnowe wasn't moving, and as far as Haggis was concerned, this was a bonus. He was feeling rather travel sick, and wasn't going to let go of a stationary perch without a fight. Thoralda DeSnowe screamed. Her fur stole dug its claws in deeper. Several youngsters in the crowd shouted encouragement. 'Hooray for beauty without cruelty...'

Odious smelly creature! Fur, Thoralda DeSnowe firmly believed, belonged on the catwalk and in the closet. She reached up with red talons to remove the offending article. Haggis struck. She screamed a second time. The billionaire, untouched by the turmoil around him, turned his colourless eyes on the unfortunate tomcat. Haggis yowled and shot off across the market square, paw pads burning, whiskers brittle with sudden frost. Warwick DeSnowe raised his acute eyes to the laughing crowd.

Silence! ...

No one could say for sure afterwards where the disembodied command had come from, only that it seemed to come from nowhere and everywhere: from inside their heads. Several people shivered with a sudden chill as if cold water had run down their necks. The air cracked. Thunder rumbled in the distance. Several heads glanced to the west. Black clouds were swiftly gathering on the previously bright horizon. The bodyguard helped his dishevelled mistress back to the car and turned to his employer.

'The Lodge, Sir?'

'Immediately. Then return for me. I have some small matters of business to complete.'

'Sir!' Chesterton all but saluted. Summoning the unfortunate Mr Hatchet, the billionaire entered Ratchet & Hatchet WS to complete his purchase of the Old Grange. That he had owned it many centuries ago was a small irony but not one he intended to reveal. *Little people!*

They would pay for that, oh yes, they'd pay – for that and past debts. But not yet. Not quite yet. Not after all these long, long centuries of planning. As he disappeared from view with a swirl of his short cloak, he didn't notice the large, broad-shouldered bear of a man who silently arrived behind the ogling crowd.

Lucy lay flat on her back on the cold hard cobbles, her heart frantically galloping, barely contained by the cage of her ribs; an inner voice in her head crying...

Danger!

She tried to remember why she was lying on the ground, but like a dream the details were fraying as the threads of consciousness returned. She had been watching Haggis when strange magic had flared nearby. Just the merest tendril, snuffed out in the blink of an eye, but it left her sickened and shaking. Tendrils of frigid air and water had washed around her, raising a deadly chill that frosted her fingers and toes and made her teeth chatter. Seeing with her fragmenting inner self, rather than her eyes, Lucy felt the fleeting presence of a deadly shapeless form, hidden within the dark heart of the man who had just departed from sight. Pain splintered in her head and adrenaline fizzed through her veins, fear following hard upon its heels. As her senses recoiled, the young girl felt faint. Lucy's legs had buckled beneath her and she crumpled to the cobbles.

'Lucy, Lucy?' A gentle voice broke commandingly into the dream. *Warmth* spread from strong hands that held hers within their comforting embrace. Earth Marks of *calm* and *quiet* washed through her. Her heartbeat slowed. Lucy focused her attention on the familiar voice, reluctantly shedding the shroud of unconsciousness. In the background, she could hear the sounds of her brother's distressed crying. High above, unnoticed by everyone, an osprey keened as it swooped towards the loch and faded from sight.

A tongue like hot sandpaper rasped Lucy's skin. Whiskers tickled her nose. There was the vague whiff of pilchards. Lucy could feel the weight of Truffle on her chest, anxiously treadling, the prick of claws demanding attention. Her lashes flickered. Kindly grey eyes that held the wisdom of a hundred winters held her gaze. A cool hand brushed her brow.

'Sis, you OK?' Beside her, Oliver looked scared. He wiped away errant tears and tried to grin at her.

Always pale skinned, Lucy's freckles now stood out in stark relief against her white face. Grey eyes flecked with sunlight were dilated with shock. She smiled weakly, chilled to the bone.

'Gently now,' encouraged Professor Thistlethwaite, helping her to sit up, spilling the protesting black and white cat to the cobbles. 'Nice and slow. A migraine?' Lucy nodded, making her head thud sickeningly.

So it has finally begun the Professor thought sadly, taking his jacket off and placing it around his grand-daughter's shaking shoulders. He glanced up to where Warwick DeSnowe had disappeared. *We hoped for more years to prepare her, as we prepared her mother. Why has he returned now? What has he planned?*

'Can you stand?'

The teenager wobbled to her feet. Others were now rushing to help.

'I-'

'Hush!' Lucy's grandfather cautioned, finger to lips framed by a wiry, white beard. 'We can talk about it later. Let's just get you home for now.'

The Guddler's Arms was packed to bursting. Rumours were flying round the inn faster than George McFeeley had ridden that very morning. Hard information was proving difficult to come by, which merely served to fuel both interest and imaginations... The Lodge had been completely rebuilt over the last decade; the mystery of who owned it had finally been solved.

Was it truly *the* DeSnowes whose wealth and pedigree ran all the way back to the first settlers of the New World? Why on earth would America's most powerful and glamorous couple want to come to Thistleburr? The Old Hawthorne Estate and Grange had been bought for a fortune! ... Ratchet & Hatchet have made a mint out of the sale. Old Mr Hatchet is going to retire on the proceeds! ... Did you see the size of that driver? ... Poor George ... nasty crash ... bicycle was a write-off ... Hadn't the papers hinted at rumours of connections with the criminal under-world? The son's been expelled from Eton College ... drugs, would you believe ... Surely not? Well I never!'

Alternately scandalised and fascinated, the speculation continued late into the night.

CHAPTER TWO

The Fifth Dimension

Overlooking the Sorcerers Loch but in another dimension entirely, it was also growing late. The light in the sky had faded to rose, then deepening twilight blue. Outside in the growing dusk you could see the lamplighters going about their rounds. The city criers could be heard ringing their bells as they trod the cobbled streets. *Ten bells and all's well. Ten bells and all's well.*

The Grand Master of the Seven Lodges was tired, and all was definitely not well from where he was sitting. Professor Thistlethwaite, the White Sorcerer, had yet to return after his sudden departure thirteen bells earlier, though a message borne by his osprey, Brimstone, had arrived at noon. Within an hour the Guild Council had been hastily recalled.

In front of him, the Outer Chamber was seething with anxiety, a riot of pointy hats and squabbling. Rumour and counter-rumour fed imaginations and tempers like a rising storm. Sparks were literally flying, and here and there, there was a flash and counter flash of energy as tempers got out of control.

Well, the Grand Master grumbled to himself as he hid a yawn beneath a cough, t*ime they woke up, even if it was a mere five centuries too late. At least with the advent of modern technology, they had discovered the truth where magic would have failed.* The bells on his seven-starred hat tinkled in unconscious irritation. Standing, he thumped his wizard's staff on the flag-stoned floor. Cut from a single hairy mammoth tusk, it was rune-carved in the shape of a leaping dragon and shod with powerful white gold.

'Order! Order!' he growled, his voice the distant rumble of thunder, both a promise and a threat. A resonant voice the Grand Master's, used to giving commands. Used to obedience. Normally it worked a treat. Not this time. His power was sucked in like a pebble and disappeared without a trace into the raucous hubbub below. In all his 101 years as Grand Master, Rubus Firstfoot had never seen anything like it.

Resuming his seat, he glowered down at the chaos in front of him, his beetling white brows knitted together under the shadow of his soft-brimmed hat. Ever watchful, his adjutant, a grizzled gremlin of some 45 years' military service with Gremlin Intelligence 6, GI6, who was devoted to his ageing master, picked up the early signs of a headache and sent downstairs immediately to the kitchens for a soothing cup of elderflower and bramble tea and, as an afterthought, a chilled bottle of Druids Draught 70/- beer. It had undoubtedly been a long day, and it was going to be longer still.

The Grand Master shifted petulantly on the knuckled, yellowing ivory of the Dragonbone Chair, hunching his shoulders like an aged raptor. He was getting old, well past his 350th year now, and his bones and bottom ached in equal measure. He gazed longingly at the cushion the court scribe was sitting on and debated whether to demand it. One way or another he would get this wretched chair properly upholstered after this meeting, and damn tradition.

There was a discreet cough from behind as his adjutant arrived bearing a glass of steaming tea set in a silver holder, and – oh blessed relief – a cushion!

'Thank you, Grimhelm.' The Grand Master smiled gratefully as he settled himself down. 'You anticipate me as ever.'

The tips of Grimhelm's green pointy ears glowed emerald with pleasure. 'Farthingweed, Lord?' He smiled toothily, presenting a well-worn wallet stuffed with fragrant tobacco leaf. 'I took the liberty of broaching a barrel of the 1163...'

'Yes, yes, why not?' Lighting up the offered pipe, the Grand Master relaxed a notch or two and sipped his tea.

The Outer Chamber of the Sorcerers Guild where the Grand Master was seated was a wonder of woodwork and stained-glass windows. It nestled in the centre of the Guild of the Seven Lodges, itself an architectural creation of stunning proportions, a fitting home for the most powerful Guild in the Celtic Sea Kingdoms of Britain, rebuilt after the Great Fire tens of thousands of years before. Why, Master Mason 'Hammeritin' Stoneman himself had designed and built the Guild after the fashion of the citadels of the immortal Firstborn, the dragons. It was unique in the Fifth Dimension.

At the heart of the City on the peak of the hill were the ancient Guild Hall and the Inner and Outer Chambers, rising like cathedrals to the sky. The Grand Master and his household lived here surrounded by sumptuous courtyards, gardens and the renowned Guild Library, overshadowed only by the mighty Skye Keep, spiralling so high that its dragon pads were shrouded in clouds. Below, where the air was clear and the views still unimpeded, lay the magnificent stone palaces and mansions of the nobility and the very wealthy, nestled amidst the formal gardens, courtyards and fountains of the Boulevard Circle.

Each Lodge had its apartments and households comfortably housed in the third ringed wall of the Lodge Circle, conveniently close to the Theatre Circle, where dozens of pubs, inns, theatres and song halls entertained witches and wizards. Visitors walking further down through narrow wynds and coiled closes came upon the Artisans and Merchants Circle, where hordes of dwarves, trolls, gremlins, gnomes, elves and imps thronged the streets, selling their over-priced wares to gullible tourists and visiting sorcerers. Shoving and pushing their way along these crowded medieval thoroughfares, visitors could sample breweries, butteries, cheese-mongers and bakers; or purchase finely crafted gifts lovingly smithed and smelted from rare and precious metals by the dwarf-smiths, jewellers, chandlers and glass-blowers; or purchase spices and vanilla from the Far Indies and Madagascar; try the latest remedy for nose warts from apothecaries; or browse in bookshops, hatters, kilt makers and cobblers. And for those stinge-bags who found the prospect of parting with their money stressful – why, they could get their pockets picked for free!

Stinging smoke billowed out of blackened forges as the
ring of hammer on steel filled the air in the Griffon Circle
with a cacophony of sound. Down here near the city
walls, the tanners and fletchers, saddlers, broomstick-
masters, blacksmiths, coopers, armourers and veterinary
surgeons practised their trades and plied their crafts.
Here, too, the magical beasts and dragons of the Fifth
Dimension were stabled, filling the air with pungent smells
and noise.

And finally, lapped by the restless seawaters of the
Sorcerers Loch, was the seventh Battlement Circle. High,
crenellated city walls, fifteen feet thick it was said, with
broad, stone-paved battlements so long it took the visitor
three whole hours to walk around, or four if you were a
short-legged dwarf or a gnome. Facing north towered the
Dragonstone Gate leading down wide, worn steps to the
thronged harbour, with its long stone jetty and high-sailed
ships, to the dry docks and ship-wrights; and to the seven
causeways linking the Guild to the Sorcerers Glen and the
Celtic Sea Kingdoms.

The Grand Master sat back in his chair with his blue eyes
closed and sent a small prayer earthwards. The White
Sorcerer had finally returned a little after the hour of the
sabre-toothed rabbit, having encountered difficulties no
greater than an ageing broom; but the news he brought
was the worst possible; their fears justified; the WarLock
known as the Black Raven for his totem had indeed
returned to his ancient lair in the realm of men. DNA
from a crystal glass of whisky accepted at Ratchet &

Hatchet had been spirited to GI5, and notwithstanding this, the White Sorcerer's grand-daughter and other sorcerers in Thistleburr had felt ill from the sickening aura that emanated from the billionaire.

Final irrefutable evidence was being presented: human forensics proving what magic could not.

'DNA analysis...' the auditorium shuddered and held its collective breath as the cryptanalyst reluctantly paused, unwilling to be the harbinger of such evil news. 'Although there are a dozen DNA strands,' the gremlin felt sick at the thought of so many consumed by one avaricious warlock. 'We believe he is ... The Black Raven.'

Gasps of horror and incredulity sighed round the Chamber. Shaking hands sketched the symbol of the One Earth as if to deny what they had just heard. Then the gabble of voices broke into a clamour of curses and fearful cries.

'But how? He should have died centuries ago...'

'Maelstrom magic!'

'How can he survive these centuries past? We saw him fall, broken -'

'By the Four! No one can survive the Curse -'

'He has preyed on others to survive? Taken their bodies?'

The Chamber was in uproar. Some were hiding their faces in their hands; a few, mainly young apprentices, were crying. Maelstrom magic: the very thought of tapping such unstable, malevolent power made any sane man shiver.

The Grand Master's calm voice cut through the noise. 'Order! By the One Earth.' His voice resonated with sudden *power* as he projected his will upon them. 'Order! I bring the Council to order.' Abashed and calmed in equal measure as the Master's magic settled upon them, members retook their seats. 'May I remind the Council that no one has ever breached the Warding Runes? The Black Raven may have survived but he cannot return to our world, and we have long since taken steps to fight him in his chosen world.'

And yet as Rubus Firstfoot said those words he felt a trickle of ice crawl up his spine. No one had ever before survived the Banishing Curse to the mortals' world. He stifled a shiver of apprehension as he returned to his chair. As the chamber settled, the White Sorcerer signalled his analyst to continue. Half an hour later the five-dimensional displays faded into darkness and the chandelier candles rekindled into a blaze of dancing light. There was silence. Normally silence doesn't actually mean silence. There are always people coughing, or scratching, or fidgeting.

Not this time. No, this time there was a hollow silence, heavy with dread. Even the sceptics held back, beaten by the weight of evidence just presented; they might not understand technology themselves but they knew its power. They glanced furtively towards the benches of the Wildcat Lodge to see how they were taking the return of their most infamous son. The cryptanalyst seconded from the Stealth Dragon Services (SDS) to Guild Intelligence 5

(GI5), a gremlin with a joint first in Cipher Breaking & Hacking from the Virtual University, looked up amazed from his plasma display and glanced at his mentor.

The White Sorcerer sat down heavily and relinquished his staff to a servant. He was feeling rather wobbly, and his hat was wilting in sympathy. He hadn't eaten since lunchtime, and that was now lunchtime yesterday, not lunchtime today ~ it was quite unheard of. He looked as pale as his white robes.

Hardly surprising, the Grand Master thought. *Peregrine has lost more at the Raven's hands than any other.* The first glimmer of dawn was already creeping furtively across the night sky, illuminating the windows with a pale light as he stood to bring the meeting to a close.

'Why has he returned to his old lair and for what fell purpose? What does he know about our capabilities in the mortal world? Has he regained any part of his power and how? The Council is adjourned to allow your Lodges time to consider this grave news. The King's Inner Council will meet in two days on Dragon Isle to determine our response. It goes without saying that this information is classified. We must not,' he cautioned, pausing to make his point, 'set off a panic in the Kingdoms such as we have witnessed here today. Lodges must take responsibility for their own members. The Faculty Guard and III FirstBorn Regiment have been put on alert as a precaution, and the SDS is to hold war exercises in the Glen. In the meantime you will find all the information presented at today's forum available through the usual channels in the

University's Arcane Library.'

Unusually subdued, the sorcerers poured out of the Chamber. Once outside, anxious groups congealed out of the milling throng. There were several broom collisions as distressed sorcerers leapt into the air to get out of the traffic jam, or headed for home without putting their flying lights on.

'You'll stay what's left of the night, of course?'

Peregrine nodded, as they walked back in the early dawn through the dew-laden gardens surrounding the Grand Master's Hall, leaving the tangle of witches and wizards behind. High overhead, the first rays of a hidden sun caught the criss-crossed vapour trails of SDS Imperial Black dragon traffic in a soft pink light. Below them the city was beginning to stir.

'They're even more afraid of the Raven now,' said Rubus heavily. 'He has taken another's life by force; who knows how many mortal lives stolen to extend his own. Who knows what twisted evil creature he has become?'

His companion nodded glumly as he paused to clean his dusty silver spectacles with the corner of his cloak. He peered critically at his handiwork. 'And they don't know the worst of it, Rubus. Not by half.'

The Grand Master threw an anxious glance at his friend. 'There's more?'

The White Sorcerer nodded. 'There's more,' he said flatly. 'I thought it best to confine this news to the Inner Council.' He sighed deeply, as if gaining some inner strength from the unravelling dawn. 'For two years our best gremlins in GI6 have tried unsuccessfully to break into Nemesis Armaments and to crack DeSnowe's encryption systems. Two years, Rubus! They're some of the best in the world – both his and ours!'

'But you have cracked the codes,' the Grand Master guessed, eyes narrowed. 'Or at least partially. Haven't you? That mysterious hacker of yours?'

His friend cast him a startled glance.

The Grand Master shrugged a little self-consciously. He could not understand this fascination with technology, but it was all the rage these days amongst the young, in particular those like gremlins who had no magic of their own, yet demonstrated considerable aptitude for technology. The Guild's brightest students spoke a language so riddled with jargon that he couldn't begin to understand a word of what they said ~ pulsed plasma thrusters, cubesats and EPS. Traditional sorcery was fast becoming a thing of the past, as many crossed into the mortal world to study at Yale or Oxford or St Andrews. Even the Virtual University was changing its syllabus in an effort to keep up with demand, introducing degrees in theoretical fractal encryption and other mind-boggling subjects that he had never heard of. With this power at their fingertips, had mankind truly caught up with the Sorcerer Lords? Had technology surpassed magic?

'I do my best to keep up with the youngsters,' the Grand Master smiled ruefully. 'It isn't easy! But the world is changing fast, old friend, and so must we.'

The White Sorcerer nodded. He had a Chair in Counter-terrorism and Counter-insurgency at St Andrew's

University and Yale. 'My ... hacker got inside one of DeSnowe's labs supporting the US military space programme and copied enough to keep GI6's encryption team busy for years. They were on to him, but their counter measures weren't good enough. We haven't been traced. But-' He abruptly faltered, voice cracking. 'Rubus-'

The Grand Master put out a steadying hand to grasp the arm of his oldest and dearest friend. 'Tell me,' he invited softly.

'Rubus,' the White Sorcerer began, taking off his glasses and rubbing his tired eyes, 'Apart from Nemesis Armaments valued at billions and supplying countless wars across the world, including the American military, he owns a vast network of companies in biotechnology, the space programme, pharmaceuticals and banking, all hidden and controlled through a web of holding corporations and off-shore accounts. His wealth in the mortal world is vast beyond our imagining. His power there is recognised, and yet its true measure remains unseen, and all are blind to their danger.

His scientists are on the brink of understanding the theories of creation itself. They dabble with the multi-universe and hyperspace. They are probing the boundaries of dark matter and black holes; the power of the maelstrom! Quantum physics is at their fingertips. The Raven's biochemists tamper with genetic manipulation, the building blocks of life itself,' he sighed.

'Mankind now wields weapons beyond their ken and without caution both. I cannot yet discern the Raven's purpose, but I do believe that ultimately he plans to bring down the inter-dimensional barriers and unleash havoc across both our worlds. He will fight magic with technology, and technology with magic.'

The Grand Master was a powerful man, but at this news he hid his head in his hands. Such awesome knowledge was rightly denied to mankind and to all but the greatest Scholars and Dragon Lords of the Fifth Dimension. For countless aeons the Guilds upheld the laws of the Immortal Firstborn across two worlds to ensure that it remained so. The Sorcerers had chosen long ago to govern the One Earth as stewards, protecting the land, the oceans and its peoples; foregoing their right to rule. The alternative ... was war ... and chaos; what humankind called Armageddon.

By the Four! He cursed mentally. *We should have seen it coming. Technology, many scoff derisively, no match for sorcery. But they are blinded by prejudice and a complacency born of tens of thousands of years. It may be a new millennium for mankind,* the Grand Master mused, *but the story of greed, destruction and failed ambition is as old as the One Earth itself.*

CHAPTER THREE

Lucy Pemberton

Oliver had first realised that his sister was different when they were both very small. That was when the family lived in Lost Scowerthorpe, a pretty little village in the remote Yorkshire Dales. It was a few weeks after Lucy's sixth birthday. She had been playing outside on the village green close to the old millpond, attempting to scoop out several rather mushy pumpkins with a spoon and a blunt knife. Oliver and a friend were nearby with a rugby ball when four other young boys sauntered over to the pond.

'Here little ducky ... come and get it...'

Laughing, they had waited till the ducks came waddling round in anticipation of bread crusts then pelted them with pebbles.

'Jerks,' Oliver muttered, looking round as the ducks

scattered, frantically quacking. A movement caught his eye. 'Oh, no!' He should have known. Head down and hotly clutching her pumpkin with its bucktooth grin, his sister hurtled towards the unsuspecting boys and deposited it very firmly on the nearest offending head whilst its owner was occupied gathering stones.

Splat!

The boy sat down unexpectedly with a resounding thump. There was a ... squidgy kind of silence. Aghast, no one moved. Pumpkin oozed down.

Oliver sniggered and hurriedly turned it into a cough. That broke the spell.

'You little...' Struggling to his feet and throwing the broken pumpkin to the ground, the boy turned towards Lucy, balling his fists. Desperation drove Oliver to place himself protectively in front of his sister. The vicar's son, Henry Ramsbottom, was big for his age, stocky and strongly built. At eight years, Oliver was reedy and gangly, and very short-sighted. Shoving the younger boy and his friend effortlessly out of the way, Henry and his cronies started kicking their ball around.

'Give us our ball back,' Oliver had shouted with frustration, picking his broken spectacles from the grass.

The older boys had smirked dismissively. 'Who's going to make us?

'I am.'

'Oh yeah? You and whose army?' Henry knocked Oliver so hard the young boy was in tears. It was more than Lucy could stand.

'Henry Ramsbottom, you're a ... you're...' Enraged,

Lucy had tried to think of the very worst insult known to six year olds – and came up with her brother's favourite: '... a toad. You're a horrible little toad,' she had screamed (although she personally liked the amphibians in question), jumping up and down in helpless rage. Not very imaginative perhaps, but the image lay there in her mind...

In the next second there was a muted pop and when the smoke thinned, Henry wasn't there anymore – but a confused looking natterjack toad was. The ducks closed in. Croaking loudly, the toad had plunged into the pond pursued by a determined feathered flotilla hot for revenge, and Henry's friends had taken to their heels screaming at the tops of their hysterical voices.

By the time anxious parents had been summoned, Henry was sitting in the pond covered in muddy duckweed. A few ducks still hovered hopefully nearby, pecking at his feet. Oliver and his friend were innocently playing ball over by the swings, and Lucy was fiercely attacking her remaining pumpkin with a certain air of smug satisfaction. Within the week, Mistress Pemberton posted a letter that had sat on the mantelpiece for five years gathering dust. Then she began to pack up her unruly household. Five weeks later, barely days before Christmas, the entire Pemberton clan moved north to the tiny burgh of Thistleburr deep in the Scottish Highlands. There on the shores of the Sorcerers Loch they found the Nook & Cranny cottage ready and waiting and Mother set up her business – *Mother Earth's Natural Remedies.*

Transmogrification was a rare skill and one she herself

did not possess: children needed to be taught how to wield magic wisely. Lucy needed a tutor to temper and mask her magic in the human world. It had always been only a matter of time.

Lucy herself had no such clear recollection of the incident. Earth Magic in its many facets had always been part of her life as long as she could remember, and came as naturally and effortlessly to her as breathing. She learnt how to talk with the birds and beasts before she learnt to talk to her own family. And she learnt how to swim with the otters before she could walk. Magic held no mystery for Lucy. To her, the very landscape was enchanted; every stream and stone had a story to tell; every creature was a unique character given form and colour by fur and fins and feathers. Seen through the eyes of her imagination, the world took on a hidden enchanted dimension, opening the door to a realm of magic and mystery that adults with their closed minds could no longer see.

This was clearly because Lucy had always shared her world with two gnomes from the Fifth Dimension who had guided and guarded her as she grew up in her human world. Inexplicably, Tantrum and Truffle didn't conveniently disappear as they should have when she graduated from primary to secondary school, although they grudgingly transmogrified into cats whenever other people were around. Nor yet when she grew from a girl to a young lady of thirteen. Not a chance! They rudely hung in there and offered their opinion on anything and everything, whether it was asked for or not.

Not that Lucy told anyone else about the Folk from the other world any more, of course. That much she knew would have been decidedly 'uncool.' Teenagers didn't have imaginary friends. Only Oliver knew the gnomes weren't imaginary, and his best friend Kealan, who never quite approved of that sort of thing. But whether Kealan did or he didn't, Lucy's feline guardians were here to stay. And so were her unusual talents.

But ... Lucy did remember when she first saw through the dimensional divide into that other world that she could sense was so close, and yet remained so tantalisingly still out of her reach. She and Oliver were lazing down on the harbour wall watching the anglers out in their bright painted boats bobbing on the sluggish swell. It was their second summer in the highlands, and it was a scorcher. Overhead, gulls were idly wheeling and bickering, their raucous cries carrying out over the still loch. Further out to sea, eider ducks crooned in the drowsy heat.

'It's so hot,' Oliver complained. 'Fancy a swim?'

Lucy nodded, grinning. 'OK! But only if you go home and get our gear.'

Oliver groaned and drooped his shoulders theatrically; he was feeling too lazy for that. Then the chimes of an ice-cream van on Goose Green tinkled enticingly, galvanising Lucy into sudden action.

'Race you? Last one buys the ice-creams?'

Oliver scrambled to his feet enthusiastically. He was saving his pocket money for something special. A free ice-cream was his for the taking.

'Hey!' his sister pointed loch-wards. 'Isn't that old Mrs Fairfax water-skiing?'

'What!' Oliver instinctively turned towards the boat before catching himself with a growl. 'You cheat!' he protested futilely to his sister's departing figure as he sprinted after her. 'I'll get you for that!'

Walking along to the end of the harbour pier the pair stripped off their trainers and socks, rolled up their jeans, and dangled their toes in the cold salty water.

'Cool!' Oliver sighed blissfully as Lucy handed over the melting ice-cream, before scrambling down to sit beside him. They sat in companionable silence as the sun beat down on the bleached weather-beaten boards, and the heady smell of seaweed and tar hung heavy in the iridescent air. Lucy idly watched as a paddle steamer packed with tourists in search of the Sorcerers Loch Monster began its laboured journey around the vast sea loch, its creamy wake rippling beneath the mercury surface, washing feathers and flotsam towards the sand and shale of the undulating shore. Black cormorants shrieked and showered like arrows around the boat, their fragile peace disturbed by the lazy chug of the diesel motor.

Oliver dug out the NeXus 5 he had bought at a bargain price on E-Bay and began to play The Mage Wars: Black Ops. Lucy surrendered her mind to a different rhythm, infinitely older, infinitely more powerful. She slowly let out a deep breath and closed her eyes in quiet meditation. She became One with the world around her. Gaia coursed through her body.

The sea, Lucy had once tried to explain to her brother with the inadequate vocabulary of a seven-year-old, had a language and harmony of its own. It flooded her senses, filling her nose and mouth with the bitter, salty taste of an ocean choked with life. She could feel the distant gravitational suck of the tides between her toes and the sting of salt on a careless scratch. Beyond the sheltered headlands she could hear the ocean deeps boom and crash against the rocks and felt its strength dissipated as the foam exploded into a million prisms of light, only to withdraw, regroup and return time and time again, as inevitable as the passing of the seasons.

She opened her eyes and gazed out at the Black Isle, a craggy midge-infested island in the loch. Fleetingly through the haze, a spiralling city shimmered into view. Sun beat off unfamiliar spires and red tiled roofs. Distant sounds and strange smells carried faintly on the breeze, the clang of hammer on steel, the cry of street hawkers selling their wares, the clip clop of horses' hooves and the crack and groan of laden wagons trundling across arched causeways. Swarming around the city and over the loch were sorcerers on broomsticks: darting specks of colour, their plumage bright as parrots in the sunlight. And yet, Lucy's eyes widened, in the lazy swell of the loch the mirrored reflection remained that of a barren black rock and a cloudless blue sky.

Finally noticing his sister's sudden stillness and her mouth hanging open, Oliver followed her gaze but couldn't see anything interesting. He pulled his earphones off.

'What? What is it?' Oliver was getting used to the fact Lucy could 'see' and 'hear' things that he, or most other people for that matter, couldn't. Except for their grandfather, nicknamed 'the Bear,' and of course mother.

Lucy's heart leapt with the question. Goosebumps shivered up her spine and down to her fingertips as she answered him. 'Another world…' There was no fear in her voice, only a fierce exultation and the realisation that this world was waiting for her. 'A world of magic.' Her voice dropped to a whisper as if teasing loose an elusive memory. 'A world far older than ours.'

Oliver could not share it with her. Its shape and form were beyond him, but generosity of spirit and love for his sister made him clasp her hand as if to anchor some small part of her in the world that he knew. He found a smile for her. A shadow suddenly fell across Lucy but not across Oliver. She looked up to the cloudless sky and smiled.

The dragon's colour was the deepening blue of dusk with a slender tail that streamed out behind. Four leathery wings cracked and billowed as they caught the spiralling thermals. And then the dragon was gone with a careless flick of its tail, fading from her sight. For a brief moment Lucy existed in two places. Then the Fifth Dimension also faded, leaving the young girl holding out her hand in mute appeal. From that moment on, the Fifth Dimension remained with Lucy like a waking dream, around her, within her, softly veiled, and she could see and hear, always, faintly, the vibrant shadow it cast across her own world.

Their first winter in Thistleburr, six years ago, had been unusually cold, but coming from Yorkshire the Pembertons were used to snow. March had just given way to April in a riot of primroses and blustery winds when the children's grandfather arrived home after a very long absence. Mrs Kirkwood, who lived down Runckle Lane, heard the put-put-BANG-put-put-BANG of what sounded like a runaway lawnmower. Mindful that she had recently dislocated her neck prying over the high holly hedge that bordered the lane, she bent to peer through a small hole that she had carefully cut out for this very purpose and saw the most bizarre thing. Wobbling into Thistleburr like a medieval knight on his charger was a stranger on a motorbike. He was, as Mrs Kirkwood told a gratifyingly attentive audience later that morning in the village post office, 'quite the most peculiar fellow I have ever seen!'

His craggy face was hidden under an open-faced helmet and old-fashioned flying goggles. A long-stemmed pipe poked out from under a bristling white beard that looked like a haystack after a storm, and a ragged ponytail waved in the wind. Faded baggy jeans were tucked into two bright fluorescent socks (of different colours – can you imagine!) and high-laced walking boots that had clearly done a great deal of hard work. Knobbly knees and elbows poked out in conflicting directions maintaining a precarious and improbable balance. A tweed jacket flapped open to reveal a well-stuffed T-shirt bearing the legend *Wizards Parking Only – All other vehicles will be Toad,* with a vile depiction of a mottled green toad for the benefit of anyone who hadn't appreciated the pun.

The motorcycle itself was evidently a museum piece of an antiquity matching its rider. Even Mrs Kirkwood, who knew nothing about bikes beyond the fact that they had two wheels instead of four, could tell this because of the old-fashioned chrome dials on the shining handlebars, and the vintage number plate TWS 1 set in silver on black, mounted on the front mudguard.

Suddenly taking his pipe out of his mouth and driving with one hand, the big man bellowed, 'Good morning there, Mrs Kirkwood!' giving the hidden recipient of his good wishes quite a fright. And riding shotgun on the baggage piled dangerously high on the pillion seat was the biggest wildcat Mrs Kirkwood had seen in her life; twenty pounds of brown and black striped fur with claws like crampons and a thick, black-banded tail. Fierce golden eyes set in a scarred face stared at the hole in the hedge as the bike passed, as if the cat too could sense her sharp prying eyes. The chuckle receded along with the sound of the motorbike, as it turned right onto the High Street.

The visitor passed through the village, so gossip reliably had it, and later his bike was seen parked outside the Nook & Cranny Cottage, where it remained for most of that weekend, before heading further down the loch-side to Osprey Cottage. Professor Thistlethwaite and Catastrophe had arrived.

From that moment on, Lucy and her grandfather were quite inseparable, and if the villagers spotted the Professor and Catastophe they knew that Lucy and her two cats would never be far behind. The locals would spot them deep in the Wychs Wood collecting mushrooms and berries, mosses and lichens for Mother's herbal remedies, or sitting outside Osprey Cottage at dusk, studying the stars and planets of the night sky, or rowing across the loch to the Black Isle with its pristine shoreline and primeval forest. There, under the protection of the ancient trees and free from prying eyes, Lucy's tempestuous and headstrong nature was first subjected to the rigid discipline and calming meditation of *The Way of the Dragon* that allowed Sorcerers to touch upon and focus the wellspring of their power: Gaia.

The villagers even became used to the sight of Lucy and her grandfather taking off around the loch on the Professor's ageing BSA Bantam, leaving behind familiar clouds of blue oil-smoke and a chorus of ear-splitting bangs on their way to goodness knows where.

The Professor, nicknamed 'the Bear' by his grandchildren both because of his size and because it was 'always time for a little something,' was fondly regarded as a slightly extrovert and occasionally accident-prone academic. He was said to have a 'Chair' at both Cambridge and Harvard, but whether he had a table too was unknown. His was a profile that mapped perfectly onto the townsfolk's understanding of what an eccentric, unworldly professor should be, although no one was quite sure what his research was into. There always a delicious air of mystery about him, which was put down, according to the village gossips, to the fact that he was a peer of the realm who had a seat in the House of Lords, which explained his frequent absences from Thistleburr on 'important business.'

CHAPTER FOUR

Trouble on the Horizon

As Lucy stepped outside into the pre-dawn gloom, sunlight brushed the frozen mountain peaks to brilliance, casting dark shadows against gold and white. Pausing lightly on her feet she took a deep breath of cold air. There was no trace of the appalling migraine that had confined her to bed the day before and which had so distressed Mother, and worried her grandfather till his brows met in the middle like an eagle owl. Mother's bitter potion had at least given her daughter a good night's sleep. Naturally gregarious and cheerful, unlike her shy introspective older brother, Lucy broke into song as she bounced towards the stables to muck out.

Then she noticed: the Wychs Wood behind her lay unnaturally silent, the sky above empty of feather and song. There was a strange tension gathering in the air, stretching its fabric and texture tighter than a drum, as if it were about to thunder. Only there were no clouds. Nonetheless, the promise of a storm hung heavy over the glen. Lucy's hair crackled with magic and goose bumps chased each other up her spine and down her long slim arms to her fingertips, flexing in the eddying air.

Lucy had learnt long ago under her grandfather's astute guidance that the One Earth harboured many interwoven dimensions for those who truly looked and listened. And what the young girl saw and heard told her that there were at least two worlds on the One Earth.

There was the modern digital world of space tourism, wearable computing devices, 3D printing and clouds. And then there was that other world, a far, far older, primordial world that lay slumbering beneath the first, around it, within it, overlaying it: the Fifth Dimension.

These two worlds were once intertwined. Not any more. They had drifted apart as surely as the great continental plates countless millennia before. During those dark centuries when few could read or write, history turned to myth, and myth had become legend. Now the scientific world of the new millennium scoffed at the primeval superstitions of the old, marginalising ancient traditions and cultures. Technology buried tradition beneath a web of fibre optic and copper cables, just as the earth itself was smothered beneath a suffocating blanket of bitumen and concrete. But underneath, deep down in the subconscious, that old world still lingered in the minds of humankind: the world of magic that drew upon the elemental forces of the One Earth itself.

And so Lucy stopped by the paddock gate and closed her eyes. Quietly she assumed the relaxing stance of meditation and felt herself growing lighter. Forming the four elemental symbols of Earth, Wind, Fire and Water clearly in her mind, she reached out to the One Earth, harnessing the power of Gaia to her will. As it flowed through her, her quivering senses unfolded like flowers, filling her with colour and light and energy. As the physical world faded around her, the young girl relaxed and allowed her acute senses to radiate outwards.

Her spirit soared with the sunlight and early thermals

to touch the snow-capped peaks of the Five Wizards three thousand feet above the loch. Tumbling with the snowmelt through the crashing waterfalls of the Spinning Gorge, she descended swiftly to the Wychs Wood, where the ancient elms and oaks whispered their secrets through mossy beards, and fungi sprouted from the rich mulch floor of the forest. Her sense that there was something unusual, something wrong, only grew in the leaden silence.

Reaching beyond the land itself she eddied through the air, lightly touching the spirits of the myriad birds and beasts who shared her highland world. Around her in cottages, stables and fields, her mind swiftly sought out the countless tiny spiders, earwigs and insects before rippling outwards past the mice under cottage floor-boards, over cats curled by the range and bats clustered in the warm dark of the loft, and beyond. She huddled with the dew-laden sheep behind the doubtful shelter of dry-stane pens then moved through the flatulent warmth of the byres and barns on outlying farms where the highland cattle rasped salt licks and quietly chewed on hay and turnips.

Brows furrowed with concentration, Lucy quested downwards to where the rabbits were digging in the loamy earth and the blind moles hunted for earthworms. Swiftly now she reached out further, still letting her mind drift like a rolling mist through the woods: over the hedgehogs preparing for hibernation, past the squabbling pheasants and the hunting fox, and out onto the moors where the red deer drank from the peat bogs, and the standing stones of the Sentinels stood sentry. Still she found nothing out of place. Turning seaward past the mouth of the Loch, Lucy felt the seductive pull of the tide as otters played tag in the kelp beds and the seagulls screeched ... but somewhere, everywhere, she sensed a furtive presence brooding on the horizon.

Returning to her surroundings, Lucy opened her eyes and flexed her stiffening limbs. Puzzled, she turned to her tasks. It was beyond her experience. Her grandfather might be able to help. She would go round to see him as soon as she could: he would know the answer. He always did.

Inside the still dark cottage, under the eaves of the Wychs Wood, lights came on one by one as Mother Pemberton rushed around like a mini-whirlwind, setting the untidy and cluttered rooms to rights for a new day.

Mother was short, plump and jolly; with a large beaky nose and round gold spectacles that were so thick they looked like bottle bottoms, no question where Oliver got his short sightedness from! Her chaotic silvery hair looked as though she had fallen through a hedge backwards, which she occasionally did after too much of the Professor's home-made birch wine. Trusty broomstick in hand, Mother made short work of the muddle. In a flurry of sparks and dust, books were whisked back to the small study. Spiders and assorted insects were rescued out of baths and sinks and tipped out the windows; toys gathered and CDs stored.

Cats were dusted where they slept. Curled up in companionable heaps on beds, chairs, bookcases, and even in old boots, they twitched slightly as the feathered duster swept lightly over them. As Mother continued to spin round the cottage with her broom, tables were cleared, dishes were washed, and fires set. And as the first sparks curled up the rickety chimneys, Mother turned through the flag-stoned entrance hall and swept into the kitchen.

In the village, as cockerels greeted a new day, few people were up yet to see the convoy of large removal vans trundle through on their way to the North Lodge, followed barely an hour later by an army of construction workers with JCBs and articulated lorries. Kealan McLeod saw them as he tramped through the village on his Sunday paper round.

By the time Lucy came in after putting the two Shetland ponies, three goats and two pigs out to forage in the large paddock, Oliver was just stumbling downstairs in his pyjamas. Thin and peely-wally from far too many hours indoors glued to his keyboard, and not enough sunshine, Lucy's brother feebly fended off slobbering dogs and an equally wet kiss from his mother and shuffled over to huddle pitifully next to the glowing range. Lucy grinned. Oliver was definitely not a morning person. By the time she had changed into clean clothes he was absorbed with his new iPad, a birthday gift from their grandfather, and was heaping food on his plate without paying a whit of attention.

'You gannet,' said Lucy, shaking hay out of her hair and seeing the devastation on the breakfast table. 'Leave some for me!'

'I'm just a growing boy, aren't I?' Oliver protested, stabbing a rasher and grinning toothily at his older sister; his brace was fighting a losing battle.

'But growing into what?' Lucy poked her brother good-naturedly in the ribs. Pulling out a chair next to the stove, she helped herself to porridge and toast.

'You're feeling better, Lucy?' Mother smiled, looking at her daughter's clear eyes and relaxed face.

Lucy nodded, her face tightening with remembered pain. Unconsciously she touched her hand to her temple. Turning away quickly, Mother bit her lip. Lucy's reaction was all the proof they needed that evil really was again stirring in the Glen. She too had felt a disturbance in the magical plane. Much as Mother wanted to deny the time had come, no matter her personal fears that her daughter was far too young, the Guild could no longer afford to delay Lucy's apprenticeship proper. It was time for her daughter to enter the One Earth's magical domain and attend the Virtual University, just as her true mother had before her. No one knew when the day of reckoning with the Raven would arrive. Until then, every second was suddenly precious beyond belief.

Mother turned back to her children with a cheery smile.

'What - time - are - you - going - out?' she asked, expertly juggling with charcoaled toast and raising a smile from Oliver and Lucy. The truculent toaster was one of many aging electronic appliances around the house that needed replacement. 'Is it still ten o'clock? Fergus rang to check.'

'Harf-nine,' Oliver mumbled between mouthfuls of bacon.

'But you said ten yesterday,' Mother corrected him. 'That's what I told him.'

'Did I? Ohdearwhatashamenevermind!' replied Oliver, grinning wickedly at his sister who smiled conspiratorially back.

'You meanies.' Mother shook her head. 'Fergus isn't that bad,' she added, but without much conviction. Fergus McGantry was a wild and angry young man who sucked everyone around him into trouble, and it was only going to get worse. Already at fifteen he had taken to roaming the streets with older teenagers and had been in the thick of several disturbances, including fighting, stealing and joy-riding. She shook her head and sighed. Youngsters today were increasingly unhappy with the limited attractions of rural small town life. Broken marriages seldom helped.

'Kealan's coming round, too, Mum,' Lucy reminded her, breaking into her reverie. 'We're going to take the bikes up Gorse Hill Lane. Then we thought we'd go round by Goose Green to see if Mr McFeeley needs a hand fixing up his bike.'

Mother hid a smile. The postman's antics of the

previous day were the talk of the burgh, but from what she'd heard from her dear friend, Moraig McFeeley, the bike was only fit for the scrap heap, and poor George wasn't in much better condition.

Halfway through breakfast there was a loud knocking on the door. The dog shot through the hall and jumped up to release the latch. A few seconds later, Kealan ducked under the door beam and into the kitchen followed by Midge barking excitedly. 'Hi, everybody.' He stretched up as high as the room would allow, clanging his head off one of the copper pans hanging from the ceiling. Oliver winced and shook his head. Honestly, if he had a pound for every time his tall friend had done that he'd be a millionaire.

There was no denying it, Lucy thought. Kealan had been at the head of the queue when legs and feet got handed out. Already six feet tall with feet like a duck-billed platypus, Oliver and Lucy's friend had to stoop to get around their cottage with its fifteenth century rafters and low doors. He had been Thistleburr Primary's champion swimmer and was the current Highland Under 16s cup-holder because his feet were the size of flippers; size 12 going on 13 with no end in sight. Finding trainers was becoming a stressful task for Kealan's dad. Thank goodness for the internet!

'Kealan, you're way too early,' Oliver observed, glancing at his iPad whilst continuing to eat. 'Do you want some?' He pointed optimistically to the toast rack stacked with slices of charcoal.

'Err ... no thanks.' Kealan evaded the burnt offering diplomatically. 'I'll have some of that hot chocolate, though.' Dumping his cycling hat and jacket on top of a pile of cats, Kealan gathered in his long legs and pulled up a stool. 'Anyway,' he sighed, 'I'm early 'cause I've got a puncture.'

'Bummer,' Oliver said sympathetically. He, too, had a paper round Monday to Friday, and the stack of newspapers with its supplements and magazines felt like it was growing heavier by the week.

'So,' Kealan continued, finally succumbing to temptation and pinching a rasher of bacon off Oliver's overcrowded plate, 'I had to do the last part of my round on foot. I'm bushed. I thought, rather than push the bike all the way home, to save time I'd just come here and dump it. I can sort the puncture out later if that's OK?'

He turned to Mother, who had just put a plate and knife and fork in front of him. 'OK if I use your phone, Mrs Pemberton? I'd better tell Dad what happened in case he gets in a panic.' No one knew why but mobile phones didn't work in the Sorcerers Glen, it was a network blackspot.

'Don't you worry, dear. I'll give your Dad a ring. You just tuck in.' Mother bustled off to the phone. Oliver grinned at Kealan. Mum was always trying to fatten him up. The McLeod family could never quite make ends meet since Kealan's mum had moved out to live with another man.

'Anyway,' Kealan said, chewing cheerfully while waving a fork in the air, 'guess what happened this morning?' He furtively checked to see that Mother was now out of earshot before leaning forward. Lucy shrugged, preoccupied with putting an enormous house-spider out the window.

'OK.' Kealan's hushed voice made her look over her shoulder. 'I was out doing my paper round as usual. It was still dark and I was taking the short cut over to the Andersons when I saw a flash of light deeper in the woods'

The hairs on the back of Lucy's neck prickled.

'There's nothing that way except the old ruin and you don't normally get people walking their dogs so far from the footpaths. So...' he added, as casually as he could, 'I decided to go over and take a look.'

Now he had the undivided admiration of his friends. Everyone in the village knew the old wives' tale of the Sorcerer's Leap, where a Puritan army supposedly captured a warlock and threw him, chained, over the waterfall, and the rumours of strange lights at night and people disappearing into the Wychs Wood never to be seen again. Superstitious twaddle, locals laughed, as they introduced Ghost and Hallowe'en Tours for the tourists. They didn't believe in witchcraft any more than they believed in the Sorcerers Loch Monster. The puritan witch hunts were a long time ago.

But, although they all scoffed at the stories in the light of day, not many of the locals would go near Old Hawthorne Grange, especially after dark. Just thirteen years ago, on the night of a terrible storm in late October, a party of five hunters had disappeared in the glen. Only

Old Charlie, their ghillie, had been found on the scorched lower slopes of the Five Wizards. Badly burnt and half-blinded, he was airlifted to hospital in Fort William. As Charlie lay in a coma battling for life, the mountain rescue futilely searched for the missing men. It was far too early in the winter season for avalanches, and the weather, apart from the ferocious storm at Hallowe'en, had been unseasonably mild.

The local police, namely Constable McFeeley, had even called in Scotland Yard. But no trace of the five English-men was ever found, except for a melted shotgun half buried under piles of scorched rubble inside the Grange, where they might have camped, and a torn jacket in the pools beneath The Leap.

Pleased with the reaction, Kealan pressed on with his tale. 'I left the bike after I got a puncture because it's so overgrown you can hardly move. I crept along really quietly…'

Lucy rolled her eyes. A six-foot walking crane with feet that arrived five minutes ahead of their owner wasn't going to be creeping quietly anywhere.

' … I could just make out this dark figure moving around one side of the ruin. His clothes must have caught on brambles because he was swearing and tugging. I heard something rip. Then I stood on a branch or something and it cracked. He froze and looked around really carefully – I thought he must have spotted me – but then he just put up a hood and slipped off into the woods, heading quickly for the village. I waited five minutes and then went out to where he had been. Guess what I found?'

Kealan made a show of rummaging through his pockets. Lucy yawned theatrically. Hastily Kealan brought a clenched fist out of his jeans pocket. He held it up in the centre of the table and opened his ink-stained hand up with a flourish. There, in the centre, was a damp, crumpled piece of paper, and what looked like a gold coin.

Chapter Five
The Old Grange

All thoughts of biking and the unfortunate Mr McFeeley were banished, as Oliver, Kealan and Lucy considered Kealan's find in the privacy of Oliver's tree house.

'You mean you actually went *into* the Old Grange on your own when it was still dark?' Oliver was seriously impressed as he settled onto a branch above the rope ladder.

His friend hesitated. 'Nnooo', Kealan admitted reluctantly. 'Not exactly *in...*'

'Maybe what you saw wasn't a real person,' Oliver suggested helpfully. 'Maybe it was a ghost – a real live ghost!'

Kealan paled. In all the excitement that thought hadn't even occurred to him.

'Oh, come on,' Lucy giggled. 'Have you ever heard of

a ghost that trips up into bramble bushes and swears? Or is carrying a map … do ghosts get lost?'

'Yeah, OK, OK.' Her brother grinned sheepishly. 'Bad suggestion.' He flipped the gold coin in the air and caught it. 'You really think this is gold?'

'Yeah!' Kealan and Lucy said in unison. Lucy's natural optimism had reasserted itself despite the tension she felt in the air. 'Course it is!'

She inspected the rough-edged coin Kealan gave her, eyes narrowed with concentration. It was heavy, its circumference coarsely cut. On one side, a worn bearded face and perhaps part of a cross. The inscription was mostly worn away. Perhaps Latin, she thought, remembering Mother's lessons on the Latin names for plants, or at least something similar. Old Spanish? It was the kind of heavy coin that, in her expert thirteen-year-old opinion, felt like it should be worth a lot. She moved over the rough planking to where Oliver and Kealan were poring over the other find, which in their minds, at least, had been promoted from 'a torn bit of paper' into a much more exciting and cool 'map.'

'- must be. What else can it be?' Kealan was arguing.

'OK,' Oliver conceded. 'Even if it's a plan of the old ruin, it's tumbled down and overgrown. And what exactly are we looking for?'

'And how about these bendy lines?' Lucy pointed out. 'What're they for?'

No one could work that one out. The crudely drawn straight lines were almost certainly a floor plan. But then there was a maze of squiggly lines radiating outwards from the ruin beyond the outer walls. Lucy shook her head. They appeared as random as slug trails after rainfall. *Slug trails after rainfall!* She frowned. *Or...* now she thought about it, *just like the network of ramblers' paths in the Wychs Wood, continually crossing and re-crossing each other.*

'Paths...?' Inspiration struck. 'Tunnels! How about tunnels?'

Kealan shrugged. 'Does it matter? Maybe we can work it out when we get there and -'

'Get there?'

'Yeah. Why not? Let's go and take a look while we still can. They're already putting up security fences, and they're widening one of the paths with a JCB to begin rebuilding the Grange. It's the size of a road already. Look.' He drew in a deep breath and marshalled his arguments. 'We've got a long in-service weekend,' he wheedled, 'and no homework.'

'A look for...?' Lucy deliberately teased her friend.

'Maybe the map leads to a treasure trove,' Kealan persisted doggedly, despite the obvious lack of an X to indicate where that treasure might be found. One of Kealan's favourite childhood books had been Treasure Island.

'Yeah, that's it!' Oliver responded excitedly as if it were his idea in the first place. 'Maybe there's a treasure trove hidden in the ruins and all those ghost stories are designed to keep people away.'

Long before Lucy, Oliver and Kealan set out for Old

Hawthorne Grange, long before the first construction trucks rolled through the village on their way to the North Lodge that quiet Sunday morning, the billionaire CEO of Nemesis Armaments and Nebula Communications walked through the silent woods of his memory. The subterranean complex of caves far below his feet had been forgotten long ago, although the memory of a sea dragon had not. DeSnowe smiled grimly; dragons tended to have that effect. When the billionaire first returned from America after a centuries long absence he had been amused to discover his sea dragon had become a major tourist attraction in the Highlands ~ the Sorcerers Loch Monster!

The scientists in his high-tech bio-weapons labs did not know the origin of the venom toxin they researched, and several had died before they fully understood its properties. But they had discovered that sea dragon toxin contained within tiny nano-sized particles had the potential to reknit their target host body by camouflaging toxic particles from the host's immune system. His scientists had unknowingly perfected the perfect parasites to prepare a new host body for him: soon, he would become two people, able to change guise at will.

Warwick DeSnowe laughed. Mankind didn't believe in dragons any more, and yet the creatures they didn't believe in were everywhere: toys and films, songs and stories. If all went to plan and the Fifth Dimension was his, their noble dragons would all be bound into servitude and unleashed on mankind ~ who would discover the error of their ways. As would the Sorcerers Guild ~ who had long forbidden subjugation of the Elder dragons.

DeSnowe breathed in the darkness, his green eyes flaring. Soon these caverns would be transformed, far from the prying eyes of the press, into the secret hub of a dark network linking his companies across the globe. A supercomputer – the Nemesis XE7, with a capacity of about 40 petaflops – would be installed down here and the underground river that plunged through the Black Wych Mountain would prevent hyper-fast electronics and miles of copper wiring and fibre optic cables from overheating. Hidden by the most sophisticated network-centric security system in the world, no one would look in this backwater, especially as the magical field that ran the length of the glen created a communications black spot. Only he had been able to penetrate this dampening field with his tiny cubesats, part of his critical satellite dynamic communic-ations network using enhanced signalling software from the development laboratories of his space programme.

All financed by his other ... decidedly illegal, but delightfully lucrative activities: oil from the once pristine wilderness of Antarctica, timber from Siberia and the Far East; mahogany ripped from the green depths of the Amazon; and ivory from the dwindling herds of elephants that once filled the dusty African plains. Conflict diamonds from Sierra Leone and the Congo were plucked from the bowels of the earth by impoverished miners in exchange for weapons. His companies were stripping the earth bare of its riches, and still no one stopped him.

Mankind was greedy and reckless. In fact...he pondered; there were many in this world who would serve him well; they all had a price. But the Guild, too, had clearly changed ... sending their spies into the world of men to seek his purpose, to divine the true extent of his power; their spies had disappeared. One had got close ... so close ... but she was dead now ~ he would not make that mistake again.

A sunken helicopter pad would be built so that he could come and go, unseen by prying and curious eyes, and one of the huge sea caverns of the Sorcerers Loch transformed into a yacht berth. At this very moment his pilots were testing a prototype bladeless helicopter in the Navaho desert for the American airforce...but the first would not go to them, it would come here.

He stood behind the Sorcerers Leap, listening to the thundering water which had nearly killed him. He had been weak, vulnerable when banished to this wretched mortal world, devoid of magic that swiftly became only a memory. But there was power of another kind in this world of men where anything could be bought with gold. Now, finally, technology was the match of magic. Soon both worlds would regret casting him out.

* * *

The drizzle intensified as the three friends pushed through the dripping undergrowth, unaware of resentful eyes watching them leave the village. High estate walls loomed that had taken a mason and his apprentices seven years to build in the reign of Elizabeth 1 of England, at a time when Scotland was gripped by religious turmoil. But inevitably, over the centuries, enterprising peasants and local lairds had lugged off cut stones by the barrow load to build their crofts and keeps. Now, in the gathering gloom, the wall lay tumbled and broken. The trio easily clambered through gaps and set off, following a familiar latticework of tracks formed by mountain bikers and people walking their dogs, avoiding the area where building contractors bulldozed their way through the woods. But they could hear the muted grumble of chainsaws and diesel engines growing slowly closer. Soon this would be a building site and they wouldn't have another chance. They followed a track close to where cast-iron gates lay red and ruined beneath a fallen tree.

'OK, here goes.' Oliver squeezed through the widest gap, followed by Kealan. A waving sea of stinging thistles and weeds swallowed them up. Lucy followed, trying to avoid getting stung. The small group fell silent. The ruined grange appeared deserted of all living creatures; not even birdsong broke the silence. Lucy whistled, brushing her hand through tangled hair. Despite scoffing at Kealan, this was the first time she and Oliver had ventured so far. Around them, a cobbled courtyard lay thick with the neglect of centuries. The only sounds were the crack and groan of the pines above, and the moan of the wind as it embraced the derelict building.

'Why on earth would anyone want to live here when they could live anywhere in the world?' Oliver frowned. 'It's ruined. It's a total dump.'

Overgrown ivy smothered the crumbling stonework, coiling like an anaconda around every lintel and doorway, crushing the stone. Slowly the arched windows and doorways were being claimed back by the woods. The once beautiful facade had been peeled away layer by layer by rain and wind until whole sections of the wall had collapsed. Looking around, Kealan clambered across the courtyard to where mistletoe clung thickly round the blackened broken entrance.

'This is where I saw that person this morning.' Kealan pointed at the trampled ground. 'Look footprints. And I found the coin just... here.'

The three of them started poking around with sticks.

'There's nothing here,' Kealan sighed after twenty minutes. He sat down on a tumbled block of stone. Lucy moved past him to inspect the entrance, where a rusting chain barred the boarded-up doorway and a council safety notice warned visitors away. The planks looked rotten; she tentatively poked a sodden piece. It disintegrated.

'Come on.' Without looking behind, she gestured for Oliver and Kealan to follow and scrambled through a gap and into the hallway. 'We can get through here. Watch your feet, though,' she called. 'There's broken tiles everywhere.' She disappeared from sight.

Lucy wrinkled her nose as ivy tickled her face and the pungent smell of decay grew stronger. She looked around, letting her eyes slowly adjust to the gloom whilst she appraised her surroundings with her inner sense. The hall she was standing in was thick with shadows. Weak light from the overgrown doorway and clogged windows barely illuminated the remnants of a vaulted ceiling high above, where shrubs sprang out of the shattered roof and tumbled chimney-stacks. In front of her the remains of a stone staircase rose up to a gallery that ran around the entire hall; everywhere, musty layers of dust and dirt and mouldering leaves lay in the damp silence.

There were memories here, etched into the stone by sorcery for those sensitive enough to read them. They crowded thickly round Lucy, but their stories were old and weak, fading echoes of battle and death and smoke. Crumbling to dust like the stones that held them, soon to be obliterated completely. *Wait...there was something...*

'Don't you -' she turned round in mid-sentence. No one else had moved. She could see the boys still at the entrance, silhouetted against the bright outdoors.

'Oh come on,' she called impatiently. 'Where's your sense of adventure?' she challenged.

There was a bit of sheepish shuffling. 'We were just, err ... studying this, err...' Oliver groped frantically for a plausible excuse that might appeal to his sister, rather than admit in front of Kealan he was scared. 'This, err ... fascinating toadstool. Yeah, this fascinating toadstool.' He pointed feebly to where Lucy clearly couldn't see. 'Weren't we, Kealan?'

Kealan looked down at the milk-white brittlegill his big foot had just squashed and smiled unconvincingly. 'Err, yes,' he agreed lamely. 'Err, sorry...' He was used to putting his foot in it. Wiping the mush off his boot he followed Oliver inside. Hidden eyes watched the small group as they clambered over spars and rubble. *Patience. Patience. Just a little longer...*

Oliver ducked under the wet ivy and tentatively stepped onto the broken tiled floor of the hall. It was so dark he could barely see Lucy, although he could hear her moving around. A sudden premonition made his sister step backwards. Kealan cursed. Everyone stopped dead still, listening intently. Kealan tried to balance with one leg in the air. Plaster sifted down from the cracked and peeling gallery. Lucy's eyes watered. She blinked furiously, trying to clear her contact lenses.

'Sorry!' She moved ahead slowly. 'False alarm. It's just some bats settling down to hibernate.'

'How can she *see* them?' Kealan began, knowing the answer full well. 'I-'

Shapes rose up from the dark in front of them. Wailing and groaning in the billowing dark, the figures rushed towards Lucy, Oliver and Kealan.

Leaves ... debris ... dust all swirled in the roiling gloom. Instinctively Lucy turned away, but her legs refused to obey the urgent command to run. Oliver and Kealan milled around in a panic and cannoned into each other. Falling over, Kealan grabbed at Lucy. Lucy screamed. Oliver screamed. Kealan screamed. Everybody screamed.

Chapter Six

Ghosts and Ghouls

High-pitched laughter ricocheted rudely off the barren walls, an unaccustomed sound that had not been heard in the Old Grange for centuries. Lucy stopped screaming as two boys moved into the light and sauntered carelessly towards them, laughing and sniggering.

'You!' she snapped, instantly recognising the pale-faced, stocky boy from Oliver's class. She tried to suppress the tingling thrill that raced through her to her fingertips, itching for release, flushing her face hotly with its energy and warmth; the urge to give them a real fright in return.

'Yeah! Whhhooooooo, I'm a ghost.' Fergus McGantry laughed loudly, waving his dark jacket in her face. Oliver slapped it away angrily.

'Get lost, Fergus. What are you doing here, anyway? I don't remember anyone inviting you.'

'Not scared, are you?' Fergus taunted, poking Oliver

hard in the ribs. Behind him, the other boy sniggered. Oliver fumed silently. Duncan always hung out with Fergus, causing trouble. He wasn't very bright, but what he lacked in brainpower he made up for with muscles. Long arms trailing down towards the ground had earned him the unkind nickname, Neanderthal Man. Kealan moved forward to intervene. 'Why don't you pick on someone your own size,' he challenged, 'and without someone to back you up for once?'

'Oohh. It's daddy-long-legs. Now we're really scared, aren't we, Duncan!' Taking his well-rehearsed cue, Neanderthal Man turned towards Kealan and shoved him hard. The tall boy fell over, cracking a knee viciously on a rusty spar. Kealan cried out with pain, trying to blink back hot angry tears.

'Oh, get stuffed, Fergus.' Lucy had had enough. 'C'mon, let's get out of here. The company stinks.'

Fergus bridled. 'Oh, too good for us, are you? Is that why you sneaked out early this morning?'

'Fergus,' Lucy retorted. *Oh, it would be so easy,* she thought. *So very, very easy.* Her hands clenched and unclenched with the effort of control. *And it would serve them right, always taunting, always hurting someone at school.* Lucy hated bullies. Gritting her teeth, reaching out to the One Earth, she sought the peaceful wellspring of meditation and forced down the bubbling surge of magic that would have changed the boys into pumpkins. Calm returned, and with it common sense and memories of dire warnings not to misuse her magic. 'No one invited you in the first place, and second, given how scared you are of the dark, of insects, the woods, the grange, ghosts and -'

'Scared? Who's scared? You were the ones screaming, not us. We're not scared of ghosts, are we?' Neanderthal Man nodded, truthfully for once. He hadn't the imagination for ghosts. Fergus moved forward suddenly to grab the torch out of Oliver's hand. 'Now we'll see who's afraid of the dark.'

'Give that back, Fergus. This isn't a game. We need that torch.'

'Oh, yeah? And who's going to make me give it back? Not daddy-long-legs, surely?' Neanderthal Man moved forward threateningly, just in case Kealan was stupid enough to rise to the bait a second time.

'And not Pipsqueak Pemberton?' Fergus smiled, sensing victory. 'No?' He sneered dismissively. 'You couldn't fight your way out of a wet paper bag.' Neanderthal Man guffawed.

Oliver fumed silently, his face burning with shame.

'C'mon, Duncan.' Turning on his heel, Fergus swaggered off, waving the torch around. Pumped up with adrenaline he failed to notice that he was leading them both deeper into the massive house.

'Forget him, Oliver,' Lucy put a sympathetic hand on her brother's shoulder. 'He'll get fed up real quick and go. There's-'

'But he's got the to-'

'And...de, de...' With a mock flourish, Kealan produced another front light. 'I always carry a spare when I'm out on my paper round. Come on,' he studied the map before heading for a corridor to the left of the main staircase. 'Let's try this way.'

In the gathering gloom summoned by Lucy's unspoken thoughts, the resident ghosts contemplated the two groups of children with keen interest. With great difficulty and long practice they managed to tumble a coin to the floor to see who would go first. Harry Frobisher, one time captain in Oliver Cromwell's Puritan army, chose heads and lost. Was he never going to learn? He knew he should have picked tails – at least they didn't get chopped off.

'I never get to go first,' he pouted. Or at least his head held in the crook of his arm did.

Gloating, one-legged William Simpson, corporal and regimental cook, adjusted his helmet and buffed up his dented armour. Satisfied that he was looking his spectral best, he picked up his broken pike and drifted down several floors to hover in ambush. Such summons were a rare opportunity for some fun.

Secretly stung into action by the long and all too accurate list of things he was scared of, Fergus was clambering over the rubble towards the light of a broken doorway, Neanderthal Man reassuringly behind him. To tell the truth, they were both a little scared. The screaming reaction to their joke had un-nerved them, and now they were looking dubiously from side to side at the shadows that lurked in every corner. Ducking under a low lintel, Fergus moved into what must have been an inner courtyard garden. An ancient, gnarled yew tree almost blocked out the light, its restless roots and the passage of time cracking through the heavy slate paving stones as if they were made of paper. A half dozen doorways bordered the garden. He chose one at random.

This particular door led down to the cellars once used for storing vats of wine from France. It also led down to where one-legged William was lurking, hopping up and down with barely contained impatience (not that he really had a choice). It had been a long time since the ghosts had had a visitor; a visitor, that is, who might be scared of them – and not, embarrassingly, the other way around. Fergus shone the torch around the stone-vaulted roof. Large rusting hooks hung from the ceilings, and the decomposing remnants of wooden trestles and barrels lay collapsed on the floor. He kicked a decomposing plank and squealed as another rat shot out through his legs. Swallowing hard, he turned back to the doorway to find his path blocked. Or at least, to see someone dressed in a leather tunic, breastplate and helmet, and with a manic toothless grin; someone transparent – with a faint lumen-escent aura. The apparition opened its mouth to utter an appropriate wailing noise, but before it could say anything, Fergus let out one of his own.

'AAAAARRRRRGGGHHH!' Fergus screamed. Then he fainted.

For the first time, Duncan didn't have someone to tell him what to do. So copying Fergus's example, he screamed as well. One-legged William screamed back, his ears ringing with indignation. He'd never met an example of Neanderthal Man before, and Duncan looked as if he could tear your head off, ghost or no ghost. Fergus lifted his head up in the middle of this vocal match and fainted again. Duncan slowly considered his options. Since fainting wasn't in his repertoire, he took the only obvious alternative left and charged straight through one-legged William, up the stairs, across the garden, through the hall, and into the woods. One-legged William smiled smugly as he departed through the ceiling. One group down and out – one to go. As the spectral glow faded, Fergus panicked in the dark. He bounced into the wall twice before he clambered beneath the broken door and up the stairs. By the time he made it out of the Grange he had two black eyes ... and a bruised knee ... and scratched legs ... and worse than all those put together – a badly battered ego.

Up in the old library the headless ghost was not doing nearly so well. Children and teenagers were no longer the timid superstitious creatures they had been when he had first lost his head to a sharp, spell-charmed sword. He had floated through the fireplace for maximum impact. When no one noticed, he popped up through the floor behind Lucy, Oliver and Kealan, and his head had given voice to its best bone-chilling scream, whilst the rest of him stood nonchalantly in the doorway. The results had been disappointing to say the least, perhaps even a touch embarrassing. They hadn't even looked up.

'Oh shove off,' had been the contemptuous response. 'You'll not catch us out twice!'

'Yeah,' Oliver had added for good measure, 'go boil your head. We're not falling for that one again.'

Boil my head? Confused and miserable, Harry had slunk off … Pulling himself together, at least pulling most of himself together – where had that dratted head wandered off to this time? – Harry headed (so to speak) down into the crypt for a major career rethink.

Lucy, Oliver and Kealan ignored the wails and screams until they also heard the sound of beams being overturned and rapidly disappearing footsteps. Clambering hastily through several rooms to get back into the hall, they were just in time to see Neanderthal Man exiting through what, up until that point, had been a boarded-up side door. They were still standing there gawping when Fergus entered from the opposite direction and, leaping over rubble and broken spars with the aplomb of a professional hurdler, also disappeared, although he at least went out by the main entrance.

Lucy frowned. 'What's got into them?'

'They're just clowning around trying to scare us. Ignore them, Sis.'

'Yeah,' Kealan added, 'good riddance to bad rubbish.' But all the same, he surreptitiously looked around behind Lucy's turned back.

'Let's go see what they were looking at,' Lucy suggested, pointing at the doorway.

An unproductive half hour later, they were getting bored when Kealan's torch picked up a flash of metal half hidden by leafy mulch in front of a huge fireplace. It was another coin.

'What's it doing down here?'

A further search turned up absolutely nothing.

Disheartened, Kealan turned to leave.

'Ouch,' he shone the torch beam down to see what he had stubbed his toe on. 'Hey,' he said, as realisation dawned, 'take a look at this, guys.'

Giving his torch to Lucy, Oliver bent down to help Kealan move the heavy slab to reveal more of the writing on the floor beneath. Lucy swept the leaves and rotting wood aside and stood back.

> *For those who wish to come and go*
> *Through hidden door you must bow low*
> *Beneath both tree and mountain high*
> *To where the water meets the sky*
> *The dragon's breath will point the way*
> *And whither then, well who can say?*
> *But should you seek forbidden gold-*
> *Beware the guardian of old ...*
> *So mortal man you must beware*
> *Of stepping in the dragon's lair*

'It's a riddle,' Kealan decided.

'Oh, you think?' Oliver asked sarcastically. 'Of course it's a riddle. But what does it mean?'

'Look it says gold! I *told* you there was treasure here!'

'Ssshh.' Lucy silenced them both with a finger to her lips. 'Let me think.' OK, she said slowly, 'a *hidden door ... beneath both* ... that must mean the door comes out beneath the woods, the Wychs Wood and goes under the mountain? A tunnel or....'

'That's it,' interrupted Oliver excitedly, pulling out the

piece of paper and waving it. 'The curving lines on the map, here, look. Tunnels!'

'-and *the water meets the sky* might be the Wychs Leap?' Lucy finished her train of thought before looking again at the crumpled map. 'Maybe that's this long tunnel here,' she mused, tracing a squiggle on the map, 'and where it ends here is The Leap.'

'*Dragon's breath.*' Kealan grimaced. 'I don't like the sound of that. What does *dragon's breath* mean?'

'Who cares?' said Oliver, unfairly, thinking exactly the same thing and glad Kealan had admitted to it first. 'It's there just to scare people away from the gold. You're not scared of a fairy story, are you?' he challenged. 'Dragons don't exist in our world.' He looked suspiciously at Lucy. 'Do they? Lucy, do they? Well not any more, do they?'

Kealan sniffed. 'They don't exist, full stop. I was just mentioning it, that's all.'

'*Bow low, bow low,*' Lucy was muttering, playing the torch over the fireplace and up the chimney. '*Bow ...* there!' she shouted making Kealan and Oliver jump. Look!' Bending down under the mantelpiece, the boys could just make out a rusty lever in the wavering torchlight. The chimney was thick with cobwebs, but around the lever they had been brushed away. Soot lay disturbed on the floor beneath.

'Right,' Lucy said decisively, and she pulled on the lever.

CHAPTER SEVEN

A Creature that Doesn't Exist

In deep caverns to the north of the Sorcerers Glen a creature that didn't exist slumbered in an inter-dimensional pocket between the worlds of magic and men, trapped and tamed by maelstrom magic to guard a secret. It was but a heartbeat in his long life since he had rampaged along the storm-lashed shores of the Sorcerers Glen, leaving havoc and ruin in his wake. When the veils grew thin he escaped his captivity and would stir and stretch his armoured webbed wings so they touched the edges of his huge cavern. Then he would slip silently into the freezing waters, his black webbed talons guiding him effortlessly through the winding maze of tunnels that led out to the open sea. There in the deeps of the blue world where he was spawned countless millennia before he would hunt for prey, his savage songs echoing far through the oceans.

Down here, far removed from the sun, no humans disturbed him as he ghosted through vast underwater mountain ranges and caverns, camouflaged by a forest of leafy appendages that looked like fronds of seaweed. Deeper yet, in canyons where the darkness was absolute, he glided gracefully like a phantom, eerily lit by flickering blues and greens. Flashes of colour streamed from his coiled tail like a thousand lamps, luring the curious and the careless to their doom, snapped up by a long pipe-like snout.

At other times he would swim through the maze of tunnels connecting the deep sea-lochs gouged out by the retreat of glaciers at the ending of the last ice age. He would come up to the surface to seek a new kind of prey. As villages grew and clustered around the lochs, sometimes this ocean wanderer was seen on All Hallow's Eve, and in their primitive fear the Lodges had named him The Sorcerers Loch Monster.

He yawned, bearing rows of ivory fangs yellowed with time. Smoke ghosted out of his mouth and nostrils, drifting over the surface of the water like a sea-haar. Yellow-flecked eyes smouldered with angry fires, undimmed by the passing of time. Green and black-scaled armour glinted in the dark. Brooding, he turned to the sky iron collar that bound him to endless service and lifted his head to call. Surely his kindred had not forgotten him?

CHAPTER EIGHT

The Sorcerers Leap

'I *told* you!' Kealan preened in satisfaction. 'I told you. This is just like Indiana Jones. There's treasure here. Didn't I say there was treasure hidden here?'

Lucy shone her light into the musty gloom; the cellar behind sank into immediate darkness. Hastily, Oliver and Kealan followed on her heels.

'It is a tunnel, but what's that strange smell?' Lucy sniffed the air.

The wide beam of the halogen bike light revealed an upward sloping tunnel festooned with cobwebs and pallid tree roots. The yellow air lay thick and foggy like sea-haar. Beneath their boots, finely laid flagstone steps led the trio steadily upwards, ducking the tangle of twisted roots that reached down through the roof with groping fingers to tug at their hair and shower dirt on their heads. Then they came across a natural crevice in the bedrock on their right, it was narrow but huge, easily big enough for a person. The air flowing over them was bitterly cold and laden with salt.

'This is where the fog is coming from,' Oliver put a hand out to stir the air.

'It must lead to the sea.' *Sea...sea...sea..* Lucy's voice echoed as she moved forward into the opening. 'We c-'

Whatever Lucy was about to suggest froze in her throat as an eerie keening cry reverberated through the caverns, thrumming through the air.

'W-what was that?' Kealan reached out a shaky arm to grab her. 'Lucy? What was t-that?'

'*That* was a dragon...' Somehow Lucy knew, as the despairing call full of sorrow and rage rose and fell. *But how? How could Oliver and Kealan hear it too? That means it's in our world!*

'Whatever it is,' she said, not sharing that last thought, 'It's a long way away. Listen to those echoes.'

There was an unconvinced silence. Lucy found a smile. 'Even a tiny dragon can't get through here, Kealan; this tunnel is *far* too small. Come on; let's go further up this main tunnel. We might not have another chance to investigate. And...if there is a dragon down that way, then maybe there is also gold! Just as you said, Kealan!' Lucy waved a hand in front of his face. 'But we won't go anywhere near it. Are you OK?' The youth's face was frozen in a rictus of a smile.

> *But should you seek forbidden gold-*
> *Beware the guardian of old ...*
> *So mortal man you must beware*
> *Of stepping in the dragon's lair*

'Kealan?' Oliver repeated, trying to keep the wobble out of his own voice. 'Lucy's right...it's far away!'

'Do you want to turn back?' Lucy asked kindly, keeping the disappointment out of her voice. Kealan shook his head mutely. He couldn't find his voice.

Taking their time, the three youngsters continued on steadily. The air here was clean and sharp in their faces.

The steps, too, became steeper as the passageway burrowed up through the roots of the mountain itself. Conversation stilled as they concentrated on putting one step after another. The flagstones became wet and slippy. Soon their breath fogged in the moist air. At the same time Lucy became aware of a new sound, barely audible above Kealan's heavy breathing. It was deep and still distant, but persistent and powerful. She could feel the river vibrate through the heart of the mountain as it wore down the granite stone, smoothing its tumultuous and timeless passage down to the loch and the open sea.

'We must be g-' Just as she recognised what it was, there was a loud crunch beneath her feet. 'Yikes!' Lucy swung the torch beam down to see what she had stepped on and cried out in horror.

'Whowa...' Oliver sucked in a startled breath, jumping backwards. Forewarned, Kealan was already turning away to run. As the others didn't join him, he returned reluctantly. The brittle broken bones of a skeleton lay scattered across the floor of the tunnel. Long dead, it had given Lucy no warning of its premature demise, three and a half centuries ago. Barely ten yards ahead was another. And where the tunnel narrowed, they came across the bodies of his companions.

Here and there, patches of rotting jerkins and rusting mail still clung to the bones. Back to back, they had evidently made their last stand here beneath the depths of the woods, far below the dappled sunlight. They embraced death together as they had life, facing outwards in a ring, their swords and pikes raised. It had done them no good when confronting an enraged WarLock. His powers may be a pitiful remnant of his former strength, but here in the realm of men he struck fear and death; beneath the soldiers' bodies, glazed stone caught the light.

Lucy knelt down and touched a rusting sword near the severed hilt. It vibrated slightly at her touch. Faint though it was, Lucy could smell and feel the traces of powerful magic burnt into the notched metal. It repelled her touch and she lifted her stinging hand with a muted cry, the shards of sword clanging to the ground where they shattered.

'I,' Kealan croaked and tried again. 'I think we should be getting out of here. It's getting a bit creepy,' he admitted when this didn't elicit the response he was hoping for. 'I –'

There was a click. They froze, staring wide-eyed at each other. The unmistakable sound of stone grating on stone echoed up the passage; then the faintest rasp of a match being struck. Distant footsteps echoed.

'We can't go back now! What do we do?' Aghast, Kealan switched the bike light off and promptly stumbled in the dark.

'Sshh.' Grabbing blindly for his jacket, Lucy put a finger to her mouth in a gesture no one could see. 'We might be heard,' she whispered. 'Listen, the map showed dozens of tunnels forking from the main one; it's like a rabbit warren down here. There must be one we can hide in. Put the torch back on. Shade it.'

Looking behind, the others saw the distant light of a torch. Softly they padded up until they found a narrow cleft in the rock face.

'We'll hide down this one,' Lucy decided. 'Wait till whoever it is has passed us. Kealan, watch your head.'

Judging they were out of sight, Lucy stopped. Crouching low, the three listened, hardly daring to breathe, blood pounding in their heads. It took ages for the newcomer to reach them. Although Lucy could sense no threat nor thread of magic, every grim fairy tale and ghost story they had ever read went through their minds as the steps came relentlessly closer, and closer, and... Light flared up the side tunnel briefly and then was gone. Kealan tried to get up but his long legs wouldn't work. His hands were shaking.

'Come on,' Lucy whispered. 'Let's follow.' Whatever Kealan thought, he couldn't raise even a squeak of protest.

There was a thundering noise now that made talking difficult, and the air was damp, but daylight up ahead lit the way. It was more than five minutes' steep climbing before they found out why, as they rounded a bend and found themselves in a cave. To their left a curtain of water hammered down to crash on hidden rocks far below.

Spinning Gorge! Lucy had to put her face close to Oliver's ear to be heard. 'It's Spinning Gorge. We must be somewhere behind The Leap!'

'C'mon,' Kealan urged, shivering fiercely. 'L-let's t-turn back. I don't like this at all. It doesn't feel right...'

Examining the far rock face, Lucy saw where the visitor might have gone. Along a rising narrow ledge was what looked like another cave. If it weren't for the firelight faintly flickering in its depths, you might never have known it was there. Cautiously embracing Gaia by a thread, Lucy immediately heard voices as clearly as if their owners were standing next to her. Probing gently forwards, Lucy could see the two figures in her mind, although both remained indistinct and hazy, shrouded by a dark mist she couldn't penetrate. That puzzled her. Instinctively she shuddered. *A shield woven from Air and Water?* Sorcerers, then, and they wished to hide their identity. Studying its construction she wove a cruder shroud of the same mould and cast it around herself.

'M-master,' a reedy voice quavered. Its feeble owner cowered in a flatteringly appropriate manner before the commanding presence of the second figure. 'I came as quickly as I could. I have begun the tasks you commanded, but ... b-but ... ' The first voice trembled and fell silent.

A laugh: cold and mirthless. 'But...?' The single word impaled the hooded man. Frozen to the spot, he wriggled frantically to no avail. 'But...?'

Lucy felt a fierce shiver of recognition creep up her spine. *Flee*! Her head began to ache again. The feeling of danger began to take palpable form as sweat beaded her head. The shadow of the hooded messenger flickered and wavered on the cave wall.

'I -' the figure breathed deeply, anxiously entwining his long pallid hands. His pale tongue darted out to lick dry lips. 'It – it will be hard to do all as you desire, Master. The policeman here is an overweight bumpkin, easy to mislead. But should more people disappear ... at the same time of year ... suspicions will arise. Should there be any mistakes...'

'*Mistakes?*' Deceptively quiet, the powerful voice was thick with malevolence and power. The messenger recoiled and tripped on his own shoelace, falling clumsily to the floor.

'*You are being well paid for your troubles.*' A bag landed with a clink on the floor of the cave. Gold spilled out in the firelight, and was hastily gathered up and hidden away. *Kealan's coin!* Lucy thought. *But should you seek forbidden gold-*

'P-perhaps someone from another village to the north? Or from the big cities: Glasgow. No one would miss a vagrant or a beggar...?' The hopeful thought lingered in the brooding silence.

'*No! The villagers must pay for their past betrayal ...*'
Lucy leaned forward, her head cocked to the side. Muffled though it was, she was sure she had heard that voice. A name hovered on the tip of her tongue.

'Please, I-' the man blubbered, saliva dribbled on his doughy chin.

'By All Hallow's Eve!' the voice lashed out. 'One will suffice. Do not fail me, else you will find the price too high. Now go.'

Lucy couldn't help it. The smooth rock of the floor was coated with a thin sheet of ice. Her loud cry reverberated round the cavern mouth as she slipped, cracking her knee. Concentration broken, Gaia and the cloak that hid her slid from her inexperienced grasp.

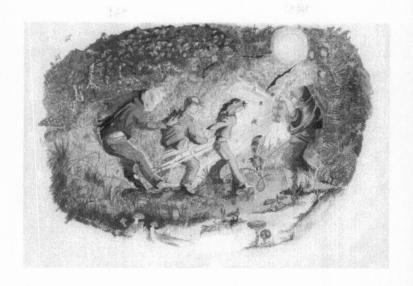

CHAPTER NINE

The Wych Elm

What? A predatory mind leapt out, searching hungrily. Lucy's hair stirred and lifted as she felt it fleetingly fixing its powerful attention on her. *A man-child. How delicious.* 'You fool! You have been followed, but no matter. These three children will serve my purpose as you are too cowardly to do my bidding. They are young and strong...take them!'

'Children? T-take them? H-how?'

'Fool! I shall call others to do my bidding since you will not. I need to feed! Go, if you wish to live!' The Raven desperately summoned his body's failing strength and drew on the powerful sorcerous venom that pulsed through his decaying veins. Could he summon a vortex and open a bridge to his army, secretly gathering beyond the borders of the Old Kingdom? *One small enough to evade detection by the SDS and their prying gremlins?*

Adrenaline fizzed, driving Lucy to her feet. The young girl staggered as the strength of the mind's cold avarice enveloped her. Clumsy as a broken puppet she turned smack into the path of Oliver and Kealan, rushing forward in concern.

'What happened?' Oliver helped his trembling sister up. 'Why did you scream?'

'Run!' She felt sick.

'Run?' Oliver frowned. Water flecked his glasses; he took them off to casually wipe on his sleeve. 'Where? Which way? Why?'

'I don't know.' She grabbed his arm, trying to convey the sense of urgency that pounded in her head. 'Run!' She spun on the ice, looking for a way out. Could they go back the way they came in? Panic rose, blocking her frantic efforts to touch Gaia.

A wind rose about them. Spinning, it began to suck in water like a spout.

Follow me! A sodden ball of fur hurtled through the thundering spray, its thick fur flattened by the downpour. Claws gripped the ice effortlessly as the huge wildcat skated to Lucy's side. Amber eyes beneath flattened tattered feline ears fixed Lucy with an urgent stare. *Follow me! Now! There is darkness here...*

Time stretched. Everything decelerated to slow motion. Water droplets sprayed from the shaking cat, each drop caught by the light. A thousand exploding prisms... falling ... falling...

'Catastrophe!' Lucy sobbed with relief.

This way! This way! Follow me...

Lucy could hear Catastrophe's frantic appeal, but she felt as if she was moving through sucking mud. As the cat vanished once more through the curtain of water, the spinning vortex began to pull them towards the dark aura forming at the back of the cave.

'T-h-a-t w-a-y.' Lucy tried to speak clearly, but her voice slurred with the effort. 'T-h-a-t w-a-y. T-h-r-o-u-g-h t-h-e w-waterfall. R-u-n-!'

'T-h-r-ough t-that?' Kealan balked, and as time suddenly, unexpectedly, returned to normal, he fell forwards. Pulling him to his feet by his rucksack straps, Lucy tried to run, but Kealan was paralysed by what was taking place behind him. His teeth were chattering. The dark shimmered and seemed to fold in on itself. A vague simian outline began to take form. As the vortex coalesced, the apparition within it held back its head and howled. Finally that was enough for Kealan. He leapt wildly at the wall of water, disappearing with a wail that swiftly receded into silence. Oliver was already gone. Lucy followed.

There was still light in the sky, but under the trees the shadows clotted and thickened. Helping Lucy out from the freezing pool, Kealan slipped and fell repeatedly on the water-soaked shale that peppered the thundering gorge.

'This way!' Turning away towards the woods, Lucy followed Catastrophe's catcalls. Gasping and sodden through, Kealan and Oliver pounded blindly after her through the deepening twilight, hands bloodied and torn by the spiteful thorns of tangled brambles and branches. As they turned this way and that down little-used, overgrown paths, they imagined the sounds of pursuit behind growing closer and closer, until it seemed the heavy panting was right on their heels.

Woof! Woof! A huge dog was on them, smelly breath hot on their faces. It yowled as Catastrophe spat and raked its nose in warning. The children went down in a tangle of arms, legs and screams. A hobbling shabby figure lit by a lantern loomed over them. The dark scarred face was more twisted and gnarled than lightning blasted bark. Oliver bit back a scream, but Lucy knew there was no danger here.

'Doon, Ambush, doon lad...' The dog subsided, grumbling. The lantern was lowered.

'Charlie!' Lucy sagged with relief at the sight of the ghillie. They were safe!

'This wae, this wae.' Following Catastrophe, the near toothless ghillie shepherded them across the clearing to where a massive tree stood, its leaf-laden branches radiating outwards above roots thickly carpeted with leaves and fungi. Around them, Lucy felt the forest grow alive with the potency of another world. With unexpected strength, Charlie lifted them up to where the knotted trunk branched out, before gathering up his shuttered lantern and passing that up to them too. Catastrophe leapt nimbly above them.

'Y're nae hurt, are ye?' One milky eye stared blindly ahead. The other searched the forest behind. They shook their heads mutely.

'Stay here, keep quiet. They cannae hurt ye as long as ye stay up yon tree. Haud on tight. D'ye understand?'

Kealan and Oliver didn't have a clue, but Lucy understood the ancient power of the generations old trees in the Wychs Wood that protected all the forest's creatures. Earth Magic danced across her skin like a warm caress, lessening the fearful pounding in her head. Looking closely, she could see the Earth Marks of *protection* and *nurturing* that rose throughout the heart-wood like sap.

'Dinnae climb doon, no matter what. Your grand-father will be here soon enough.' Charlie pulled a long gralloching knife from inside high boots. 'Here.' He handed the knife to Oliver haft first. 'Take this. Lassie,' he looked directly at Lucy, 'nae magic. For your life, nae magic. You don't want to attract his attention!' The crippled man returned to the ground and hobbled across the clearing. Planting his feet firmly on frost cracked leaves, he picked up his shotgun, plugged in two cartridges from the full belts that crossed his chest, and closed the breech with a reassuring click. 'Sit, Ambush, sit.'

The tension in the air hummed and snapped. Catastrophe's hackles rose and his thick, black-banded tail fluffed out dandelion fashion, each hair fine-tuned to the magical ebbs and flows in the air. Lucy could feel the hairs on her arms and neck rising in sympathy as dark magic rolled forward over the forest. The pressure in her head grew and grew, pulsing upwards until she could barely breathe. The sound of splintering wood was drawing rapidly nearer. She struggled for the inner calm of Gaia, fear blunting her efforts.

The clearing was briefly lit and then died back into darkness.

BANG!

The sudden sound was deafening. Kealan screamed. Oliver screwed up his eyes and covered his ears. Something thudded onto the ground. Charlie ejected the cartridges and swiftly reloaded. Ambush was growling, hackles up.

BANG! BANG!

A mucklegrub slammed into Charlie, spinning him brokenly round. The gun flew up in the air, landing near the bole with a dull thud, and the man didn't move. Ambush cried out once as a claw sliced into the dog's fur, then fell into silence. At the edge of the clearing the injured creature was screeching its frustration, ripping branches off trees and beating the ground. It could not ignore the scent of Earth Magic that lay hung in the clearing like a ground frost. To cross these ancient wardings would mean death, and the relentless mind that summoned it from the Fifth Dimension had turned to other tasks. In the distance other voices answered its call. The mucklegrub hunkered down to wait.

'Oliver,' Lucy appealed. 'I have to do something!'

'Lucy?' Oliver waved a hand in front of his sister's unseeing eyes. 'Lucy?' he repeated desperately, reaching out to touch her still form. 'Don't go. Please don't go.'

'You're safe it you stay here, they can't touch you!'

A warm flush flowing through the wood told Lucy she had crossed the threshold between the physical and spiritual worlds. She opened her eyes. Beneath the corpulent moon a raucous cacophony of sound rose to greet her. A bat swiftly answered her urgent summons, and within moments she was flitting through the forest searching for pursuit. *There!* Heavy-set shapes bulldozed through bushes, stopping only to scent the air, tearing a rent through the floor of the forest. Manlike after a fashion, but the build of gorillas with spiked spines, they had long muscled arms that hung to the ground. They were barrelling forwards with the same swift knuckled gait as a chimp. Only these creatures were armoured and carried wicked weapons. Their leader paused to sniff the ground. With a guttural bark it leapt forward.

Lucy had never seen a mucklegrub but her dream-memories recognised one. She felt their innate loathing for all things that moved in the bright light of day, blending with the mindless lust of the hunt. Yet Lucy also sensed another strong emotion, a deep reluctance. *What are they afraid of? What can three children and a cripple do?*

CHAPTER TEN

Scramble, Scramble, Scramble!

High among the clouds, the landing pads at the top of the Sea Dragon Tower on Dragon Isle were a flurry of activity. The Rapid Reaction Air Wing (RRAW) had been scrambled, and an Imperial Black stealth battledragon of the elite SDS was being prepped for immediate take off. The time was at T minus 10 and counting. Three harriers had already flown.

Visible only against the rising moon, the Imperial Black stretched its carbon-coated wings, under-armoured with titanium scales, and sheathed its claws, ready for take-off. Imperial Blacks were as dark as the empty space between the stars. No running lights betrayed their presence in the night sky. Over-powered, over-armoured and densely shielded by ancient magics, they were invisible in both the Fifth Dimension and the world of men. Perfect for inter-dimensional missions.

'Go, go, go!' The mission commander, a mountain dwarf from the Weeping Glen, urged her troop of BoneCrackers to mount up.

Landing lights flashed amber, warning all non-mission personnel to clear the pad. Powerful tendons cracked as huge wings slowly powered up. T minus 5 and the Black Knights of 9 Commando Brigade were going into combat.

5-4-3-2-1...The landing lights turned green. 'Thunderbolt Tornado, Thunderbolt Tornado... You are cleared for immediate take off.'

'Roger that, Sea Dragon Tower. We have lift off.'

So saying, the top-gun pilot, a Dragon Lord with five hundred bells on Imperial Blacks, activated her helmet-integrated display and sight system (HIDSS), and gathered the reins of her battledragon. Thunderbolt Tornado rose silently into the night sky, twisted gracefully through three axes and climbed swiftly towards the Wychs Wood. On board, the SDS strike team checked their equipment and braced for drop-dead.

The Imperial Black reached the stratosphere high above the Sorcerers Glen, and only a fleeting iridescent flare like a shooting star in the night sky marked its passage through the Jump Gate into another world. Tightly strapped on between the dragon's armour spine plates, it was nonetheless a roller-coaster ride. No matter how many jumps you made, you never got used to the gut-churning drop. Rookies always carried a 'barf' bag. Those who forgot had to wash their helmets out.

Buffeted by the turbulent air, the dwarves doggedly gritted their teeth beneath their matt-black full-face visors and braced themselves in readiness, with the stocks of their spelled weapons against the dragon's armoured plates. Passing fleetingly through the vacuum of dimensional-hyperspace, the dragon shuddered heavily before popping out into the mortal world like a cork out of a bottle of champagne. The pilot wasn't worried. She knew her stealth battledragon would register no bigger than a bumblebee on human military radar.

She held Thunderbolt in a hover as she considered the

terrain on her monocular display. Far below her, the empty road from Thistleburr wound like a curving pale scar that hugged the contours of the loch. Spots of marigold light picked out the houses and crofts that flecked its northward path. Thunderbolt dropped out of the sky. Below, flashes winked through the forest canopy close to the drop co-ordinates. Stalling heavily, Thunderbolt hung above the dense woodland, his huge wings effortlessly maintaining a hover over the targeted drop zone.

'Go, go, go!'

Ropes were thrown and forty seconds later the Strike Team had abseiled down and gathered round their commander. The dragon melted into the night sky, the massive downdraft from his wings fading like a passing storm.

'Deploy deflector!'

The Strike Team split into predetermined pairs and disappeared through the tangled undergrowth. Within a minute the first team checked in.

'Team One, check.'

'Team Two, check.'

'Team Three ...'

Yanking up her helmet-mounted display visor, the mission commander checked the readouts on her wrist display and depressed a spell icon.

An invisible Shield Bubble formed around the inter-dimensional rift (IDR), isolating it, and them, from the rest of the mortal world.

'Shield deployed,' she growled into her voice-activated

comm. 'Team One: Bluntaxe, Grikjum, Kneecracker, Heed-Banger and Pumplestomp. You take the IDR and clear the caves. Team Two: Heartburn, Rorgstone, Battlehammer, Chisel and Gimlet – secure the children. Stormbringer, Hornblower – you're with me.'

Pulling down their battle blast shields and readying their chosen weapons, the Strike Team closed in on their uninvited guests.

A dim red light in Command in Control (CIC) at the heart of Dragon Isle revealed banks of tactical displays. This was where the integration of technologies and magic was at the forefront of evolving military strategy and tactical decision-making. The soft whirr and click of equipment was overlaid by the calm voices of dozens of gremlin technicians tracking events as they unfolded. The Night Watch supervisor, himself a gremlin of some twenty years' experience in the SDS, swallowed nervously as he scrutinised their work; he had scrambled the RRAW on his own authority. He fervently prayed that he had done the right thing.

He moved over to where a horseshoe bank of consoles was tracking the Strike Team. Live feedback, from night-vision helmet-cams lit up thirteen split-level displays. Individual trooper sensor feedback scrolled down the right hand side. The forest was too dense for the visual sensors to reveal any new data yet but this was the realm of magic.

Seated in the centre on a mono-railed chair, the young SDS officer in charge of tonight's operation thoughtfully stroked her braided hair rings: two pewter and one silver denoting the rank of Major. The Supervisor watched as the dwarf toggled a few knobs, frowned, and then keyed data into the powerful computer. The sophisticated complex of panels and screens in front of her was awash with digital readouts constantly acquiring, processing and analysing data. A welter of white-blue icons and dwarfish glyphs were inset into the banked desk next to the inbuilt ergonomic keyboard, specially designed for stubby dwarf fingers. No one could match the dwarf clans when it came to battle tactics.

'Mission Control to Black One,' she growled. Check your helm-cam.' A thump from Black One and the grainy feedback cleared.

'Mission Control to Black Leader. ETA IDR – two minutes and closing. Multiple intruders: grid 36A:92C. Locate and destroy. Be alert for incoming friendly fire ...'

The Supervisor shook his head fretfully as he moved across the room. The gremlin automatically checked the pilot's acoustical telemetry signature; fluctuating, but within acceptable parameters. Satisfied, he moved on down the line. Hearing footsteps, he hastily turned to greet the incoming figures, instantly recognising the tall broad-framed BattleMage, Lord Twyholm Somerled, who was Guardian of the SDS Battle Academy, followed by his white Siberian wolf, passing through the security access tunnel.

'Sire!' The gremlin bowed nervously.

'Grotbag,' The Guardian acknowledged the officer on duty. Three senior members of the School of Aerial

Tactical Warfare and the Dean of the Faculty of Interdimensional Studies from the Virtual University followed behind him, radiating nervous energy that sparked and snapped.

'Status?'

'IDR, Sire.' Grotbag moved to a transparent tactical display that took up half a wall: a small-scale topographical map overlaid by a neon reference grid. A pulsing star indicated the epicentre of the rift. Icons inset to the right flickered to life as the young gremlin's hand swiftly passed over them. He selected one with his long black fingernail, and the map zoomed in to an individual grid sector on a scale of 1:500.

'The Wychs Wood!' The Guardian's eyes narrowed as he took a closer look. The epicentre was barely a half-mile from the source of The Leap, but the quake was barely registering 0.2 on the IDR scale display and already closing.

'There are also trace signatures, Sire, here and here, but they are very faint.'

'So?' The Guardian still did not understand. Interdimensional rifts occurred naturally and fairly frequently. As any self-respecting sorcerer knew, squashing multidimensional worlds into a finite amount of space, for instance the One Earth, inevitably had consequences. Like planetary tectonic plates colliding or pulling apart, the multi-dimensional worlds of the One Earth were both drawn and repelled by magical shifts. These shifts tended to cluster around dimensional fractures like the Sorcerers Glen, creating huge magical pressures. Sooner or later these pressure points blew like volcanoes, causing what gremlin techno-speak referred to as inter-dimensional rifts or IDRs. One such fault line lay along the length of the Sorcerers Glen.

'Sire....' The Supervisor nervously bit his lower lip with sharp pointed teeth. 'This rift was *summoned*: the energy traces are very faint but we detected it. As there are no authorised jumps scheduled for this evening I ran a check against the Sea Kingdoms database. Initially it could not identify a match. We ran secondary level diagnostics. No problems identified. So I ran a check against all known sorcerers past and present.' He touched an icon and a sub-display overlaid the map. 'The *Summoning* Signature here was initially shrouded by a rune-blind. But just for a second, the rune wavered then stabilized, and look, Sire – look at the signature!'

The Guardian hissed. Magic had a particular dimensional signature as personal and unique as a fingerprint, and the identifying glyph that leapt out of the screen was known and feared throughout the Fifth Dimension. His throat suddenly felt dry. *He is reaching into the Fifth Dimension! How? Whose magic did he draw upon?*

The gremlin keyed another icon. The board came alive with movement.

'These are?'

'Mucklegrubs, Sire.'

Mucklegrubs? The Grand Master started. They were brutal and stupid; and that made them unpredictable. Like the larger apes, but with a viciously spiked backbone used to disembowel their victims. Only a Mage could command them so the Raven had recovered some vestige of his former power. What on the One Earth was going on? At least a dozen such contacts were converging relentlessly on a now stationary group of four a mile to the south of the rift. The Black Knights were on an intercept course. 'And these are?'

'We think they are children, Sire. Only there is an anomaly,' Grotbag drew the data aside and called up another diagnostic panel. 'There are very faint traces of an unidentified composite in their immediate area. And,' he went back to his original sub-display. 'This one here, setting up a defensive perimeter, is most probably the White Sorcerer's manservant, for he has set them under the protection of a wych elm. We should be able to make a positive identification in...' The gremlin glanced over to the lead team digital displays, '... less than three moments.'

Children? Has the White Sorcerer's grand-daughter been discovered? Was it possible the Raven had learnt of her existence? No, if that were so he could easily have killed her long ago.

* * *

'Lucy! Lucy!' The sheer terror in Oliver's voice drew Lucy back into herself with such force that she slammed into the trunk and nearly lost her grip. She looked down to see Kealan, half blind with panic, scrambling to the ground. Gathering in his long legs beneath him Kealan stumbled to his feet and was swallowed by the forest. With a howl of triumph the wounded mucklegrub gave chase. Catastrophe dropped silently to the ground in pursuit.

'Lucy!' Oliver cried as his sister leapt from the tree. 'Lucy, they'll kill you. Lucy! Don't leave me again. He told you not to use magic! Lucy!'

'Stay up there and you're safe. I promise.' Swiftly casting symbols of *protection* and *calm* in the smoking air, Lucy was gone, leaving her brother weeping in the wych elm and Charlie motionless beneath its sweeping branches.

Catastrophe hissed in warning and sprang as a shadow loomed out in front, barring Lucy's path. Growling with frustration, the enormous creature flailed at the spitting hissing fur-ball that kept it from its larger tastier prey. In that moment of confused confrontation, magic totally failed the young teenager. Throwing back her fist instead, as she leapt, she instinctively rammed it forward with all the force she possessed. Eyes crossed with pained surprise, the huge mucklegrub grunted as it fell to its knees in a jangle of chain mail.

Lucy immediately knew she would have to do better than that. One lucky strike on its sensitive bulbous nose was not enough, and although Charlie's shot had peppered the mucklegrub's left shoulder and arm with lead pellets, the creature was already lumbering angrily to its feet. And by the sound of it, several more were also giving chase. Tilting her head to listen, Lucy easily detected and isolated the crash of Kealan's frantic flight. Knowing her friend was nearing exhaustion, she fell back instead on her grandfather's martial arts training: The Way of the Dragon.

'Heeeeyaaaah!!!'

Spinning lightly on her feet, she felled the mucklegrub with *The Whirlwind*, landing both her feet on its chest followed up by *The Striking Adder* which was meant for its throat, but hit its face. She hadn't the strength or the experience to fell the creature for good. Instead the mucklegrub gave a strangled gurgle and went down once again, clutching its nose in anguish, feebly trying to fend off Catastrophe's frantic attack as the wildcat danced just out of reach of its bristling spine-crest.

In an effort to ease the pounding that threatened to dilute her magic, Lucy took a deep breath and sought the inner calm of meditation. The young girl had no idea that what she was about to attempt was only taught at post-graduate level at The Virtual University, and with good reason. Both University Senate and the Guild considered it far too dangerous for untried apprentices or even the majority of sorcerers under the rank of Mage. Too many never returned: trapped forever in the mind of the creature they had temporarily *bonded* with. But Lucy had loved animals all her life with all her soul. Beginning with bonding with small creatures like mice and hedgehogs at the age of six, she had swiftly progressed through the field and hedgerow to smaller mammals, bats and birds and, once when she was eleven, a whale. She had found herself swimming in the freezing sea for days after that and had learnt a valuable lesson in over-confidence. But she had never before imposed her will upon an unwilling host, albeit a fairly primitive one.

Biting her lip with concentration, Lucy turned towards the east for higher awareness, drawing the apex point in the air. Describing the second symbol, Air itself, for increased power of the mind, and finally the subtle mark of *bonding* to complete the triangle, she drew the points together. With a whispered word she cast her Earth-Spell, and her body faded silently from view, becoming a gnarled branch invisible against the bark of a tree while her spirit *searched* for her unwilling host.

Beside Lucy, the massive mucklegrub that had been reaching up towards her inert body, spraying droplets of blood from its fractured nose, found its knees unexpectedly buckling. It blinked and shook its head as if adjusting to a new and puzzling thought. Growling softly in confusion as Lucy battled to control it, the creature sluggishly attempted to struggle to its feet, only to collapse a third time. Summoning the full force of her will, Lucy impatiently urged the primitive body to obey her simple commands and grasp the two-bladed axe that lay in the long grass. Bred for battle, used to unthinking obedience, the mucklegrub obeyed the imperative that whispered in its tiny mind.

The axe fell through uncooperative fingers, wielded by a girl unused to the sheer weight of the thing. As the heavy weapon cleaved half the creature's foot, Lucy repressed the explosion of white-hot pain that threatened to overwhelm her. If she fainted, she would lose what little control she had gained and would be as good as dead.

'Up! Up!' she screamed frantically in a guttural mockery of a voice, as three more mucklegrubs barrelled through the trees behind her. She would never know where the ancient language of the Elders came from. 'By Earth, Wind, Fire and Water I command you.' The air pulsed and boomed. Lucy's borrowed mucklegrub turned to face its newly arrived companions. Ignoring the stench of foetid breath that filled her borrowed nostrils, Lucy's mucklegrub lobbed the head off the first and the axe hand off another and had shrugged off the unwelcome body before the remainder of the troop had rallied and turned their lethal spines on their fellow.

As strident squeals and steel sparking on steel rang out, Lucy, with Catastrophe at her heels, was already running swiftly and silently after Kealan. In her euphoric haste she neither sensed nor saw the spell-warded SDS troopers until she fell tumbling into their arms, where a panicking Kealan was already struggling against the iron grip of an armoured dwarf.

'Lucy!' He gasped in relief. 'Wh-'

There was a sudden gusting of wind and they both looked up to see the largest dragon imaginable dropping out of the wind-churned night sky.

Kealan fainted.

* * *

Moran stood stock still, too afraid to move. What he had just witnessed was like something out of a horror movie. About to flee the way he had come, the sight of whatever those creatures were which leapt out from the back of the cave had changed the Deputy Headmaster's mind in no uncertain terms. Now he stood, soaked and uncertain. Then he had the second fright of the day as an unearthly cry of rage ripped through the tunnels. Despite himself, compelled by some inner madness, Moran tiptoed back up to the cave and stole a quick glance. Warwick DeSnowe was standing with his fists balled as his outline seemed to wobble and change, but even worse was the man's face: it had sagged like melted candlewax. Covering his mouth, desperately trying not to be sick Moran had all but fallen down the steps. A second furious scream had galvanised him into action. Jerking, stumbling like a puppet on broken strings, Moran fled for his life the same way as the children; for by now he was in no doubt that he would take the departed children's place.

CHAPTER ELEVEN

The Vice-Chancellor

The Grand Master Rubus Firstfoot and Vice-Chancellor the Lord Barnaby Rumspell were old friends; indeed, their friendship could be traced all the way back to their apprenticeships at that renowned scholarly institution founded in the century of the Grumpy Capercaillie by the Sorcerers Guild: The Virtual University. And so it was not surpris-ing that, immediately following the arrival of a cloaked Imperial on the landing pads above, bearing a message from the Guardian of Dragon Isle, they ensconced themselves in the study at the heart of the Master's residence with a vintage port and a pipe rack, and orders not to be disturbed. And it was there, because the Lord Rumspell was a dear and trusted friend and because he was necessary to their future plans, that the Grand Master revealed that the White Sorcerer had a grandchild raised in the mortal world, and how by sheer chance she had nearly been captured by the newly returned Black Raven.

The enormity of that thought silenced them. The corpulent Vice-Chancellor, in tartan robes, pulled off his wet boots with a grunt and warmed his feet at the fire. He had a hole in his right sock. Rumspell considered the offending toenail for a moment before replying.

'I did not know Caitlin had a child.'

'Very few do. She apparently lived only long enough to give birth, then she and her husband were buried near

Franconia in New Hampshire, where he came from.'
Peregrine said Caitlin loved that open vista surrounded by
mountains almost as much as here. Midwife Mistress
Pemberton took Lucy to be brought up with her son in
Yorkshire, whilst Peregrine stayed in Harvard University
in Boston, and Washington.

'He has not been the same since his daughter's death.'

'No,' the Grand Master shook his head. 'But he loves
his grand-daughter dearly. And although Oliver is not
truly his grandson, no one is any the wiser.

'He, too, is important?'

'Yes. Oliver will also have a role to play by Lucy's side,
for he is a gifted...err...err...' Rubus Firstfoot sighed with
exasperation. *Technology!* 'Programmer..err...coder. A
problem solver, Peregrine says.' The Grand Master
grimaced. 'He says the boy can take on DeSnowe in his
own world by breaking into his computer networks. He
can infect them with a virus...err...'

Rumspell's eyes crossed, making the Grand Master feel
much better. So he was not the only one to find
technology baffling.

'So she is to come here to be trained?' Rumspell asked.
'Will she not be in danger?'

'None save you and I and the Guardian know of her
existence. The Raven does not know Caitlin lived long
enough to have a child, and above all else we must
conceal that from him.'

Rumspell looked at his friend and frowned. 'Rubus,
what if Lucy chooses not to take up her mother's mantle?
Or if she is not as gifted as Caitlin?'

'Then we will have to do the best we can. Once we may have had time to find another, but the Raven has put plans in motion, I am sure of it. Why return to his lair in the Highlands? He is openly challenging us. Something has changed. Peregrine says that his holdings in the mortals' world are vast, that it is his hand behind countless wars as he sets them one against the other.'

'Well,' said Rumspell unable to stay downhearted for long. 'At least the Raven will not know that our grasp of technology is somewhat greater than it was last time we confronted him. He may even believe that we don't know who he truly is...that he killed Caitlin before she revealed his identity. Arrogance was his downfall once, it may be again.'

'I know, that wouldn't be hard, but we've done it. Peregrine's idea last century to found Gremlin Intelligence 5 and 6 has proved little short of inspired. High magic can match high technology in many fields, but our reach is limited.' Grand Master Rubus Firstfoot paused, reluctant to utter the fear that gripped the Guild and University in the latter part of the twentieth century.

'We have failed to make that quantum leap, where technology has succeeded. Technology can reach billions in the blink of an eye and is embraced by humans wholeheartedly, although they cannot control the power at their fingertips. Nuclear fusion is as dangerous as Maelstrom Magic; both have immense powers of destruction. The Raven will use it to bring them to their knees. He nearly did fifty years ago during their so-called 'cold war' and the Cuban Missile Crisis. This time he might succeed. He is a master at treachery and deceit...'

'Then we must not fail now,' Rumspell said softly.

The Grand Master nodded. 'We took a calculated risk in allowing Lucy to be raised in the mortal world that killed her parents, deeming her safer. But the Raven's unexpected return has forced our hand: it's time to bring her here to learn the other side of her heritage and I need your help.'

'Of course, of course. Anything.' the Vice-Chancellor nodded, and then a thought struck him. 'Do you think Warwick suspects the truth, that he set a trap for her?'

'No, no. Twyholm is certain of his intelligence. He believes the children were hunting for treasure in the old ruin in the woods when they uncovered old tunnels. He merely took advantage of the ... opportunity.' The Grand Master shuddered as he replayed the girl's recollection of the conversation she had overheard. 'We believe he requires ... new blood to sustain his own life. And Samhuin approaches, what the mortals call Hallowe'en.'

'Yes,' the Vice-Chancellor of The Virtual University replied thoughtfully. 'Predator and prey. The cycle of birth, death and rebirth. All such rhythms are part of the Web of Destiny and life is always the ultimate prize. It is only,' the scholar qualified, 'a question of degree.'

'Yes,' the Master replied heavily, 'and we both know what that means in his case; nothing short of the obliteration of the Guild and the subjugation of human kind. He may even sacrifice the One Earth in pursuit of the Elders.'

There was a long silence while both sorcerers sat lost in

memories. Despite the drawn curtains and the warm heavy tapestries, the Vice-Chancellor shivered.

'And the child? Is she safe and well after her adventures?'

'Yes, Lucy is safe. By the time the BoneCrackers arrived she had already taken steps to protect her brother and friend herself. The girl *bonded* with a mucklegrub and set it on its fellows.'

'What?' The Vice-Chancellor coughed as a mouthful of port went down the wrong way. '*Bonded*!' he exclaimed wiping his bushy beard with a sleeve. 'A mucklegrub, you say? Ah, by the Four, Rubus, she is truly her mother's daughter and that gives me hope!'

'Indeed. A dangerous craft. To have a novice succeed, and with a creature so brutal.' The Grand Master shook his head in disbelief. 'Brutal, but thankfully stupid. Susceptible to manipulation...

But that very achievement succinctly demonstrates we have procrastinated too long. Tundra,' the Grand Master paused to affectionately ruffle the head of the huge wolf that came to lie at his feet. 'We have sought to protect her, to allow her a normal childhood amongst men so that she belongs amongst them. Mistress Pemberton has taught her our ways since she was but a babe, and Peregrine has guided her childhood these last six years. But the time has come to begin her formal apprenticeship, to meet the peoples and creatures of the Fifth Dimension. Only here can she truly understand the nature of our world and its peoples and creatures.

'In a few weeks your new semester begins and I would

like to have her enrolled as your apprentice. Fresher's Week coincides with their schooling mid-term break. How many are apprenticed this year?'

'Around one hundred. Mostly from the Seven Kingdoms, and a handful raised amongst Otherfolk families, like young Lucy.' The Vice-Chancellor stared at the fire, waggling a ringed finger thoughtfully in the air. 'There is another apprentice, Rubus, a boy from The Gutters in the Old Quarter. The Old Quarter, I know,' the Vice-Chancellor held up a beringed hand to ward off the protest forming on the Grand Master's lips. 'Hardly where you'd expect to find such aptitude for learning, but there it is. His college entrance examination was outstanding, simply outstanding. I intend to take him as a second apprentice – with a full bursary, of course. The lad can teach our sorcerer's apprentice the ropes and do a better job than we could possibly manage. We are old men, and she needs the company of youngsters her own age. In any event, she needs to be as inconspicuous as we can make her, and that means she must become as familiar as possible with this world of ours. What better place for her to learn the base realities of life? No one will look for her in the City slums, least of all the Raven and his minions.'

The Grand Master mulled the idea over in his mind and nodded 'An excellent idea, Barnaby,' he nodded. 'Excellent!'

'When are you sending for her?'

'Tomorrow at dusk. Peregrine is introducing her to the physics of dimensionality at this very moment.'

'Then I think,' said the Vice-Chancellor of the Virtual

University, 'tomorrow evening will also serve as an opportunity for me to meet young Lucy Pemberton.'

CHAPTER TWELVE

Dragons and Stuff

The house spider scuttled up the wall and escaped out the window into a frosty world of dappled sunlight. Lucy's eyes flicked to the Bear, sitting quietly by the fire, watching her through a haze of smoke. Having eaten a whole rabbit, Catastrophe was lying on his back at his master's feet, burping with satisfaction.

Oliver and Kealan were playing cards. Kealan was still rather wobbly and had lost his appetite for adventure, at least for now. Coming face to face with a very large example of a creature he didn't believe in, he had suffered selective amnesia, and done his best to convince himself it had all been a nasty dream. Charlie was in hospital at Fort William, having suffered severe concussion, but luckily no other injuries. Ambush was at the local vets, having had twenty stitches on a gash on his flank. Inspired by the BoneCrackers, Oliver had begun designing his first computer game: The Fifth Dimension.

Damp wood in the fire fitfully hissed and hummed. Pinesap bubbled. Grey wood-smoke billowed and danced up the chimney; filling the room with a smell so thick you could almost taste it. The pine suddenly cracked and sparked in a fitful shower of sparks. Lucy jumped. Smoke...starburst explosions...screams and shouts and spells ricocheting through the woods...

Lucy! Lucy, don't go! They'll kill you!

By Earth, Wind, Fire and Water, I command you...

Sucking in a deep breath, Lucy took the plunge, knowing somehow life would never be the same again. 'Why am I so different? Why can no one else do what I do? I mean, mum does things, little things when she thinks no one is looking, but Oliver can't; Kealan can't. What's different about me and you? I- I seem to know things I haven't been taught...'

The Bear nodded. This time was always going to come.

'Every living creature, man or beast, is unique. Every one of us has unique gifts to share with those we love. Sometimes it takes time and luck to find what we are good at. Now, Oliver here works magic with his computer...he has a gift for solving puzzles, seeing patterns...he can reach out from his bedroom to anywhere in the world...a very talented young man indeed!'

Oliver glowed.

'Kealan is a gifted swimmer; perhaps will become a champion. Win a gold medal at the Olympics.'

Kealan preened, trying not to look smug and failed. For once his big feet were an asset and it was true ~ he was in his element when he was in the water.

Lucy held her breath as her grandfather turned to her.

'Many human legends and myths speak of a magical time when there were no boundaries between people and animals, and it was believed that animals forged a living link between people and the One Earth. Magic resided in every living thing. Mystical and physical were interwoven, and everyone could draw upon it. Those days are long gone, banished by science and technology, relegated to history.

Those peoples such as the Eskimo, the Native Americans, the Maori, and the Aboriginals and many others still honour the old ways. Amongst these peoples, animal spirits or totems, and shamanism, continue to play an integral role in life. They still honour that unbroken tradition that has existed from our most ancient ancestors. You, Lucy, are such a one. You have always demonstrated a deep affinity and affection for all living creatures, be they great or small. You are an Earth Child whose heart beats in rhythm to that of the One Earth in all its dimensions, and one of those is the Fifth Dimension ~ the world of magic.

Oliver grinned at his sister. Lucy rescued slugs from pavements, and spiders from getting sucked up by the hoover. Wasps were calmly removed from the classroom, and injured wildlife nursed back to health. He had always thought his sister would become a vet, like Thistleburr's Megan Anderson. Perhaps also study at the Royal Dick Vet at the University of Edinburgh.

'Would you like me to show you that other world?'

'Yes!' Lucy's grey eyes suddenly caught the sunlight, making the breath catch in her grandfather's throat. *The same eyes. The same smile.* He swallowed. *I will not lose her. By the One Earth, not this time.* His grey eyes narrowed. *No. Not again.*

'And when you say animals...' Oliver piped up enthusiastically. 'You mean dragons, too, like the one we saw yesterday? It was *huge*!!'

'Yes,' the Bear smiled. 'Why do you think we see dragons everywhere in movies, ancient artwork, fantasy novels? Man *remembers*, even if he doesn't believe! Let me show you.' Lucy's grandfather looked down to where his young audience held their collective breath. Kealan and Oliver fidgeted under his scrutiny, both acutely aware that they were being permitted to share something special with Lucy. Beside them, Lucy bounced with barely suppressed energy. She couldn't remember having being so excited before.

'The first dimension.' The Bear drew a burning line in the air with his finger. 'A simple line.'

Kealan frowned disapprovingly.

'The second dimension is the area of a flat surface – for example, a square or circle drawn on a piece of paper.'

Kealan coughed pointedly as the circle smoked.

'The third dimension is our world.'

A globe spun in the air, arcing around a distant sun, a small moon caught in its gravitational well. 'You, me, and every living thing in creation. We are all creatures of the third dimension. And to our world of up and down, forwards and backwards and side to side, we add our past and the future, or timeline if you will, to the cosmological mix. Thereby creating the fourth dimension. But....' He paused, with a craftsman's eye for timing. 'All rather boring, don't you think?'

Kealan fidgeted, silently agreeing.

Oliver nodded doubtfully, wondering what was coming. He held his sister's hand tightly, a little afraid that he was going to lose her to this other world, where, for the first time in their lives, he couldn't follow. Sensing his discomfort, Truffle parked herself on his lap. Lucy for once was motionless, held in the grip of a fascinated terror.

'Welcome, my dears - to the Fifth Dimension.'

Sparks flew from the chimney to swirl round the room, filling it with fleeting images. Towering medieval citadels and crashing waves flickered in the smoke, sharp-faced green-eyed gremlins and stout, loudly dressed gnomes, black armoured knights astride black dragons as large as a football field...huge flocks of sorcerers on broomsticks ...breathtakingly beautiful elves on feathered dragons, all the colours of the rainbow.

Kealan instinctively ducked as those feathered wings slowly unfolded and dived straight through him on hidden gusts of wind. Oliver stared awe-struck. *I wish my computer games were as good as this*, he thought, not for the first time, nor, he was sure, for the last. *I want to design holographic computer games,* he determined, envisaging the fortune that would be his. *Embedded in glasses...like Google glasses...borrow a little of Lucy's magic!*

'The Fifth Dimension is what you would call the magical dimension: an elemental world that harnesses the power of Earth, Wind, Fire and Water but also wood and metal and stone and ice. Astrophysicists and mathematicians have long guessed at its existence, but still it eludes their grasp. The power of dimensional magic remains far greater than any science or technology can devise.' He raised his bushy brows questioningly at Kealan's open mouth and beckoned Lucy forward. 'Dimensionality, my dears, is simply an attitude of mind. Observe.'

He flicked a fingertip, effortlessly weaving together elements to his design with a barely audible word. Where the wall and chimneybreast should have stood, a rectangular void blinked into existence. Beyond lay the open loch, barely visible through an opaque threshold that rippled like water.

Kealan squeaked.

Lucy leapt to her feet, curiosity and delight chasing across her face.

'A Gateway, my dear.'

The Bear clasped her hand.

'Set your sights at a right angle to reality ... and step forward into the Fifth Dimension.'

'The Fifth Dimension,' Lucy breathed softly, testing the strangely familiar name on her tongue.

Kealan, suddenly conscious of his open mouth, popped it shut. Oliver stood hesitantly in front of the void. 'It looks just the same,' he said, clearly disappointed not to find a dragon parked on the doorstep.

'Yes, my dear, yes, much of it is. And many of our cities and peoples bear the same names from a time when our twin worlds co-existed, one within the other. Indeed, it is only in the last few thousand years, as Lucy knows, that the Sorcerers' Guild and all that we stand for have finally passed beyond the ken of mankind. Except for the tribes I mentioned previously. They still honour the old ways. For them the door to our world remains open.'

Lucy reached out to touch the rippling Gateway.

The Professor watched his grand-daughter, hoping that she would learn to love this new world opening up to her.

It was so very different from the world of men. Would she blossom as her mother had? Only time would tell.

'We, you and I, and everyone else,' he explained for the benefit of Oliver and Kealan. 'We are all part of the One Earth and the Web of Destiny, bound to its intricate pattern, its future.'

'The One Earth.' A thrill of recognition ran through Lucy.

'Even if,' her grandfather continued, 'many are blind to it. There are many who wish to rule, Lucy, boys, to dominate all other creatures and peoples, to bind the powers of nature to their will and to strip the earth of her wealth. They would leave a barren wasteland for those who will follow. The Guild is dedicated to preventing that.'

If the Earth dies, so shall we all die. Gaia protect us.

'And dragons and stuff?' Oliver interjected returning to a favourite subject. 'How come we don't have any? Or,' he searched for the word Lucy often used. 'Totems. Why don't we have any of them?'

The Bear nodded.

'To the western world, to many of our close friends and colleagues, witches and their familiars – generally cast as cats, toads, spiders, owls and bats – are creatures of fiction that live only in story books and movies, or in the superstitious, over-excitable imaginations of seventeenth-century peasant England. Ironically,' a smile touched his lips, 'though few realise it or even think about it, we celebrate that which we don't believe in every Hallowe'en, and in countless children's books from *Winnie-the-Pooh* to *The Northern Lights*. Children take it for granted that animals communicate with them. Think about cuddly toys. Everyone has them, but as they grow up they simply forget why. But in the Fifth Dimension, that magical time and that link with the animal world, still exists. Animals are never subordinate to our whim nor do we own them. They are our teachers, our companions and friends; often our soul mates, more precious to us as any living soul.

Gnomes, too, as you all know, possess the ability to transmogrify into another creature's form, to shape-shift into an animal form that allows them to pass unnoticed in this modern world of ours. Now,' the Bear twanged his braces. 'Time flies and so must we. Are you ready, my dear?'

Lucy stood silently; filled with the need to hold the moment, to imprint life and love as it had been before everything changed. The Bear stood silently, understanding. Accepting a hug, giving her brother a brave smile, Lucy stepped through.

The Gateway swallowed them up. There was a faint clap of rushing air as the void collapsed with a whiff of smoke. The faintest residue of cordite hung in the air. Neither boy moved. Oliver battled between pride and envy, his taller fair-haired friend overwhelmingly grateful that he had been left behind. He had seen enough mucklegrubs and warped black magicians to last him a lifetime.

Mother poked her tousled head round the door. A tray stacked with buns and cakes followed her into the lounge.

'Ah, they're away already,' she said cheerfully, trying

to hide her worry, pouring out the hot chocolate for Kealan and handing Oliver a Pepsi-Max. 'Dear me. Never mind. All the more for us!'

CHAPTER THIRTEEN

Vampires and Vegetarians

It was more evening than afternoon. Lucy and her grandfather walked slowly along the overgrown path in easy companionship and deep in conversation. Catastrophe, the object of their discussions, had long since disappeared into the long grass to spread fear and dismay amongst the local bird and mammal population. The cut off squawk of a pheasant and the hysterical yelping of a wild dog pack showed that he was having fun.

'But when will I...'

'...get a more glamorous totem?' the Professor finished astutely. 'One that you can form a more meaningful relationship with? One that isn't quite so... *vulnerable?*'

Lucy's blush said it all. Spiders intrigued her. Their webs were the strongest threads in the world. Sometimes she would tease garden spiders with a blade of grass, tickling their tummies until they bounced up and down, shaking their webs to identify their tormentor.

'I don't know, my dear,' the Bear laid a reassuring arm around his grand-daughter's tense shoulders, pulling her within the familiar folds of his cloak. 'No one does. Your spirit-animal, as we more commonly call them, will choose you, just as Catastrophe chose me. And the choice may not necessarily be to your liking. Ah,' he put up his hand to forestall Lucy's inevitable protest. 'Not everyone could love a slug or a rat or a lobster the way you can.' That raised a smile. 'Or a large foul-tempered wildcat.'

That raised another smile. 'But they are here to guide and teach us what we need to know. It can happen when you are a baby or when you are in your nineties,' the Bear continued. 'For some it may never happen at all. For those who exist only in the Fifth Dimension, their totem will stay with them throughout their long lives. But for others, like you, and myself, destined to live with a foot in two worlds, totems live out only their normal term of life. We love them with all our hearts, but then we lose them to the Earth's Cycle of Life, and another creature takes their place. As you grow and change, so too your spirit-animals will change according to your needs. Some, like Catastrophe, will be your companion in both worlds. Others, for example a mammoth,' Lucy smiled despite herself, picturing a jaunt down to Goose Green with a mammoth in tow, 'cannot possibly cross with you to Thistleburr, and so they cross with you in spirit only, hence the term 'animal spirit.' They are there to guide and teach you. But, either way, they will always be at your side, and in your heart. Ah, here we are.'

The setting sun was already casting long shadows when the Bear stopped and whistled. The horse that cantered to a stop by the gate stood a full nineteen-hands with hooves the size of cymbals. It would have to be a big horse that could carry the Bear!

'Phew,' Lucy looked relieved and finally admitted, 'We're riding *horses*!' Strange to be nervous, but animals and brooms were two different things, not to mention her fear of heights.

The Bear chuckled knowingly. 'Ah, yes, my dear. One

thing at a time, mmnn?' he muttered as he disappeared into a tack room stuffed with hay and a jumble of equipment.

'Hello, old friend.' He selected a saddle from the rack and, stepping up the worn mounting block, threw it over the horse's broad back. 'Paladin meet Lucy.' The stallion nickered as it nuzzled at her pockets, nose soft as velvet, his breath hot and damp on the back of her hand.

'Here.'

Lucy took the wrinkled apples that appeared in her grandfather's hand and fed them to the dapple-grey.

'I've never seen a saddle like this before,' she said curiously, reaching up to touch the unusual dual-saddle design as the professor strapped it on with practised efficiency and fitted a tooled leather bridle.

'I think you'll find it quite comfortable. Our equivalent of a family car I suppose! Grab a cloak from the pegs. Right, my dear, here we go.' Her grandfather helped Lucy up the stone mounting-block and adjusted her stirrups. After checking the horse's girth he mounted himself. He nudged the horse to a trot.

'We must make the City, my dear, before the Watch close the gate for tonight. I had hoped to beat the rush hour. No matter. We should just manage in time.'

They made slow progress despite the wide gauge of the causeway that spanned the loch in eight giant leaps of stone and wood. Witches and wizards congregated loudly in groups, trading, haggling and debating, looking little different from the good citizens of Thistleburr save for their medieval dress and weaponry. Richly dressed artisans and merchants on finely caparisoned horses, pointedly clutching pomanders to their noses, looked down in disdain at the unwashed, unruly mob that blocked their passage. Wrinkling her nose, Lucy had to admit they had a point as the crowd carried them along. The colourful, rank odour painted a thousand pictures, none of them attractive. The pong was riper than a pair of Fergus's unwashed socks disintegrating in the locker room.

A few sorcerers bobbed into view, easily distinguished by their bright robes and designer staffs, but the tallest by far were the powerfully built and heavily armoured troll marines with their heavy-ridged brows and bow-legged gait.

'Oi! Stop thief! Stop thief!' There was a cry of anger as a scrawny bat-eared gremlin made off with a purse, melting into the oblivious, uncaring throng thinking only of a fire to rest by and a pot of soup against the cold. Halfway across the causeway the press almost brought them to a halt as the crowd smoothly parted to make way for several dozen dwarves heading for the glens. Wrapped in plaid and kilt, the glowering dwarves rode wild boars the size of Shetland ponies, shields at their backs, axes in belts. No one in their right senses, not even huge trolls, picked an argument with such a notorious combination of attitude and tusks.

'Dwarves!' Lucy whispered with a smile of delight. 'Dwarves! And they're riding wild boars! It's just like Lord of the Rings!' Hearing her, her grandfather smiled in quiet satisfaction. *After all, where did Tolkien get his ideas from?*

Yawning ramparts surged darkly out of the surf to greet them, climbing to where torches smoked and sparked and soldiers drilled, black against the sunset. Spray and spit caught the air, gusting back in a wash of creamy lace that drenched the packed travellers as they approached the ironbound gates. Beyond, a higgledy-piggledy forest of smoking chimney stacks, windmills and steep roofs fought for space with their neighbours within the crowded city walls.

The tightly-packed crowd swarmed beneath a wicked portcullis, bursting into a sprawling fish-market that clung stubbornly to the outer walls. Wood smoke swirled and sparked from a dozen huge braziers. Lucy started as hands reached up to the horse, thin clutching hands pale against her dark cloak. Scared, she pulled away, but the hands clung to her, threatening to pull her from the saddle.

'Lady, fair Lady. A penny, fair Lady?'

'Beautiful bracelet, Lady, to match your eyes.'

'Pots and cauldrons, Lady, mended so as you wouldn't know.'

The unwashed swarm of beggars and street urchins surrounded the horse until the Bear muttered a mild *dispersing* spell. The crowd instantly turned away, already seeking more pliable targets, and all around the bawling cry of hawkers and street traders rose to mingle with the squeal of pigs and the coarse braying of pack-mules.

Lucy wrinkled her nose, tasting the familiar eye-watering smell of salt water, fish and tar on her tongue. Her searching eyes caught a familiar scene. She caught at the Bear's sleeve.

'They're kippering today's catch!'

As she watched the split-herring being lifted from barrels of brine Lucy remembered when the Bear had first explained about kippers. They had been sitting on the old stone wall that ran around Thistleburr Smokehouse, sharing a bag of chips. A half-dozen kippers wrapped in newspaper were tucked in the saddlebags of the Bear's motorbike.

'Do you know where kippers come from?'

Lucy had squinted suspiciously at the Bear, looking for the catch to this seemingly simple question. 'From the sea?' she ventured.

'Aha!' The Bear had smiled smugly, delighting in catching her out. 'No! Kippers are smoked herring. The fishermen don't catch kippers, they catch herring, gut them and then they are pickled in barrels of brine and hung,' he pointed to the hive shaped kilns, 'on tenterhooks. Hence the expression, *I'm on tenterhooks*.' He put up a hand to forestall Lucy's question. 'Tenter-hooks are simply nails that are hammered into sticks called tenter-sticks. Watch and learn.' And Lucy had watched then, as she was doing now, as the dripping tenter- sticks were handed from fishwife to fisherman and on into huge hive-shaped kilns that became narrower and narrower, drawing the eye up to where the oak-scented smoke finally escaped into the cooling night air.

Once they broke free of the choked market-place, the crowds gradually dispersed into a myriad of crowded alleyways and dens where narrow houses reached so high their overhanging roofs shut out what little light was left in the sky. Buskers and beggars crowded thickly on dirt-packed streets choked with stinking middens, where hollow-eyed people and animals dug for scraps.

'The Gutters,' the Bear whispered as Lucy tightened her grip around his waist, frightened by the poverty and the desperate faces that ghosted in dark doorways and darker alleyways. 'One of the few places to survive the Great Fire.'

Leaving the smells of the harbour pooling in the cold air below, they made slow progress along a switchback deeply scored and rutted by the passage of countless wagon wheels and loaded barrows. Softly unfurling her senses to the growing night, Lucy could hear the crack of windmill stones grinding flour, and beneath their feet the muted gurgle of water from the city's hidden watercourse. The whisper of a thousand conversations leaked from behind darkened doorways and shuttered windows to swirl around her in a jumble of images. She pulled her hood down.

'Eek!' Lucy suddenly squealed and jumped and then was immediately embarrassed as the Bear turned enquiringly in the saddle.

'Washing,' she muttered sheepishly, shaking her head like a dog. She glowered upwards to where the crowded houses leant perilously close high above their heads, and dripping clothes lines were strung from attic to attic. At their feet a scatter of hens flapped in useless panic as they passed, and all the while Lucy gazed upwards to where the great Skye Keep spanned the earth and the darkening sky.

Paddocks and creaking windmills slowly gave way to thatched and timbered cottages, inns and dens and stable yards, and then again to grander houses with tiled roofs and glass paned windows. Even higher and the warren of streets and alleys flowed into a single paved and brightly-lit boulevard that hugged the contour of the hill in ever tightening circles. Whitewashed mansions and palaces grew larger and grander the higher they rose, and overhead dragons swept down to hover above landing-pads, their burnished scales catching the last of the westering sun as it finally disappeared beyond the black mountains in a defiant blaze of red.

'Lord, Lady.'

A groom rushed forward to help as Lucy stepped gingerly onto the mounting block, and, as the horse was led away, three servants with smoking brands ushered their guests towards the massive stone tower that dominated the Sorcerers Glen.

'What ho, there! Wait for me!!' Leaning heavily on his staff, a portly man with several chins too many and eyes surrounded by a sea of wrinkles waddled up to them, puffing and blowing. In his wake, his companion beavered along furiously trying to keep up, claws clicking on the cobbles; webbed hind feet leaving a trail of water clear across the courtyard. As the wizard reached forward to take the Bear's offered hand, he winked at Lucy. She liked him immediately.

'Barnaby,' the White Sorcerer returned the greeting warmly. 'You're back from London early. And how are you keeping?'

'Well … very well, Peregrine, thank you.' Barnaby's many whiskered chins wobbled as he spoke, and his warm brown eyes twinkled with delight as if he had just enjoyed a joke. 'Mistress Pemberton's seaweed and bark ointment worked a treat; my leg feels almost as good as new.' He smiled ruefully. 'That silver birch wine of yours – could knock a dragon out!!'

The wizard turned his beaming face towards Lucy, who had bent down to scratch the glossy plump beaver behind its small ears. 'And this young lady must be…?' He raised eyebrows that looked like small bushes, determined come what may to grow into a fully-fledged hedge.

'Lucy,' she said helpfully in case there was any doubt. 'Pemberton,' she added for good measure.

'Of course you are, m'dear. A credit to your mother, I hear.' Lord Rumspell clasped her hands in his and planted a soft wet kiss on her knuckles with an audible smack.

'Lucy,' her grandfather introduced her, smiling at her obvious squirming embarrassment. 'This is my old friend, Barnaby Rumspell. Vice-Chancellor of the Virtual University.'

'*Uncle* Barnaby, m'dear, Uncle Barnaby to you,' Lord Rumspell boomed, without pausing for breath or releasing her damp knuckles. 'And this fine fellow here is Muckle.'

On hearing its name, the beaver slapped its flat tail loudly on the stones and fixed Lucy with an interested brown-eyed stare that matched his master's. *Welcome. Do you have any birch bark?* he asked hopefully. Lucy shook her head.

'Well, welcome to our humble Guild. Has the good Professor shown you around yet? ... No? ... Wonderful! Then I shall ... We've time, haven't we?'

Lucy's grandfather nodded.

'Good, good.' Retaining a limpet-like grip on Lucy's hand, Lord Rumspell ushered them across a cobbled yard and through a small postern gate inset into the tower. 'Welcome, m'dear,' he said, 'to the Skye Keep.   Right,' Lord Rumspell smiled conspiratorially.   'Just stand here.' Shuffling obediently, Lucy looked down at the carved stone circle inlaid into the bedrock and felt the dormant wellspring of power beneath. *A porting stone*, Lucy remembered the Bear had mentioned them, *with the power to transport anyone from one site to another. Created by the sorcerers for those...how would we put it these days? Those Folk not of a magical persuasion?*

'Wonderful, m'dear. Close your eyes ... Go on now.' Bewildered, Lucy screwed up her eyes as the two men moved either side of her. The air suddenly warmed and her legs buckled slightly making her stomach lurch warningly. But the sensation barely started before it stopped. Bright light now burned her eyelids, and it was silent save for the loud hiss of wind. It was very cold.

Lord Rumspell chuckled with delight, a warm fruity sound. 'Open your eyes, m'dear. Open them!' Lucy's new-found uncle was positively jumping up and down beside her, impatient to see her reaction.

Lucy opened her eyes. A wash of adrenaline pumped through her. Swallowing quietly, she shaded her eyes and stepped forward, forcing herself to look over the stone ramparts, a familiar weakness washing through her legs. Most of the glen now lay in shadow, its contours picked out by burgeoning constellations of light as crofters and farmers lit their lamps. Immediately below Lucy, the Keep fell away steeply to the seventh gallery and the Grand Master's personal dragon pad. Beyond and beneath, landing pads and stables mushroomed out from the sixth gallery, hovering in thin air like lavender clouds. Far, far below a medieval cityscape of spires and rooftops and arching viaducts and aqueducts radiated outwards in a series of concentric circles, set in a shield of molten gold water. Lucy gripped the stone so hard her knuckles ached, trying to fight vertigo. She looked down. The world swooped. The sun dipped behind the mountains and the glen fell into darkness. Sudden movement caught her eye.

'Oh!' Lucy stepped backwards, reaching out to the Bear.

'Lesser vampire dragons, m'dear,' Lord Rumspell murmured at her shoulder, anticipating her question. 'Only find them here in the north. Thistles, you know.'

Lucy looked blankly at him.

'Thistles, m'dear. They only eat thistles.'

Darting through the growing dusk, clouds of the small black dragons were spiralling up into the translucent blue above, joining together into a vast swarm that gracefully swooped and soared against the saffron sunset in a synchronised dance. Entranced, as the night cooled Lucy watched as more and more tiny dragons rose from their hidden roosts. The sun fell below the horizon and the glen, and the ocean beyond fell into total darkness.

Overhead, flickering stars emerged from the deepening night, and the dancing dragons were silhouetted against the rising moon. It was breathtaking. Lucy turned to say so and jumped back with a squeal of fright. There was a soft movement in the still air behind Lord Rumspell and the Bear. What she had thought was a gargoyle rustled as it gracefully unfolded thin bat-like wings tipped with claws. Bright moonlight glinted off tiny armoured cladding and shining eyes. With a squeak of pleasure, the vampire dragon clumsily launched from under the eaves, plummeting down over the smoking chimneys and spires before catching the wind and rising up to greet the onrushing night.

'Lords? Pardon my intrusion.' A tall thin boy with the rimless hat of a sorcerer's apprentice stood silhouetted, dark against the brighter doorway, a bracket of candles held high before him. 'The Grand Master has sent to say his work is complete and you are welcome to attend him.'

'Thanks, m'boy, we'll come just now. Lead the way, Justin, lead the way.'

The air was heavy with smoking candles and magic as Lord Rumspell limped through the Moon Gardens, softly talking to the Bear. Muckle had gratefully disappeared with a delighted splash and gurgle into one of the ponds that bordered the moonlit path. The gardens were alive with the buzz of conversation and debate and the soporific tinkle of water cascading down waterfalls. Lucy walked slowly behind the two sorcerers, drinking everything in. The lanky apprentice dropped back to join her. Lucy was surprised to see glow stars dotted his hat and cloak.

'You're one of the White Sorcerer's new apprentices, aren't you?'

'Who?'

The boy frowned at her. 'Professor Lord Peregrine Thistlethwaite of course!'

'Erm, yes, I think so.'

'Lucky you,' the apprentice pouted, throwing back hair braided with bells. 'I'm apprenticed to old Prof Whittlebank,' he added. 'He's *so* boring, that is when he's not half asleep. He hibernates most of the winter and burrows in books the rest of the time. I shan't see him again till spring now – hey look! Moon spiders.' The boy pointed to where huge knobbly-kneed arachnids were delicately spinning their fine silk webs, silver against the dark foliage. 'They're really good with garlic butter and some nice crunchy bread -'

'Yeuch!' In the darkness Lucy shivered and crossed her eyes with horror. 'I'm a vegetarian myself.'

'Pardon? What's a vegetarian?'

'It's ... err, ... don't you have vegetarians?'

'No, never heard of them.' The apprentice shook his head, puzzled. 'How do you cook them?'

Their debate on relative culinary delights got no further. A sudden breeze caught their cloaks, followed by the sound of air rushing through a tunnel.

'Blood and Bone! Run!'

As Lucy's heavy cloak billowed and slapped around her face, she stared uncomprehendingly towards the bush the apprentice had dived into. On all sides, apprentices and servants were scattering in different directions, but the sorcerers, including the White Sorcerer and Lord Rumspell, were standing their ground, ignoring the commotion. Lucy could see their fingers gather spells. Tiny motes of light danced in the dark.

'Lucy!' the White Sorcerer bellowed.

Lucy looked upwards to where the darker shadow of a dragon shut out the stars as it bore down on them, and ran.

'Justin,' Lord Rumspell cried. 'Get over here, lad!'

A pointed hat poked doubtfully out of the bush. 'Lord-'

His words were swallowed by the down draft.

At the last moment the pilot pulled the dragon up from its dive. Barely clearing the trees it scraped over the roof tiles of the Hall, bringing down several chimney pots that smashed into the courtyard. There was a loud belch of smoke, and then it was gone. As two smaller dragons rose from the Hall dragon pads to give chase, people began to gather together in indignant groups.

'Not another stolen dragon!'

'By the One Earth! What does the City Watch think it's doing? Can't they catch a few wretched teenagers?'

Justin emerged from his shrub. Bits of twig were stuck in his hair. A large spider was firmly attached to his hat and refused to let go. He sidled self-consciously over to where Lucy was still staring in the direction the dragon had taken.

'Joy riders,' he explained, peeling cobweb off his chin. 'They'll have stolen it from up town somewhere,' he said, trying to get a tenacious strand off his hands. 'You're not supposed to fly big dragons over the city. The Guild introduced ordinances several years ago; it was becoming so expensive rebuilding. And quite a few deaths too!' he added as an afterthought.

'Deaths? Why did some people run?' Lucy asked, as more self-conscious bodies popped up from under shrubs and bushes.

'Ah,' said Lord Rumspell stepping up to them. 'Why indeed? Well, m'dear, it's common sense really. You see-'

A huge flame rolled over the top of the chimneys.

'Not again,' said Justin as he started running.

'Lucy,' the White Sorcerer said, firmly gripping her elbow. 'The safest place is here with us.' Both wizards watched with interest as the dragon passed overhead with barely feet to clear. It was riderless this time, reins flapping in the wind, and the saddle had slipped beneath its scaled belly. The air rumbled. Several spiders fell off their bush. There was a sonic boom as the dragon started climbing. Hot air buffeted the garden, followed by an appallingly loud vibration as something dense fell to earth.

'AAAAAAAArrrrrrrrrrggggggg-' Justin's muffled scream

was prematurely terminated. There was total silence.

'A close call there, Barnaby,' the White Sorcerer smiled happily.

'Indeed, Peregrine, indeed,' replied Lord Rumspell, considering the newly deposited mound with interest. 'Shame about those spiders, though...'

The shimmering bubble that had protected them faded.

'Yiich!!' Lucy stepped backwards, pulling a face.

The White Sorcerer coughed delicately into a handful of cloak, his eyes watering. 'Pungent,' he declared sympathetically, nodding his head. 'Pungent. It's the brimstone, ye'see.'

Lucy looked askance at the huge steaming pile.

'Fine hats those,' Lord Rumspell observed as the tip of a submerged hat poked through. 'Wandwillow & Undercloak unless I miss my guess. Ash for strength and willow reinforced for suppleness, I imagine. Foresight & Hindsight's have a most excellent collection these days. Perhaps a grade 1 or 2 spell woven in?'

'Blood and Bone!' the apprentice cursed, as his head followed his hat into fresh air – so to speak.

'Let that be a lesson, lad,' said Lord Rumspell kindly. 'Don't ever forget your basic first year spells. McGringle's Bubble is a good one to remember. Lucy, m'dear, I trust this answers your question? Good, good. Well, Justin m'lad, we have to leave you to the tender mercies of the clean up squad. Ah yes, that's them arriving already.'

A cart was rumbling towards them, pulled by a team of four drays. Dozens of dwarves armed with picks and shovels set to work immediately.

'They'll have him dug out in no time at all,' said the Bear reassuringly, smiling at Lucy's horror-struck face. 'A visit to the public baths, and he'll be right as rain.'

The party continued on their way, leaving the sound of happily digging dwarves in their wake.

It was a small entrance hall panelled in wood, the floors flagged in a flawless expanse of velvet slate. Stone hearths blazed to either side of a central staircase that wound its way up past spiralling galleries. Shields with lacquered coats of arms lined the walls, along with a business-like array of spiked battle staffs and dragon maces.

There was a sound behind, such as someone politely clearing his throat. Everyone turned. The owner of the vocal chords was a stooped grey-haired gremlin with a number one haircut. A small chain hung from his belt with a ring of keys, which his long clever fingers toyed with thoughtfully, like an abacus.

'Lady. Lords.' The bat-eared gremlin bowed his mottled head and clicked his heels. *Old habits never die*, the Lord Rumspell thought with an inward smile.

'Grimhelm,' the White Sorcerer smiled robustly. 'And how is the Grand Master this wonderful evening?' And never was a word said with more feeling. Any evening was beautiful if you had had a narrow escape from incoming dragon dung. Leading the way up past paintings of dragons; sabretooths, spitting adders, Imperials for the most part, then along a very long corridor decorated with a single hanging that reminded Lucy of the Bayeux Tapestry, Grimhelm ushered his master's guests through an open door.

Lucy paused on the threshold to take in the scene. Windows were thrown open to the cool night air, making the candles gutter and smoke. A figure dressed in cobalt robes stood idly in the trembling shadows, looking out over the dark loch, smoking a pipe. Next to the window a darkly polished desk was covered in a scatter of scrolls and books. A young gremlin was bent over a parchment, dusting the ink with sand. He rolled it up, sealed it with smoking wax, and going over to the casement he selected a bat from a cage hanging there. Attaching the carrying pouch he threw the homing pipistrelle bat into the night. Gathering up the remaining scrolls and bowing towards the turned back of the Grand Master, the scribe silently left. The door closed with a soft click. The man at the window turned.

Doffing their hats, Lord Rumspell and the White Sorcerer swept them to the floor. Lucy bowed as well. A poorly stitched button popped off Lord Rumspell's robes, ricocheted off the wall and clanged with a metallic ping against the fireguard. Lucy fought to stifle a giggle. She ventured a quick glance at the Grand Master.

Her heart thumped. He was watching her; heavily lidded eyes glinting from the depths of a hood, which still hid his face. A hawk-like nose protruded into the light. There was a short silence. Lucy fought the urge to fidget and quietly held the gaze of the man before her. The air crackled and sparked with anticipation. Unexpectedly, the smoke from his pipe changed hue. Rings all the colours of the rainbow chased around the room and out the window.

They were followed by a flock of rainbow birds swooping and diving before dissipating into the night. The Grand Master was rewarded with a delighted giggle.

'Come, child,' he said gently, in a deep voice. 'Come and talk with an old man.' Offering her his ringed hand, Rubus Firstfoot led the girl to where a bench and high-backed chairs were gathered round a cheery fire. Sitting, he dropped his hand to scratch the head of the white wolf that silently followed to lie at his feet, and then paused to consider the girl in torn patched jeans and faded T-shirt who knelt sat beside him.

She was of middling height and slim, all sharp angles and elbows and feet; still gangly and gawky and covered in bruises and scratches from her recent rough and tumble adventures in the woods. Her eyes were grey, as her mother's had been, framed by long lashes and delicate brows that swept upwards. Curious eyes that now quietly held his gaze and openly returned his scrutiny. Shame about the spots though – they were beginning to outnumber the freckles scattered on her nose and high boned cheeks by a ratio of two-to-one, but they, too, would doubtless pass in time.

As for the silver nose stud and the vivid purple toenail polish, well, he had been forewarned – thankfully! – that fashions had changed, and young people today did all sorts of strange things that his generation never dreamt of. But that was life, after all, and it kept the old from growing dull and complacent.

The fire hissed and sang. The White Sorcerer plumped himself down with a thud and a sigh at the other side of the hearth and stretched his toes to the fire; Catastrophe wrapped himself around his boots. Lord Rumspell bustled noisily off to a cabinet, and Lucy heard the clink of glass and the glug, glug of drinks being poured.

'M'dear?'

Surprised, glancing at the Bear who looked pleased with himself for bringing a bottle or two along hidden in his cloak, Lucy took the offered Coke gratefully. 'Thank you.' She smiled shyly and sipped her drink, bending down to stroke the huge wolf behind the ears. It closed its yellow eyes and gave a deep rumbling approval.

She's like her mother at the same age, no doubt about it, but not as tall. The Grand Master glanced quickly at his friend, sympathy softening his gaze. *I wonder*, he thought, as he accepted a Druids Ruin 80/- beer, *how he manages to keep the anger caged so deep inside.*

Pushing back his hood the Grand Master turned again to the girl, revealing a face at once both young and infinitely old with electric blue eyes. 'So,' he said smiling, and laughter lines wrinkled his face. 'Your grandfather tells me you are ready to go to University?'

CHAPTER FOURTEEN

The DeSnowe Dynasty

At school the next day there was another surprise. General studies was the S3s' first lesson after assembly. Miss Strang was just going over homework when there was a quiet knock on the door. The popular headmaster came in, followed by a dark-haired boy.

'Good morning, class.'

'Good morning, Mr Bruce,' the class dutifully chorused. The headmaster turned to Miss Strang, ushering the tall slim boy in front of him. 'This is Mortimer DeSnowe,' Andrew Bruce said, rather abruptly, 'who will be joining your class. Do make him welcome.' And with that, the headmaster left the room.

Hands in pockets, leaning carelessly against the teacher's desk, the boy lazily turned to look at his new class, a mocking smile playing on his lean tanned face. He was wearing designer jeans and T-shirt. Broad shouldered and graceful, he had the look of an athlete, and he was, Kealan grudgingly thought, looking down at his own long gangly legs, incredibly good-looking.

'Well, Mortimer,' Miss Strang beamed and waved in the general direction of the class. 'I'm Miss Strang, and these are your new classmates.'

Turning towards the teacher, Mortimer held out his hand. 'A pleasure to meet you, Ma'am.' There was an immediate rustle of interest round the class. The Etonian inflection was pronounced and deep, but underlying it was the unmistakable drawl of an American accent. *This must be the family all the fuss in the village was about!*

A heavy gold bracelet caught the light as Mortimer firmly shook the teacher's hand and looked directly into her face. For no accountable reason that she could think of, Miss Strang found herself blushing under the boy's close scrutiny. 'Well,' she said, flustered, shaking off those strangely hypnotic eyes that were so dark they were almost black. *Like a shark's...a predator,* where *on earth did that thought come from?* 'We'd better find you a desk, hadn't we?' Turning to the class she flapped her hands around distractedly. 'Now, let me see...'

Several hands went up around the classroom. Fergus hissed at Duncan sitting next to him. 'Take a hike, move over there,' he demanded. 'Quick!' He shoved hard with his elbow. As the heavily built boy clumsily took to his feet and lumbered to the empty desk behind, Fergus shouted.

'Here, I've a place free next to me. Miss Strang, I have a place next to me.' The new boy turned to look at Fergus jumping up and down.

'Fine by me,' he drawled, moving towards the desk at the back of the classroom. 'That is,' he turned to look over his shoulder, 'if it's alright with you, Ma'am?'

It would not have been Miss Strang's first choice. Fergus was consistently a troublemaker, forever disrupting classes and breaking all records for double-detentions – but she felt that in some inexplicable way she was no longer really in charge.

During morning break the S3s crowded around

Mortimer, instinctively knowing that their classes were likely to be more interesting now that the American had arrived. For starters, their new classmate had three diamond studs in his left ear and one through his nose, and his dark hair was tied back in a long ponytail. All three were against school rules. He was deluged beneath a sea of questions.

'Are you really an American?'

'What school did you go to before here?'

'Are you living in the old Lodge?'

'Are you very rich?'

'Are those bracelets real gold?'

'Is it true that you have stacks of servants to do everything for you?'

Used to being the centre of attention, Mortimer answered their questions carelessly with a smile, but amidst all the fuss only Lucy, talking to Oliver and Kealan out in the playground, noticed that the smile never quite reached his eyes. Wherever Mortimer wanted to be, it was clearly not Thistleburr. And there was something unsettling about him that disquieted Lucy.

Warwick DeSnowe stood in the glass penthouse suite of his Snowe Tower and looked down over London. Small people, the Black Raven told himself, looking at the milling masses heading for the subway and home, until recently hardly a worthy challenge. The last rays of the setting sun glinted off the ribbon of the Thames River as it wound its way sinuously through the noisy city, past that other more ancient white fortress which until recent centuries had also dominated the skyline: the Tower of London. But whereas every Anglo-Saxon had known the power and threat that the Norman tower posed, few could even begin to guess the greater threat that loomed high over them now in the early years of the 21st century.

From this eyrie that soared higher into the darkening sky than any other in London, even overlooking the Shard, the Black Raven could see the distant suburbs of the capital. And the military spec. satellite dishes and radar antennae that crowded the top of the skyscraper ensured that he could also see anything else he chose in this world. Anywhere on earth and beyond; even out into the cold depths of space. Technology was undoubtedly the new magic for a new millennium, and those fools in the Fifth Dimension who had chosen only to act as stewards had no idea what mankind was now capable of...what *he* was capable of.

Warwick splayed his hands against the cooling glass, trying to quell the anger that rose hotly. He had had to flee the Sorcerers Glen without feeding, leaving him weakened. Well the beggars that fed his appetite in London would not be missed in a city so large as this. Fresh blood and dragon venom elixir kept him alive – for now. But he had wanted a petty taste of revenge ~ the bloodline of one of those villagers who had condemned him all those centuries ago.

'Sir?' the young man crossed the floor with a smoking goblet. He wore a glove; else his hand would have been instantly frostbitten, and to drink would have spelt death, such was the cold power of the maelstrom. His elixir ~ a toxic blend of sea dragon venom and nanobots ~ represented the first true blend of technology and magic.

As the youngest son of one of the Black Isle's greatest patrician families in the Sea Kingdom, the Lord Warwick had been trained at the Battle Academy on Dragon Isle. A natural soldier who rose rapidly through the ranks of the SDS, he soon tired of endless battlegames. Turning to advanced combat and battle magic, he surpassed even the battlemages in four of the seven military disciplines, and became the youngest ever to command a regiment; the elite IV ShadowBlades. A regiment, however, with no worthy adversaries, no battle honours to add to the three-headed dragon standards...no glory...no fame...no enemies...the Sorcerer Lords had grown feeble and fat when there were worlds for the taking.

Not for him the weak, inept magic permitted by the enfeebled Guilds, but the raw unfettered magic of creation itself: maelstrom magic, more commonly known as chaotic magic, from which the very crucible of the Earth was forged: powerful, predatory magic, always seeking dominion ... always seeking susceptible minds. Long outlawed by the Guild, all knowledge was long since destroyed and scattered to the four winds, but whispers of its power lay hidden, waiting to be found. Clues were discovered in old castles, rune stones, fragments in grimoires and libraries. The dark of night...the cold of winter...death: chaotic magic lay hidden in deep shadows for those who looked.

He had thrived on its power, soaked it in hungrily like a black hole sucks in light and energy, destroying everything he touched. In the empty wastes of the frozen north he began to build an army held together by the power of the maelstrom. Secretly, he laid his plans and started to recruit other like-minded SDS officers to his fledgling army. *Why serve when we can rule?* And still he fed on the chaotic magic like a drug until its corrosive song pounded through his veins, filling him with its awesome destructive power. The price was high but payment lay in the future.

But there were many faithful to the Guild whom he knew he could not corrupt, whose strength was untested, whose collective power was undoubtedly greater than his, and one in particular of whom he was uncertain – who in the depths of the long night he feared, despite their bond of blood. That fear, and the rash confidence of youth, drove him to indiscretion and haste. Rumours of rebellion and betrayal reached the Guild. Summoned before the Guardian, the Lord Warwick fled to his northern castles in Caithness and Orkney; and, as another century turned and a bitter winter froze the highlands, he unfurled his banner and unleashed his ravening armies. Battle raged across the Celtic Sea Kingdoms for nigh on two hundred years. Spilling into the mortal world, it fuelled a fear of witchcraft across two continents that would take centuries to die, and blackened the name of witchcraft and wizardry. And then the Guild had caught him.

Dragged in front of the council, Warwick was condemned to exile and ultimately death after a mortal's hand-span of years. His twin brother made no move to save him. His raven was killed, and he was banished to the petty warring world he had sought to rule. Injured and diminished, he preyed upon the scattered farming settlements that clung tenuously to life in the shadow of the Sorcerers Glen, consuming their human flesh on All Hallow's Eve to extend his own life. Fear rippled through the highlands and beyond. Far to the south, whispers of witchcraft and necromancy reached the English Lord Protector Oliver Cromwell. Gripped in a frenzy of witch-hunting, the WitchMaster General and his puritan army marched north. They pursued their elusive quarry throughout the brutal winter months, finally trapping him in the depths of the Wychs Wood. Bound in deadly chains of iron that drained his power, he was cast over the massive waterfall in the Spinning Gorge, but not before he had killed some three score in the tunnels riven out of the black rock beneath his lair. Then they fired the Grange, hoping to erase the Raven's name from mankind's memory. But the legend of the Sorcerers Leap was not so easily forgotten.

He should have died. His broken body almost did. But chaotic magic's power hung on to damaged life, and by sheer effort of will his spirit triumphed; hovering on that stark boundary between life and death, lingering between the worlds of magic and man. He took sanctuary within the Sentinals; an ancient stone henge by the moor, an open portal between the dimensions where Wild Magic ran like quicksilver in the living stone crown.

For decades he nursed his hatred in the shadows, building his strength slowly, watching and waiting. Finally, on All Hallow's Eve, when the Wild Magic hummed and sang between the stones, he surged out from the henge and took another's body to make his own. After a century of struggle he was free. But one life was not enough; because the parasitic maelstrom devoured bodies like cancer. As each host was consumed the Raven was forced to take another and another, giving the henge its infamous name of the Necromaners Ring. Finally strong enough, he fled to the New World with his gold, where for generation after generation he continued to feed on human life to maintain the illusion of this broken husk that he now occupied. Not for much longer. Technology and magic combined would serve his will and impose it across two worlds.

It became clear during his first week at school that Mortimer, Mort to his friends, was both clever and charming. During class after class he impressed the teachers with his knowledge and quick learning ability and soon became a favourite. Even 'Old Prune-face', the dour history teacher who normally loathed children on sight, was giggling foolishly at his jokes. Mort spent money lavishly, showering his classmates with small gifts, generously sharing heaped bags of the most expensive sweets from the Chocolate Cauldron at break times, and treating everyone to ice creams and sticky buns from the Muffin & Bagel after school.

By the end of the week he had attracted a large group of admiring followers. The youngsters were bewitched. Their lives had rarely extended beyond Thistleburr and the Sorcerers Glen, and Mort's photographs of his family homes in New York, London, Paris and Monte Carlo brought glamour and excitement to the burgh – not to mention the expensive toys at the North Lodge: quad bikes, gaming PCs and to Oliver's envy ~ a Sony KD Ultra HD TV. But Lucy alone noticed that he gave nothing of himself to anyone, and nothing that he could not easily afford. By the Friday of his first week, Mort had already been allocated a place on the S1s rugby team gathered for practice in the afternoon gloom.

'Tackle! Pass the ball, pass the ball!' Mr McGill, ex-rugby international player and voluntary school coach, shouted encouragement. 'Andrew, get out to that wing, remember where you should be .. Duncan, *both* hands on the ball ... Sandy, which side are you playing for? Tackle, Fraser! Tackle!'

The first game of the season was in two weeks' time against the Fort William Foxes. Bereft of proper training and a place to practice, the Thistleburr Thorns were struggling to keep a team together. The coming match was crucial if they wanted to stay in the Highland League. Oliver shivered in the early October drizzle and tried to wipe his wet and steamed-up glasses with his muddy shirt. The small park beside the school, which doubled up as a sports ground, was churned into a quagmire, painting the players in their motley selection of old clothes and hand-me-downs a uniform shade of dirt. Only Mort somehow seemed to stand out from the crowd. His brand new Scotland rugby kit and natural athleticism, not to mention professional private school coaching at Eton (before he was expelled for drug taking), made him conspicuous by comparison, drawing admiring looks from the gaggle of spectators who braved the eternal Scottish autumn drizzle.

Wearing the white team bib, S1's number one try-scorer and team captain looked down at his mud-spattered knees, white with cold. Kealan's old size 7 boots were pinching his size 8 feet and letting in damp. His one and only proper rugby shirt had seen better days. But he didn't want to make a fuss; he knew how hard up his family was. Out on the right wing he stamped his feet to keep warm and waited impatiently for the ball to come his way. It was starting to get dark, and soon they would have to end the practice session. The teams stood even at one try each.

Suddenly the ball was coming his way. One pass – a second – now it was surely his. Kealan passed the slippery ball to his friend. Gripping it with both hands, Oliver steamed up the right wing, wholly focused on the approaching try line.

'Go on! Oliver! Run!' He heard Kealan's warning shout. He never saw anyone coming, but he briefly heard the pounding of feet in the squelching turf. Suddenly there was a horrendous jolt and he thumped to the ground, gasping for air like a stranded fish. The ball bounced out of his grasp, was scooped up, and a pair of brightly studded boots splattered him with mud as they sped away. Seconds later he heard a ragged cheer. Mort had scored a second try for the blue bibs. The whistle blew. Session over. A muddy hand was thrust down to help him to his feet.

'Tough luck, country boy.'

The crowd applauded the sporting gesture as Oliver looked up into triumphant dark eyes that belied the spoken sentiment.

It was now six o'clock and the dark school grounds appeared almost deserted. The last parents had left half an hour ago, heading for warmth and dinner. A light breeze chased some rubbish across the playground. A few windows glowed dandelion-yellow in the dark. Down in the gym, the janitor was moving equipment for a coming inter-school competition, humming loudly as he went about his tasks, his dog following at his heels. In the upper corridor, Mrs Anderson was mopping up the floor and trying to prise a stubborn blob of chewing gum from the sole of her shoe. Neither of them noticed two tiny pinpricks of light behind the bicycle shed.

'Twenty pounds a week for cleaning and maintaining the bike.' The taller boy took a deep drag of his cigarette and blew the cloud of smoke into his companion's face. The second, heavy-set boy hacked and coughed.

'Thought you knew how to smoke?' Mort observed with a sneer.

'I do,' Fergus protested. 'Course I do. It's just,' he swallowed down another choking fit. 'It's just they're a bit strong.'

'Yeah, right. Well?'

Underused mental gears ground into action. Eighty pounds a month! Fergus didn't hesitate. His pocket money was two pounds a week, all of which went directly into the jingling tills of The Chocolate Cauldron. This was easy money.

'Yeah,' he said, aping Mort's American accent. 'Yeah, that's cool.'

Disappointed as he was, Oliver was by nature both forgiving and generous. He wasn't entirely sure he wanted to be captain. Scoring tries for his team was what counted and, to be honest, rugby was beginning to lose its thrill. Coding had stolen his heart and all his spare time. He'd already decided what he would tell Mr McGill when he padlocked his bike outside the newsagents the following Sunday. If Mort became captain, that was OK with him. Collecting a huge pile of Sunday papers, Oliver stuffed them untidily into the fluorescent paper bag, strapped on his helmet, kicked up the side-stand and set off. Kealan was still down with the flu, and Oliver was covering for him.

It was hard work; Thistleburr was built on the lower slopes of the surrounding mountains. Then skirting about the Wychs Wood, his round took in all the cottages that lay at the fringe of the forest or around the side of the loch. By seven-thirty, both paper bag and the dawn were considerably lighter, so Oliver kicked up a gear. He raced along the old railway track and up over the banking, heading for the kirk. At that point, where the tarmac turned to rattling cobbles, a screw holding the back mudguard on sheared, and the mudguard whipped down under the tyre. The bike stopped dead in its tracks with a screech of hot protesting metal that catapulted Oliver head-over-heels onto the hard road.

The bell rang and the playground reluctantly emptied as people headed back for afternoon classes. Fergus cursed, using a word that he had once heard his father shout before he had stormed out and never come back. He was fiddling with the complicated gear spindles. Mort had told him to tighten the chain – before school broke at three o'clock. For some reason it was thick with grease, and he already had liberal amounts plastered over his sweatshirt and hands. Fergus groped around the asphalt, looking for the blasted spring link that had pinged off goodness knows where. He growled with frustration and threw the spanner bad-temperedly at the bicycle shed. Given that it was a brand new bike he hadn't thought his part of the bargain would actually entail any serious work. Fergus avoided serious work like the plague.

'McGantry.' The clipped precise tone froze Fergus to the spot. 'Doing a spot of maintenance, are we?' Sarcasm dripped from every word. 'To someone else's bike? It's becoming a bad habit. Over here, if you please. Now. And bring that with you.' The Deputy Headmaster pointed to the boy's feet. 'No, not the spanner, the hacksaw.'

The hacksaw? Fergus was genuinely confused and looked round to where Moran stood smiling nastily, pale eyes as sharp as his nose. '*That* hacksaw, McGantry, *now* if you please, or you'll get double detention.' Fergus stood up in horror, aware that a growing number of people were lingering at the school door trying to listen in on the one-sided exchange.

'But I don't have one!' he protested hotly. He threw down the spanner and watched in horror as it bounced and caught Moran's shin. Seeing the mean expression forming on the Deputy's face, Fergus stepped backwards – onto a hacksaw. Now everyone was watching, hanging out of open windows. With fresh humiliation, Fergus was marched off by the scruff of his neck to the staff room, protesting his innocence loudly to anyone who would listen.

'But it's not mine. How many times do I have to tell you?'

'Oh, I know very well it's not *your* bike, McGantry. And that is precisely the point.'

'But –'

Fergus looked over his shoulder and threw an anguished glance at the crowd as if he expected a lifeline. Lucy followed his eyes but was unable to see who he was looking for. The onlookers broke up into smaller groups to speculate on the fate of the hapless Fergus. Lucy was still waiting and watching when someone chuckled softly in the gloom of the bicycle shed and a cigarette flared. Grinding the stub underfoot, Mort sauntered off to his next class. Lucy realised suddenly that he had done this deliberately. He was enjoying the spectacle too much.

'Have you heard, Oliver?' Lucy was horrified.

'What?'

'Fergus has been suspended for tampering with Mort's bike. Sawing through a mudguard bolt!'

'Yeah,' Kealan added. 'Weasel-Face caught him red-handed at lunch break. He's going to be suspended.'

'But that's what happened to my bike! Oliver unthinkingly reached down to rub his broken leg, even though the cast wouldn't let him. 'That's why I crashed. A bolt had been sawn through!'

'Yeah, that's what they think h- ' Kealan nodded.

'But why would he sabotage Mort's bike?' Oliver shrugged. 'They're mates.'

'Well he was caught in the act by Weasel-Face – '

'- with a hacksaw. There were loads of witnesses -' Lucy added.

'Mort says Fergus is jealous of him...'

And then two days before half term week and Hallowe'en, Fergus disappeared. For two days his desk sat empty. Mort didn't appear at all concerned. 'He's skiving,' he had said casually when asked by Mr Bruce. 'He's done this before, hasn't he?'

The headmaster of Thistleburr School coolly considered the boy standing in front of him. There wasn't anything he could put his finger on, but he didn't like Mortimer – not one bit. Nor, as he had demonstrated, was he remotely overawed by the wealthy DeSnowes, unlike his Deputy, Mr Moran, who was practically grovelling in front of the boy and had made so many foolish promises to the father. The Headmaster had had strong words with his obeisant deputy following the billionaire's unexpected visit during his absence the week before, and Mr Moran had been in a filthy mood ever since. The Headmaster frowned with distaste and turned to the policeman standing beside him.

'Mr McFeeley. Do you have any more questions?'

Mr McFeeley didn't. Not for the first time, he was completely perplexed.

'Can I go now?' Mort was looking thoroughly bored. 'I *do* have to go to rugby practice, you know,' he drawled. 'After all,' he added, smiling in a self-satisfied kind of way. 'I *am* the captain now, and without me the team doesn't stand a chance.' Mr Bruce reluctantly agreed.

'That boy knows more than he's saying,' he said as he showed Constable McFeeley to the door. 'But,' he admitted, 'his explanation seems entirely plausible. Fergus *has* played truant many times. He's even run away from home, but sooner or later he always turns up, unrepentant and disruptive as ever.'

CHAPTER FIFTEEN

Gertrude

For Lucy, half term could not have come soon enough and Fergus was the furthest thing from her mind as she set off round to her grandfather's cottage early on Saturday morning. The loose dark breeches, soft boots and heavy dark jerkin Mother had laid out for her felt a little strange, but not so odd as to make her stand out in either world.

'Many children from the age of ten or eleven upwards are enrolled at university,' the Grand Master had explained, as the young girl sipped her Coke and stroked his huge wolf. 'But the Fifth Dimension is what your history books would call a 'medieval society', one similar to your world hundreds and hundreds of years ago. Generally speaking, those who are enrolled at our university come from wealthy patrician families or from the merchant guilds. They are often younger sons and daughters who will not inherit the family wealth and lands.

'So...' the Grand Master planted large hands on his knees. 'The twin concept of school and compulsory education as you know it does not exist here. We only have, as once you had, universities as seats of learning and discourse, and nothing like as many as exist in your world today. Although,' he smiled, 'you do have virtual universities, first founded by one of the OtherFolk like yourself who move between worlds.

'The majority of children become novices who study for six years to gain a basic education in the sciences, mathematics, history, languages and elementary sorcery. But those who show greater potential are enrolled as apprentices to a Professor. You, my dear, are such a one.'

'Given that I am often away on business,' the Bear said. 'We three have agreed that you are to be apprenticed to no less a person than the Vice-Chancellor of the Virtual University!'

'Uncle Barnaby?' Lucy's smile was one of relief. Mother had already warned Lucy it could not be her grandfather and the young girl had been really nervous of finding her way in this new world without his guidance.

'When? When do I enrol?'

'I suggest one week from now,' the Grand Master

replied. 'When your grandfather himself has to attend the University for the first meeting of the Winter Senate. He has been appointed to a new Chair in Stealth Magic and will be taking up the position immediately. An auspicious occasion that neatly coincides with Freshers Week.'

Uncle Barnaby nodded. 'Quite so, m'dear. That will give you a little time to prepare yourself, sort out your gown and books, and so on and so forth.'

The Bear had his head buried in a cupboard and was tugging something out. It flew out over his shoulders. Lucy held it up. A black gown patched with brightly coloured squares! Red spots on white...green and yellow stripes...purple...mnnn.. .not exactly cool!

'Try it on! Try it on! It was mine when I was your age!'

Lucy shrugged into it. 'It feels very strange. It's a bit long...'

'Well, lots of universities still wear robes...St Andrews, Oxford, Cambridge. You will get used to it in no time at all!'

'Right, well.' He glanced at his watch. 'Time we were making tracks for the University; we're running a wee bit late. Ceremonial robes for me today, I think.' He coughed. There was a muted bang. Gone were the bright patterned braces, the broad-rimmed explorers hat with pheasant feathers stuck in the band and the trademark boots with mismatched socks and laces.

'Well, my dear?' The White Sorcerer tried not to preen and failed dismally. He was dressed in flaming red from head to toe. Tiny runes in gold threaded the fiery material in arcane symbols and Celtic patterns. The robe's frayed edges and the moth-eaten rim of the truly spectacular five-pronged ceremonial hat only marginally marred the overall impact. And, Lucy noticed, one or two of the stitched red-gold stars on the cloak had fallen off or were hanging by a thread, but who cared? It was quite magnificent!

'Wow!' Lucy managed admiringly.

'The Stealth Magic School,' the Bear explained, 'comes under the joint auspices of the Faculty of Fire and the Faculty of Wind. I think red suits me so much better than blue, don't you agree?'

'Err...' Lucy mumbled her assent, wondering what on earth 'auspices' meant and mentally filing it to look up later. Leaning forwards to the mirror, the Bear adjusted his hat, the topmost point of which was sadly crumpled and hanging onto a swinging crescent moon for all it was worth. Seemingly satisfied, he selected a staff and satchel from his hat stand. The staff was white as bleached bone and carved with the head of a roaring bear at the top. He slipped the leather thong over his wrist and handed Lucy a satchel.

Lucy realised her mouth was hanging open like Kealan's often did, and closed it just as hastily. The Bear chuckled. 'Impressed my dear, mmnn? Time to fly! I'm afraid, given how late we are, we must take a broom. Do you think you can cope?'

Lucy's stomach churned with nerves but she nodded brightly, holding her hands to stop them shaking. *Please,*

please don't let me be travel-sick. Please, please, don't let my fear of heights make me fall off or do anything stupid...Please, please...

As the Gateway from Thistleburr closed behind them with a muted pop, the Bear ushered Lucy out through his peeling front door. His broomstick raced round from the back where she had been gossiping with the trees. Catastrophe leapt from the roof onto the generously bristled broom with surefooted feline smugness and settled himself down. Despite his injuries, the cat seemed as sure-footed as ever. Lucy took a second look at the broom. A few pipistrelles and one hedgehog were hanging out in the bristles.

'Right, Gertrude, two up today, and one's a novice, thank you.' The pale, broad-handled broom immediately grew several feet in length, and a saddle with deep stirrups appeared in front of Catastrophe. Lucy instinctively stepped backwards before she remembered her grandfather's unexpected revelation that brooms were alive: crafted from living wychwood. Sensing her hesitation, the broom jinked and rustled by way of invitation, earning Lucy a baleful glare from Catastrophe. The girl stretched out a hand and touched the shaft. It was warm to the touch and silver Earth Marks flowed through the grain.

'She's an old girl, quite gentle, m'dear.'

The idea of mounting anything that was just hanging suspended in thin air took some getting used to – let alone talking to it. Lucy felt more than a little daft and for once was glad that Oliver wasn't there to see her. *It felt like talking to your wardrobe!*

'Right, my dear,' the Bear encouraged. 'Give it a go. Nice and gentle, no, don't leap – '

Lucy landed awkwardly as the broom shied away. Catastrophe yawned pointedly and swatted half-heartedly at a cloud of midges.

'Here, my dear,' the Bear beckoned her to a mounting block embedded in the garden wall. 'Try this way.'

Lucy approached the broom a second time, angry with herself.

'Gently, gently,' the Bear offered, 'Broomsticks are just like people and horses. They have different temperaments. Now Gertrude here is an old lady, very stiff and prickly these days, and rather sedate. She won't buck, but she doesn't like rough and careless handling, and she is not particularly fond of children. That's right ... foot firmly in the stirrup ... yes I know it seems a bit strange at first but you'll get the hang in no time...'

Time passed... quite a lot of it.

'OK?'

Lucy nodded, swallowing dryly, unable to speak.

'Gert-'

Finding he could barely breathe, the Bear adjusted Lucy's limpet-like grip so that he could suck in a lung-full of air.

'Gertrude, The University, if you please. Nice and slowly, and keep low.'

Gertrude rose gently above the lawn and pivoted towards the Loch. As the broom climbed up over the still water, the faint sound of shouting carried up to them on the wind. Lucy looked nervously down. There was a fierce argument taking place down beside the causeway. A witch in the fir green robes of the Pine Marten Lodge was standing next to her bent broomstick, hat askew and hair sticking out wildly. A child of about four or five strapped into a child carrier was bawling loudly.

'Why don't *I* look where I'm going?' shouted the outraged wizard standing next to his parked stick. 'If you hadn't been paying so much attention to your child, Madam, you might have noticed that you were speeding as well as driving without due care and attention - '

'If you hadn't been flying a broomstick as old and decrepit as you clearly are...'

'Madam! I must protest...'

As they rose higher still, Lucy looked over to where the cottages and houses of Thistleburr normally clustered round the south end of the Loch. The shore lay pristine and undisturbed, save for a scattering of crofts betrayed by thin wisps of chimney smoke that hung in the still air. It took Lucy a moment to realise that there were also no telephone wires. Not a road or a single tourist bus in sight. Instead, the dense Wychs Wood stretched as far as the eye could see. She had never seen anything like it save in glens inaccessible by roads.

Suddenly, Lucy's skin prickled as an eerie cry rose and fell to echo off the mountains. A sound not heard in Scotland for centuries. Clutching the Bear as hard as she could, Lucy turned awkwardly on the broom to eagerly search the woodlands passing beneath her feet.

'Wolves!' She grinned, fingering the wolf pendant that hung on a fine silver chain around her neck. *What other creatures were not extinct in the wild and untamed prehistoric landscape of The Fifth Dimension? Bears? Beavers? Wild boar? Elk?*

'All of those and many more, my dear.'

Lucy blinked. The Bear was a mind reader!

Sweeping out across the sparkling water, the Black Isle city rose to greet the travellers like a medieval fortress ghosting on the loch. The colourful spires and heraldic devices of the seven Lodge towers passed quickly beneath; then they were passing through the drifting smoke hanging over the dragon pads. She caught a fleeting glimpse of a huge scaled body glinting in the weak autumn light, and then they were past and the rushing cold air made her eyes water.

'Arrggh!' The Bear cursed, almost dropping his pipe.

An apple had bounced off his hat and landed in Lucy's lap, followed by what looked like a cheese sandwich and several chocolate biscuits. Gertrude slowed as the Bear temporarily lost concentration, and Lucy risked a glance up to where a stationary broom hung suspended in the air above them. Two sets of feet dangled in the air. The broom had 'L' plates.

'Sir!' The exasperated voice clearly belonged to the wizard with the bright red safety helmet on. 'You don't slam on the brakes – you glide to a stop slowly and safely. Otherwise you might cause an accident. As it is, I have just lost the contents of my lunch box. Now let's try that again, shall we?'

The smooth sardonic voice slowly receded as the broom rose steadily.

'Open your eyes, my dear.'

Obeying reluctantly, Lucy peeked over the Bear's shoulder to look at the rapidly approaching headlands. The low cloud thinned. Gleaming white in the sunlight, the university towered above them. Lucy was almost speechless.

'It's...'

'My dear?' The Bear reined Gertrude in, giving Lucy time to collect her thoughts.

'It's...'

'It's carved out of the White Mountain!' she explained to Oliver late that night, struggling to find the right words to convey the impossibility of what she had seen. 'They call that range the Dragons Spine, just like we do! It's... the university is built *into* the mountain! Like a honeycomb. People on brooms darting in and out like bees. It's... a tangle of blue turrets and spires and spheres and stars – all sorts of different shapes just hanging there in thin air! And dragon pads,' she scrawled a shape like an upside down mushroom on the cover of one of her brother's computing magazines. 'Floating like lavender clouds around the spires. And-'

'And dragons?' interjected Oliver hopefully.

'Oh, yes! Lots of dragons,' agreed Lucy, warming to her topic and still awash with excitement. 'Not just the huge one that saved us. There are also small ones the size of dogs. But only the SDS get to fly the big ones. No one else.'

'No!'

Yes!' Lucy nodded. 'Really! They're called Imperial Blacks. They're noble dragons and have magic of their own-'

'And then what happened?'

Lucy pulled a face remembering. 'And then...'

Below, cobbled yards and wharves were crowded.

Gertrude slowed down and descended quietly to hover several feet above the ground. The Bear slid effortlessly off the front to be greeted by a colleague. Behind his back and taken unawares as the broom tipped slightly, Lucy caught her foot in the stirrup and fell off, kicking Catastrophe on the way down. As the cat snarled a protest and spat in reprimand, Lucy could feel a red flush rising determinedly up her neck and into her cheeks. Despite her stinging hands, she tried to get up too quickly. Unused to long garments, Lucy stood on her own hem and fell over again.

'Here,' a sympathetic voice offered, 'let me give you a hand up.'

Mortified, Lucy took the offered hand and stood up awkwardly, brushing the grit off her cloak. 'Thanks,' she muttered, ears glowing pink.

The owner of the voice turned out to be a small suety boy wrapped in a faded and frayed cloak, also two sizes too large and tied with string. Two hazel eyes blinked owlishly in a pale face framed by sticking out ears and a riot of spiky brown hair.

'Apprentice?' he ventured hopefully.

Lucy nodded, too embarrassed to answer.

'First year?'

Lucy nodded again.

'Me too.' The boy's face broke into a wide squint-toothed grin. 'My name's Douglas, Douglas Archibald, and this here is Bucksturdie.'

Momentarily confused, Lucy started as a lithe and graceful red fox darted out from beneath the boy's shabby cloak to consider her with bright, intelligent amber eyes. The vixen was gorgeous, all the glorious colours of autumn: russet waistcoat picked out by white muzzle and belly, black socks and a creamy tip to her bushy tail. Despite herself, Lucy was instantly envious. A fox was a powerful totem for any child to have, imbued as they were with the power of shapeshifting and camouflage.

Her own last totem had been a very large house spider which Miss Strang, secondary two's modern studies teacher, had unceremoniously flattened with a textbook amidst a chorus of hysterical screams. A spider might well weave the Web of Destiny, but a fox was decidedly more glamorous and less likely to get squashed underfoot.

Douglas continued without pausing for breath. 'And that's my parents over there.' The boy pointed through the milling crowds to a slight wispy woman with sandy hair, standing next to the quayside, and a tall, strongly built man standing nervously beside her, clutching a paddle in large weather-beaten hands. A small coracle bobbed in the swell beside them. 'I'm the first in our family to go to University,' Douglas said proudly. 'I won a scholarship from the Guild. I – '

Signalling Lucy to follow, the Bear had turned to the broad steps winding in sweeping loops up the craggy rocks to the main entrance of the University, his huge wildcat at his side. Douglas waved a hasty goodbye to his parents and rushed after her.

'You know the ... White ... Sorcerer?' Douglas was already puffing, but that didn't disguise the note of admiration in his voice.

'Err,' Lucy ventured, as she struggled with her robe up the steps, not paying as much attention as she might. 'Who?'

Douglas looked pointedly at the Bear, barely a few steps in front of them.

'Oh, yes,' Lucy answered, nodding her head. 'I'm just not used to calling him that yet. He's my grandfather. 'We, err, we just call him -'

'Newt & Toad!' Douglas was so excited he forgot his mother's admonishment not to swear. 'I've never met anyone who even knew anyone so important.'

Lucy couldn't help smiling at Douglas's sheer enthusiasm. 'We, we call -'

'Ssshhh!'

Lucy and Douglas looked up suddenly to find themselves surrounded by an absence of professors. The scholars had congregated in droves beneath the university gates to welcome Professor Thistlethwaite to his newly established Chair. Preening and competing in their brightly coloured faculty gowns and elaborate belled and feathered hats, the bickering scholars assembled strictly in line according to their pecking order. Guarding the gates were colourfully cloaked Faculty Guards bearing the University's coat of arms on their shields. First in line was the elderly Chancellor, Professor Arbuthnot Conundrum, with a monocle balanced at the end of his hawkish beaky nose and robed in unexpectedly tasteful university tartan. He strode forwards with his gangly hand outstretched. His long kilt swayed as he walked, and his woolly mammoth sporran inlaid with silver bounced a tattoo upon his knobbly knees. His animal totem, a woolly mammoth which also served as University mascot, was grazing nearby.

'My dear chap!' He seized The White Sorcerer's hand with a gorilla-like grip and shook it vigorously. 'Wonderful to see you, dear chap, quite wonderful – and the ESRC [European Sorcerers Research Consortium] grant for 10,000 gold guineas! Quite overwhelming! What, what?'

'And this must be Barnaby's new apprentice, Mzzzzz Pemberton?' he murmured, ignoring Douglas hopefully hopping up and down behind Lucy. 'Welcome, my dear, welcome. Your grandfather was president of the students union here, you know, so we're expecting wonderful things of you, what, what?'

Lucy hadn't a clue how to answer 'what, what' so wisely stayed silent. Douglas gave up trying to look over her shoulder and stuck his head round the side of her. The Chancellor looked momentarily offended, then continued smoothly.

'So ... quite a family tradition, eh? Well, say no more.

All cloak and dagger stuff, what, what?' Pointedly turning back to the Bear without waiting for an answer, the Chancellor continued, 'Allow *me*, my dear chap...' They moved away.

Lucy frowned. *What on the One Earth was he talking about?* She dropped back to rejoin Douglas, who was still jumping up and down.

'The Chancellor spoke to you!' he squeaked. 'He actually spoke to *you*!'

'Ssshhhh!'

Douglas swallowed hard as a wave of disapproving glowers washed over them both, leaving them stranded in the wake of the welcoming committee. They could hear snatches of Professor Conundrum's introductions as the chancellor waded through the lengthy welcoming committee.

'The Bursar, Mistress Campbell ... Professor Diphthong, Spell Master...'

At the end of the line, the Chancellor was turning away when a determined voice bellowed, 'Sir! Staff Sergeant Major Pounder, sir! Of the Faculty Guard!'

Douglas, who had the misfortune to be right behind the owner of the voice, tried to clear his ringing ears. Everybody flinched. The Bear turned back. Professor Conundrum smiled through gritted yellow teeth.

'Yes ... how could I forget ... Err, indeed ... Allow me to introduce Wand Sergeant Major Pounder in charge of Novice Instruction. He will make a sorcerer out of your apprentice. Oooh, yesss, the Sergeant Major can sort out the elves from the goblins, the fairies from the dwarves ...

the -'

The Bursar elbowed him in the ribs.

'What?' The Chancellor jerked upright. 'Yes, right... ' he mopped the sweat from his brow. 'Well, must get going, what, what? Meeting of the Senate, don't you know?' He turned to the Bear. 'Professor, I'm sure that colleagues would like to welcome you officially? ... And Wutherspoon here will be delighted to look after your apprentices and take care of details like registration, show them round and so forth. In fact, Wutherspoon,' he finished, turning to a familiar young pimply apprentice named Justin hovering nearby, 'I do believe you have some kind of programme worked out for Freshers this year, what, what? Good, good.'

Amid murmurs of ' ... *so* delighted that you accepted ... Oxford and Cambridge ... frightfully jealous...' the welcoming committee passed beneath the shadowed stone archway into an inner courtyard, where dozens of novices and a scattering of apprentices were aimlessly milling around. There the official party ground to a halt.

With a slight sniff of disapproval, the Chancellor muttered to his Registrar, 'Oh do get a grip, Mistress Bentwhistle; they're blocking the doorway. Can't be having *students* all over the place; this is a University you know.' Firmly ushering his guest in front of him, the Chancellor disappeared with his entourage through a small oak door, pointedly marked 'Staff Only' in a half dozen languages.

Lucy looked around, bewildered.

'I haven't a clue either,' Douglas murmured in her ear.

'OK, Freshers,' Justin shouted. 'Freshers, over here, if you please.'

'I think that's us,' Douglas said. 'C'mon.'

CHAPTER SIXTEEN

Why Serve When We Can Rule?

While the Freshers tried their hand at the best the Students Association could throw at them, and the Senate continued with its scholarly deliberations, another more sinister meeting was taking place in the Virtual University. High up the mountainside of the Sorcerers Glen loomed the Cauldron Snout Tower, centre of the School of Weather Warfare; the military research wing of the School of Strategic Studies. A protective, dampening shroud hid their deliberations from view and from listening ears. It was two bells since Strike Commander Calin of the elite ShadowBlade Regiment and his escort had put down on the landing pads, ostensibly to discuss the latest spells to enable dragons to fly in all weathers..

'The maelstrom has been seeded in the Arctic of mankind's world,' the Chief Scientist of the Met Office in London addressed the large gathering of the Raven Brotherhood. 'As you instructed, my Lord Strike Commander, according to your inter-dimensional spell. Even as we speak, it creeps south, disguising the mark of the maelstrom. We can test our strength against the mortals and the Guild both. As the winter solstice approaches, its power will grow... when the sun barely rises it will cast its mantle over the entire land, and our Dread Lord will be able to return unseen to his rightful realm.'

'There is no danger of discovery?' Lord Calin

demanded.

'My Lord, no. Our hand in the last Arctic Vortex and Polar Vortices over America remains hidden. If anything, both the mortals and the University will blame global warming. When the war with mankind finally begins, we will unleash an ice age not seen for 10,000 years, and this time we will not fail.'

'You must move soon or we risk discovery.' A Professor of the Economics of Weather Warfare sounded breathless and panicky. 'I am willing to support you only so far,' she said as she brushed a damp strand of hair from her face. 'But you promised easy success. If things go wrong, I do not intend to lose my Chair, nor my seat on the Senate.'

Several of her colleagues from the Centre for Strategic Communications nodded, a little too fervently.

Scholars! Lord Calin had known the academics would be trouble sooner or later. *Curse them for their weak and faint hearts. The offer of Vice-Chancellor is not enough? Well, if they turned allegiance once they could do so again.*

'Do not fear,' his contempt was clear. 'The Faculty Guard will be taken down...' *and so will you....once you have played your part...* The young Strike Commander paced restlessly to the leaded window and looked down over the jumbled roofs of the University. From this high vantage the original Pentangle could be clearly discerned, despite the rambling additions of later centuries.

With all the impatience of youth, the commander returned to his seat and turned his eyes towards those around the table. The golden eagle totem perched on his high backed chair screeched harshly, spreading his massive wings. The academics cringed involuntarily under the scrutiny of those piercing raptor eyes, eyeing the fearsome talons with growing unease. Their totems were for the most part also birds, but had grown into plump and sedate creatures like themselves: pheasants, doves, a capercaillie and a hare, although there were two bobcats and a lynx as well as several other small mammals. One, a dormouse, squeaked hysterically with fear and scuttled out of sight into the depths of her mistress's university robes.

'And the Department of Military Encryption & Codes,' Lord Calin queried softly, 'have you anything new to report, my friend? Anything you might like to share with your colleagues and fellow conspirators?' Around the table, warwitches and warlocks shifted subtly in anticipation.

'Umm,' the elderly Professor began, his voice trembling as he avoided eye contact. His bird-totem took the form of an impudent and intelligent magpie that casually sat on the back of his chair, dipping its head up and down. It clacked in warning. Surreptitiously, the Professor of Quantum Encryption wiped the sweat from his trembling hands on the side of his robes and gathered Thatcher's Defensive Shield under the table. 'We, um, I, um, that is we -'

The bolt scorched across the table. Meeting the barely moving defence of the professor's shield, it engulfed both spell and scholar. As his charred body crumbled to dust on the floor, his fellow academics screamed, their horrified gazes locked on the pitiful remains of their colleague. A roast magpie thudded to the floor. The acrid smell was ghastly.

The Lord Calin smiled coldly at the academics' disarray. At a signal, his equerry handed him a saddlebag. He tossed the limp corpse of a tawny owl pierced by a black-fletched arrow onto the table. Feathers fluffed across its surface, blood splattering several of the scholars, who cringed. The owl had a dark bloodied ring around its one remaining leg, bearing the university seal.

'Members of our brotherhood intercepted a coded message to Vice-Chancellor Rumspell hidden amongst University despatches. We have a number of cryptanalysts as our... guests along with their families. Your good colleague here promised proof of conspiracy in return for further promotion and gold. Luckily he had not yet betrayed our plan. He wanted his reward first. Should there be any further betrayal,' His fierce gaze swept the now attentive group of academics like a blast of withering wind. 'The price will be beyond your reckoning.'

Eyes wide with shock, each held his scrutiny in turn. They had probably never seen a spell fired in anger. You could hear their ragged breathing louder than an October gale. Good. There would be no going back. He turned to the Warwitch on his left, who bore the badge of Major of the BearsPaw Brigade.

'Major, time to draw upon the sea dragon's venom and then release him at Samhuin to draw the White Sorcerer to recklessness; the fool will be unable to resist protecting his precious mortals.'

'Strike Commander. The potion needs only this final reagent. We need only the final casting and once drunk, he will fall into a coma...awaiting only our Dread Lord to claim a new body.'

'You have your orders. Report back. I now have to suffer the Senate dinner. Do not fail our Lord!'

The Ravenswing Brotherhood assembled in the Cauldron Snout Tower did not, technically, exist. Outlawed by the Guild, its members had been hunted down and given the choice of exile with their master – or death. To wage war broke the oldest and greatest of the Sorcerers' laws. Most chose exile and died anyway.

But power is addictive. Like a rapacious weed, the Brotherhood had simply taken root on the lawless dark fringes of the realm. Now its poisonous tendrils reached out across the Celtic Sea Kingdoms and beyond, burrowing into the heart of The Virtual University itself, finding converts amongst the young ambitious students of Praetorian College.

Why serve when we can rule?

The chilling words were whispered on the wind as the university prepared for the winter semester and the weeklong fire festival of Samhuin, known in the mortal world as Hallowe'en.

CHAPTER SEVENTEEN

The Rescue

The last candle had burnt out. It was utterly dark, and it was silent. And now it was growing cold outside as night fell. Mort had flown to join his parents in London for the half-term. The Raven's servants, human or otherwise, rarely came to these medieval gold-mine shafts deep in the Black Sorcerer Mountain of the Sorcerers Glen. The entrance had long since collapsed and had been smothered by centuries of vegetation so that few save the beasts and birds of the forest knew of its existence. Its day had passed. Nowadays, only bats hung out here, plus the occasional creepy-crawly and an extended family of rodents, currently numbering three hundred and thirty-two. As stars appeared high above, the mine's nocturnal occupants departed to forage for food in the Wychs Wood, and silence descended. Well, almost. Something broke the undisturbed peace of this mountain lair. It was a rather feeble noise, really. Somewhere between a snivel and a hiccup. But the self-pitying tone was instantly recognisable. Gradually the noise quietened and was replaced by soft snoring.

Half-term. It was freezing cold. Already daylight leached through cracks in the curtains and cast the room in a cold pale light. Downstairs, she heard the faint murmur of conversation and the clink of plates in the sink. It was Saturday, the last weekend of half-term. The excitement of her elevation to apprentice was still new-minted and bright as she struggled into horribly cold jeans and a jumper, and raced downstairs for breakfast.

'We're going down to the loch, mum,' Lucy tumbled into the kitchen and headed straight for the deliciously warm range. 'We're taking out the boat with Kealan.' She peered out the kitchen window. It was windy, the clouds scudding across a wolf-grey sky, but the forecast of rain held off. Halfway through breakfast the doorbell rang. It was Mr McFeeley, wearing his policeman's hat.

'Oh dear, George,' Mother said, 'I am sorry to hear that. Fergus has always been a bit of a handful, but I'm sure he didn't mean to really hurt anyone. Well, I hope he returns home soon for the sake of his poor mother. She must be terribly concer-'

'Hi, Sis.' Entering the kitchen in his pyjamas like one of the walking dead, Oliver knuckled his eyes and peered myopically at Lucy. He had been busy on his computer into the early hours of the morning, coding. It was difficult work infiltrating the US space programme, using carefully constructed code to search for Nebulae Communication's embedded Trojans, without falling into a trap himself. 'Are you ... what's wrong?'

' Sshh! It's Fergus,' Lucy said. 'He's still missing.'

'What makes you think he hasn't run away?' Oliver asked later, as they sat in his tiny attic bedroom watching Game of Thrones. 'Everyone else thinks he has.'

'Yeah,' Kealan added, trying to clear a space between circuit boards, memory chips and flash drives to sit down and stretch out his long legs. 'Who cares, anyway? Look what he did to Oliver.'

'Yeah,' Oliver echoed with feeling, looking round from his keyboard and leaning down to rub his ankle and leg in their bright yellow cast. 'Look what he did. Let him stew if he's in trouble.'

For the first time since Mortimer had arrived at Thistleburr, Oliver had been the main centre of attention at school and he felt he struck a rather heroic pose as he manfully limped around saying, 'Oh, it's nothing really.' Secretly, Oliver was rather proud of his cast. It was only a minute fracture and didn't hurt too much, and he had been intending to give up rugby at the end of the winter term anyway. Only, he wasn't going to admit that to anyone.

He had other more exciting things to do with his time now, but that really wasn't the point, was it? And the plaster cast *was* itchy, and he'd stubbed his wretched big toe a dozen times if he'd done it once. He turned back to his PC to scan the endless lines of code compiling down his screen.

'I don't know.' Lucy looked thoughtful, remembering the ugly frown that had contorted Mort's normally handsome face when Oliver was surrounded by admiring onlookers, for once oblivious of the American boy standing alone in the corridor except for Fergus and Duncan. 'It just doesn't feel right. Don't you think it's a wee bit strange that the person to gain the most from your crash is Mort, not Fergus? And now Fergus has conveniently disappeared just when everyone is really fed up with him, and – '

'Everyone's always fed up with Fergus,' Kealan inter-jected before wilting under Lucy's glare.

'*And* couldn't care less where he is. I think...,' Lucy paused, frowning. 'I think Mort set Fergus up deliberately to be caught tinkering with his bike.'

'You think?' Oliver said, doubtfully, only half-paying attention. He was rebuilding his computer.

'Oliver?' Lucy prompted, waving a hand in front of her sibling's glazed eyes. Honestly, Oliver was in another world half the time. Her brother scrubbed through his hair and yawned.

'Mort?' Oliver took his dusty glasses off and gave them a vigorous polish to mask his frustration. 'He seems such a nice guy,' he offered with a shrug, 'although I've only spoken to him once or twice. Why would he do a thing like that? And anyway, you know I've been wanting to give up rugby for ages.'

Lucy gritted her teeth. Was she the only one who saw the other, darker side of Thistleburr Secondary's star pupil? 'Well...' she rationalised, 'it's no secret he wanted to be captain instead of you, Oliver. And now he is.'

Oliver was silent, listening to the soft tattoo of rain on the roof tiles. Rumours had been flying round school that the billionaire had offered to sponsor the Thistleburr Thorns if his son were to be captain of the S2 rugby team. Mr McGill had told the class that Warwick DeSnowe had already completed a deal to sponsor the Scottish Rugby Union to the tune of millions. But that didn't mean Mort had anything to do with his accident.

'And anyway,' Lucy added, relentlessly driving home her point, 'Fergus is a show-off. He likes to be the centre of attention. But you know he's all talk and no action. He's full of hot air. It's not like him to really hurt someone.' *But would Mort? Or was she imagining things?*

'OK,' Oliver surrendered with a sigh. Lucy was generally right about people. 'Where do you think he is, then?'

Lucy shook her head. 'I don't know, but I bet Weaselface does. Those voices I heard in the cavern behind the Sorcerers Leap? I've been thinking about them. I wasn't sure at the time, but now I know one of them was Moran's.'

'So ... what if it was?' Kealan didn't understand. 'We don't know what they were doing and what's this got to do with Fergus?'

'I'm not sure,' Lucy said slowly, as if she couldn't quite put her finger on the connection, 'but I think it must be tied up with the coin you found. There's something going on.' She paused. 'I mean, who pays with old gold coins? They must be worth a small fortune!'

'Yeah!' Oliver unexpectedly perked up. 'Moran's also the one who gave Fergus detention, so he was the last person to see him.'

'OK,' Kealan grumped, disappointed at the change of plan. The weather was vile and he was quite comfortable. Switching Game of Thrones off, he sighed. 'OK. What now?'

It had been a long, boring Saturday morning. The sense of

excitement was rapidly wearing thin in the incessant downpour. Tempers were beginning to fray as the three met together under the doubtful shelter provided by some huge rhododendron bushes, assorted planking and leaky green tarpaulins that collectively made up Oliver's old tree house. He couldn't climb up the rope ladder to their family tree house. Lunch was sandwiches and soup.

'Zilcho!' Kealan flopped heavily down on the water-proof rug, banging against a large branch and showering himself, Lucy and Oliver just as they had taken their waterproofs off.

'Same here,' Oliver reported as Lucy turned to him. She had Truffle curled warmly round her neck like a scarf, and Tantrum attempted to groom despite his soggy fur. 'There's hardly anyone out in this.' *Except us,* he didn't add, as water trickled down his neck. *It's cold and I'm bored. This is a wild-goose chase.* He itched to get back to his coding. His toes sticking out the plaster cast were bright pink. He rubbed them back into life and replaced the sodden sock. He shivered and sipped the steaming soup.

'Maybe you were wrong, Sis?' he cautiously suggested, to break the heavy silence, half-hopeful that she might call it a day. 'The water was really noisy. We were scared. Those voices you heard might have been anyone.'

'No,' Lucy insisted. 'I know one of them was him.'

'Well, maybe, even if Weasel-face has something to do with Fergus's disappearance, it's probably nothing to do with the hidden passageway. Maybe we sh – '

Truffle growled softly, ears flattened, nose scenting the

air.

'Sshh! Get down!' Lucy suddenly ducked, signalling everyone to be quiet. 'Look,' she whispered, turning to see if the other two could see where she was pointing through the dripping leaves.

Crouched in the wet undergrowth, they could all now see the hooded, darkly dressed figure walking swiftly up the old footpath and straight towards the seven-foot construction boundary fence that was being raised around the Old Grange. A bulky dark rucksack was hitched over one shoulder. Stopping at the heavily barred gate, the figure looked furtively around as if checking to see if there were any other walkers nearby, but the dripping woods appeared deserted. Softly opening the padlocks with barely a clink, the figure slipped through and into the murky woods. He kicked out viciously at a plump white-and-black cat that slipped quickly through behind him. A second scaled the fence and shot off into the undergrowth.

'Damned cats.'

It was forty minutes later. The rhythmic sound of rain falling on leaves was unrelenting. Moran switched off his torch and dumped it in the now empty rucksack, fastidiously brushing telltale cobwebs and dust from his wet anorak. He glanced at his watch. Half three. Time to get going. Sunday walkers would be out with their dogs before dark fell. Wouldn't do to get caught in this neck of the woods. He caught a movement at the edge of his vision.

'Who's there?'

Silence. Eyes narrowed, the man softly laid down his rucksack and picked up a large branch, carefully weighing it in his soft pale hands. A twig snapped. Stepping aside, the figure raised his weapon.

Silence. He shook his head. He could have sworn -

What? The pungent smell made the man's eyes water. Another sensory organ kicked in, telling him his foot was getting warmly wet all of a sudden. He looked disbelievingly down as his shoe filled. With a final satisfied squirt, the huge grey cat shot off into the bushes.

Cursing loudly, Moran hurled the stick and swore.

'Damned cats.'

'Right,' Lucy decided after Tantrum and Truffle told them where Moran had gone. 'That's settled then. We'll leave as soon as Kealan gets back from his paper round tomorrow morning. And we'll use Kealan's bike and paper bag as cover in case we get spotted by Weasel-face.'

* * *

The blackbird chirped as it sensed a change in the air. It was the first chirp of a day that was not even a distant gleam on the horizon. It broke enthusiastically into song – unlike Oliver, who stumbled around shivering and stubbed his toe again on the end of his bed, then slipped in the bathroom. It went downhill all the way after that.

'Well, I managed to pick the front door once,' Kealan said defensively, pocketing the bent piece of wire. He let the padlock drop with a plaintive clang. 'I'm not a magician, you know.'

They both turned on cue to Lucy.

'What?' she protested weakly. 'But I don't know how,' she shrugged hoping it would put them off. 'Magic just happens.'

'Great. Well, make it just happen now,' Kealan suggested. 'You've had a week at university, haven't you?' he added uncharitably.

'It was Freshers Week,' she protested. 'We spent most of our time joining clubs and looking around. We only had two lessons on grinding reagents.' None of which came close to the real reason behind her reluctance.

The boys looked unimpressed.

Lucy sighed, glaring furiously at her feet. 'I can't,' she reluctantly explained, face flushing. 'I can't just use magic whenever I feel like it, the Bear warned me. He said it's not for petty use and temper tantrums.' She winced as she remembered the long litany of mishaps that had befallen those who annoyed her. For example, when Ross Dunsmore's bike wheel had buckled somehow, after he soaked them all by deliberately riding through a puddle. Or when Mrs Wright's stew had turned to tripe after she chased Truffle out of the house for helping herself to Mr Wright's dinner. Or the time Fergus developed boils on his bottom following a fight with Oliver. Forgiven, and even indulged at first when she was very young and did not even know what she had done, such mishaps increasingly became the focus of lessons aimed at preventing childish outbursts and attendant loss of control. It had been a long hard struggle and had led to some spectacular tantrums.

And then there were the more recent times when she had used her burgeoning magical powers to avoid a tedious task or complete her homework, or to rid herself of an untimely outbreak of spots on her nose, or to change the colour of her hair to match her toenails. Any score of different tasks made easier by the twitch of a nose, or a look, or a quietly murmured word.

Lucy winced as she remembered the furious dressing down the Bear had given her, after she had decided that Janice Porter was a total cow for picking on her in class because she was so skinny. Janice's Gran had fallen down the steps in fright and broken her hip when a black-and-white Galloway cow in their front garden spoke to her, begging to be let into the house. Luckily everyone thought old Mrs Magnusson had been at the bottle again, but Mother had insisted that Lucy visit the old lady every day for the six weeks she was in hospital following her hip replacement, and the Bear's rare anger was punishment enough.

'Magic, madam, is not yours to manipulate for foolish and fickle purposes. It is not conveniently there to be carelessly cast in pursuit of small personal gain, to trip a friend or spite a foe, to change an outcome in your favour. It is not a game to be used and then quickly discarded because it did not achieve your intended outcome, or indeed because it led to unanticipated and inconvenient consequences that you did not think of. Magic is a powerful art that carries with it great responsibilities, and it behoves you to temper its use with learning and discretion. Since neither appears evident despite my painstaking instruction to the contrary, you are grounded for a week. You are not to use magic for any task for a month, and you will learn the first twenty Precepts of McConnell's Law of Unintended Consequences. And, madam, make no mistake, I will know if you do.'

'Meeeeowl?' Tantrum broke into her train of thought. The grey cat had returned from chasing a wood mouse and was rubbing up against Lucy's legs.

'Oh, all right,' Lucy consented grudgingly as Tantrum transmogrified. The grey dressed gnome rummaged around in the pouch that hung round his waist, pulling out some pieces of wire. Several seconds later, the padlock parted with a satisfying click. Tantrum smugly repacked his assortment of picklocks. In a blink of an eye the gnome's outline shivered and shrunk and the grey tabby slipped through the open gate ahead of the three friends, and disappeared into the woods.

Far from the beaten track, hidden by overgrown bushes and brambles, the narrow mine entrance was certainly well hidden, Lucy thought. Squeezing through the tangle of brambles, they crowded into the mineshaft one by one.

'I wonder if this connects with the tunnels we were in the other week,' Lucy said, thoughtfully, remembering the warren of tunnels on Kealan's map. That gave them all pause for thought. 'But we're nowhere near the Sorcerers Leap,' she added for Kealan's benefit. 'Ready?' Muted nods were the best she was going to get. Lucy stepped forwards.

Picked out by the braided light of their torches, the

tangle of broken roof beams and rubble stretched off into the unwelcoming gloom. Motes of dust filtered down from the planked ceiling, clouding their torch-beams as if they were underwater. Their warm breathing blossomed into sparkling clouds in the frigid stale air, catching painfully in their throats and steaming up Oliver's glasses. Lucy stood quietly. No threat lurked here, the dark presence of the Raven had flown, but she sensed there was someone. The signals were a little murky. *Snoring?* She started to move forward. Ahead, shapes slithered and moved and tiny feet clicked on petrified spars. Behind Lucy, Oliver and Kealan's torch beams flicked anxiously left and right.

'Rats!' Oliver let out a sigh of relief, feeling a bit daft that his heart was pounding. Truffle was already halfway out of sight, chasing an early morning snack. Lucy frowned and wondered whether the gnome actually liked raw rodent when she was her cat-self and how she reconciled that with her vegetarian gnomish-self.

Stepping back into the clear air and cupping his hands to his mouth, Kealan shouted. 'Fergus! Fergus!' The sound echoed and bounced down the twisting mineshaft, coming back loudly to mock them. They listened for a reply. Silence. Nearby an owl hooted. Everybody jumped this time. 'Fergus! Fergus!' he tried again. 'Fergus! Fergus McGantry!'

Lucy looked exasperated. 'Kealan, how many Ferguses are you expecting to find in here?'

'Yeah, err, right.'

'OK,' Lucy said reluctantly, taking a calming breath.

She disliked confined spaces and was hoping Fergus wasn't too far from daylight. With a marginally plumper Truffle now curled comfortably again round her neck, she started cautiously forward. 'C'mon.'

Tentatively, the boys followed Lucy down the debris-choked shaft, clambering over broken spars and around boulders. Lucy's bootlace snagged the jagged edge of a beam and tripped her. The beam tumbled with her, kicking up a choking cloud of dust. Coughing, everyone turned away, rubbing stinging eyes, and waiting till the dust settled, before continuing.

'Arrggh!' Behind Lucy, Kealan cracked his head on a low beam. Oliver ducked in time.

'Mind the low beams,' Lucy called belatedly over her shoulder.

'Yeah, great, thanks!'

They arrived at the first fork in the shaft. To the left, two tunnels continued on into darkness. To the right, a small barred door stood barely four feet away.

'Look.' Lucy fingered a candle and box of matches poked into a recess in the wall. Lifting the box, Oliver read out by torchlight, *'The Guddlers Arms, Thistleburr.'* They grinned at each other. Heaving the plank out of the iron door sockets, they crowded through the rickety entrance.

It was a small chamber dug out of the mountain and shored up with dark timbers. The earth floor was hard as stone, stamped down centuries ago by the passage of countless feet. And in the middle, curled up under a pile of blankets, someone was snoring loudly. Crumpled biscuit and chocolate bar wrappers littered the floor, and a half-empty bottle of *Irn Bru* lay drunkenly on its side. A bucket covered with a cloth stood in one corner. Lucy wrinkled her nose. There was no mistaking it. The rescue expedition had found Fergus.

'Don't leave me! Don't leave me again!' Fergus leapt up and thrashed around in the blankets when they woke him, cracking Kealan on the head for the second time in less than five minutes. Kealan howled with pain. Oliver barely managed to hold his irate friend back from thumping the errant prisoner in retaliation.

'Fergus! Fergus! It's us,' Lucy shouted, playing the torch over everyone's faces so that Fergus would recognise them. This hardly helped. All Fergus saw were hooded dusty white faces, eerily lit by torches so that their eye sockets and nostrils looked huge. He screamed again right in Lucy's ear. Truffle had had enough. She hissed loudly and swiped at him. 'Gerrrrrroffff!' That was the last straw for Fergus. He fainted. There were an anxious few minutes of silence before the screaming resumed.

'Fergus! It's me – Lucy.' Lucy gritted her teeth and was considering a judicious slap on the face to end the hysteria when, disappointingly, realisation finally dawned.

'Lucy?' Wide-eyed and pale, Fergus could barely believe his luck. 'Oliver?'

'We've come to rescue you.' It sounded grand and daring until Fergus threw off the blankets. As they fell to the ground, Lucy saw that he was chained to a stone flagstone embedded in the floor. She deflated like a burst balloon. *Another padlock! Oh bumble! Why hadn't we thought of that?* Tantrum was somewhere outside near the perimeter fence, standing guard.

'It was Moran,' Fergus was whimpering. 'He said he ... what?' He looked at their worried faces. 'What's wrong?' Fergus gripped Lucy's arm anxiously, pinching it hard.

'The chain, Fergus,' she pointed wriggling out of his grip. 'We don't have a key. Calm down; we'll see if Truffle can sort it. Fergus, let go,' Lucy added as she tried to unclamp his fingers. 'You're hurting me.'

'Truffle? Are you nuts? How can a ca-'

As Truffle wrestled with the lock, Fergus just stood with his mouth hanging open, looking from the plump gnome to Lucy and back again. 'It was a cat,' he burbled at Kealan. 'It was a cat.'

'*She* was a cat, Fergus,' Kealan delightedly corrected him. '*She* was a cat.'

'Rats,' Truffle swore, as her final hairpin snapped. 'It's no good, Mistress. I don't understand how to open locks. That's Tantrum's speciality.'

'It talked!' Fergus grabbed at Oliver. 'It talked!'

'Course it talked,' Oliver said unkindly. 'Didn't you know gnomes could talk? I thought everybody knew that.'

'Now what?' Kealan asked.

Lucy played her torch over the rusting ring bolted into the stone. Finding no obvious weaknesses, she knelt down to examine the padlock. Oliver joined her, probing for a weak or rusty link in the chain. Kealan wandered round the room, playing his torch up and down the walls and over the floor. He moved back out the door and into the passageway beyond. 'Got it,' he shouted triumphantly. Grinning broadly, he held up a key. 'It was on top of the door.' Within seconds, Fergus was freed, and the group were turning to leave when they heard a noise.

THUMP!

Everyone froze. Truffle, a short distance down the tunnel, skidded to an ungraceful halt.

THUMP!

Lucy turned to the others. 'Someone's trying to bring the tunnel down!'

'Weasel-face!' Kealan said. 'He must have seen us! Run!'

This time the very air seemed to shake. Grit sifted down from the roof to pile up in little heaps on the floor, and the timbers trembled. They peered out of the door. Truffle hastily reversed gear.

THUMP!

With a growing rumble, a cloud of debris raced towards them. Truffle leapt for her life. Spars snapped, and the roof of the shaft caved in. Horrified, they looked at each other before tumbling back into the little prison. Slamming the door shut, Oliver, Kealan and Lucy leant against it as the earth rumbled. For what seemed a long, long time, the boom and crash continued. As silence slowly returned and the choking dust settled, the rescuers turned to each other, wide-eyed with shock. Oliver and Kealan pushed against the door, but it was firmly jammed.

And mobiles didn't work in the Sorcerers Glen.

'Now what?' asked Kealan.

CHAPTER EIGHTEEN

Water Flumes

'Help! Help!' Ten minutes of fruitless shouting had gained them nothing but sore throats. Everyone was trying their utmost except Fergus, who was working himself into a self-pitying frenzy. 'No one's going to hear us in here,' Lucy finally admitted defeat. 'We'll have to think of something else. Fergus! Fergus! Oh, sit on him, someone. We need quiet to think.'

With a cursing Fergus firmly pinned down by Kealan and Truffle, Lucy and Oliver carefully inspected their prison. Testing every part of the wall with her hands, Lucy swept the torch over every crack in the ceiling and around the blocked door. Walking backwards, she tripped over the ring inset into the floor.

'That's it!'

'That's what?' Fergus frowned irritably.

'What's it?' Oliver asked.

'What's what?' Kealan was thoroughly confused.

'A trapdoor,' Lucy answered triumphantly. 'Why have a ring set into the stone otherwise?'

Crowding round, they swept the debris off and gripped the edges of the stone. 'Ow!' Kealan yelped as a second fingernail broke. 'Look, look!' Hopping up and down, he offered his injuries up for inspection.

'It's too heavy,' Oliver gasped, sitting down defeated, nursing his throbbing leg. 'It's impossible to get a grip.'

Kealan grunted as he moved the heavy chain out of the way so he could sit more comfortably. 'The chain!'

'Ye-es,' said his friend slowly. 'It's a cha-in. Well done, Kealan.'

'It's a chain,' Kealan glowered, 'which means it's for pulling the slab up. Isn't it?'

'Fergus, don't just stand there,' Oliver complained before Lucy or Kealan could. 'Give us a hand.'

With grinding reluctance, the slab moved to reveal a dark hole. Everyone peered down into the impenetrable gloom.

As the architect of their ruin wiped his hands fastidiously with a clean handkerchief, Moran reflected on a task well done. That was the entire bunch of brats all holed up together. They would never realise there were other ways in and out of the mountain. His master would be well pleased – four children for the price of one. Good thing his watchstrap had broken after all, or he would never have come back in time to see them disappearing into the mine. Gloating openly, Moran headed back circuitously towards Thistleburr, taking care to avoid paths frequented by dog-walkers. A pair of feline eyes watched him go. Tantrum slipped away in search of Charlie.

The musty silence from the dark hole seemed to grow and envelop their little prison. Fergus snivelled loudly. Lucy leant forward, absorbing the silence. She sensed no direct threat, and yet her instincts were clamouring to be heard. The scent of something powerful lurked far beneath the mountain tunnels, and her sense of foreboding blossomed. There was darkness of an altogether different nature down here. But they had no choice. The billionaire was in London, he had been on the news talking about bringing satellite broadband internet to the Highlands, so surely the immediate threat was gone? But there was a dragon ~ they had heard it...smelt its sulphurous breath.

> *Beware the guardian of old ...*
> *So mortal man you must beware*
> *Of stepping in the dragon's lair*

Yes...but a dragon couldn't get through these small tunnels could it? If it were guarding gold then it had to be big! Wherever it was, it wasn't close. Lucy nodded and took a deep breath. 'We'll go down here and find another way out.'

Fergus balked at her plan. 'I'm not going down there,' he insisted. 'You're crazy. You don't even know where it goes.'

'Well, we can't stay here. No one knows where we are,' Lucy said flatly, unbuckling her rucksack and upending the contents on the floor. 'We never told anyone.'

'You never told anyone? You mean – '

'Oh, put a sock in it, Fergus,' Lucy snapped, stung by the injustice of his criticism. 'We've no idea who's in league with Weasel-face. Who could we trust?' *And anyway*, she thought, *we thought it would be simple*. Ignoring his glare, she continued brightly as if it were all going according to plan. 'Look! We brought ropes and stuff with us – penknives and torches.' Taking the rope, Oliver knotted it to the rung and threw the remaining length into the gloom.

'I'll go first,' Lucy said, much to his relief. 'You can't go, not with your leg in plaster. I'm light. I'll find it easier to come back up if the rope doesn't reach to the bottom. Kealan can you play out the rope?' Oliver nodded to acknowledge the hidden message.

Putting on a head torch and adjusting the angle of the light, Lucy was soon swallowed by the dark. Watching anxiously, the others saw its beam swivel round, searching like a lighthouse in the dark. Hidden from Fergus's sharp-eyed scrutiny, Lucy relaxed and focused her mind, becoming one with the One Earth. Lucy's long hair resonated to the music of the river that carved its way through rock. The hairs on her head twitched like antennae, each one alert to the faintest of shifts in the eddying air, combining to describe the boundaries of their prison, painting a picture in her mind of the heart of the mountain and the flowing artery that would lead them to safety. Calmly casting the symbol for Wind in her mind, she embraced Air. Her skin tingled as she shrugged her body and swept like a gale through the tunnels under the mountain.

The heart of the mountain was very cold and thankfully empty. Lucy explored the passages, clefts and caves that twisted and turned, some upwards, others slanting deeper down into greater darkness where the light of day was never seen, searching beside the river and a way out which her friends could take. She found it following the river as it cascaded down and down, finally reaching the loch.

'Where's she gone? Where's she gone?' The rising twang of hysteria underlying Fergus's repeated questions grated on Oliver's strung-out nerves. His cold foot was aching.

'Oh, shut up, Fergus,' he snapped, wishing he knew the answer himself. He glanced anxiously at his watch. 'She'll be exploring to see if it's safe. Do you want to go down to help her? No? I didn't think so.'

There was a short, anger-laden silence.

'I'm back, I'm back.' Lucy's voice made them all jump. 'It's OK to come down.'

Oliver struggled with his cast, so climbing back up, Lucy knotted the end of the rope to form a loop and she and Kealan carefully lowered her brother down foot-by-foot. Fergus whined and was more hindrance than help. It took ten long minutes to persuade him to climb down the rope by himself, and only their threat to leave him stung the complaining boy into action. The small group studied the six tunnels that radiated out from the cavern where they stood.

True to form, Fergus started to hyperventilate. 'It's a maze,' he groaned in dismay. 'We'll never get out.'

'Some of us might not,' agreed Oliver darkly, closely watching his sister, 'if I have anything to do with it, anyway...'

Practical as ever, Kealan quietly gathered the remaining two ropes and repacked their rucksacks. He handed the heaviest to Fergus, ducking his head so that the other boy couldn't see the smile that twitched on his lips with silent revenge. Lucy chose her tunnel. They set off hastily down its steep incline, with a reluctant Fergus tripping behind. His footsteps followed them like an unwelcome echo.

'My torch battery's fading!' exclaimed Kealan worriedly. They'd made slow progress over the last hour, with Oliver hobbling along as fast as he could. His leg was beginning to really hurt but he tried to hide it. Lucy was getting worried; they still had a long way to go.

'Mine's stuffed, too!' Oliver confirmed, playing the fading beam over the tunnel walls to the front.

'You were supposed to put in new batteries,' Lucy said. 'What happened?'

'I thought you were going to do it,' Kealan glowered at Oliver.

'No I wasn't. That part was your job,' Oliver protested hotly. 'I-

'Oh, c'mon,' Lucy intervened. 'There's no point arguing about it now. Put your torches off and save them.

We'll just keep one on at a time to make them last.'

They redistributed their belongings a second time, shedding Kealan's pack so that he could help Oliver. To begin with they made steady progress. Then Fergus started to slow down and fall behind. Lips pursed, Lucy ignored the loud theatrical sighs and mutterings until she heard Kealan cursing richly as he and Oliver stumbled over a length of dropped rope.

'Can't someone else carry this rope?' Fergus whined. 'It's heavy.'

Lucy had had enough. Concern for her brother gave free rein to her anger.

'Fergus, if you whinge again, we'll leave you behind,' she snapped. 'In fact, we can just take you back to where we found you and let you find your own way out of here. Pick it up! We might still need it.'

Fergus turned his anger on Kealan. 'Stop treading on my heels.'

'Well move faster, then,' Kealan urged through gritted teeth. 'We keep falling behind because of you. You don't want to get caught again, do you? In fact,' he ordered, elbowing Fergus out of the way, 'we'll move in front. That way you only have yourself to blame if you get lost, and you won't have me tripping on your ankles.'

'No, no, please.' Fergus was suddenly contrite, finally realising that he had pushed too far. 'I don't want to be last. I'll go faster.'

'I thought you weren't scared of the dark?' Kealan queried sweetly.

'No, no!' Fergus shook his head frantically, hanging

onto the taller boy's T-shirt. 'I'm not really – scared – you know. I – not really. Here, let me help you.'

Turning back into a cat who could see better in the dark than the children, Truffle, followed by Lucy, led the small expedition deeper down into the mountain, following the rambling song of the river. The spill of rushing water grew louder and louder, swallowing their footsteps. Beneath their soaking feet they could see its frantic rush through cracks in the tunnel floor. Lucy considered the passages that forked in front of them, trawling her memory for the best way through the granite-veined labyrinth.

'Rest here for a moment,' she suggested. 'Put one of your torches on. I'll check this passage if you can check that one, Truffle?' The dark swallowed her and the cat.

Kealan and Fergus sank down to the floor. Oliver felt chilled to the bone and his teeth were chattering. He remained on his feet, trying to get some warmth back into his fingers and toes. Eyes closed, neither Kealan nor Fergus noticed as Oliver hobbled out of the protective circle of yellow light. Lucy was turning back as her brother's scream tore through the tunnels.

'Oliver!' Lucy ran to where Kealan was hanging on desperately to his friend's jacket, his feet wedged against a rocky outcrop. The torrent below was relentlessly sucking them into its freezing embrace.

'The rope!' Lucy screamed frantically, slipping and trying to regain her feet on the treacherous ledge. 'Get the rope!' She seized hold of Kealan's jacket, while Fergus struggled with the rucksack clips. Arriving back, Truffle seized the rope and looped and knotted it about herself before handing the end to Fergus. 'Brace yourself to take my and Oliver's weight!' the gnome curtly ordered the shocked boy. 'I'm going to have to reach down to him as I'm the lightest.'

Truffle reached down to the petrified boy and hooked herself beneath his armpits. 'Pull! Pull!'

'Fergus,' Lucy cried, trembling with the effort, 'pull the rope, pull the rope.' She could barely hang on any more.

'Pull! Pull!' Sodden through, Oliver was finally dragged up over the lip and into the passage. He lay gasping on the ground, shivering uncontrollably. Lucy knelt beside her brother and pulled his wet jacket off. Abandoning it, she helped him into hers. Together with Kealan, she rubbed life back into his cold legs and arms, while Fergus held the torch. Kealan dug out his balaclava and gloves for his friend, while Lucy carefully inspected the hole that had ambushed them. Somewhere she had taken a wrong turn.

The ragged void in the floor of the passage yawned the width of the tunnel. Flecks of foaming water sprayed high, catching the light as the river thundered underneath, disappearing into the bowels of the mountain. Oliver could never make the jump, she decided, ropes or no ropes. The other passage was difficult but it was better than this one. She quickly made a decision. 'Let's turn back. We'll take one of the tunnels we passed a few minutes ago.'

Wearily, the shaken group clambered to their feet and retraced their steps to the last junction. The sound of water gradually receded. They tramped onwards, taking only a short rest to eat some chocolate from Kealan's rucksack. Another passage, another tunnel, another hour passed. To Kealan the tunnels all looked the same. He had no sense of direction any more; they could be going in circles, and he wouldn't have noticed. He tried hard to show he wasn't scared as the afternoon wore away. The tinkle of water broke into his thoughts barely moments before his torch's beam was dissipated by a huge cavern. Ancient stalactites hung almost to the ground, creating an eerie arched vault with huge shadows. Here the shallow river gently meandered, lapping quietly over the smooth stone bed. Then they had their first stroke of luck. As Lucy played the torch over the cavern, the light picked out something bobbing in the water beyond large boulders. Kealan scrambled over.

'There's a rowing boat tied up here!' he shouted, pointing down to where a small bleached craft bobbed in the current. Sure enough, a small boat was moored to a rusty iron ring sunk and bolted into the stone. Two paddles lay carelessly flung in the bottom, along with a reflective orange lifejacket.

'A boat in the middle of a mountain?' Lucy and Oliver looked at each other. 'Why would anyone do that?'

Fergus frowned, impatient at the delay. 'Who cares? It's here. Let's use it.' Without waiting for the others to agree he jumped in, setting the boat rocking dangerously.

'It comes out under the mountain into the loch,' Lucy quietly reassured the other two boys, nodding meaningfully so that Fergus wouldn't see.

'What have we got to lose?' Kealan added gamely.

'Let's give it a go.'

Lucy's brother only nodded. He looked poorly, his teeth chattering with cold. Truffle jumped up to warm him.

They clambered in cautiously, moving around carefully until they had a feel for the boat's balance. Lucy insisted her brother take the life jacket, only after a huge row with Fergus, who had grabbed it for himself and refused to take it off until forced to by Kealan. Fergus then huffily refused to help with the paddling, sparking another war of words. Disgusted, Lucy, Oliver and Kealan divided the tasks between themselves; Oliver taking the tiller, and the other two one oar each. That settled, Lucy untied the rope, and the boat slowly slid out into the river and threaded its way through the craggy cave. Resting his leg comfortably on the rucksack, Oliver played the big torch over the cavern roof and lit the way ahead.

The boat carried them down through a labyrinth of glassy channels that turned and twisted sinuously through the mountain. Sometimes the flume spilt out into bowl-shaped caverns, where the boat gently spun like a pebble before being released to continue its downward journey. Lucy and Kealan made no attempt to paddle. They simply let the craft choose its own course and used the oars only when they got too close to the side. Then the channel unexpectedly divided.

'Which way?' Lucy muttered to herself, momentarily lost. There wasn't much time.

'Left,' said Oliver.

'Right,' Kealan said decisively

Fergus, with an opinion about everything, remained stubbornly and unusually quiet.

Lucy chose left.

At first they hardly noticed any difference, but gradually the river dropped more steeply, propelling the boat forward. The caverns and caves rushed by faster now, flecks of spray thrown up by the bow soaking those in front. Fergus angrily sat up to complain. The spray caught him again full in the face. He spat water.

'Um ...' he muttered as the boat pirouetted in the current, dancing round a rock all but invisible through the deep green water.

Kealan, paddling furiously to avoid the odd boulder here and there, glowered at him. 'Sit down, Fergus. You'll tip the boat.'

The prow of the boat surged up and then lurched down as the boat dropped over a series of small waterfalls. Fergus banged his head.

'Oohhh,' Lucy, never a good traveller moaned. 'I feel a bit sick...'

'Um...' mumbled Fergus again as the boat brushed a rock and spun faster. Kealan's unsympathetic smile began to freeze on his face.

Truffle retreated to the floor of the boat. Fergus took a reluctant look over the bow and scuttled to the stern.

'Um...' whimpered Fergus. No one heard him. The growing noise of white water drowned everything out. The boat bounced hard off the smooth side and plunged down into a swirling pool before being spat out the other end into a narrow funnel. Here the boat raced along and the river began to froth and foam. Feeling sicker than ever, Lucy squealed as their craft dipped down and up over a series of larger waterfalls. She and Kealan now struggled with the oars, fighting to keep the boat steady.

Fergus groaned, hiding his head in his hands. 'UM!'

'*What?*' Everyone rounded on Fergus collectively. Whatever Fergus was doing, he wasn't helping steer the boat.

'Um ...' he pointed uncertainly with his torch.

The boat whirled like a-merry go-round as Lucy hauled in her oar and took the large torch from Fergus. The noise was deafening, and the river began to boil like a cauldron. Spray clouded the air. Torch beams revealed the disturbing news that the river suddenly dropped out of sight. The penny finally dropped, moments before the boat and its five occupants were due to do so.

Oliver looked stunned. 'A waterfall,' he screamed. 'Sis, it's a waterfall!'

I took the wrong turn!!

Screaming loudly, Fergus dived for the bottom of the boat, landing heavily.

'Oh, no!' Kealan groaned, frantically trying to row against the current. His paddle splintered on a submerged rock, numbing his cold fingers with the shock.

The boat hit another and everyone bounced. Truffle found herself unseated and scrabbled for purchase. An early bath had not been on her list of priorities for the day. Transmogrifying in mid-air she grabbed for the nearest thing in which to embed her considerable claws, and found the ample shape of Fergus's bottom, which was handily sticking upwards whilst the rest of him quaked at the bottom of the boat. The cat landed with unerring precision.

Truffle clawed her way up Fergus, who was hysterically hanging onto Oliver's lifejacket and trying to pull it off the smaller boy. Kealan tried to turn the boat with the pitiful remains of his paddle. Heart thumping, blood fizzing in her veins, Lucy tried to focus her mind whilst everything around her unravelled.

'Lucy,' Oliver screamed as the boat teetered on the edge of the booming waterfall, tipping everyone head over heels towards the prow. 'Lucy!'

'Oliver!' Lucy lunged at her brother's orange lifejacket, but the wet material slipped out of her hands as Fergus's weight pulled the lighter boy down towards the churning water below.

'*You are not to use magic*'...*but surely this was different? This was a matter of life or death*....Lucy's breath caught in her throat and instinct took over. Her fingertips tingled. Tendrils of nectarine light cracked in a wild blaze that lit the huge glassy cavern with a million prisms of water. Desperately, she tried to control the threads of raw magic that radiated out from her fingers, weaving them to her chosen pattern. The cooling strands caught the small boat and slowed its gut-churning descent. Above, canvas sails cracked and billowed as an unseen wind caught them, and the small boat righted itself back to an even keel. Having reached Fergus's head and found reasonable balance, Truffle leapt for the rigging and Lucy's more accommodating lap. As the sparkling light died, a stray tendril tickled Fergus with an audible crack. Howling with fright, he let go of Oliver's lifejacket and tumbled to the bottom of the boat.

The children cheered and whooped. Slowly the boat floated down through the tumultuous spray to settle gently in a quiet pool beyond the reach of the waterfall. In the blink of an eye, the mast and sails were gone.

'Way to go!' Kealan punched Lucy on the arm in unfeigned admiration.

'Cool,' declared Oliver, taking his glasses off and trying to wipe the lens.

'Fergus,' Kealan said, impatiently aiming a half-hearted kick in his direction, 'you can stop screaming now…'

Five minutes later, the boat swept out under a low cavern into the Loch and into the teeth of torrential rain. It was already dark.

Fergus sneezed and blew his nose in a loud, meaningful way on his sleeve. Everyone ignored him, trying to paddle with their hands and the remnants of one oar. It was too dark to see and they had no idea what direction they were going in. As the rain gusted across the loch, Fergus dabbed pitifully at the raw scratches that showed through rents in his jeans and T-shirt and snivelled loudly. Everyone still ignored him.

Fergus tenderly traced a set of five scratches that came down from his hairline to his ear and showed up vividly against his pallid skin. His bottom was also killing him, both cheeks felt like fire, but even Fergus drew the line at dropping his jeans to garner sympathy. The source of his discomfort groomed contentedly on Lucy's lap. He glared at the cat. He could swear it was smirking. Just wait till he told someone, that would wipe the smile from their faces.

'Well,' Kealan managed with a weak smile, as a small wave whipped over the prow and soaked him once again, 'it could have been worse.'

'Yeah, right,' Fergus snarled, as welling anger replaced self-pity.

Kealan was seriously contemplating shoving the obnoxious Fergus off the boat when they heard the chug of an old diesel engine. A dog barked. Suddenly a spotlight cut through the rain, and Tantrum's voice called to them. 'Mistress? Mistress?'

'Tantrum! Charlie! We're here, we're here!'

'Ouch!' 'Ouch!'

Down in the kitchen, Lucy, Oliver and Kealan listened appreciatively to the muffled cries of anguish and tried desperately not to laugh too loudly.

'Fergus, dear,' Mother insisted upstairs, 'if your bottom is hurting so much you must let me have a look. We wouldn't want the scratches to become infected now, dear, would we?' Mother reached for antiseptic ointment in the bathroom cabinet.

'Here you are, dear,' Mother said consolingly, as a newly scrubbed and doctored Fergus was propelled into the kitchen for a special hot chocolate doctored with herbs. 'This will make you feel *much* better.'

Ten minutes later, Fergus closed his eyes sleepily. Removing the empty mug, Mother intoned, 'You ran away from school...'

'I ran away from school...'

'You were hiding out in the woods...'

'I was hiding out in the woods...'

'You fell into some brambles on the way home...'

'I fell into some brambles on the way home...'

'You don't remember a thing about today's rescue...'

'I don't remember a thing...'

'Well,' Mother said briskly, 'I think that should do the trick. I'll just give Mrs McGantry and Mr McFeeley a ring and tell them the good news.'

CHAPTER NINETEEN

Magic, Mischief and Mayhem

Highland goblins have a well-earned reputation in human folklore, despite the fact that they have not been seen in our world for untold centuries: they are big, mean and nasty, almost as big, mean and nasty as a highland bull with a headache. Crowding together in bickering tribes and clans – Overhangs, Blubberguts, Fungalfoots and Hangbellies, to name but a few – they live in squalid and overcrowded underground caverns called middens, and tend only to come out at night in small herds to make mischief and rake through people's rubbish bins. Endowed with great cunning and guile, goblins are, however, not very bright, and can generally handle nothing more complex than a weighted cosh. Their speciality therefore lies in cunningly crafted booby-traps and sneaky ambush. Physically strong, and tenacious as bull terriers, they like nothing better than a good brawl so are readily available for hire. But like many thugs, they are basically cowards at heart and will turn tail if the odds aren't stacked hugely in their favour. So it should come as no surprise to learn that they are notoriously unreliable. Their busiest time of year is always All Hallow's Eve, when the dimensions drift together and anything can happen – a traditional time of magic, mischief and mayhem.

It was one week till Hallowe'en and the Pembertons'

annual party. Thistleburr was gripped by a frenzy of excitement. At Thistleburr Primary and Secondary, art and craft classes were wholly given over to painting masks and pumpkin carving. Competition was fierce, and there was more than one deliberate act of sabotage. Old Mr Finney's prize pumpkin got slashed in the middle of the night, and the Johnson family down by the Green deliberately bought up every last spangle and bolt of black cloth from the haberdashery, which led to an unexpected run on black bin bags.

Five days to go till the Pembertons' Hallowe'en Party. Dawn crept across the pale sky in the Fifth Dimension as Clan Blubberguts were settling down in their subterranean caves after an unsuccessful night's hunting. The larder remained empty, and the goblins were hungry and bad-tempered.

Cattle-rustling had become a hazardous occupation after the farmers hired dwarves to guard the herds, so the clans had turned to illicit distillation and smuggling and grew fat on the proceeds. Illicit stills cropped up all over the Highlands and coppersmiths grew as rich as lords. The excise men turned a blind eye in return for a keg or two. Then the crop failed after the cold wet spring, and bolls of grain could not be bought at any price. Stills lay abandoned and the clans went hungry. Finally they resorted to touting for work in every dive, hovel, public house and tavern in the Old Quarter.

Not that it had done much good so far for clan Blubberguts. Gargoyle was sitting disconsolately picking gunk out of his broken black toenails. Steam gently rose from his foetid feet. He sniffed deeply, sucking in a hapless cloud of midges. His holey and peeling hobnailed boots yawned hungrily like crocodiles. So did he, revealing a set of incisors that would have done a great white shark proud. Too restless to sleep, the tall broad-shouldered goblin belched enthusiastically and had a good scratch before returning to his personal grooming. Finding an extra choice globule, he pinged it across the cavern. It smacked into Fungus like a splattered blue-bottle. Unmoved, the pudgy, short purple-haired hobgoblin continued to clear out his earwax in order to make some candles for Grandma's birthday. Fungus was very fond of his sixty-one-year-old Gran, who had taught him how to mug small furry animals and how to casserole tunnel dwarves with cider, apples and parsley, just as all good grannies should.

In the gloom of another cave, several of Gargoyle's Deputy Chieftains – Manky, Mac the Knife, Toemould, Pharrt and Short-tooth McGoofgulf – were digging disconsolately through rubbish in search of some particularly tasty rotting morsel that may have been overlooked or had just ripened sufficiently. Toemould twitched. Her hairy mammoth-hide jerkin was itching more than usual. Something uninvited was scuttling around in there. Well, maybe it was time for the Annual Winter Shakedown, a reliable source of food when all else failed. Who knew what choice titbits might fall out? And, as all good goblins knew, if it moved it could be eaten.

On guard duty up by the midden entrance in an old

disused quarry, Gibbergiest was honing his razor-sharp nails with a huge metal file. Bored, he reached out and tested them by gutting a passing furry-footed rodent. Times were lean, but ... things were about to change for the better.

Four days to go. Megan Anderson, Thistleburr's young vet, stared glumly into the full-length mirror and considered her handiwork. She moved to the right. Then she moved to the left. That was the only way the mirror could cope.

Mirror, mirror on the wall, who's the plumpest of them all?

She sighed and adjusted the black conical hat. A star fell off, to lie sadly on the floor. No, it wouldn't do. In five acres of black sheeting she looked more like a billowing black hole or an approaching storm front than a witch. She could hear the unkind laughter and whispers that had plagued her through her school years, as if she were deaf and blind as well as plump. Not until she studied at the Royal Dick Vet at the University of Edinburgh, where who you were was far more important than what you looked like, did she find any peace. When she returned to the Sorcerers Glen five years later, she found nothing had changed.

'Catherine and Hazel ... such *beautiful* girls ... lovely figures ... so talented...' And the pitying glances in her direction hastily turned into insincere smiles.

'A changeling ... so different from the rest of the family ... the size of her nose! Look at that bottom ... *Super* girl,

Megan, mind you, very practical around the house, and *so* very good with animals. I hear she got a first?'

Well, she was the first to admit that her nose would look more at home on a moose, and as for that wretched boil – overwhelmed by the enormity of its task, the inadequate plaster was peeling off already.

I wish...Let's face it, she thought angrily. *Fairy Godmothers don't exist for people like me any more than Prince Charming does.*

Better to pretend she wasn't well and spend the evening in the company of a hot bath, a microwave dinner and a good book – as usual. She sighed, dropping her Hallowe'en outfit into the laundry bag. She could cut it up into rags later.

Three days to go and plans were being laid in the Fifth Dimension. Water dripped from every branch and cascaded down the mountainside into the churning burns below. Thunder rumbled softly in the distance, and a flicker of white light momentarily revealed a cloaked figure with a shuttered lamp hurrying through the sucking ankle-deep mud on the foot-hills of the White Corries out on the moors. Three bodyguards took up tactical positions around the perimeter on their sure-footed garrons. Their presence was purely a matter of status: only a fool would challenge their boss.

The figure turned into the tumbled quarry entrance and a damp cluttered passageway. Pulling back his hood the tall assassin gagged. The stench was quite unbelievable, even by back-alley standards. Whoever their client was, he must be very powerful and very rich to order an inter-dimensional raid with the risks that entailed for revealing their intervention in mortal affairs, but that information was on a 'need to know' basis and he did not need to know. The sooner this odious commission was completed and the promised bags of gold were in their hands, the better.

Shaking himself like a dog, the sodden visitor un-shuttered his lamp and confidently moved swiftly down the incline and over a pile of rocks and dirty rags that blocked his way. Confidence rendered him careless. Sensing a sudden movement behind, he started to turn, but it was too late. Within seconds, the second in command of the Shambles Assassins Syndicate was cracked over the head and trussed like a chicken for the pot.

He woke up several minutes later when a pitcher of dirty water was unkindly thrown in his face, making sure that any part of him not already wet would be now. A ghastly plook-marked face with a nose like a soggy prize cucumber, surrounded by a shock of yellow hair, swam into view. It was attached to the dirty rags and a nasty looking spiked cudgel.

'Password?'

'Dolt,' the assassin cursed, 'don't you know who I am? Cut me loose.'

' 'ere,' Fungas bellowed down the tunnel. 'Got som'un 'ere who don't know who 'e is!'

'Dolt! I'm Twentwo Grimwold! See this eye? No! Not this one! The patch? Now set me free!'

Fungus nervously considered his victim's request. He knew the one-eyed assassin by reputation. Anyone who moved in the murky underclass of the Gutters did, though most that met him didn't survive to tell the tale. All the more reason for not compounding the first error by adding himself to that long list. Hastily despatching a trained rat down the tunnels to summon reinforcements, Fungus fell back on familiar routine.

'Password?'

'Password?' The dazed victim glared at his tormentor and tried to focus both his mind and his eye. He managed neither. 'Err ... three times the moon will rise and then the petals will open.'

'Nope,' said the goblin, helpfully fingering his cudgel and considering whether his victim would be better casseroled or baked to remove all incriminating evidence.

'Four times the moon will rise and then the petals will open?'

'Nope.'

'Five?'

'Nope.'

Petals. Portals. Separated by two lousy letters. Despite a hammering headache, the assassin stood and tried to forget how close he had come to being skewered by this unwashed bunch of vagabonds. Clarity had come to his rescue just in time, unlike those useless bodyguards out in the pouring rain who were about to have their contracts prematurely terminated.

Waving his arms in a magical sort of way Grimwold made appropriate mystic noises and dropped some magnesium powder on the fire. There was an impressive flash and a bang. He smiled inwardly. He was no mage, he fought from the shadows with steel wire and poison darts, but goblins were so gullible. You could be saying any old gobbledygook and they fell for it. Should anyone care to ask they would assume their orders came from a chapter within the Guild. He paused for dramatic effect to ensure his efforts were making the desired impact, cleared his throat, and launched into his prepared piece; an old lullaby his Ma used to sing on All Hallow's Eve:

> *The moon is waxing,*
> *The time is near,*
> *When mortals walk,*
> *In mortal fear.*
> *The mists grow thin,*
> *Night matches day,*
> *Then ghosts can walk,*
> *And ghouls can prey.*

He paused to gauge the reaction of his audience. They were staring at him in rapt attention. Well, he had been warned they were none too bright a bunch, but that was the understatement of the millennium. Telling them to gather round, he gave them a one-day rune pass for the Necromancer's Stone Portal, and their instructions.

'Newt & Toad!' Lucy unthinkingly echoed one of Douglas's favourite oaths.

Oliver gawped at his sister. 'Newton did *what?*'

Diligently cutting eyeholes in an old sheet, Kealan looked up.

'Err, nothing,' Lucy mumbled, sucking her pricked finger before applying herself once more to her bright orange needlework. Oliver and Kealan exchanged pitying glances; Lucy's choice of costume was...unusual to say the least. Kealan considered his own choice to be 'cool'. Oliver declared his was 'scary. Like Darth Vader, but with a pointy hat.' He'd been practising heavy breathing for days now to complete the overall effect. Lucy's was just... orange...and circular...just as a pumpkin should be.

The outside of the woods around the Nook & Cranny echoed to the industrious sound of wooden mallets hammering on pegs and the occasional finger. Two days to go and the frantic and chaotic party preparations were well in hand under the watchful and critical eye of Mrs McFeeley. The big marquee used by Thistleburr Nook Hotel for weddings and summer parties had arrived on a lorry, and some local lads were hoisting it up in the large paddock behind the cottage. Inside, the kitchen was baking in both senses of the word.

'Thank you, lass.' Mother took the meringue from Megan, casting a shrewd eye at the morose girl. Her bounce – metaphorically at least – had definitely gone, and her puffy eyes and pale face told a story of their own. Mother cast a pebble into the pond.

'Why, Moraig,' she said, turning to her good friend, who was up to her elbows with suds in the kitchen sink, 'isn't this magnificent?'

'Aye. You've a rare talent, Megan,' Mrs McFeeley agreed with sincerity, looking at the splendidly sumptuous array of hams, pickles, breads, cheeses, cakes and pies that decorated the kitchen like a medieval banqueting hall. And so Megan had. The lass could cook. And she had a rare gift with animals – in that one respect she and Lucy were alike. Once upon a time the local farmers would have been queuing up to marry a woman with biceps like a bull who would think nothing of calving a cow or shoeing a Shire horse. Once upon a time...

Nowadays, inexplicably, glamour seemed to count for more than a good plate of heart-warming stew. Perhaps, Moraig McFeeley mused with sudden insight, that explained the high level of divorce. When passion turned cold the last thing you wanted was a badly cooked, cold dinner on the table. Right or wrong, however, Megan was destined for spinsterhood and was relentlessly hurtling towards it at full steam.

'You've baked a feast fit for a king, or,' Mrs McFeeley added, venturing reluctantly onto unknown territory, 'fit for at least half the population of Thistleburr! Ha, ha!'

That barely raised a weak smile.

Ears wilting with failure, Mrs McFeeley gruffly turned back to the comforting familiarity of dirty bowls and plates and gave a dirty pan a right drubbing to cover her embarrassment.

Right, Mother thought. *Time for Plan A.* She surreptitiously nodded at her friend.

'Kealan, Oliver,' Mrs McFeeley said on cue, briskly taking off her apron, 'let's go and see how they're getting on with that tent, and then I'll need a hand moving those sacks of crab apples for the 'dookin' contest.' So saying, she departed, leaving the hot kitchen to Mother and the miserable young vet.

'Megan, dear,' Mother began, looking appropriately apologetic, 'I need to ask a particular favour from you.'

'Oh?'

'Yes. What with Mr Fairbairn being down with the flu and Mrs Gibson away down in London visiting her sister, we're short of judges for the fancy dress competitions. Just myself, the Bear and Mr Bruce.'

'Oh?' There was some genuine interest this time.

'Yes. We need someone younger on the panel. I know it's asking a lot – you're bound to have your costume all sorted out – but we were wondering if you would consider being on the panel – to help us out? I'm afraid it means you couldn't take part in the fancy dress yourself ... don't want you outshining the winner!'

The answering smile was more than enough.

The Hangbelly midden was also a hive of frantic activity, only partly due to the perishing cold in the caves. The Lodge had denuded the surrounding hillside, introducing the concept of clear-fell logging to the Fifth Dimension. Now there was nothing left to burn apart from mammoth dung. That at least kept the midges away – and most other folk with a nose of any description. Bowls of dye lay scattered like colours from an artist's pallet. Scissors snipped and trimmed. Fights broke out over the curling tongs.

Goblins, as you know, have a wild and unkempt thatch of hair, which they love to colour brightly and decorate with moss and beads, or feathers and the bones of little furry victims. Amongst the middens, haircuts are a matter of status, hairstyles a matter of fashion and lifestyle choice; and collectively they clearly denote which clan you belong to and which territory you control.

Gibbergiest was working on his nails again, which he had painted the same bright red as his hair, and as an artistic afterthought he had added little black spots to complete the ladybird effect. His large hooked nose was also colour-coordinated and dripped incessantly in the cold like a melting icicle. Sitting on his bedding pallet, Gargoyle strapped on his black armoured knee and elbow pads (in-line rollerblade accessories, obtained illegally on the black market) and stuck a fifth knife down the inside of his left steel-capped boot. He belted his sword and buckled a second over his back, checking that he could lift the blade cleanly over his shoulder. A couple of weighted coshes nestled reassuringly under his shirt, and a helmet hung around his back. It was in fact a modified old steel saucepan, but it looked the part and handily doubled up as a reserve war hammer in a fight. Gargoyle looked over the preparations and nodded with satisfaction; the lads and lassies wanted to look their best for All Hallow's Eve.

It had been a long time since any goblins had crossed a Portal into the human dimension, but like all goblins he had listened avidly to the childhood human stories told at his grandfather's knee, and his father and grandfather had before him. One couldn't be too prepared for gate-crashing a party.

Two days to go. Weasel-face licked his thin lips in apprehension. Despite his bringing down the mineshaft by kicking in a few brittle supports, those interfering brats had somehow escaped, bringing that whingeing child with them. How on earth they had discovered the mineshaft in the first place remained a mystery, and finding his boat had not been part of the plan. Luckily they had not found the bags of gold stored nearby. The only saving grace was that the McGantry boy had suffered a mild concussion and couldn't remember a thing. Maybe the brat had somehow broken free before the other children found him, and they didn't believe his ridiculous story of being kidnapped. Fergus had cried wolf far too often for anyone to take his wild accusations seriously.

Reluctant to flee before his plans had been fully realised, Weasel-face had waited fearfully for the arrival of the police. But Mr McFeeley had cheerfully said 'hello' as he delivered the morning post. That, however, was now the least of his problems. His patron was unlikely to be so accommodating, and the bottom line was that he had failed to provide a single suitable victim – for whatever it was the dreadful man was planning on All Hallow's Eve. Weasel-face shivered with apprehension. It didn't take a great intellect to work out that he was in serious trouble and his dreams of a villa and a five-series BMW in Costa del Crime were slipping out of his sweaty grasp. He glanced at the clock over the mantelpiece. What to do? Wiping his clammy hands on his ill-fitting trousers,

Weasel-face debated what would redeem himself in the eyes of his terrifying master. He didn't want others to succeed where he had failed.

One day to go, and Granny Pemberton arrived by train from Edinburgh. In the village, the grocery shop was clean out of pumpkins, and only rock hard turnips were left for the luckless latecomers. Bent spoons and temper tantrums resulted. And all over Thistleburr, children and parents, grannies and grandpas, aunts and uncles, teachers and pupils preened and pouted in front of mirrors as final touches were put to bat masks, spangled wizard's cloaks, white ghostie sheets, sparkly outfits and an amazing variety of imaginative pointy hats, cloaks and wands. Oh, yes – and one bright orange pumpkin with dark green tights. Competition for prizes was, to put it mildly, fierce, if not ferocious.

CHAPTER TWENTY

All Hallow's Eve

All Hallow's Eve. As dusk and the dimensional barriers fell, magic tingled in the frosty highland air and flowed down from the dark peaks of the Sorcerers Glen to pool in the brooding Wychs Wood below. The night deepened to dusky lavender. Deep in the woods a tawny owl hooted, his searching call echoing softly in the still glen. His mate shrieked in response. As gloaming descended, a steady stream of cars and jeeps from outlying farms and crofts headed into Thistleburr for the party, their sweeping lights touching the heathers and bracken of the moors to sudden colour.

In the paddock, a green-masked imp in ripped tights slipped furtively under the awning and into the huge white-and-red-striped tent, lit by the yellow glow of fifty-six carved pumpkins. 'Phew!' Fergus whistled in appreciation as he walked round the trestle tables groaning under the weight of goodies. Poking a finger in the pumpkin pie, he frowned with distaste and moved instantly on towards the toffee spider's web cheesecakes, jellies, and a trick or treat chocolate cauldron, full of awesome sweets from the Chocolate Cauldron sweetshop: first prize for the best child's pumpkin competition! Surely no one would miss one or two. Carefully lifting a meringue and a spoon, Fergus slipped under the tablecloth and set to work.

Out on the moors all was now silent. A plump pair of

225

ptarmigans pecked the frozen crackling ground. A soft rumble caused them to pause, alert brown eyes sensing danger. Hoarfrost bounced and sifted from the ancient stones of the Necromancer's Ring, old aeons before even the Romans came. Weather-blasted runes carved upon the outer stone ring of Sentinels came to life one by one as if filled with liquid gold. The final glyph clicked softly into place, and a pool of neon blue briefly lit up the central stone cromlech. As the ptarmigans took flight, the air within the central arch shimmered and the ancient Portal between worlds opened. Once the ripples settled, you would never know it was there. Shadows moved murkily beyond. Dark figures leapt heavily through and took off at a run in the direction of the glen. The sound of heavy feet and clinking armour gradually faded. Five minutes later, as the last light faded, only footprints in the frost remained to tell the tale.

The goblins quickly discovered that the world of man had changed a great deal since the mid-seventeenth century, even in this remote highland glen. Pounding over the frozen bogs they had entered the familiar Wychs Wood and come across their first tarmac road.

'A black river!'

Teetering at the edge of the tarmac, Foosty tried to keep his balance. The clan crowded helpfully behind him.

'It disnae look like water,' a voice offered. 'It's no moving.'

'Aye,' multiple heads nodded agreeably. 'Let's check it oot.' So saying, in time-honoured goblin fashion they collectively shoved Foosty hard. Seeing that he didn't disappear, and suffered nothing more than a hard landing on his armoured knees, they suspiciously ventured out one by one. Ten minutes later, following its winding course, they came upon a herd of armoured creatures lining the road on the outskirts of the village.

'Maybe they're only pretending tae be asleep,' Gibbergeist offered, with the natural caution of his race. From the safety of the woods Pharrt fletched an arrow. There was a metallic thunk as the steel-head embedded itself in the boot, but the car didn't move. He dispatched a second. Warily hanging on to each other, they crept out of the comforting cover of the trees to investigate. Gargoyle was just reaching out to touch the frost-licked metal when, belatedly, the car alarm wailed like a banshee. The goblins fled towards the village, leaving a trail of abandoned weapons.

'What's that?' Heads stilled, listening. The growl of thunder grew. Out on the open road, the goblins frantically searched the clear night sky for an incoming broom. Suddenly a blinding beam of light swept round the corner behind them, and a deafening roar filled the night air. Bawling with fright, the hill goblins leapt into the undergrowth. The noise suddenly stopped and the lights went out. The clan stared wild-eyed, ready to flee again at the first sign of serious trouble. Tentatively, their Chieftain poked his perfectly camouflaged mop out from the safety of the frost-cracked rhododendron bush. Under the spotlight of the full moon, a helmeted vision dismounted.

Kicking out the side stand, the driver effortlessly parked the huge motorbike and shook out her wild red hair. Moonlight winked off silver studs and buckled steel toe-capped boots. Dressed in snug fitting black leathers, she was big bottomed like a hippo and every bit as graceful. Gargoyle felt an unaccustomed rush of adrenaline and his toes tingled. It was love at first sight.

The fancy dress party was in full swing by the time Megan arrived with a score of admiring goblins in her wake. The cottage and tent were full to bursting. Taking advantage of the perfect weather, the crowd had spilled out into the pumpkin-lined paddock where Second Fiddle, the local band from the Guddlers Arms, fired up with fiddle, pipes and bodhrán. Just outside the entrance to the tent, Mrs McFeeley was busily in charge of the 'apple-dookin' contest, maintaining discipline with the help of a large broom and Haggis. Mr McFeeley had a rare night off and was sampling Professor Thistlethwaite's Thistleburr Thunder home brew with gusto. Underneath the trestle tables now surrounded by revellers, Fergus licked the last crumbs from a plate of chocolate muffins and turned his attention to the cheesecake.

The goblins could not believe their eyes. Dozens of brooms lay abandoned in an untidy pile at the gate, guarded by a 'humongous' scarred wildcat that arched and spat as they passed through the ghost-fence of pumpkins guarding the paddock. The field was absolutely heaving with wildly whooping witches, wizards and sorcerers dancing gaily to the Dashing White Sergeant. It wasn't often sorcerers let their hair down like this. And there amongst them was an odd and lavishly dressed assortment of imps and elves, goblins, fairies and little people running round all over the place! With a mind of its own, Gargoyle's right foot began to tap the beat. Pharrt took up the rhythm on his helmet – another saucepan – with a spoon. Before they knew it, the whole midden were adding their own distinctive sound to the band's. As the last note hummed into silence, the witches and wizards all clapped loudly.

When the eightsome reel struck up, Gargoyle handed his helmet and warhammer to a deputy. Fluffing his hair up and straightening his body armour, the chieftain strode across the paddock in pursuit of the black leather-clad bottom.

'Umm,' he said to Megan. 'Umm, Lady. I wonder, umm, if you might like to dance?'

Megan looked up into a face that might have been her own when she looked in the mirror. The warm brown eyes above the prominent bulbous nose gazed at her in frank adoration, and an uncertain mouth full of teeth all trying to go in their own individual direction smiled at her. Her would-be suitor was dressed in similar fashion to herself: dark leathers, patched and roughly stitched, sported the very latest thing in goblin graffiti, wild green hair hung to his waist and boots jangled with bells as he moved.

Of its own volition Megan's mouth opened. 'Oh, yes,' she breathed.

An hour later, the Reverend Cashman took a break between judging 'best pumpkin' and 'best turnip lantern' to wander over to the tables and get a bite to eat. The crowd seemed more rowdy than usual, in particular a bunch of guzzling, belching and grunting goblins – or trolls? Playfully kicking, tripping and punching each other, they were methodically working their way around the tables, having demolished three roast hams, a vat of stew and a mountain of sausages, not to mention two barrels of the Professor's Thistleburr Thunder without passing out.

'Must have the constitution of an ox,' the Minister muttered, as he joined a table of friends with his bowl of soup and bread.

'Biker friends of Megan?' Thistleburr School's Headmaster Mr Bruce queried Mrs Anderson, as they watched the leather-clad helmeted group. 'I saw them arrive just behind her.'

'I don't recognise any of them,' Megan's mother admitted with a frown. 'But then, that's hardly surprising.' She looked down her long nose disapprovingly. Biking was yet another fault she found with her youngest daughter, to add to a growing list.

'It's a fine job they've done with the costumes,' Reverend Cashman was impressed. 'Perhaps they're from over Braewood way.'

'Aye,' the Headmaster nodded. 'Take a look at that strapping fellow bringing over a drink for Megan. Is he a new boyfriend? Who – '

Their reveries were interrupted, as somewhere close by

there was the loud sound of someone being copiously sick.

The goblins had just collected their mallets and were gathered near the tent where they were trying to muster up some enthusiasm for the task in hand; namely to fell the tent, vandalise houses and make off with some of the villagers back to the Necromancer's Ring or the Old Grange. However, they had never been to a party before where they fitted in so well, where folk didn't scream or faint or set the dogs on them. And as for the food and drink ... gold or no gold...

After Megan had reluctantly left to take part in the pumpkin and fancy dress judging, it had taken Gargoyle the best part of an hour to round his clan up. Barfbag couldn't remember when she had had so much fun. 'Apple-dookin' was new to her, and by the time Gargoyle found the short plump goblin she was in the queue with two-dozen assorted junior witches and wizards, waiting to have another go. Attempts to remove her forcibly resulted in a loud temper tantrum, and a huge witch had sent him packing with a clip round the ear for bullying.

Scruffbag, Heedbanger, and Bamboozle were finally tracked down to the lounge of the Nook & Cranny, packed in with the under-teens, watching a Hocus Pocus DVD. Upstairs, Fungal was having a field day on Oliver's NeXus and had flatly refused to come. And Goodgulf had been well and truly cornered in the lounge by some old biddy, who had him firmly hooked round the neck with a brolly. She wouldn't let Goodgulf go and seemed to be trying to understand their language!

'Right, lads.' Gargoyle shuffled his feet and gripped his mallet more tightly, just as Second Fiddle struck up again and the paddock exploded into life. 'Let's take a vote,' he suggested. 'Who wants to knock the tent down? I said – who wants to knock the...? Who wants...?' Gargoyle bowed to the inevitable and followed his clan into the thick of the ceilidh.

CHAPTER TWENTY-ONE
Pure Dead Magic

Professor Thistlethwaite tightened the belt that girdled his robes and graciously thanked yet more guests for complimenting him on the authenticity of his outfit and the strength of his home brew. Signalling a bright orange pumpkin, a wizard, and a tall ghost in large trainers, he headed for a covered trailer of fireworks down by the loch.

Hens have very long memories, longer than humans in any event. Goblins mean trouble. Goblins mean being plucked and roasted or boiled. However, hens are also the closest living relative of dinosaurs ~ take a look at those talons! Hearing a stramash in the hen shed, Granny Pemberton peered myopically out the back door. One of the biker laddies was talking to the rescued battery farm hens. How sweet ... probably one of Lucy's vegetarian friends.

She listened in. There was a lot of squawking and a language she didn't recognise. Granny Pemberton banged her hearing aid. Dratted thing must be broken. She couldn't make out a word. Ah ... Maybe it was Gaelic? She always wished she could speak the language of her Stornoway forefathers. Perhaps the youngster would teach her – never too late to learn! As the hen-pecked goblin screamed and fled out of the pen, she expertly tripped Goodgulf with her Zimmer-frame.

Boom! Bang! Bang! Crack! Crack! Crack!

The goblins careened into each other in fright – finally they had been rumbled! Everywhere witches and wizards were casting spells with sparkling wands; even the children! But as they scrambled to flee before being turned into turnips for their impudence, every other head had turned skyward to where a radiance of multi-coloured dandelions bracketed the night sky. The crowd surged lochwards for the famous highlight of the party: the firework display!

Back in the nearly deserted paddock, an uninvited guest emerged out of the leafy shadows of the Wychs Wood; he'd show them for not inviting him. Petty malice twisted Moran's features as he methodically sawed through the guy ropes of the marquee one by one, leaving a few strands that began to fray and snap under the increased tension. That should do the trick. As he smugly departed along the lochside path towards Goose Green, he never noticed the glint of moon on weapons in the woods behind him. Nor did he see the flutes of hot breath condensing in the frosty air about a group of ape-like creatures gathered under the dark cover of the trees. He did notice that an uninvited haar was rapidly blowing in. Too late to spoil the fireworks, he thought sourly, as he headed for The Guddlers Arms; perhaps he might find a suitably drunk victim for his master here?

Pop... pop... pop... the final rocket fizzled out and the staccato boom and thunder fell silent. Cordite dispersed rapidly in the face of a rising westerly wind coming from the sea. Clapping and cheering broke out. The Bear doffed his wizard's hat in a theatrical bow. Chatting loudly, the crowd began drifting back to the marquee and the promise of hot food. A few spots of freezing rain pattered down out of a clear night sky; feathers of fog following in their wake, hastening them on.

'Come on!' Oliver frowned. 'That storm's blowing in really fast.'

The Bear paused, suddenly alert. *All Hallow's Eve... what madness has he unleashed?* Green flared dimly in the fog's depths and he could feel the rage rolling in, bringing the promise of death with it. A few children turned back, thinking there were more fireworks. 'Lucy! Oliver!' he ordered. 'Get everyone back to the paddocks – **now!**'

'What?' Lucy asked. The children were frightened by the sudden urgency of his voice 'Why? How?'

'Something has been released that doesn't belong in this world. Go! Run! Get everyone up to the paddocks and the band going. Don't come looking for me! Find Charlie and tell him. He'll know what to do.'

Half a mile away on the deserted west loch road, a local crofter named Jamie Harper stumbled out of The Foosty Bannock and into the teeth of that very storm blowing in from the sea. Wrapped in a warm cocoon generated by one pint too many, he hardly noticed the piercing cold. But the sheets of horizontal rain stung his watering eyes, and the rising wind buffeted him, so that he was flung around like a scarecrow. Head down and collar up, he didn't see the obstruction on the road until he lovingly embraced it like an old friend. Bouncing robustly, he sat down in the streaming gutter.

'Ma dose,' he whimpered pitifully, fumbling in his pockets for a handkerchief to stem the bleeding. 'S'a stupid place tae leave a...' A what? Jamie Harper was not a man overburdened by the weight of his own intellect at the best of times, and this was definitely not the best of times. Staggering backwards, he blinked.

It was impossibly huge, of Jurassic proportions, outlined by a phosphorescent aura. So vast, its true size faded upwards into the howling storm. Rain hammered off a scaled body; a vast undulating body stretched far out into the water as gracefully as any suspension bridge. Barnacles clustered about huge webbed claws that crumpled a Land Rover and two cars as if they were made of paper.

'Damn me … iza lizard … iza bloody big lizard…'

As if it had heard, the sea dragon raised a dripping maw the size of a rail tunnel from the seething loch; letting the tasteless remnants of a yacht fall from its mouth. Somewhere in the depths of Jamie Harper's pickled brain, a primordial warning bell began to clang and he stumbled into a futile run. A frond of kelp took his feet out from under him and the drunken man went down heavily and everything went dark.

'Boom!'

'Crack!

The fog roiled with flashes. Boom! Crack! Crack! Thinking it was more fireworks, people began to turn back towards the loch.

'Lucy! Do something!'

'What?' The pumpkin raised its arms and glared at her brother. 'How?'

'Err…Lucy's going to play!' Oliver shouted. 'Lucy's going to play!'

Witches and wizards slowed. Children turned back to the paddocks.

Out on the loch-side, white light blazed and sparked in the heart of the fog. Freezing seawater cascaded down, drenching Jamie Harper to the bone, bringing him rapidly round. He opened his eyes just as the vast mouth packed with three rows of serrated teeth was dipping towards him. But … he was to be a more fortunate man than he perhaps deserved. Crack!

F-f-fireworks....? Jamie blinked and rubbed his eyes in disbelief. Bathed in incandescent light, a wizard stood beneath the towering monster, hands raised as if in appeal. *A wizard; with a huge cat dancing about his feet? Hallowe'en*! Jamie Harper belatedly remembered with relief. He wasn't going mad!

'Go back to the ocean deeps where you belong!' the wizard commanded. 'Go in peace...noble one. Only death awaits you in this world.' Heat shimmered, vaporising seawater as the White Sorcerer held back the leviathan, forbidding it to step on land.

*You are no Dragon Lord to deny me...*the enraged voice roared in the Bear's head.

Jamie Harper heard none of it... but he felt the strength of the creature's rage and cowered.

No, I am not...my path is one of peace, but I wield great power. Go! The Bear threw all his might into that command. *Mankind kills what he does not understand...*

They are puny... no match for me...

They are now...they have weapons that can kill even you. They can swim the ocean depths, they can reach the stars...mankind has always been your mortal enemy... why your kindred departed this world long ago. Go now... return to the ocean deeps...

I cannot...I am compelled to obey...dark magic binds me...these mortals are to pay with their lives...my master commands it. The sea dragon turned inland.

A single soothing note alighted on the stirring air. It hung quivering for a moment above the quietening crowd before catching the sea breeze. The sea dragon's great head suddenly stilled then turned towards Thistleburr. At the Nook & Cranny, all eyes were drawn to where a bright orange pumpkin with green legs and arms plucked a fiddle from Second Fiddle and improbably proceeded to draw from it a haunting tune. As the melodic notes rose and fell to the rhythm of the sea, a mesmerised hush descended. Caught up by Lucy's spell, Gargoyle felt the hairs on the back of his neck prickle in ancient recognition: a lullaby of the Elders. One-by-one the spell-bound guests in the Nook & Cranny stopped what they were doing and turned their heads to listen. Gathering their children to them, they headed for the paddock. Abandoned bat balloons escaped into the starlit sky.

Lucy could not say where the tune came from, only that it seemed urgent that she sing it. Beneath the harvest moon, rippling streamers of music wove their magic, threading through the crowd and out across the loch and headlands beyond, drawing them together in a net of silver notes. Faster and faster now, the fiddle sang in Lucy's hands; the strings began to smoke. Lucy lifted her hand. The spell broke. For a moment nothing marred the perfect silence; then the crowd sighed with deep contentment.

'Now that,' someone said, as the applause died and the crowd slowly dispersed, 'was pure dead magic!'

The coiled tail was rapidly unravelling into the loch like a ship slipping its mooring as the Professor fell to his knees, shaking and retching: *A sea dragon collared by chaotic magic!?* Scales rattled off shale, and boulders the size of cars bounced down the hill into the churning water, before the White Sorcerer had the first hint that another dragon had taken its place: a cloaked battledragon. Tarmac sagged and several more cars were crushed. The bolt that hit him at the same time as an Imperial Black materialised above him was the last thing the White Sorcerer remembered, as he was seized by rough hands and dragged up a wing. Within moments, both dragons were gone and the unnatural storm faded into the night.

Jamie Harper tentatively raised his head. As the Land Rover braked in front of him, the dazed crofter rubbed his eyes with his knuckles and attempted to stand. He looked around. He was alone with his imagination. The rotund and familiar outline of Constable McFeeley swam into view.

'Consternoon aftable,' Jamie managed, before fainting into McFeeley's arms.

CHAPTER TWENTY-TWO

Best We've Ever Tasted

After the stupendous fireworks and Lucy's haunting ballad, faced with a squall blowing in from the sea, the villagers and goblins were crowding into the marquee for some hot food and drink when the guy ropes finally snapped. Muffled shrieks and cries for help issued from partygoers trapped beneath the heavy canvas, and the tent began to smoulder in places. One-by-one the stronger goblins crawled out and shook their hairdos back into shape; not one had spilt a precious drop of Thistleburr Thunder.

It took a few moments before the band ground to a jangling halt and spectators rushed to help. Mrs McFeeley got there first. She charged across the paddock in black spangled regalia, complete with hat, cat and a cauldron brimming with water. The goblins ducked as a torrent of ballistic apples passed their heads en route for a fire ignited by a crushed pumpkin lantern. For her part, faced with a flock of multi-coloured bikers, Mrs McFeeley came to a sudden stop. Well, her feet did, but the rest of her considerable self took a second or two to catch on, and threatened to give those goblins in the front of the pack a black eye for their trouble. Unabashed, Mrs McFeeley dropped the empty cauldron with a clang and weighed up the assembled group with an experienced eye. The goblins quailed under her scrutiny. Goblins, and indeed all peoples and creatures of the Fifth Dimension, have an instinctive and deep-rooted respect for sorcerers. A tradition firmly based on the fact that any disrespect might entail a change of shape and a change of career. The clan fell back in disarray, tugging their greasy forelocks in respect.

'Good morrow, o-o-old cro-o-o-oh, oh-err-esteemed mother,' Gargoyle frantically corrected himself, looking anxiously to see if the old hag had noticed. She hadn't. Instead she was looking at their warhammers.

'Jolly good. Mallets. Just the thing,' she barked. 'You chaps, follow me. Pip pip. You there,' she ordered, pointing at Heedbanger and the offending cauldron, 'don't just stand around. Fill this with water and get those fires out. You there, take this broom and get beating.' So saying, Mrs McFeeley turned to assist dazed guests without checking to see if her orders were being followed. After a heartbeat's hesitation, the midden fell dutifully in behind. They recognised authority when they saw it.

'Gran?' Lucy frowned at the lavender-haired reveller trapped on the sofa. 'Have you seen the Bear?'

'No, sweetheart,' Grandmother Pemberton's Zimmer frame edged forwards to trip the goblin attempting to rise beside her. 'Perhaps he's preparing to judge the fancy-dress? I must say,' she turned twinkling eyes on the desperate goblin, favouring him with a display of her dentures. 'This young man of yours has the most marvellous outfit!'

Goodgulf threw a frantic look of mute appeal at Lucy, but she was already turning away. She couldn't find the

Bear anywhere.

'Charlie! Charlie!' Finally, a frantic Kealan and Oliver had found the ghillie talking with local crofters by some parked cars, and told him what the Bear had warned. Immediately calling Ambush to his side, clambering into his Land Rover, Charlie left for the loch to talk to the locals who had spilled out of The Foosty Bannock to join the party

'The Sorcerers Loch Monster?'

Jamie Harper nodded and winced. He was remarkably sober given how much he had drunk. 'Aye! That wa' it!' The monster! We're doomed. Doomed!'

Scout Leader Dr Wyatt had patched up the shaking crofter's grazes and bumps. Wrapped in blankets, seated by the stove in the kitchen of the Nook & Cranny and gulping down a steaming bowl of cullen skink, Jamie's teeth were still chattering from fear; although his audience were putting it all down to passing out in the middle of freak sea-storm and hypothermia. Constable McFeeley winked at Mother Pemberton and shook his head, mimicking drinking a dram.

'You saw a wizard? You realise it's Hallowe'en, Jamie?'

'Aye! No! I mean he was a *real* wizard. He was fighting the monster! It was going to eat me! I was doomed! Doomed, doomed!'

Constable McFeeley shook his head. A monster didn't normally feature at Hallowe'en. Witches and wizards... brooms and cauldrons, apple dunking and pumpkin pie, but not, generally speaking, monsters in the loch!

'A wizard? Lucy had arrived after failing to find the Bear anywhere. 'You saw a wizard? It was the Bear; he was dressed as a wizard! Where is h-'

'And it was how big did you say?' Constable McFeeley was oblivious to the underlying tension.

Jamie spread his arms wide and hiccupped; he was beginning to enjoy being the centre of attention. 'Fitball pitch...the Forth Road Bridge! Aye! We're all doomed! Doomed!'

'Mmmnn...' Constable McFeeley nodded knowingly...' and where did this monster of yours vanish to, did you say?' It was hard to miss a monster the size of a football pitch.

'It went into the loch, of course!' Jamie was indignant.

'You've had a dram too many, Jamie, haven't you?'

'And the wizard?' Lucy pressed. 'What happened to him? Where did he go?'

'Maybe he got eaten?' Jamie suggested. 'Aye, must've been eaten. He was doomed...do-'

Lucy screamed.

'Hush, darling.' Mother glowered at the crofter.

Mrs McFeeley caught her friend's eye and shook her head in disgust. *Really!* Jamie Harper was always spinning far-fetched stories. A night in the police station's only cell might sober him up.

Charlie arrived carrying a bruised and unconscious wildcat. A search down by the loch had revealed a white pointy hat, ripped and torn and bloody at the side of the road where the loch wall lay in rubble. Wherever the Bear was, it was almost certain he was no longer in this world. Wide-eyed with shock, the ghillie shook his head in answer to Mother's silent question. 'He's nae here.' The words had hidden meaning. Lucy burst into fresh tears.

'Wheesht child,' Mrs McFeeley didn't understand. 'I'm sure your grandfather is just talking to someone. He'll be along any minute now.'

'Megan's on her way over to stich Catastrophe up,' Charlie turned to go. Tantrum and Truffle in feline form were still out at the loch side searching for clues.

'No place for a wild cat to be out and about when there are fireworks,' Mrs McFeeley said disapprovingly with a sniff. 'Excepting Haggis, of course; he *insists* on coming out. Glad to see Tantrum and Truffle are shut up safely somewhere, Lucy, dear.'

Half an hour later the tent was back up. Bruised party-goers and one broken arm were still being treated in the Nook & Cranny by Dr Wyatt, and the party was back in full swing. The fancy dress competition was drawing to a close. With all the excitement, no one noticed that one of the judges was missing and Mr McGill, the wealthy local antiques collector, had quietly taken his place.

'And...' the microphone boomed, 'first prize for the adult fancy dress to the...' whisper .. 'The goblin with the green hair.' Envious heads turned, searching for the prize winner amongst the rainbow mops that crowded the tent. Already in seventh heaven, Gargoyle could scarcely believe his wrinkled lugs. For the second time that evening, an unfamiliar sensation surged through him as the congregated revellers clapped and cheered. No one had ever thought him worth a handclap before, let alone a crate of silver birch wine. Elbowed forward by his fellows, and glowing with pride, he self-consciously adjusted his nose bone, wiped the grease off his chin and a tear from his eye with his 'manky' jerkin sleeve and stomped up to the platform to collect his prize from Megan.

Back at the midden the hooded messenger from the syndicate listened in growing disbelief as the anxious goblins answered his questions with reluctance. For a start no villagers had been seized or delivered to the Old Grange. Why was becoming more obvious.

'You did *what*?'

'Em, we put the white-and-red tent back up.'

'Because...?'

'The big witch told us to. She was huge, wasn't she, lads?' Heads nodded dutifully.

The messenger groaned. 'She probably wasn't a real witch. Can't you tell the difference? They all dress up at Hallowe'en – you know – like the theatre?'

'Could've fooled me,' muttered someone. 'And she had a muckle great cat too!'

'And then she gave you what?'

'Home brew.'

'Home brew?'

'Aye.' Gargoyle nodded. 'Thistleburr Thunder – a whole crate – best we've ever tasted. Wasn'y it, lads? And then there was the pumpkin pie.'

'Pumpkin pie?'

'Yeah. Best -'
'You've ever tasted... '

CHAPTER TWENTY-THREE

Rune Blind

A cloaked Imperial Black had summoned the Grand Master and the Vice-Chancellor to Dragon Isle with all haste, putting down just as a battlegroup was being scrambled. The situation room deep in the island was shrouded by dense battlemagics, as they were admitted to find SDS battlemages deep in conversation. There was the clash of armour from guards outside as the Guardian arrived.

'SitRep?'

'My Lord Guardian!' The Duty Officer saluted before turning to where a battlemage was seated in the centre of a spinning globe of light. Plucking symbols out of the whirlpool, the battlemage threw them into the air to form a multi-layered tactical display.

'The White Sorcerer is missing and a human is claiming to have witnessed their Sorcerers Loch Monster here.'

'Maldock?' The Guardian turned to his senior SDS officer.

The Strike Commander of the III Firstborn leant forwards. 'We scrambled three Imperials to the lochside but they were too late; it is clear a cloaked Imperial made an unauthorised jump, shrouded by sophisticated battle-magic, at around the same time. We detected a decaying signature of chaotic magic.

'A cloaked Imperial?' Rumspell asked, his voice flat

with shock. 'Then there are traitors amongst the SDS!'

'This confirms G16 intelligence that the Raven has allies amongst us,' Rubus Firstfoot reported with a heavy heart. 'There have been whispers of the Raven Brotherhood's return, but no more than that. We could find no proof.'

Rumspell frowned as a sudden thought took him. 'An eminent academic from the School of Military Encryption and Codes recently disappeared, and there have been others who have met with accidents.' He closed his eyes in inner contemplation. 'It seems there are also those in the University who would betray us.' He shook his head. 'Who knows how long the Raven Brotherhood has been gathering its strength?'

'And they are cloaking their activities with the maelstrom? How?' The Grand Master demanded. 'That knowledge was long since destroyed.'

'Yes,' the Strike Commander Maldock confirmed. 'We barely detected the jump and we could not identify a signature. It was hidden behind a rune blind.'

'The White Sorcerer?' The Guardian asked.

'I fear he is dead.' Some of his bloodied garments were recovered, and his totem is, as we speak, being operated upon. He -'

'No,' the Grand Master denied it. 'We can give out that we believe he is dead, but I do not believe it,' he shook his head. 'Why risk discovery by using a dragon? An assassin would have left no clues.'

Rumspell nodded thoughtfully. 'Because he almost certainly now knows we have finally unearthed his true identity. Returning to the Sorcerer Glen would have betrayed him, even if the forensic evidence did not. And yet he took that risk. Why? There is evil abroad in the world of man.'

The Guardian agreed. 'I fear the White Sorcerer has a role to play in the Raven's plans; he has some fell purpose and whatever it is, it will happen soon. The fact that he risked this dragon being seen bespeaks confidence and suggests he is about to make his move. But I think it was not intended to be seen, that it was merely a lure to trap the White Sorcerer. Perhaps also intended to take revenge upon the descendants of those who betrayed him to the mortals' armies. The influx of the world's media to the Glen is almost certainly not to the Raven's advantage. I suspect he thought himself safe here from the public eye.'

'And the dragon; a sea dragon?' Rumspell asked. 'The Faculty of Water have long believed them driven to the edge of extinction by the goblins eons ago.'

'Almost certainly the same collared sea dragon wrought havoc amongst our fleets in the Raven Wars, causing devastation from the Isle of Midges to Cape Wrath, the Guardian answered. 'It vanished during the battle of the Runestone: believed dead. This surely must be the same dragon that has since given rise to the mortal's legend of their *Sorcerers Loch Monster*.'

'Binding a noble dragon into servitude.' Rumspell shook his head worriedly. 'It is against all our laws. Who knows what price we may pay for that? And where has he hidden it, that we have failed to find it all these centuries?'

'That is a puzzle we have yet to solve,' the Guardian

said grimly. 'The chess board is set and the players are in motion. We have been caught unawares. I fear we are in a race against time to uncover his true intent.'

'My Lords,' Strike Commander Maldock reminded them. 'With a rune blind the Raven *cannot* return to our world. No matter where or when, he would die the moment he set foot in the Fifth Dimension. It has never been done before.'

'Let me remind you that he should have died after a mortal's hand span of years in their world. No one has before survived the Banishing Curse, and yet survive he has,' Rumspell said chillingly. 'That has never been done before either.'

'I shall order both GI5 and 6 to turn all their attention to this and only this,' the Grand Master said, 'but with the greatest secrecy. We can let it be known he was killed by a sea dragon, let them believe they are safe from scrutiny, and see if over-confidence betrays him. It gives us a chance to identify those who aid him.

'Meantime I shall send word to Mistress Pemberton, and bid her say that Peregrine has been called to London on urgent business. We do not need a bumbling murder investigation to hinder us.'

CHAPTER TWENTY-FOUR

Your Time is Done

The White Sorcerer felt nauseous as consciousness returned. His head ached and blood was clotted about a wound above his swollen right eye. Otherwise his body was bruised and nothing felt broken, but he was frozen to the marrow and his wet robes were stuck to the ground. He swam in and out of consciousness several times before he managed to stay awake. Trying to move, he found his hands and feet bound. Eyes still closed, the White Sorcerer listened for clues as to who in the SDS had taken him, and why. There was the clash of armour and some muted conversation of soldiers, but where were they? He could smell the sea. He opened his good eye. The cavern was so vast he couldn't see its roof or sides. He turned his head and adrenaline surged through him. The sea green eye was half lidded and still, but the sea dragon was aware, he was sure of it: awake yet sleeping. Like him, the dragon was bound to another's will by chaotic magic! This was the chill kiss of the maelstrom: cavern and dragon were cloaked, but the power and skill it must have taken! The White Sorcerer shivered; he was so very cold.

Dawn was creeping across the night sky when there was a subtle change in the air. Glimmers heralding a massive incoming jump gate warped the air: battle magic combusted. A dragon was decloaking inside a mountain? How? The smoking sulphurous air triggered by the

Imperial's arrival lay leaden in the cavern, and made the White Sorcerer hack and cough. Without looking up, he immediately sensed the power of the young Warlock BattleMage, as he dismounted. He lifted his head defiantly to look his enemy in the eye, recognising the young Strike Commander with a shock he failed to hide.

'You? Why?'

Dark eyes flashed. 'Why? You ask why?' Strike Commander Calin spat his contempt. 'The Guild grows soft and the regiments rot in their barracks. We are forgotten. Our blades grow rusty while the merchants grow fat and rich, and the university opens its doors to peasants from the slums. It is time for the natural order of life to be reasserted. Why serve when we can rule? The Fifth Dimension is ours by birth-right and all other worlds on this One Earth. We shall crush mankind with their vaunted technology; they will die in their millions beneath our dragons, and the power of the maelstrom!'

'You serve my brother.' It was not a question. 'One of the Raven Brotherhood?'

The warlock smiled in the growing light. 'His is a power you cannot defeat. Already he has the mortal's world in his grip. Their greed and pride will be their downfall, as your lack of ambition and misguided paternalism towards them will be yours.'

'I do not fear death. Return my staff and I will fight you.'

'Death? Oh no, old man. You do not get off so lightly. Yours is to be a different fate.' The mouth twisted mockingly. 'Yours is the body that my master needs so that he may return to the Fifth Dimension, so that he may assume the mantle of Dread Lord that is rightfully his, and fashion his powers into the instrument of your downfall. Yours and all you hold dear. And none shall know … until it is too late. A … Trojan horse, as your precious mortals would say? Now, be silent. We must prepare. My master needs more than blood to run in your veins before he can take your body.'

The White Sorcerer's blood ran cold and his guards murmured restlessly, openly afraid as one of the sea dragon's poisoned spines was milked for venom, smoking drops captured by a metal drinking horn carved with strange runes. Sky metal! The White Sorcerer noted this with a detached part of his mind.. Somewhere he had read that only sky metal could withstand the cold of maelstrom magic. A soldier screamed as a tiny droplet ate through his armour; as his skin began to boil through to the bone the soldier thrashed and gurgled and then swiftly rattled into silence as his body dissolved into glue.

'Bring him,' Calin ordered as he took the drinking horn.

The White Sorcerer was roughly pulled to his feet. He could hardly walk, his legs were so numb, so the soldiers dragged him. The porting stone inlaid at the back of a small cavern passed in a blur. The windowless room they found themselves in was furnished only with a chair with straps, a table covered in instruments, and a cauldron hanging above a lit fire in the centre of the room.

'Old man,' the young warlock's voice intoned, trembling with power as the spell was cast and the toxin added to the cauldron. 'Your time is over. Ours has yet to come. Bid your life farewell, for when you wake it will be as a living host to another.'

The White Sorcerer flinched as he felt the awesome power of the dark spell gather about him, and he felt afraid. He was one of the greatest scholars of his generation, eldest son of his house, but treachery had dealt his captors the advantage of surprise. The White Sorcerer felt the wash of baleful power before he heard footsteps and knew who it was. The soldiers all went down on one knee. Calin saluted, fist on heart.

'Brother mine,' the voice flat with menace made him shiver. 'We are finally reunited after all these centuries.' Warwick DeSnowe smiled, though neither face nor voice was familiar, both borrowed from unwilling hosts. Behind him, a technician in a biohazard suit unpacked a small clear cylinder from a padded case and poured it into the brew. Then the Raven stretched out his hand and drew a blade across his thumb; as the drops fell into the cauldron it began to seethe and boil. Then he raised powerful symbols: forbidden, arcane spells of binding and imprisonment, of slavery and submission. Dark shadows swirled like ink in water. Tendrils of frost covered the room.

The technician selected an injector with a long needle and drew in the deadly brew. As the liquid entered his bloodstream the White Sorcerer screamed then thrashed about as the nanites swarmed through his body, bearing their deadly cargo, knitting it to a new and deathly design.

'Nanotechnology...brother, dear,' the Raven smiled.

'You have not heard of them? Nanites keep me alive when this tired body has frayed. Sub-atomic nanobots encapsulate a toxin that would normally kill you instantly... they hide the toxin from your immune system whilst changing you at molecular level to prepare you as my living host. But this time I will have the power to change aspect from one body to another. I can be you in the Fifth Dimension, and the reclusive billionaire in this world. He smiled coldly. . 'As the mortals say, I shall have the best of both worlds! You see, they do remember the Fifth Dimension deep down. Well, I must leave you. I return to London and then to the States. My helicopter awaits me. When the power of magic in both our worlds reaches its zenith on the winter solstice, I shall return to claim you and my rightful realm, both! Sleep well...brother!'

But by then the White Sorcerer couldn't answer, couldn't protest, as the paralysing venom robbed him of reason.

'You know where to take him.' DeSnowe left.

The paralysing venom crept relentlessly forward. The White Sorcerer's legs were numb now and he felt sick to his soul. Floating in and out of consciousness, he no longer knew where they had taken him, save that it was dark and cold. So very cold. The muscles in his chest locked and he sank into a deep coma.

CHAPTER TWENTY-FIVE

Aye! We're Doomed...Doomed...

Thistleburr was the centre of a media scrum. Scores of vans with satellite dishes crowded the loch, despite the atrocious seasonal weather. Bus-loads of monster hunters spilled out, with field glasses and cameras at the ready, and both the Guddlers Arms and the Foosty Bannock had run out of beds. Overhead, a helicopter with thermal imagers hoped for a sighting to match the BBC News scoop. Every palaeontologist in the country was giving their scholarly opinion as to what the creature might be and how it might have survived.

On the back of this world coverage, VisitScotland was already planning a Sorcerers Loch Monster Visitor Centre with lottery funding, and the Official Sorcerers Loch Fanclub was running inaugural Loch Monster trips, despite the lateness of the season. Jamie Harper was revelling in his lucrative, new-found fame.

'CNN, Mr Harper. This will pick up Thistleburr's tourist trade...'

'BBC News, Mr Harper. Can you tell our viewers what...'

'Mr Harper, you say you saw the Sorcerers Loch Monster? Can you describe it, sir?'

'Och Aye...Aye, I can,' Jamie spread his arms wide. 'Muckle great beastie it was...all scales an' seaweed. Muckle great teeth...longer than a man! It glowed in the dark! Aye! We're doomed...doomed....'

The tills in Thistleburr belied his sentiment; the small burgh was firmly on the map!

CHAPTER TWENTY-SIX

Potions and Toxins

The Head of Potions and Toxins had privately sent word to Barnaby Rumspell of important news that might have a bearing on the search for their absent colleague and friend. Given that GI5 & 6 and the SDS had failed to uncover a single clue as to where the White Sorcerer was, or why he was taken, the Vice-Chancellor immediately left the meeting of the University Court and found his way with all haste to the Potions Cavern.

Scores of cauldrons were suspended over fires or hanging in the air. Weird and wonderful contraptions funnelled and heated and blew up potions and poisons. Cauldrons bubbled and popped. Dozens of apprentices were weighing and grinding, seeping and stewing roots and berries, flowers and minerals. Here spell-masters and alchemists at the cutting edge of research were construct-ing the spells and cantrips for future generations.

Bang!

Everyone within earshot, including Rumspell, ducked, then looked around sheepishly to see if they had been observed; the potions cavern was protected by a force-ten shield bubble, so they were quite safe. Professor Bumble-weed appeared out of a toxic haze, talking earnestly with one of his staff; his hat was singed and his robes full of holes. Spotting Rumspell, and raising what was left of his eyebrows, he passed through nexus three.

'You found something?'

Bumbleweed nodded. 'Come to my study. Fetch Towald, would you, please,' he asked one of the apprentices working at a bench.

Piles of books and parchments were littered over the floor...Bowls of seeds, barks and bones. Unidentifiable things hung suspended in jars. Bowls of sweets, half eaten dinners. Bumbleweed swept a pile of accumulated papers and two donuts off a chair. 'Sit, please. I think we might just have made that breakthrough you've been looking for. Not told anyone else but you.

'Towald is one of our brightest and best pathologists, on secondment from GI5; she is one of Peregrine's protégées. She specialises in toxins; gremlins are remarkably immune to many that would kill us, did you know? Not many people do. Got to thank Peregrine for that, it was his suggestion to open the University up to them.'

'Lord Rumspell,' the young gremlin at the door bowed. 'Professor? You wished to see me?'

Bumbleweed nodded encouragement. 'Come in! Come on in now! Don't be shy. Now tell the Vice-Chancellor what you've discovered.'

'When you told me the White Sorcerer was missing I thought I might take a second look at the DNA sample used to identify the Raven. Without our recent advances in analytical forensics, this minute trace would have passed unnoticed,' she held up a tablet to demonstrate.

The Vice-Chancellor watched in total, cross-eyed incomprehension as the display zoomed in from a sequence of cells to a spiral helix. The pathologist again split the screen. Algorithms flashed, breaking the constituent parts down into their chromosomal structure.

'Venom,' the young gremlin said, selecting an amino-acid linkage with her laser pen. 'But there are several things which I do not understand. See how this chromosomal chain splits and replicates? I think the toxin is displaying a virus-like behaviour, but in reverse. Normally a virus co-opts cells from the host body in order to replicate itself and so overwhelm the host and maximise potential for successful transmission to others. But,' she continued, clearly confused, 'this venom absorbs its victim's genetic code for its own use. Anyone infected is altered at a genetic level themselves...I am not sure how or why. Because,' she added, perplexed. 'The toxin is fatal. It would kill anyone who came into contact with it instantly,'

'And the toxin?' Rumspell queried, although he thought he already knew the answer.

'Sea dragon venom, Sire,' the pathologist confirmed. 'A noble sea dragon.'

CHAPTER TWENTY-SEVEN

Sea Dragon's Bane

At 409 years, Sedgeburt was the oldest academic in the Celtic Sea Kingdoms. Head of the School of Oceanic and Aquatic Predator Studies, and research director of the Guild Nautical Institute at the Virtual University, he also held the Chair of Marine Mammal Studies at Oxford University and the Sea Dragon Chair at Harvard. In fact, he had so many chairs he didn't know which one to sit in and had plumped for a sofa instead. And given his extreme age and the long uncomfortable flight from Boston on an Imperial Black at mach-one, he could be excused for falling asleep in the comfort and privacy of the Grand Master's study. His animal totem, a truculent marine iguana dragon befriended on a recent trip to the Galapagos Islands, lay at the Archmage's feet. One heavy lidded eye opened to return the Grand Master's scrutiny. So, Sedgeburt was not truly asleep. Time, perhaps, for some gentle persuasion.

'Ahem,' the Grand Master coughed politely. The gentle snoring continued. The Grand Master nodded at Grimhelm, who poured a malt whisky from a crystal decanter and held the goblet under the white-haired professor's nose.

The nose twitched.

The iguana opened both its eyes and flicked out a tongue.

The snoring ceased.

The nose twitched again and, with his eyes still closed, Professor Sedgeburt smacked his toothless gums and raised a shaking hand. Grimhelm carefully placed the goblet in it.

'Aaahhh,' Sedgeburt belched luxuriously as he slurped the amber whisky with enthusiasm. 'Inversnekie Gold! You keep a fine shellar, my boy, a fine shellar.' The wizened old man smiled beatifically and opened two shrewd blue eyes to study his host.

'Well, my boy,' said the world expert on sea dragons, 'what exactly issh it you want to know about sea dragons?'

Professor Sedgeburt shook his head in disbelief.

'Shhea dragon's venom, my boy?' The old man's voice had trembled. 'How is that possible? Mmnnnn...it was so very long ago.' The professor was silent for a time, gazing unseeing at the fire. Sensing his companion's disquiet, his totem raised its scaly head, and bared curved serrated teeth to hiss at the Grand Master. A log shifted, sending a flurry of golden sparks up the chimney.

'I'm sshorry, my boy.' The old man shrugged off distant memories and reached for his goblet. 'Be patient with an old man.' He took a sip to wet his blue-veined throat and waited till the dragon had soothed him, and helped him gather his thoughts.

'You will not know this story because it was buried lest others be tempted to folly. When I first graduated I was apprenticed to Mycroft, one of the greatest healers and minds of his generation. It was a sshingular honour to be chosen by him. His shcientific research had led him to tales of the fabled elixir of the sea dragon realm that was said to return life to those struck down with illness or infirmity. The Shhea Dragon Lords of the First Age were blessed with long life and great powers before their dragons were hunted to extinction by the hobgoblins, or so we believed. Mycroft believed it was the venom which held the key; although it was a deadly toxin he believed that if it were bound by spells it could prolong lives. But it proved dangerous work, and the old, the weak and the ill, those it was shhupposed to heal, shuccumbed to the venom and died.

'Mycroft discovered his sshpell was parasitic; it did not extend life as he had hoped, but it allowed those strong enough to claim another's healthy body as a host, and so continue to live through them. The Shenate instantly forbade his research and Mycroft was ordered to destroy all his work.'

For a moment, the professor's eyes clouded. 'But Mycroft did not heed their warnings and continued in sshecrecy to recklessly pursue hiss dream, his purpose now warped by the power and potency of the spell's casting and the promise of eternal life. He took the body of another, only to discover the spell was too virulent, a host body had to be prepared, else it was consumed. Who knows how many lives he took in his desperate drive to find a suitable host before it killed him? His research was destroyed, his name removed from the scrolls. The elixir he conjured was called Sea Dragon's Bane for the many lives it took.'

The Grand Master listened in horror as Rumspell shared his news. 'Sea dragon venom in his blood? What can it mean?'

'Perhaps,' Rumspell had been asking the same questions, trying to make sense of Sedgeburt's information. 'Perhaps the sea dragon is far more than a ruse to lure Peregrine? That the venom is what has kept the Raven alive all these centuries?'

'Is that possible? How could anyone safely milk a sea dragon for venom, when the tiniest drop of kills instantly. Everything...man and beast, ship and armour dissolve on contact.'

'I know! I know! It doesn't make sense!' Rumspell's totem stopped his frantic gnawing on the chair leg and thoughtfully fixed the Grand Master with a reproachful white-toothed stare. 'To drink venom would mean death, yet I fear venom is the key to this riddle.' Rumspell sat down heavily; bowing to the inescapable forces of gravity and engineering, his chair collapsed with a satisfying clatter about the plump beaver's head.

The Grand Master ushered his friend to a new chair. 'But perhaps, Barnaby,' the Grand Master was grasping at straws. 'Perhaps the Grimoire of Seahenge might give us some answers?'

Rumspell sat forward, his dark eyes intent. 'The Grimoire of Seahenge! Yes, yes, if it truly exists' he murmured almost to himself, 'it could be the very thing. Many of the old scrolls refer to the book crafted by the first Dragon Lords themselves, in their city beneath the sea.'

The Vice-chancellor pitched his voice like a wordsmith:

'They say that the sea kingdom of Atlantis is a fairy story for children, a mortal kingdom that fell beneath the sea following some great calamity, but they are wrong. The citadel of Atlantis still rises from the ocean canyons of the Fifth Dimension. The whales sing of its glories as they glide beneath its mighty bridges and spires, but the sea dragons are gone. The Grimoire of Seahenge is a wondrous book. It contains all the wisdom that is known of the great ocean deeps and those creatures that inhabit them. It was given into the keeping of the sorcerers when the immortal dragons and their citadels faded from the human world thousands of years ago.

'Seahenge is bound in rare, white sea-dragon scales and clasped by white gold. The fragile pages are crafted from the translucent scales of great fish long extinct. Its words are written in the inks of giant squids and the grimoire bound shut with elemental symbols of water. The secrets of creation are contained within its pages, for truly the great oceans from whence all life sprang still girdle this One Earth of ours. For this reason the exact location of the Seahenge Grimoire is known only to a few; it is hidden in the perilous depths of the Arcane library.'

Lost in thought, Rumspell fell silent, absently stroking his bushy beard. Lavender clouds of smoke wreathed around him as he pulled hard on his pipe. The Grand Master watched his colleague anxiously as conflicting emotions flitted across the Vice-Chancellor's face. Rumspell looked up and nodded.

'Exploring the theory and practice of dimensionality

and the great grimoires is my lifetime's work, Rubus, yet I have charted only a fraction of the Arcane library's depths, and we can only guess what knowledge lies there beyond our feeble reach. Scholars have spent a lifetime trying to find the Old Grimoires without success.

'But! You are right, Rubus, as ever,' the plump scholar whispered, so softly that the Grand Master had to lean forward to catch his words. 'Where there is life there is always hope. Yes! My field trials are not yet complete, but... ' The Vice-Chancellor came to a decision, and the colour flooded back into his face. He looked up with something like his normal enthusiasm and energy.

'Rubus, I have been constructing a tool to assist scholars and researchers, indeed the librarians themselves, to locate grimoires by presenting virtual options and a map of their possible locations. Given specific parameters, this spell can explore thousands of possibilities in a heartbeat, narrowing the options and increasing the chance of success by a factor of thousands. I have completed a primary spell, and early results in the Library look promising, but remain infuriatingly inconsistent. With your permission, I shall immediately try to find the grimoire to see if it can unravel this mystery, offer some hope for Peregrine,' he nodded determinedly. 'I shall take all apprentices and set them tasks to divert attention should anyone be watching us.'

'Perhaps,' Rumspell continued thoughtfully, 'I should engage the services of the redoubtable Mrs Bracegirdle. Yes, indeed...' He brightened noticeably.

The Grand Master held his face poker straight and

attentive. So ... the rumours were true? Well, well. Good for him!

'Then, Barnaby, I must ask you to take this task on – as discreetly as you may. I know the danger I am placing you in. How widely the Raven has spread his wings we cannot guess, but there can be no doubt that we are being watched. We cannot betray our doubts or reveal to any but a trusted few that we hope Peregrine is still alive. Hide in the open, Barnaby. Hide in the open.'

Good advice. Given Lord Rumspell's considerable bulk, this was merely common sense unless a handy mammoth lurked in the immediate vicinity, and generally speaking you didn't find many of them in the Library. They wouldn't get past the eagle eyes of the redoubtable Mrs Bracegirdle for a start.

'How's it going then, love?' Mrs Archibald took in the miserable pair, picking half-heartedly at a supper fit for a Michaelmas feast. It took a great deal to put Douglas off his food; in fact, if his mother were honest, she couldn't remember the last time. Lucy was valiantly wading through her soufflé, stabbing the broccoli with all the apparent enthusiasm of a heron in a salmon farm.

'It's not.' Douglas paused with a forkful of potatoes halfway to his mouth. 'No one knows where the White Sorcerer is. And all the books say that sea dragons are extinct...although there have been sightings in Lucy's world.' He stopped when he saw his mother's expression.

'Sea d-'

The knock on the door was unexpected, making Mrs

Archibald spill water over the table. The Archibalds didn't go in for much entertaining. Feeding themselves was a difficult enough task, and times were hard. Mrs Archibald looked anxiously at the children with an unspoken question on her face; they both shook their heads. Still clutching the earthenware water-jug to her chest, Mrs Archibald stepped through the curtained doorway into the front room.

Lucy and Douglas could hear low murmurs of conversation followed by a crash. Mrs Archibald came scurrying in sideways like a boiled crab – face bright red and arms going in all directions as if the two she were allotted were entirely insufficient for the dual tasks of curtseying and ushering in their guest. A large man with a small cheerful face barrelled in after her, pursuing the aromatic promise of a second dinner. He was plainly dressed under a dark-hooded cloak beaded with pearls of water, and if he had come with an escort, as befitted his rank, there was no sign of them.

'Children, err...' Douglas's mother was at a rare loss for words as the stranger's cherubic face wrinkled with smiles. She curtsied as the man threw back his hood. 'The Vice-Chancellor needs your help.'

'M-m-more mutton, Lord?'

'Mmmmmmnnnn!!! Magnificent!!' Deftly avoiding the three-pronged fork waving enthusiastically under her nose, Mrs Archibald carved another slice from the small roast ... then another ... Nervously biting her lips she laid the carvers down on the empty platter and turned to the pots on the range.

'More rosemary potatoes?'

'Mmnn... Delicious..., dear lady!! Quite... delicious!!'

'More apple dumplings?'

'Mmnn... Splendiferous!! Stupendous!!'

'Cranberry bread?'

'Mmnn... quite...delectable!!'

Having got the general idea, Mrs Archibald piled on additional helpings from the remaining dishes without asking.

'Douglas!' She fetched a gentle kick at her son sitting boggle eyed on a chair, riveted by this example of culinary demolition. 'Out to Aunty Maggie at the Greasy Spoon, dear, and see if the kitchens can spare a tray of dumplings, a pan of gravy and a loaf or two.'

'Annnannotherbottleofaleperhaps?!'

Mrs Archibald winced and shouted behind her son's departing back, 'and a keg of Sorcerers Shilling, dear.'

Two happy bells later, Uncle Barnaby successfully hitched up his embroidered robes over two dinners and three layers of tummy and tightened the cord in an unsuccessful attempt to keep them there.

'M'dear lady.' His plump face wobbled as he mopped his greasy chin with a sleeve and looked regretfully at the empty plates. 'Indebted to you.'

Mrs Archibald summoned a weak smile from the bottom of her boots and the bottom of her equally empty larder. What on the One Earth were they going to eat for the rest of the month? What would her husband think when he came home tomorrow after a week's hard fishing, to find nothing on the table but the catch his crew had landed? That mutton had been a gift from a wealthy merchant passing through The Greasy Spoon who had found her cooking to his liking.

The solitary tallow candle brought out for the Archibalds' illustrious guest spluttered and went out, returning the kitchen to near gloom. As the Vice-Chancellor quietly spoke, Mrs Archibald shifted uncomfortably on her wooden stool. Having lived all her life in the Old Quarter, she had never heard of the Arcane Library of The Virtual University, and given the Vice-Chancellor's description she was beginning to wish she still hadn't. High magic was not for the likes of her folk, and she struggled to understand how her son had suddenly become embroiled in such dangerous statecraft.

'Grimoires are no ordinary books, child,' Uncle Barnaby cautioned, cherubic lips pursed with thought. 'Theurgies, enchantments, spells and potions cannot be solely bound by parchment, leathers and rare metals. They would burn to ashes. Magic leaches into the very air and stone that bounds the Library. These grimoires are sentient creatures bred for this one purpose. They are living guardians of ancient magicks and forgotten peoples, opening their pages only to those with the knowledge and wisdom to appreciate their power, to recognise their potency ... and their danger. Earth Magic has a will of its own that few save Mages, Loremasters and Lords can truly master. A little knowledge, my dear, is a dangerous weapon in the wrong hands.'

'Err,' said Douglas uncertainly.

'Young man?' Face dimly lit by the dying fire, Rumspell encouraged the boy with a friendly yellow-toothed grin and raised eyebrows. He looked genuinely interested.

'Em.' Douglas was still in awe of Lucy's easy familiarity with 'Uncle Barnaby' and her powerful and famous grandfather. 'If it's so dangerous, why are you taking Lucy with you? And,' he added, with pleading in his eyes and voice, 'and – can I come, too?'

'Douglas!' Rising to her feet, Jean Archibald was instantly apologetic and afraid on behalf of her forward son.

'But of course – if your mother permits it. Madam?' Instinctively Rumspell deferred to the boy's mother. He could sense the fear and concern for both children in her eyes and heavy unspoken words.

'Mum,' Douglas pleaded, reaching out to touch her arm with a gesture beyond his years, 'Lucy can't go on her own. She needs me … she, she needs someone from here to show her around. Please?'

'I shall protect them, Madam! Do not fear!'

The Vice-Chancellor rose to leave.

'M'dear lady.' Lord Rumspell gallantly hovered in the rain over an embarrassed Mrs Archibald's hand, planting an extravagant kiss on her rough chapped knuckles. Then, having successfully frightened the pair out of their wits for their own good, Uncle Barnaby finally turned from Lucy and Douglas into the damp night. 'Get a good night's sleep.' His bushy eyebrows knitted together fiercely under the hood. He looked like an eagle owl. 'We go in at first light.'

CHAPTER TWENTY-EIGHT

The Arcane Library

Words. The most elementary magic of all that the Vice-Chancellor had taught his apprentices on their first day: secret, potent, and brimming with power. Enough to set the imagination on fire, to make men dream. Living words and stories etched into silent metals, stone and wood in a bygone age where few could read or write. Never to be taken for granted.

Spells, cantrips and incantations: a combination of technique and talent used to allow the reader to control or manipulate the elemental powers of the One Earth. Often gathered together and bound into grimoires, thus creating books of great potency and power.

Books. Words of power lovingly scribed onto expensive sheaves of vellum, papyrus and parchment using rare blended inks and colourful pigments, then bound together with magical hides and potent spells. The oldest magic in the world: conferring prestige and priceless knowledge upon their owners.

Libraries. Costly and rare collections of books: owned by kings and princes, emperors and powerful city-states. And of course, Universities...

The Arcane Library buzzed with quiet activity and fairly tingled with suppressed energy as a ragtaggle clutch of yawning apprentices stumbled up to the Reference Desk to join the half dozen groups already waiting there. Endless aisles of bookcases stretched as far as the eye could see in every direction, including up and down. More magic books than the imagination could imagine rested here, along with a goodly portion of woodworms, bookworms and Scholars who burrowed away with surpassing diligence in pursuit of higher learning.

The largest recorded captured bookworm weighed in at 15 feet and five tons, with a mouth like an expressway tunnel. That was magic for you. So was the revival of Old Perkins, who had managed to get in the way of the browsing worm and, being rather dense and wooden himself, had got mistaken for yet another tasty morsel. It took three weeks to de-goo him, but the Professor of Tornado and Storm Studies had pulled through. So had the bookworm.

Wandering off, Douglas goggled at the hovering, long-snouted glow drakes that flew around after scholars, illuminating their way into the Library's wild untamed depths. There were no windows here in the bowels of the Glen. Not so much to keep the uninitiated out, oh no, the unwary and unwise would quietly (or sometimes very noisily) disappear and wake up to find themselves on the other side of the galaxy, communing with little whistling wool creatures on a barren moon. No, the perfect seamless sphere of the Arcane Library was designed to keep its troublesome tenants in. After all, such a concentration of spells and magical lore naturally distorted mundane mortal rules of physics – having the same effect, generally speaking, that a Sorcerer has, but magnified by a factor of potency.

The air was thick with spells that had broken free from their bindings or had yet to be trapped and tamed within the confines of a grimoire by an accredited Spell-Binder, whose complex and exacting profession meant they were always much in demand across the Celtic Sea Kingdoms. Nuclei of pure magical energy awaiting a Master's touch to transform and mould them to their ultimate purpose, spells zipped through bookcases, floors and students alike with wild abandon, occasionally exploding in a potent shower of colour that wrecked havoc upon the unwary and inexperienced. Elderly grimoires, tired and tetchy and worn out with the constant effort of containing their wilful charges, queued up for rebinding by overworked library staff. Rainbow-hued spells that painted the full spectrum of magic crowded curiously around the delighted apprentices, hoping for careless crumbs of magic.

Several aisles away, Douglas yelped. Finally over-whelmed by the sheer quantity and potency of the spells it contained, a panicking treatise on Agoraphobia scrabbled beneath his feet in an undignified gallop for the safety of the bookshelves. Seconds later, an elderly tome on The Effects of Magical Fields on Gravity also succumbed to its charges and fell off the 78th shelf, knocking Douglas off his feet just as Lucy found him.

'Arrghhh!' Douglas squealed indignantly as yet another indigo plasma bolt zapped his backside. Sooty sparks glowed like thousands of eyes, then winked out. The smell of burnt wool filled the air as Lucy damped down the dying embers.

'Ssshh! Stop fussing,' she admonished. 'We're not supposed to be drawing attention to ourselves.'

'We're not supposed -?' Douglas fumed. 'I'll have -.'

'Fire! Fire!' Alerted by the apprentice's scream, Lavender Morrison, assistant under-librarian standard grade, was homing in on the tell-tale indigo sparks, clutching a small portable water-drake.

Crying, 'Make way, make way,' she elbowed through Lord Rumspell's entourage with practised efficiency. 'Don't panic, don't panic. Everything's under control.' There was a muted percussive sound like a two-hundred-year-old plumbing system flushing, followed by the gush of high-pressured water escaping. The small teal-green dragon burped happily at a job well done.

'Err, sorry 'bout that,' the young lady said. He's still being trained ... bit, err, over enthusiastic ... only seven weeks old ... Fires you know ... um, books ... bad combination ... Err, can't be too careful ...' Alerted by the glacial expression solidifying on Douglas's normally good-natured face, she faltered.

'Um, would you like a towel? Let me – Dougal, no. The fire's out. NO, DOUGAL! NO!!!'

Following in Lord Rumspell's comfortingly large wake, Lucy and a very soggy Douglas pressed on deeper into the Library. Wild Magic sparked from volume to volume, sizzled from bookshelf to bookshelf, zapped from aisle to aisle, and arced from all of them towards the unfortunate Douglas, who discovered a hitherto unknown and unwanted affinity with lightning rods.

Lord Rumspell's dozen apprentices had scattered noisily to several different tasks, which would keep them going for days, if not weeks. Hopefully they would distract any prying eyes from the true purpose of their master and mentor, who now strode purposefully with no sign of stopping. Shooing away several persistent glow drakes, Lord Rumspell had chosen to light the way with his staff.

'Ouch.'

'Sorry.'

'Ouch.'

'Sorry ... sorry.' Douglas rolled his eyes nervously as Lucy turned round to hiss, 'Get off my heels.'

'This place gives me the creeps,' Douglas apologised miserably. He'd so wanted to be brave, but mischievous spells clustered round them as if sensing their lack of experience. Douglas could hear their unsettled whispers all around, and occasionally red, amber or green oval eyes winked owlishly on and off.

Until then, the few books that Douglas had encountered had been ... normal. Pages bound between two covers that you opened and closed and placed on a shelf somewhere until next time you needed to know how to bake goblin bread for that special birthday party, or needed Mrs Newtlett's remedy for banishing unwanted neighbours, or wanted to understand Taylor's Theorem of numerical methods.

Certainly Douglas had never encountered the kind of book that sprouted legs, wings or fins and deliberately moved every time you got near, or opened itself at exactly the right page you were wanting even before you knew what you wanted to know. Certainly not the kind that bit hard or slammed shut on careless fingers; or disagreeably refused to open at all; or were as opinionated as you and loudly disagreed with everything you said. Magical spells did that to books, collectively they wore on their nerves, ground them down until grimoires, even relatively young ones, became as cantankerous, snappy, and unpredictable as a two-hundred-year old crocodile.

Here and there they passed by a foosty cloak and faded pointy hat crumpled upon the floor next to an empty pair of slippers, as if their owner had been unavoidably detained somewhere else and had not yet returned to collect his or her belongings. Sometimes there was a distant squawk followed by silence. 'Whoops.' Lord Rumspell smiled enigmatically. 'There goes another one.'

Another what – where? Douglas mouthed silently, hanging on to Lucy's cloak.

And then there were unexplained scorch marks that blackened the floor and surrounding shelves...

Deep in the maze of books, far from prying eyes, Rumspell finally halted.

'Right, m'lad, you're going to act as a gimbal reality anchor for us. A lighthouse, so to speak,' he added, seeing the boy's confusion. 'In case we can't find our own way back home.' *In case Lucy has to find her way back without me.* 'And Lucy here will come with me.'

'Stand here.' Rumspell pointed to a dark star inlaid

into the floor. At its centre was a small slot. 'And,' the Vice-Chancellor placed one of Douglas's hands round his staff, 'whatever happens, don't move away or let go of the staff. Think you can manage? It's not an easy task I'm asking of you.'

'No problem,' Douglas squeaked, puffing his chest out like a wood pigeon. He coughed. 'No problem,' he said in his deepest manly tone as he reverentially accepted the wizard's staff. The wood felt cool beneath his fingers. A faint tremor ran its length as if it were exploring the unfamiliar hand which now held it.

'Time to plug in,' Uncle Barnaby smiled reassuringly, 'to our ancient Fifth Dimensional equivalent of the Internet. Oh, yes,' he said, noting Lucy's surprised expression, 'you're not the first! Who do you think gave you the printing press; the steam train, or virtual universities? Good Sorcerers, one and all. Great scholars, engineers, scientists... I, in my own humble area of culinary expertise, gave mankind bacon and maple syrup, and peanut butter and Jell-O...'

Peanut butter and Jell-O? Douglas mouthed silently and frowned at Lucy. She shrugged and stuck her tongue out as if to say 'yuck'.

Placing his sandaled feet firmly on the smooth stone floor, grasping his staff with one hand, Rumspell planted its silver shod end into the groove between his feet. It softly clicked into place and the star began to glow gently. Holding Lucy firmly by his free hand, Rumspell closed his mind to the wider world and its myriad distractions. He pushed all thoughts of roast pork, ice cream, chocolate and … He sighed audibly and muttered, 'Barnaby, son of Winklethor, get a grip. No time for trifles…'

Closing his eyes again, Rumspell focused on dimensionality. His toes tingled. Gradually the mood of the Arcane Library flowed into his mind. Around him the physical library grew dark and the rustle and whisper of the magical books grew louder. His staff began to vibrate. Multiple conversations flowed around him in languages and tongues long vanished in the living world. The tingling spread as the momentary paralysis of inter-dimensional merging took hold, and he and Lucy began to fade in front of Douglas's eyes.

Later, Lucy could barely recall how she felt as the Library faded, casting her adrift in inter-dimensional space. Afraid certainly. Excited. The boundary between natural and supernatural merged and blended. Deep currents of Earth magic held her like an unborn child in their liquid embrace, as she fought for air before realising she could still breathe in this place that was nowhere and yet everywhere. Lucy fought down the familiar feeling of vertigo. She opened her eyes to endless fathoms of night. Her wretched stomach lurched downwards with a sickening familiarity, not that it or Lucy could tell which direction was up or down, but it lurched for good measure, anxious to make its feelings known to anyone who might be paying attention. Did it feel like this in the International Space Station? Was she going to be space sick?! And where had the brooms magically appeared from?

At her side Rumspell remained reassuringly large and motionless, allowing his young apprentice time to adjust. Eyes tight shut again, she clung gratefully to him, feeling the contours of his arm around her shoulders but strangely not its weight. Slowly the feeling of falling settled. She took a deep breath. For the first time since the Bear's disappearance, Lucy was doing something that might just help him, by helping Uncle Barnaby to find a special book, a grimoire that he said might provide answers to the Raven's plans and her grandfather's role in them.

Jerkily, Lucy moved first one arm and then the other, kicked one leg and then the other, testing the fluid bounds of her new-found buoyancy before tentatively letting go of Rumspell's hand. Floating backwards, she managed an uncertain smile as he reached forwards to pull her effortlessly back to his side.

'Right, m'dear.' Rumspell anxiously squeezed her hand. 'I don't mean to rush you but I must concentrate. Are you ready? Trust your broom, they have great empathy and she will give you a smooth ride.' Rumspell took a deep breath and sketched a spell, his hands dancing gracefully through complicated manoeuvres of high magic. Normally portly and clumsy, the heavyset Rumspell was clearly in his element, finding a grace and fluidity of movement that transformed him from man to ArchMage. One spell flowed into another so smoothly that Lucy could not see where the one ended and another began. She stayed respectfully silent, watching, remembering.

'At least the elemental parameters are locked in,'

Rumspell murmured to himself, wiping the sweat that beaded his brow with the back of a hand. Glancing at Lucy, he explained, 'Web parameters, m'dear, in this context, mean framework, the widest scope of the search engine spiders, i.e. the elements of Water and Air. The others words cast define the scope, your meta-tags if you will.' Lucy pulled a face, clearly showing she hadn't understood a word. Uncle Barnaby was sounding alarmingly like Oliver! With a small smile, Rumspell returned to his task.

Saucer-eyed, Lucy unconsciously fidgeted on her broom, absorbing the boundless world around her, her fears forgotten. A wave of Earth magic took her unawares as a creature coalesced. Despite her passion for arachnids Lucy screamed. The spider in front of them was big; large enough to eat Rumspell and her and still wonder what the main course was. Its cephalothorax bristled with dozens of eyes in four rows, used for detecting minute changes within the magical spectrum of light, and its abdomen was virtually translucent. Lucy swallowed, more than a little afraid.

'Not quite complete, m'dear, in either form or substance.' So saying, Rumspell drew signs and symbols in the air and murmured a few more words. Lucy recognised the symbols for *search, command* and *urgency*. The spider dipped slightly and then scuttled away at unbelievable speed, leaving a thread for them to follow its path.

'The game's afoot!' Rumspell cried, waving his hat in the air. 'Come, m'dear,' his mount bucked, eager to give chase. 'Follow me.' Giving full head to his broom,

Rumspell swooped away in pursuit, robes billowing about him. Lucy, without remembering that she hadn't yet learnt to fly solo, leapt after him. Ten times the spider stopped where green and blue hued clouds hung. Each time Rumspell refined his search and pursued a hopeful lead, only to reach another dead end. They continued on, following the silken thread the spider spun as it hunted down possibilities. Then the creature scuttled into a huge bank of vivid red cloud. Gusts of unseen energy knocked their brooms sideways, then swept them back again. The Vice-Chancellor easily corrected his course. Behind him Lucy struggled to hang on, let alone control, hers. White lightning flashed across their bows, and the heat blasted them like a furnace.

'Hang on!' Uncle Barnaby bellowed helpfully as his broom bucked. 'Just a small nebula; they're always rather lively.' As the Vice-Chancellor suddenly dipped below her, Lucy opened her mouth to reply but just as suddenly they burst out into clear cool air. Ahead of them the spider slowed. Bringing his broom to a smooth stop, Uncle Barnaby studied the grimoires that swirled and flashed in the flickering space around them.

'What now?' Lucy called, as she caught up with him.

'We're close, m'dear. I can feel it in m'toes.' So saying, Uncle Barnaby hiked up his sock to let her have a look at his toes. There was no doubt – they were definitely toes. And quite hairy ones, but beyond that, Lucy felt, one couldn't say.

Unabashed, Uncle Barnaby wiggled them excitedly. 'Search, my dear. We search.' So saying, he grasped a book. Lucy joined in, finding that if she gently put her hands out, the books came to her. Soon they were clustering around her broom, competing for attention.

'How will we know which one it is?'

Rumspell smiled. 'I'll know, m'dear,' he said, tapping the side of his head. 'Lifetime of experience.'

Holding a large leather-bound grimoire, Lucy was amazed to find it as light as a feather, easy to hold with a single hand, and when she let go the book just floated away. Gravity barely existed in ten-dimensional space. Gravity was far too ordinary. Sensing that the quarry they sought was close by, Rumspell drifted on the eddying currents, letting them carry him in their chosen direction. Beside him, for the first time, Lucy relaxed a little. Absorbed by their task, neither master nor apprentice noticed a distant speck of light until the books yammered and jinked from their grasp.

Turning too late, the Vice-Chancellor sank sickeningly into a bitter arctic undertow that clawed at his senses and froze his fingers. Behind him, the cold numbed Lucy. Once, for a dare, she and Oliver had dived from the end of the jetty into the icy loch on New Year's Day. By the time they surfaced from their dives their limbs were leaden, and Charlie had waded into the icy water to drag them blue and chittering to the shore. She felt like that now. In front of them the search engine spider shrivelled and folded in on itself, disappearing in a wink of green powder that glittered as it hung in the air. The maw of the cloud turned towards the ArchMage and his apprentice. Yanking back both brooms by sheer force of will,

Rumspell evaded the enveloping green cloud, but searching tendrils groped in pursuit.

'An ambush,' he shouted. *How long ago did the Raven set wards to prevent the book's discovery? But that means we are on the correct path and he failed to find it!* 'Get clear, Lucy. NOW!' As Rumspell urged her away, a tendril brushed his broom, sending a jarring electric shock through the living wood which splintered. With a cry of pain Rumspell tumbled away head over heels into the darkness, and his broom bolted out of control. Lucy wrenched her own round in a tight loop and raced to round up the broom and overtake Rumspell's spinning body.

Douglas stood alone in the rustling library and tried his best to look brave. The staff cast a weak light, barely penetrating the shadows that danced along the shifting aisles. As a bell rang the hour of the inquisitive stoat, being brave became harder and harder. His tummy rumbled and nature called – increasingly loudly. He wished he'd brought a flask of water to wet dry lips. Then the golden star turned sickly green. The heavy soles of his reinforced hide boots were smoking. Douglas needed help! Reading her companion's mind, Bucksturdie raced away, a russet shadow enveloped by the dark. The staff began to smoke. Hanging on determinedly, Douglas started jigging with the aplomb of an experienced Morris dancer minus the bells. Where was an assistant librarian with a water-drake when you needed one?

'Thank you, m'dear,' Uncle Barnaby puffed as he rested on his broom and examined the burns on his hands. 'I wondered if any obstacles would be laid for those who came looking. How foolish of them. Now we know for certain we are on the right track.' He looked ruefully up at his young protégée. 'The books have scattered. We'll have to begin our search again.'

Lucy had a sudden thought. The book could not have gone too far. 'What if -'

'M'dear?'

'When I'm at home,' Lucy said in a rush, 'and I want an animal or a bird to come to me, I sing, or play the fiddle. If I sit on the rocks at the edge of the loch, the seals and otters come to the surface to listen ... '

She trailed off uncertainly as Rumspell stared at her thoughtfully. *Has she inherited her grandmother's skill?* 'The very thing, m'dear,' he smiled. 'Why not? Music runs in the veins, y'know. Sing! Focus your thoughts upon the book and give it your all!'

Taking a deep breath, the young apprentice obligingly gave it her all. The grimoires rustled breathlessly as Lucy sang softly, soothing their ruffled pages, calming their fears. Once again they began to congregate around, fluttering close for attention. The odd note chimed in response. Soon notes sprang into the air all around the singing girl.

Rumspell closed his eyes. 'Ahh,' he breathed, 'music, the greatest magic of all.'

Rumspell sat quietly as Lucy sang. He knew the ancient grimoire had come, he could feel the change in the magical tides eddying about them, but he waited until Lucy finished. He simply held out his hands and the grimoire came to rest on them. He handed it to Lucy. 'It's perfectly light!' And so it was.

At the very moment when Lucy closed her hands around the large volume, Rumspell cried out and swung his broom round. The books scattered as an apparition of smoking emerald hurtled down upon them.

'An emerald wraith,' Rumspell groaned, seeing for the first time the fine silken spider thread that was attached to the book. They had just rung the doorbell and sprung the trap. 'And I am without my staff!' He rummaged frantically in his pockets and pulled out a small wand with the logo DisposAWand embellished along its length. 'Woefully inadequate,' he muttered, looking at the closing wraith, 'but I have some small skill in the matter.'

'Fly,' he cried to Lucy. 'It's guarding the book. Fly to safety, or your grandfather will be lost to us.'

'Where?' Lucy cried, looking wildly at the featureless space around them. It all looked the same to her.

'Home,' Rumspell barked, 'if our young friend has managed to hold the fort.' So saying, he muttered words of summoning, and a light bloomed in the dark. 'Thank goodness,' Rumspell sighed. 'He's still there. Fly straight at the light. I'll delay the wraith.' He waved the wand and fired it. The wand sparked fitfully then fizzled out. 'Drat,' Lord Rumspell cursed, 'it's a dud.'

Throwing the wand away, he executed a rapid U-turn and raced up beside Lucy. 'Now,' he cried urgently. 'Follow me, stay in my slipstream.' So saying, the Vice-

Chancellor took off at breakneck speed, with Lucy's broom obediently in tow.

'Nearly there,' he cried as they hurtled towards the growing light. Lucy looked over her shoulder. The wraith was gaining. Now she could see its black eyes and the glint of sharp teeth as it coldly smiled.

'Dragons Teeth,' Lord Rumspell glanced behind. 'Almost there but not quite.' He swung his broom and looped out behind Lucy. She slowed.

'No,' he cried, 'your friend is there. Go, fly through.'

Lord Rumspell turned towards the wraith and hastily threw up a warding shield to protect her. Lucy obediently swooped towards Douglas and safety. Behind her she heard the detonation of contact as the wraith smashed into the Vice-Chancellor's shield; explosive light showered down over her head. Hurling the book at the apex of the funnelled light, she struggled to turn her broom around. Neither Rumspell nor Lucy saw a second wraith slip swiftly through the open door to the library.

There was a massive explosion and a book thudded to the floor on top of Douglas. The stunned apprentice lay flattened on his back, with only his smouldering boots sticking out and the charred remnants of the staff still clutched tightly in one hand. Without the staff it was now pitch dark. He struggled up, horrified, as a luminescent green vapour began to billow out of the star and ooze towards him. Dragging the book for all he was worth, Douglas tried to pull it and himself to safety, but the green was rapidly taking shape and form. Fingers formed into a claw that beckoned him back. A sickly sweet odour filled the air. He felt faint; his head nodded.

A flash of red-gold and a snarl announced Bucksturdie's return as she bounded over her master's prone form. Snapping and yelping with a shaggy blur of wicked white teeth she drove the liquid creature back in on itself. Only dimly did the drugged young boy become aware, through a fog, that the vixen had gripped his cloak and was pulling him inch by agonising inch away from the man-like thing that bubbled and oozed with green malignancy.

Something hurtled over their heads. A second explosion knocked him flat again. Suffocating smoke roiled and eddied. Coughing on the floor, the apprentice could barely see. A hot tongue rasped on his ears and chin and neck, the touch of a cold nose reviving him from his stupor. Frantic paws dug at his chest as Bucksturdie covered the apprentice with lavish kisses. Blinking furiously to clear his vision, Douglas stumbled up to his feet and looked around in confusion. In the dying glow there was no sign of Lucy or the Vice-Chancellor. Greasy particles of soot floated in the air. Suddenly a globe of soft white light threw back the darkness.

'You there.'

A furious sooty vision in sensible, silver-buckled black boots, red-and-white-striped knickerbockers and a volum-inous body barely contained by a billowing robe and a dozen lace petticoats hurtled down upon him. Douglas cringed. It was an entirely natural reaction under the circumstances.

'I say, you,' the apparition bellowed, 'you there. Take my hand, young man. And don't let go of that grimoire.' The confident words carried the imperious weight of generations used to commanding lesser beings. Douglas obediently raised an arm, desperately clutching the heavy book under the other.

The reinforced Willowswitch Multi x 4-Bristle Drive slowed to a hover. Douglas took this opportunity to disentangle himself from the suffocating petticoats, only to be poked in the eye by the pointy tip of an enormous hat, upholstered like its owner in university tartan.

'Off you get, young man.'

Bucksturdie had already sprung lightly off as Douglas hastily obliged, barely avoiding the size 8½ hobnailed boot that parted his hair as its owner dismounted with a delicate and distinctly feminine grunt and turned to face him. White-rimmed eyes blinked owlishly in a sea of soot. The apparition removed its pointy hat to reveal steely grey hair pinned back into a severe bun, held in place by a vicious looking array of hatpins bearing the University's coat of arms. A pair of pince-nez spectacles perched on the end of a fine Roman nose were removed and furiously polished with a lace handkerchief, leaving sooty streaks.

'Righty-ho, young man,' said the formidable Mrs Bracegirdle, heartily clapping Douglas on the back and raising clouds of soot. 'You're all right there, are you?' she asked, as Douglas fell coughing to his knees. 'Jolly good, jolly good. A fine animal you've got there,' she glanced at Bucksturdie, who was grinning broadly with her tongue lolling out. 'A jolly fine animal. Alerted me to your peril, wouldn't take no for an answer. And you have the book? Jolly good. Lavender here will look after you. Cuthbert,' she bellowed, without pausing for breath. 'Cuthbert, don't dawdle off somewhere.' As the broom whisked up to her, she leapt on it and disappeared into the depths of the library.

'Um, would you like a wash?' a small voice asked hopefully.

Douglas turned to see Lavender, with her water-drake, Dougal, in tow and several towels at the ready.

The wraith no longer felt quite so certain. The plump sorcerer in University robes who had looked like such easy pickings was putting up a tenacious fight, for an academic. He might be overweight, but it was becoming increasingly clear he was far from over the hill. It hesitated; after all the grimoire was no longer here. The sorcerer's apprentice was having a go, too, although most of her shots missed completely. Staring at one of Lucy's bolts, which actually went backwards over her shoulder and nearly set her broom on fire, the wraith got caught. Emerald exploded, splattering Lucy and Rumspell with sizzling globules. As the smoke thinned, the sorcerer and apprentice found themselves alone in glittering space. Lord Rumspell tried to wipe the goo of his chin. 'Right, M'dear! Time to head for port!'

They turned to find their beacon gone.

'What do we do now?' Lucy asked in a small voice.

'When lost at sea we must look, my dear, for the metaphorical lighthouse to guide us to safety.'

Somewhere in the dark of hyperspace, the second wraith was preparing to have another go. It had just about emerged into the library when someone had slammed the door shut in its face with a fistful of magic that had made it see stars, and not the ones in multi-dimensional space. A long, long time ago, this grimoire had been hidden so that its secrets never fell into the wrong hands. Unable to find it, the warlock who set the trap should anyone else find it, had been...persuasive and he was not one to forgive failure. Its eyes glittered coldly as it poured through the star portal and prepared to retrieve its prize.

'Oh no, you don't. We won't be having with any of that in my library.'

The wraith turned towards the sound.

Mrs Bracegirdle swung Cuthbert like a cricket bat. In two heartbeats it was all over; and it was all over the bookshelves as well. Briskly wiping the goo off her face, the Chief Librarian of the Arcane library swept a long wand out of a petticoat pocket and plugged it into the soot-streaked star inlaid in the floor.

'There,' Lord Rumspell cried, as he spotted the distant sweeping light that winked into existence. Racing for it, master and apprentice leapt together. Temporary paralysis took hold, and the glittering dark of inter-dimensional space faded. Coloured motes danced in the air, heralding their return to the library with a bang.

We haven't managed it, Lucy thought in alarm, as a large green-splattered and sooty apparition coalesced into view, wielding the biggest broom the apprentice had ever seen. On seeing the unmistakable outline of Lord Rumspell, followed by Lucy, materialise, the apparition unexpectedly smiled, revealing a palisade of air-cooled teeth.

Lucy stepped back in alarm.

'Master Rumspell.' The apparition's shoulders sagged with relief. 'Barnaby, dearest man...'

'Dear lady.' Lord Rumspell fumbled for her hand and bestowed a grateful sooty kiss that lingered poignantly.

CHAPTER TWENTY-NINE

Code Cracking

'Oh no!' *There's nothing there. There's nothing! We've got the wrong book!* Exhausted, Lucy tearfully held her head in her hands in bitter disappointment.

It was early afternoon. Everyone had hastily washed and eaten. Lucy and Douglas were wearing spare junior assistant librarian robes, part of Mrs Bracegirdle's plan for throwing the 'hounds off the scent' as she put it.

The Grimoire of Seahenge had been reverentially placed on the dragon lectern in the Vice-Chancellor's private reading room, as befitted its venerable status. Lucy had been given the privilege of being the first to open its pages.

'Patience, m'dear.' Lord Rumspell held up an admonitory finger. 'Knowledge is not so easily gained, and what would its worth be, m'dear, if it were? Take yourself off to the city, get a bite to eat, take a look at the markets...'

He held up a finger to his lips to soften the protest he saw forming on the young girl's lips. 'Hush, lassie. Hush. I know it's difficult, but nothing will be gained by haste. We must tread softly, else we alert those who are most surely watching to see if we have uncovered their plan. In the meantime, I, with Muckle's help, shall see if we can unlock this book's secrets.'

'Young man,' Lord Rumspell placed his hands on the boy's shoulders and looked Douglas squarely in the eye. 'I rely on you once again. Take Lucy here to the city

markets and replenish your mother's empty larder. Here.'
He lobbed a soft purse tied with a thong to the boy, who
caught the clinking money adroitly. 'Go on, now, have
some fun.'

Cracking his knuckles loudly, Lord Rumspell eyed the
resting great grimoire with pleasure, in anticipation of the
battle of wills that was about to unfold. This was his
delight and his lifetime's work: unlocking ancient secrets
through a skilful blend of sorcery, guile and persistence.
It was a challenge he could never resist – but this time the
stakes were impossibly high...would this unlock the
secrets to Peregrine's disappearance and to the Raven's
plans?

Wrapping Gaia around him like a comfortable cloak,
the ArchMage studied the hitherto unseen currents of
Earth, Air and Water that eddied about the book,
ensnaring its wisdom in its delicate filaments, preserving
the power of its spells in a million coloured threads.
Every detail of the book's crafting sprang to life, given
form and texture by the power that radiated from the
rotund ArchMage. The grains that formed the illuminated
pigments on the page: the life of the great creature of the
deeps whose scales formed each precious, pearlescent
sheet, the bioluminescent black ink of the extinct giant
squid. A grimoire written in that lost citadel beneath the
sea, far from the sunlight, countless eons ago; and every
detail woven together in the ancient liquid language of
those who bonded with the immortal Elders: the dragons.
He turned a page.

Carelessly grooming his fur with the two split nails of his webbed hindfoot, Muckle suddenly stood, balancing himself with his flat scaly tail and chattered loudly. Lord Rumspell listened attentively.

'So you agree, old friend, do you? Then let us begin.'

Sensing his unspoken challenge, the grimoire's pages rustled smugly in response. This promised to be a good fight.

Two days later, the Vice-Chancellor wiped the sweat from his brow and watched with elation as light spilled into infinitesimal grooves and the smoking pages came to life. He began reading. The candles burnt down and were replaced. The fire stoked. A tray of food was left untouched. Dawn broke and night fell. Mrs Bracegirdle was called in to help. She in turn summoned her army of librarians. The Vice-Chancellor invited the Deans of Faculty to attend him, and several academics were hastily summoned from Yale and Oxford. Books and grimoires, ancient scrolls, runes and glyphs, ogham carvings and cuneiform tablets were studied. All known spells and counter-spells were referenced. Finally they found what they were looking for, written in the long forgotten language of the Elders.

[decorative script / fictional alphabet — five lines of text]

Time to see if the gremlins of GI5 lived up to their reputation: time to see what secrets the Grimoire would reveal about Sea Dragon's Bane.

'Newt & Toad!'

Lucy hardly heard her friend as she looked around the Encryption division of GI5. Under Uncle Barnaby's wing they had entered the Skye keep by a secret underground tunnel that ran from under the Grand Master's halls. Their small bright-eyed gremlin guide, Towald, then escorted them down and deeper down into this bustling subterranean labyrinth of laboratories that honeycombed the black basalt rock beneath the city, all the time listening and talking into the minute iridium-green Bluetooth headset that curled around her pointed ear.

Douglas was fascinated by the security protocols, firing endless questions at Towald as they reached the bottom of a ramp. Douglas, Lucy thought, would get on with Oliver like a house on fire. When this is over, maybe they could meet? Desperately tired, she had to bite back her impatience as the gremlin stopped yet again to explain some protocol, even if in fairness, she acknowledged it was a small delay and her friend had more than earned it.

'It's called an SSO, Single Sign-On,' Towald explained

as she punched a code into the access panel and placed her scaly palm on the hand scanner. 'Everyone has to use multiple authentication token methods or devices. This is a finger-imaging panel. Place your hands here, please. Thank you. Now stand here.' Douglas shuffled forward and peered eagerly forwards as a thin line of blue scanned his face. 'Thank you.' The gremlin courteously but firmly detached Douglas from the electronic eye. 'This device is an iris and retina scanner.' The light blipped green for the second time. Lucy followed suit. The gremlin smiled as she gestured them forward. 'You are now cleared to enter.'

The opaque glass doors opened silently.

'How,' Douglas quietly asked Lucy as they approached the operations core of the Cryptology section, 'did they get our fingerprints?'

Lucy was wondering just the same thing.

A gremlin rushed to greet them. 'Lord Rumspell,' the duty watch captain bowed, gold and crystal earrings tinkling. Lord Rumspell smiled, although his hazel eyes betrayed his gnawing anxiety. 'At ease, Morlock. Tell me, how are your lovely wife Grimelda and your fine young sons?'

'They are well, Lord,' Morlock responded, smiling with pleasure. 'This way.' He led his visitors past rooms housing a series of supercomputers and through to a large laboratory filled with teams of technicians and a myriad of workstations. Douglas was in seventh heaven as they passed by screens crammed with equations and algorithms. *James Bond*, Lucy thought, as Morlock retrieved Douglas once again and propelled him after Lord

Rumspell. They stopped beside a bank of workstations and Rumspell asked a series of questions that the team of cryptologists quietly answered.

Morlock turned emerald lizard eyes to Lord Rumspell. 'With your permission, Lord?'

The spell from the Grimoire of Seahenge was thrown onto a large Organic Light-Emitting Diode screen on the wall. A breathless whisper ran round the lab as the beautiful flowing script was instantly recognised. There was a brief reverential silence.

The Immortals, Lucy thought. The language of the Immortals! Her fingers tingled in recognition. The language of the First Dragon Lords!

Lucy and Douglas were all attention as the technicians keyed in several commands. On the top part of the screen the runes were arranged in lines. Below, letters of the alphabet scrolled down the screen at breathtaking speed searching for a common frame of reference. A letter glowed and was superimposed on the cipher text. The process became a blur as the computer recognised the language and extrapolated those runes that remained. The cryptologist typed in a few commands and the script vanished. Words began to form line-by-line-by-line:

> *Claw of dragon swimming deep*
> *Both awake and yet asleep*
> *Goblin's gob and troll toenail*
> *Hedgewitch's broom and kelpie's tail*
> *Laughter of sun shining bright*

Tears of moon in cold moonlight
In stony crown at dawn of day
Banish dark and spells away
Conjure magic old as Earth
And summon light to bring rebirth.

'Well done, Morlock,' Lord Rumspell acknowledged the gremlin's superlative skill. 'My compliments to your team.'

'It was not difficult, Lord.' The cryptologists' pride was evident in their wide grins. 'The code is old; it took a simple binary search algorithm.' Noticing Douglas's rapt expression, Morlock suggested, 'With your permission, Lord, perhaps I could show your young protégés around the labs?'

He turned to the boy, who was hopping up and down with barely restrained enthusiasm. 'We have a special purpose-built Echotech Cracker supercomputer that can test 50 billion different key sequences per second...'

Night had already enveloped the Lord Rumspell's sumptuous study in his private apartments, high in the Glengoyne Tower of the Virtual University, built on the lee side of the Dragon's Spine Mountains that formed the north range of the Sorcerers Glen. Lucy stared anxiously at the rhyme, but its rhythm and meaning defeated her. Keyed up and worn out, she was having difficulty concentrating.

'Sit down, m'dear.' Rumspell steered the yawning girl to a comfy chair by the fire. She was exhausted and no wonder! He rang for a servant. Lucy drank the hot milk that tasted of cinnamon and honey. Her head lolled as Rumspell deftly caught the glass. Pulling a woollen rug over the sleeping girl, he bustled back to his desk and set to work to fathom the secrets of Sea Dragon's Bane.

Several hours later, maps and reference books scattered over the desk, he sat back with a degree of satisfaction but also with deep dismay. Much had changed since this spell was first cast that made their task easier. Trolls, for example; trolls formed the elite Sea Reaver Marines. There would be no shortage of available toe nails! Goblins, however, were a trickier bunch, not to mention repulsive, but Mistress Pemberton knew just the person to achieve that task...and as for kelpies they were dark and dangerous...*I'll have to think on that... Hedgewitch's broom*; Celia could help him out there. He nodded to himself. *But the sea dragon?* The Guardian had suggested that it might be concealed in an inter-dimensional pocket... but *both awake and yet asleep?* The meaning of sun and moon also totally eluded him. *Stony crown...*that has to be the Necromancer's Ring ~ a place of great power...

There was not only great danger in collecting the reagents for the counter-spell to defeat Sea Dragon's Bane, but also in the casting. And yet the greatest scholars and battlemages were not qualified. According to Professor Sedgeburt there was only one person who was, through the bond of blood. All others would fail and most certainly die. But how could they pit untrained children against the power of the Raven? Writing several messages, he selected three bats and despatched them into the deepening night, and gave Lucy the last in a sealed letter for her mother.

'Giddyup, Pawkie! Up! Up!'

The broom faltered, stalled, dipped, and then began to pick up speed as its pilot finally got to grips with elementary flying.

'Hang on!' Justin cried cheerfully, as they wobbled into the night sky.

Lucy swallowed and closed her eyes. A well-scrubbed and fresh-faced Justin had just passed his elementary flying test and flew a very nervous Lucy back to the White Sorcerer's cottage. A large knock-kneed moon-spider clung to the pinnacle of Justin's hat. His totem, he confided in hushed tones to Lucy, had revealed itself in his moment of greatest need by hiding under his hat. The two were now inseparable. Lucy fervently prayed that Cobwald would teach Justin to fly properly, but she didn't hold out too much hope. Stepping through the Gateway and swiftly walking home, Lucy barely had the energy to change into her pyjamas. The Bear may have been missing in the Fifth Dimension, but life in Thistleburr had to go on. School tomorrow. Within minutes of her head hitting the pillow, Lucy was asleep.

Downstairs, as the fingernail moon rose and Thistleburr slept, Mother reread the rhyme and letter from Lord Rumspell and tried to fight down welling panic. This was going to place her young daughter and her friend Douglas in great danger; they were far too young to be facing such a dire challenge. There was only one ingredient of the spell she could readily arrange herself. Rummaging around in the Hallowe'en box, Mother dug out a photograph of the judges and winners of the fancy dress competition. Within the hour, Truffle and Tantrum had posted a most peculiar and particular message to the Most Wanted Post, in Hog Market Square of the Black Isle.

Well-endowed red-head (female) seeks attractive green-haired Prince Charming. Must like Thistleburr Thunder and have an interest in music and motorbikes and exotic hairdos. Apply Mistress Pemberton, c/o the Gnomes Guild on Baker Street.

CHAPTER THIRTY

Brooms and Dustpans

Lucy, Kealan and Oliver were gathered in the kitchen of the Nook & Cranny. They were all staring at Mother Pemberton, wide-eyed and opened-mouthed in disbelief.

'But... I don't understand,' Lucy repeated. 'How can *I* do this? I'm only an apprentice. Why can't Uncle Barnaby, or the Grand Master? Or the Guardian?'

Mother took Lucy's hands in hers. 'Firstly, because we have been betrayed and they are most certainly being watched by our enemies. We don't know who we can trust in the Guild, or even in the SDS. The Guardian is secretly preparing for the worst on Dragon Isle with the III FirstBorn Regiment, whose loyalty is absolute. Ah, hush, Lucy, love. We cannot risk revealing that we have learnt something of the Raven's plan, let alone that we are conjuring a counter-spell. While GI5 searches for your grandfather – the Grand Master is certain he is here somewhere in our world, now awaiting Warwick Snowe – we must gather these reagents unseen and without their help. None will pay attention to apprentices.

'But there is another reason, Lucy dear. Uncle Barnaby believes that only one who shares the same blood as your grandfather can safely cast the counter-spell: and it must be someone born to both the world of magic and men as the Raven now is. For anyone else it would mean death to even come into contact with Sea Dragon Bane.'

Oliver tried to bite down his fear and put a comforting

arm around his sister. 'H-how long do we have to find all these things on this list...' he raised the rhyme. 'These reagents?'

'Until the winter solstice on the 20th December: the longest night of the year. It is a time of great power when the dimensions merge in places such as the Necromancer's Ring, flooding it with magic, and Lucy will need to draw upon that magic. We are certain that is when the Raven plans to return.'

'What is a kelpie's tail?' Oliver asked. 'What's a kelpie?'

'And the dr-' Kealan coughed and tried again. 'Dragon swimming deep...? I mean...how does Lucy get a talon?'

'Well,' mother suggested brightly, 'let's collect the ones that are easiest first, whilst we work out those we don't understand. Let's begin with the Hedgewitch's broom. On Friday evening Uncle Barnaby is expecting you, Lucy, at the Guild Skye Keep. Do you think you could fly Gertrude yourself? She is a rather sedate old broom, set in her ways, but she knows you now.'

Kealan took a dubious look at the broom, innocently propped against the kitchen door.

'That is just a broom, Kealan, dear,' Mother said, looking at the boy's muddy boots. 'You might like to sweep the floor with it. The dustpan is over there.'

CHAPTER THIRTY-ONE

Hedgewitch's Broom

Mrs Celia Bracegirdle was an aristocrat descended from a long line of Bracegirdles, a ruling patrician family who had evidently been organising things since man first stood upright and lifted a club to bonk his neighbour on the head. You could imagine a Bracegirdle organising sorties on mammoth-back to catch a rogue sabre-toothed tiger; leading the tribe into battle on chariots pulled by boars; converting that old damp cave into a penthouse suite complete with central heating and running water. Their heraldic coat of arms was a mammoth quartered with a broom, a thistle dragon and a bent spoon. No one could remember where the spoon came from; that little story was thankfully lost in the comforting mists of antiquity. The latest scion of the patrician house was treasurer of the Ladies Guild, patron of countless worthy charities and chairwoman of the Racing Dragon Stud Society, in addition to holding the prestigious post of Chief Librarian of the Arcane library. Unexpectedly, all this made her uniquely qualified to assist the Vice-Chancellor and his apprentices in their quest for the reagents needed to cast the counter-spell for Sea Dragon Bane.

She was also well known for her dislike of children. Children, Mrs Bracegirdle felt, were the unfortunate kind of thing that happened to other people but never to her. And such a well-known reputation made it highly unlikely that her hand in the lowly affairs of the Vice-Chancellor's first year apprentices would be detected. Mrs Celia Bracegirdle lived high up in the Boulevard Circle, as befitted her station.

'I've never been up to The Hill,' Douglas whispered in Lucy's ear as Rumspell began his final circling descent to the broom pad located on the east wing of Thistlestone Palace. It was already dark, and they couldn't see a thing beyond the glow of light from dozens of windows and from braziers marking out the drive and entrance. Stepping down from the pad, they followed Rumspell across a stone courtyard and down dark steps to a little-used side-door. Douglas pulled the doorbell rope vigorously. In the distant depths of the house a bell rang and shortly thereafter, footsteps could be heard coming closer. Then the frayed tapestry bell-pull came off in his hand. Douglas was standing there aghast when the door opened and familiar formidable eyes skewered him. He visibly quailed.

The redoubtable Mrs Bracegirdle rallied admirably. 'Ah, yes,' she said, proffering a smile she normally reserved for dragon hunters and the intellectually challenged. 'Been meaning to replace that for years. Frightfully old fashioned. Jolly good of you to take it off, really.' She took it out of Douglas's stationary hand and flashed a rare smile over the children's heads at Lord Rumspell.

'Delighted, dear Lady,' the Vice-Chancellor said kissing his hostess's expensively ringed hand. 'Your humble servant, as ever.'

Suddenly aware that both Lucy and Douglas were

staring raptly at this little byplay, Lord Rumspell straightened and coughed self-consciously.

'Ahem. Right. To business,' he said, tucking in his tummies and raising his staff. 'Lead on, dear Lady. Lead on!'

There was a quiet knock on the door of the Nook & Cranny.

'Right, lad,' said Mother briskly, eying up the anxious goblin hovering on her doorstep, a one-day Portal pass in his hand. 'It's into the bathtub with you, and a change of clothes. When did you last wash? ... ooh, dearie-me, dearie-dearie me.' She bustled off to find coal-tar soap and a stiff brush, before depositing the goblin in the bathroom with strict instructions, toe-nail clippers, a nit-comb and a very large bottle of stringent antiseptic. Then she made a phone call to the vet's surgery. She was breaking several Guild ordinances, but as her mother used to say, 'needs must when the devil rides.' Gargoyle had something she needed, and she had the means of persuading him to part with it.

* * *

'Bracegirdles one and all,' Celia Bracegirdle said proudly, as the children quailed beneath the grim, gilt-framed stares and stuck up chins of generations of Bracegirdles, captured in oils. 'Including,' she said wistfully, hand to her bosom, 'my dearest Herbert.'

There was a huge painting over the study fireplace of 'dearest Herbert' clad in spectacular armour and a tartan plaid, wielding a nasty-looking claymore on the back of a swooping moorland thistle dragon. The nasty-looking claymore was hung beneath the painting. It was badly notched and buckled. It didn't take much imagination to work out that its owner had come to a similarly untimely end.

'That's Stormcrasher Crisp.' Mrs Bracegirdle sniffed and wiped a tear from her eye. 'Herbet's favourite battle dragon,' she added. 'Of impeccable lineage. Bred and raised him from a colt. Quite inseparable the two of them – right to the very end. Well!' She dabbed her nose with a lace hankie and adjusted her pince-nez. 'I dare say,' she said in more businesslike tones, looking down her long aquiline nose, 'that you're wondering why I invited you here?' The children nodded, awkward and tongue-tied in the face of such grandeur. Rumspell's smug smile as he followed Lucy and Douglas through buttery and bakery, wine cellar and kitchens was positively feline.

'The broom stables,' Mrs Bracegirdle announced, as if that were sufficient by way of explanation.

'Blood and Bone!' Douglas whispered reverentially as the wall-sconces sputtered into light around the hammer-beamed stable-block. Lucy stood silently, trying to take in the strange sight in front of her. A broom stable?

Dancing around with frantic glee, Douglas couldn't keep silent any more than a lapsed hermit. 'Newt & Toad! Newt & Toad! This is a Stormcloud Skywalker. They're bred from gingko wood, very rare. And a Sirocco Sandstorm.' He reached out to touch the smooth oiled wood, the perfect grain, so light to the touch. A priceless pure-bred pedigree broom. 'Oh, a Myrk-Rider Classic! …'

Windsom Cloudrider... Moonshadow Marauder... Starcluster Suncatcher... beautiful names... Half listening to Douglas's magpie chatter, Lucy wandered round. *They're so beautiful. Such strange...creatures. Why are we wasting time?* She stopped dead in her tracks, not daring to believe. With trembling hands, she reached unseeing into her robe pockets and re-read the crumpled rhyme for the hundredth time. *Hedgewitch's broom* – there it was! Finally she remembered to breathe. Spotting her stillness, Douglas rushed over.

'A Hedgewitch Harvester! You've found it!' He danced a little jig and punched the air. 'And look, a Hedge Rider! There must be a dozen at least.'

'Fourteen to be exact, young man,' Celia Bracegirdle informed him, making him jump. She moved surprisingly silently for such a large woman. 'The largest private collection in the Celtic Sea Kingdoms. Herbert's family on his mother's side came from a long line of hedgewitches,' she explained. 'A family tradition handed down from generation to generation for thousands of years. A dying art these days, I'm afraid. No one needs them anymore.' She moved forward to select a broom with wild tangled bristles. The shaft was inlaid with an intricate Celtic knotwork of coiled dragons and skulls in white enamel and gold.

'Young lady,' Mrs Bracegirdle announced, her knowing compassionate gaze boring into Lucy. 'This is a besom: a hedgewitch broom crafted from three woods. Wychwood for the shaft, silver birch for the bristles and supple willow to bind the two together. He's yours. Goes by the name of

Barking Broombuster III, but Old Ma Ragpole used to call him Napoleon.'

Lucy opened her mouth and stared, wondering what Napeoleon would have thought of having a broom named after him!

'No need to thank me, young lady,' Mrs Bracegirdle said gruffly and dabbed her eye. 'Come along, now. Grandma Bracegirdle doesn't like to be kept waiting.'

Grandma Bracegirdle turned out to be a wizened old lady with a nose like a wilting parsnip, dark gimlet eyes framed by a fine network of wrinkles, and a generous helping of hairy warts. Three hundred and forty two she might have been, but she was sharp as a whip and had ears like a bat. Dressed from head to foot in black and lace with pointed boots and pointy hat, she looked to Lucy every inch the storybook witch. And so she was, and one of great renown. For Grandma Bracegirdle was one of the greatest hedgewitches of recent generations.

'But what is a hedgewitch? Lucy had asked. 'What does it mean to be a hedge-rider?'

'Ah, little sister,' Grandma Bracegirdle's gaze was hypnotic, her voice mesmerising. 'In your world a hedge was the boundary between the village and the woods. Crossing that barrier is dangerous because who knows what creatures lie in that wilderness beyond? In our world the hedge is the barrier betwixt the living and the dead. Standing stones are one such divide, places of great power. Where there are no stones, then ghost fences are laid. This divide is at its weakest between All Hallow's

Eve and the winter solstice; the shortest day of the year. On that day, the barriers between our worlds fail, and then we must ride the Hedge, weaving Elemental threads to strengthen the barrier and keep evil at bay. It is the Hedgewitch who denies Fate his victims. Thus it is that you must deny Fate and his minions your grandfather's life.'

'Ghost fences?' Lucy had asked in a moment of inspiration. 'Is that what pumpkins do?'

'What?' Douglas had never heard of pumpkins.

'Err Turnips...turnip lanterns?'

Douglas looked baffled. 'Why?'

'Well...at Hallowe'en we all make turnip lanterns, well pumpkin lanterns nowadays, they're easier to carve. We carve them into faces like a skull and set candles in them. We put them at windows and doors. In America they set them on steps and verandas...lots of them!'

'Why?' Douglas frowned in confusion.

'Ghost fences,' Grandma Bracegirdle nodded approvingly at Lucy. 'You have forgotten why you do it, but long before the eagles of the legions crossed the sea, as day and night matched, the tribes set out skulls with candles to banish the dead, to stop them coming into the world of men.'

'Ghost fences....' Lucy grinned.

'So, deep down,' Grandma smiled with satisfaction, 'mankind has not entirely forgotten the old ways...'

For the rest of that week, Lucy spent every spare moment at Thistlestone Palace taking a crash course in hedgewitchery. And having seen Lucy crash-land Napoleon once too often in the indoor flying arena, Mrs Bracegirdle also gave her some helpful tips and techniques on how to take off and land safely, with both rider and broom intact, instead of tumbling head over heels like a booby chick.

If Douglas was enjoying Lucy's misfortune, Mrs Bracegirdle soon wiped the smile off his face. Both apprentices were formally introduced to a particular friend of hers whom they had already met briefly – Wand staff-sergeant major Pounder of the SDS – who immediately began to formally instruct both in the forms of Riding The Dragon. Smugly certain that she already knew enough about the ancient martial art, Lucy was wholly unprepared for Pounder's explosive tactics. Every time Lucy reached for Gaia, the black-wand Sergeant Major bellowed in her ear louder than a foghorn, or let off smoking coloured firecrackers, or doused her with water, shattering her composure. Lucy realised for the first time how little she really knew.

~Hedgewitch's broom~

The first item needed for the casting of the spell was now discovered. Napeoleon took very good care of Lucy and before long she felt that she could circle the Necromancer's Ring at least three times!

CHAPTER THIRTY-TWO

Goblin's Gob and Troll Toenail

The silver Ducati Multistrada 1200S motorbike parked outside the Nook & Cranny should have been a clue to anyone who cared to ask. Then there was the blue crash helmet with furry ears in the hall.

'A small gift ... from ... Gargoyle and ... and me,' Megan said with a shy smile, holding out a small stoppered vial.

'Go on,' Mother encouraged, 'take it, Lucy.'

Lucy turned the blue bottle round in her hand. It contained a small amount of foaming liquid that moved sluggishly.

'It's, err,' the young vet looked to Mother for reassurance, still uncertain about the very peculiar request. 'It's, err, goblin's gob ... err,' Megan trailed off, uncertainly.

The smile Lucy rewarded her with was as radiant and hot as a midday sun, and her hug was as fierce as a grizzly bear's.

'Two off the list!' Oliver high-fived his sister as Kealan held up the vial with a disgusted expression. 'You already have two! A hedgewitch's broom and goblin's gob! Yeuch! Which one next?'

Mother held up a small canister. 'This arrived from the SDS today. Troll toenail! From a SeaReiver Marine's boot.'

Kealan's look of horror deepened.

'Three! Lucy, that's three!'

'Now what?' Kealan asked.

'I think Kelpies tail,' Mother suggested. All three looked blank. 'Oh, dearie me!' Mother exclaimed. 'You don't know your own Scottish folklore! Oliver, dear, can you err... google kelpies?'

'Kelpies,' Kealan read over his friend's shoulder as Oliver scrolled down. 'Scottish myths, folklore and legends...... Kelpies. The...err...the mythical kelpie is a supernatural water horse that was said to haunt Scotland's lochs and lonely rivers. The kelpie would appear to victims as a lost dark grey or white pony, but could be identified by its constantly dripping mane. It would entice people to ride on its back, before taking them down to a watery grave.'

Kealan and Oliver turned to look at Lucy in horror.

'I've got to pull a kelpies tail?' Lucy asked no less horrified. 'How do I do that without getting kicked?'

Later that Friday evening, a bat arrived from Lord Rumspell instructing Lucy to cross to the Fifth Dimension first thing next morning, where Mrs Bracegirdle would be expecting her. It was only three weeks until the Winter Solstice.

~ Goblin's gob and troll toenail~

The next two reagents were crossed off the list. Mother knew the others would be nowhere near as easy, but she kept her fears to herself.

CHAPTER THIRTY-THREE

Fairy Tales

The knock on the door after midnight was unexpected and persistent. Moran had made few friends in Thistle-burr; his wife had left long ago and he was no longer in touch with his children. Asleep in an armchair in front of the fire, his heart hammered in his chest in a sudden rush of adrenaline. *The police! They must have found out about the children! That wretched McGantry boy must have recovered his memory!* Preparing to flee, he peered out through the curtains expecting to see the red and blue lights of a police car. He blinked and took a second look. There was a huge bird of prey perched on his gate, and no sign of any car.

He didn't recognise the cloaked young man standing on his doorstep, though he did recognise the type... military, except for the long strand of braided hair. His visitor dispensed with the normal social pleasantries and came straight to the point.

'You have failed my Master twice. There will not be a third time, not if you value your life.'

'W-what?' Moran blustered. 'Who are you? How dare you threa-'

'My master has need of your services. A...body will be brought here a few days before the winter solstice. My master will come to claim it at the witching hour.'

'Witching hour? A-a body? A *dead* body? I can't-'

'A little late to be squeamish is it not?' The young

man's contempt dripped from every word. 'You were quite prepared to sacrifice four children for gold.'

'But here? Why here? Why not the Old Grange as before?'

'Because that most certainly will be watched and the necessary wards are not yet in place. Thanks to you, the underground tunnels have been discovered and are no longer secure. Once the winter solstice casts its shadow over the realm of men it will be death to tread there uninvited, but not yet'

Realm of men? Moran felt a choking fear rise. 'W-whose body is it? What is he going to do with it?' Moran shivered. He didn't want to know but was compelled by ghoulish interest to ask.

'That is of no concern to you.'

'I want an advance payment. This is far more dangerous for me.'

The young man smiled coldly. 'I don't think you realise you have no choice. But my Master is prepared to be generous. Once this task is complete you will be paid half a million pounds.'

'Half a million?' Moran could not keep the greed from his voice. 'I have a cellar...but how are you going to bring a body without being noticed?

'He will be brought here by stealth dragon after dark.'

'Dragon...?' Moran burst into laughter. His visitor's expression didn't change. 'Oh, come on! Don't be ridiculous! Stealth dragons! You've been watching too many movies! I'm no child to be frightened by fairy stories.'

'Look out your back window.'

Sneering, Moran walked through to his kitchen with a view over the lower slopes of the White Sorcerer Mountain. He shrugged. 'It's still snowing. So?'

The young man pressed a bracelet on his arm that glowed briefly, and said a word that the Deputy Headmaster could not make out. The air seemed to wobble...and then Moran couldn't see a thing. It had gone utterly dark. Moving forwards, Moran wiped the glass with his sleeve. Something glinted overhead. The Deputy Headmaster stuck his face against the glass. It couldn't be! A talon shifted, crushing the garden wall. He swallowed, shaking his head. *This must be a dream...* he was still asleep!

'Oh, it's very real, believe me. An Imperial Black Stealth dragon.'

Moran's mouth was hanging open. Ice crawled up his spine. 'If i-it's a d-dragon, w-what are y-you?

His visitor smiled. 'A WarLock...Did you really think we only belonged in fairy tales? We are your worst nightmare!'

CHAPTER THIRTY-FOUR

The Kelpies

It was a clear night, lit only by a slight phosphorescent glow from the sea. Overhead, a billion stars flickered and twinkled. Lucy was nervous, her tummy churning, and she was grateful that Douglas couldn't see her face. She knew that if Douglas realised her lack of confidence he would try and stop her, to protect them both. She couldn't let that happen; the Bear was running out of time. But she was also afraid for her friend, who trusted her.

As they quietly walked around the loch to the rocky headlands on the firm tidal sand, Lucy thought back over the last week that had unexpectedly prepared her for her fourth quest, in search of one of the more dangerous reagents needed for the counter-spell to Sea Dragon's

Bane.

Mrs Celia Bracegirdle had quite clearly taken the two apprentices under her protective wing, and they were, for the 'duration', robed as assistant under-librarians. Whilst Douglas was directed to the Kelpie section of the Pentagon reference library of the Faculty of Water and instructed to identify and cross-reference all recorded sightings in and around the Sorcerers' Glen, Lucy was briskly instructed to 'follow me.'

Mrs Bracegirdle strode determinedly along the tangle of corridors, spheres and stairs of the large Faculty campus down on the lochside without getting lost once. Ignoring the luminescent 'No Entry – Experiment in Progress' sign, Mrs Bracegirdle flung the door open. Lucy found herself in a spherical acoustical laboratory with opaque white walls and no windows. It was entirely lined with moulded pyramids designed to dampen all external sound.

'Ah, Geoffrey,' Mrs Bracegirdle had boomed, as a small man stood uncertainly to greet them, his black robes puddling water on the floor. He had been lying in a huge transparent bath of water with a peculiar gadget attached to his head. That was until Mrs Bracegirdle rapped the side loudly with her wand. That made him sit up all right, so fast in fact that half the leads popped out of their housing and into the water. The water sparked and fizzled. So did its occupant. He screamed. Mrs Bracegirdle appeared oblivious to the devastation she caused.

'Geoffrey,' she barked, 'I think I've found the very student to help you with your applied research. This is

Lucy Pemberton, one of the Vice-Chancellor's apprentices.' Placing the gadget carefully on the floor, Geoffrey looked immediately interested.

'Lucy, this is Dr Unravel. Heads up UAMU – the Underwater Acoustical Music Unit. Well, I'll leave you two to it, then.'

That first evening, Lucy had been given a crash course on kelpies, including some underwater footage of the elusive sea creatures taken by a member of staff from the department of Shapeshifting, disguised as a whale.

'Kelpies, Pemberton,' Unravel had earnestly said, 'can sing. That's how they trap their victims; at least that's what we think. Unfortunately, until now anyone who tried to collect evidence disappeared. In theory, I believe we can use their strength against them. Fight music with music. We've only had limited field trials and I don't think the spell is quite right yet. And it's so difficult finding qualified students with the right combination of song and spell to experiment on, err, I mean with, err, talent so to speak.' The young wizard beamed at her. 'Right, let's get to work, no time to lose. You're a postgraduate?'

'Err, no.'

'Ah, right you are. Fourth year, then?'

'Umm...'

'Third?'

'Umm...'

'Second?'

Lucy shook her head.

'You're not a *Fresher*, are you?' Lucy felt that 'Fresher'

said in this tone of voice sounded very unsavoury indeed. There was a short silence.

'Ssooooo,' Unravel asked carefully, as if his words rested on very thin ice indeed, 'you haven't taken Kelpies 3? Ooor Acoustical Algorithms 4? Oooor,' he looked suddenly hopeful, 'read my best seller, Kelpies for Dummies? It sold 102 copies,' he announced proudly. 'Top of the list for seven months!'

Lucy shook her head again.

'Well!' He took the plunge. 'What can you do for me?'

'Sing.' Lucy smiled at him. 'I can sing. And,' she added with determination. 'I'm a very quick learner.'

And that cheerful assertion led to long sessions in the Music room and a potted history of kelpies, plus the rudiments of The Theory and Practice of Counter-spells.

'What do you think?' Lucy had stopped where a wide burn trickled down to the beach. Ahead, they could hear the waves breaking on the rocks as the tide turned. 'I think this is the right spot,' Lucy guessed, consulting the small map Douglas had carefully drawn.

'Looking good,' Douglas responded chirpily with a confidence he didn't feel. 'Just the kind of place a kelpie would lurk.'

Crouched in the sand dunes, they settled down and Lucy emptied the bulky bag she had been carrying. Douglas looked doubtfully at the helmet she handed him.

'Are you sure these things work?' He lifted one and put it on his head. The helmet looked like an upside down pudding bowl that had sprouted tendrils. Lucy tried not to laugh.

'Well, they did in the lab with the recorded kelpie songs...'

'How does it work?' Douglas asked for the hundredth time.

'It comes with three spells to get you started,' Lucy repeated patiently. She pulled out a slim black disc then fitted it back in the slot with a click. 'You will be able to buy top-up cards from the post office, once Professor Unravel has lodged the design with the patent office. This,' she explained, pointing to a black rectangular attachment, 'is the harmonics phase modulator, which err, it err, scrambles their song into random arrangements so that the wearer isn't spell-bound. The song is then rearranged with *entrapment* and *confinement* modulations woven in, and the counter-spell fires it back at the kelpies. In theory, their song rebounds on them and they are spellbound. And then we grab some horse's tail!'

'Mmnn,' said Douglas doubtfully, 'in theory... What happens if it doesn't?'

'I've learnt the counter-spell. I've been practising the spells all week.'

Douglas nodded, not entirely convinced, but unwilling to voice his doubts.

Bowl firmly clamped on his head, Douglas nibbled nervously at his fingernails. Lucy huddled in the dunes, trying to ignore the chill breeze drifting in from the sea. Neither of them noticed when two of the three tiny green runes on the back of Lucy's helmet faded, then turned red.

Cramped, she moved awkwardly in the sand while glancing up at the night sky. By her estimation they'd been here over an hour...one bell she corrected herself ... What if the kelpies didn't come tonight, or tomorrow? Or at all? Belatedly, she realised that the hairs on her neck and arms stood up, goose-pimpled as if washed by sudden cold. *Oh no!* Lucy tried in vain to shut the sound out. Over the sea breeze, a terrible song was softly keening, washing onto the shore and over the grassy dunes.

> *Come to us, come to us under the sea,*
> *Cool rolling waves will welcome thee*
> *Come to us, come to us under the sea,*
> *Swim in the oceans, cool, deep and free*
>
> *Come to our world deep under the sea,*
> *Where whales sing their song, their sweet melodies*
> *Come to our world deep under the sea*
> *Drift on the currents in our harmony.*

The thin fearful melody rose and fell like a deep-ocean swell, calling to Lucy, pulling at her, compelling as a riptide. Douglas didn't stir. He squinted at crumpled notes about kelpies in the vain hope of gleaning some new fact that might help. Lucy could feel the kelpies' cold hunger for warm fleshed victims, but the currents now commanded her. As if its task were completed, the song suddenly fell to silence. A faint drumming could be heard. It grew steadily louder.

'There, look!' Lucy pointed through the sharp grass

towards a herd of horses galloping along the shore, foam flashing from their hooves. Although it was dark, she could see each individual horse in a cold spectral light: gold, copper and silver, speckled with foam, nickering and neighing. She took her helmet off. It rolled down the dune to bump her friend's foot. It took Douglas a moment to realise what she had done. He scrambled to his feet. 'Lucy! Lucy, put it back on!'

'What?'

'Put...' Douglas scrabbled for purchase. 'Put it on!' he ordered grabbing her arm. His friend ignored him as if he wasn't there.

'They're beautiful,' Lucy swayed, dreamily rocking on her feet, head lolling back and forward. Douglas shook her urgently. Then he too heard the hoof beats drumming on wet sand and froze. Suddenly afraid, he looked down on the rapidly approaching horses and knew that Lucy had fallen under the kelpies' spell, and somehow, he hadn't.

'Dragon's teeth!' he softly swore, using his father's favourite oath. 'You're spellbound!' Beside him, Lucy moved forwards. 'They're- they're dangerous,' the boy persisted, trying to pull her back down with him. 'Oh no,' he groaned, 'they've seen us.' He could do nothing but helplessly watch as the herd wheeled and galloped up the dunes towards them. Rearing up, hooves struck sparks from rocks as the horses surrounded Lucy and Douglas in a tightening circle. He tried to protect her with his body but there were too many and they were so very big!

'Ride us,' the horses invited rearing into the night, 'ride

us. It is a beautiful night to gallop on the beach under the stars.'

A horse the colour of honey stepped forward, shaking its pale spectral mane, softly pawing the sand with barely concealed impatience. 'I am Sea Mane. These are my brothers and sisters.' Entranced, Lucy reached out to touch the velvet noses softly blowing and snorting, clouding in the cool night air. But Douglas was repulsed, somehow sensing the slimy grasping creatures inside. Their glamour had not bewitched him.

'No, don't go.' The boy grabbed Lucy's arm. 'You mustn't ride them. They're enchanting you.'

A wave of anger and crude magic rocked him on his heels. Sea Mane reared up snorting, striking hooves isolating Lucy. The boy stumbled back on the shifting sand dunes. He grabbed at the nearest thing to stop him falling, but the hairs of the horse's long tail came away in his hand and he fell heavily, rolling down amongst the marram grass, spitting sand. Stamping and snorting, the angry horses crowded round Lucy.

'Lucy,' Douglas shouted, throwing his helmet to the ground, 'don't ride them. Please don't ride them.'

'Come.' SeaMane nuzzled her. The horse knelt down making it easy for her to mount. 'Come.'

Lucy was hesitant. She could hear Douglas shouting, pleading, but it was as if she were sleepwalking and had no control over her actions, so she mounted the golden horse. Douglas stood alone, trying to knuckle the stinging sand out of his eyes as the horses cantered down into the sea. Eyes blurred with tears, the boy scrambled to his feet and followed.

As the bitter cold water surged round her ankles, Lucy woke from her trance, but it was already too late. All around her the horses were vanishing, melting into the foaming dark water; and in their stead, clammy frog-like creatures closed in on her.

'I'm coming,' Douglas screamed, tripping and falling. 'I'm coming,' he puffed, trying to regain his breath. Fighting to his feet, his hand closed on a sea-bleached plank of wood.

The horse beneath Lucy dissolved. The sea devoured her. Striking out, she surged to the surface in a burst of bubbles. Her lungs burned as she tried to shout 'Douglas!' Around her, beneath her, dark toothless mouths opened and closed like fish. Black eyes, sunken and empty, loomed through the churning foggy water. Delicate frilled gills flapped and pulsed where cheekbones should be, and fronds of seaweed swayed around them, tangling her legs. Desperately, in her panic and fright, Lucy tried to summon Gaia to blast the creatures back, but already her numb hands were bound by grasping reedy suckers, her hair pulled cruelly. She was struggling to keep air in her lungs. Waves doused her in cold searing salt that filled her nose and ears and lungs.

But Douglas was on her heels. Hefting the plank, he ran along a rocky outcrop and dived in just ahead of the disappearing herd. Treading water, he wielded it like a club, thumping into kelpies with a horrible soft splat. Inky dark liquid and jelly-like lumps spilled into the water. As the brittle plank finally broke, he reached down to the small knife always sheathed on his belt. Putting the blade between his teeth, he took a deep breath and dived.

The kelpies were all around Lucy, choking the life out of her. Slimy brown fingers pulled her down; on the verge of drowning, the girl lost consciousness. But plump though he was, Douglas had learned to swim before he learnt to walk. Working with the fishing fleet was a harsh and demanding life. Mishaps were frequent, and if you couldn't swim, you died. Diving again and again, he struck out at the hateful kelpies, cutting their smothering grasp. It was like freeing a dolphin trapped in the corded fishing nets. He'd done it before. The sea echoed with noise as the water acted as a natural amplifier. Above them, the surface bubbled and roiled like a cauldron. Gasping for air, he grabbed Lucy's limp hand and kicked hard for the surface. Gurgling with fury and spite, the kelpies struck out for deeper water, leaving the exhausted boy to drag his lifeless friend up on the sand.

Lucy opened her eyes. She felt warm and comfortable but her throat felt raw. Truffle was curled under the blankets in the nook of her arm. The room was dark. Then gradually she became aware of the blackened wooden rafters lit by flickering yellow, and realised that it was not her own bedroom ceiling. The weak light and long shadows were cast from a single tallow candle on the bedside table, and the peat fire flickering in the blackened grate. Blankets and an eiderdown were piled over her. The Greasy Spoon!

The door opened silently, and Douglas tiptoed in,

followed by his Mum. She was carrying a bowl of steaming broth. Bucksturdie leapt forwards to lick Lucy furiously.

'You're awake!' Douglas bounced happily down on the bed beside his friend. 'Tantrum is away off to tell your mum you are OK.'

His hands were bandaged, and raw red rings stood out all over his neck and arms. Lucy realised she was covered too. Then it all came back to her, the horses, and the battle with the kelpies. She knew she owed her life to Douglas. She opened her mouth to thank him.

'It was nothing, really.' Her friend beamed happily. 'Just call me the hero of the bell!'

'Douglas!' Lucy found she hardly had the energy to thump him.

'Here, young miss.' Douglas's mum leant over to plump the straw pillow. 'Up you sit, now.' When Lucy was comfortable, Mrs Archibald gave her the bowl and big chunks of black bread. Lucy suddenly discovered that she was ravenous, and the barley and leek soup was delicious.

'Mmm ... great ... thank you,' she managed between spoonfuls. Then her face fell and she pushed the bowl away. 'It's all been for nothing,' she cried to Douglas. 'I never got the horse's hair. I never - ' Tears pricked at her eyes.

But Douglas just grinned from ear to ear.

'Did you...?' A sudden hope flared in Lucy's heart.

Douglas held up his right hand. His fist was wrapped around a handful of long golden hair. Lucy leapt up to hug him. Truffle fell onto the floor with a loud flop and an indignant squawk, to be slobbered by an enthusiastic Bucksturdie.

'We've done it,' Lucy cried. 'We've done it! You've done it!'

Douglas's blush was hotter than the fire. He smiled shyly, pumped full of pride. He took the rhyme from the table and scored through 'Kelpies tail'. Picking up the candle, he handed the piece of paper to Lucy. 'That's almost it! You've got all the reagents except for the scariest one, the dragon's claw. Soon you'll be able to cure the White Sorcerer, Lucy.'

But that was not the only surprise.

'How about a hot bath?'

'A bath?' Lucy's eyes lit up then she frowned. 'But I thought you – '

'We've just had a fire-drake installed, see,' Douglas announced proudly, delighted at the surprise. 'Uncle Jamie won him dicing. He's right good with the cards. Uncle Jamie, that is, not the drake.'

'Great,' Lucy offered cautiously, not having a clue what a fire-drake meant but not wanting to appear stupid either. 'A bath sounds great.'

An hour later Lucy emerged, wrapped in warm towels. She had never had a bath in a zinc tub in front of a fire before. It was fun, much more fun than usual. Half an hour later, dressed in some of Douglas's clothes, she was sitting on a stool next to the kitchen range hugging a mug of hot chocolate.

'Want me to show you the fire-drake? We're the only family in the street!'

Lucy nodded. No point in stealing the moment by telling her friend everyone in Thistleburr had hot running water.

Holding the lantern high, Douglas took Lucy round the back to where a ramshackle stable block stood. Tiptoe-ing, she peered over the door into the gloom. Strange gurgles came out of the dark. At first she couldn't see anything but hay, and one or two sleepy hens. Then the lantern's glow caught a flash of red. Douglas unlatched the door, and in the pool of light Lucy saw a small red dragon curled snoring in the hay, with a half dozen hens perched on and around it. A large leather collar studded with brass hung round its neck.

'Drakes get lonely on their own,' Douglas explained, 'but there's no way we can afford to buy him a mate. He's really friendly, so all the other animals have moved in with him. They seem to understand when to get out of the way.'

'Out the way? Of what?'

'Through here,' Douglas ignored her question, instead opening a door into a small stone-built pen where a riveted cast iron tank stood raised on plinths. The room was very warm and musty. The tank glowed faintly in the dark and was pinking as it cooled. A spaghetti tangle of gurgling plumbing and bends stretched out from the tank and along the inner side of the stable block. It was lagged with rags. Another pipe ran in from the outside. 'It's a blast furnace. Ian, the blacksmith's apprentice, built it last week. The cold water comes in here, see, from the City cascade system, and then Digbert heats it up – to cherry red – and the hot water is pumped out here into a sink in the house.'

Lucy nodded uncertainly.

'Watch. Here, Digbert,' Douglas called, handing the lantern to Lucy. 'Here, boy. He's a colt,' he explained, as the wee drake waddled through and came up to lick his hand with a rasping hot tongue. 'He's only about four months old. Dad says he'll grow to about twice this size.'

Carefully avoiding the spikes, Lucy scratched the little dragon behind the horns. It made a queer grumbling sound and burped loudly. There was the faintest whiff of gas.

'See, he likes you.' Douglas went over to a pile of turnips, potatoes, coal and oats. As Douglas heaped coal into a small trough the small dragon began feeding.

'Now what?*'

'Wait and see.'

A few minutes later, a very plump, pear-shaped Digbert lifted a nose covered in coal dust out of the bucket and happily burped.

'Duck!' Douglas shouted as a weak yellow flame rolled across the stall. Lucy, who had been looking upwards for a duck, squealed as her bottom was lightly toasted.

'Err, sorry.' Douglas looked horror-struck as he beat the sparks out from her leggings. 'Ermm, I forgot to mention...' He trailed off into silence as Lucy slowly turned round, looking like thunder.

'You forgot to mention what?' She queried sweetly,

before she upended a pail of water over him.

~Kelpies Tail~

'Here…' everyone collected around Lucy to view a fistful of kelpie's tail hairs.

'I didn't think you would manage!' Oliver was almost in tears.

'I didn't. It was Douglas,' Lucy admitted honestly. 'He saved my life. I was bewitched and they were changing into…' she shivered. 'Horrible jelly like things with gaping mouths and suckers on their webbed hands, and Douglas dived in and attacked them!'

'He sounds really brave!'

Lucy nodded. 'He is.'

'When are we going to meet him?' Oliver felt an unexpected twinge of jealousy.

'Well, the Guild has strict rules about who may cross,' Mother warned. 'But I expect you will meet him soon.'

'He's like you, Oliver,' Lucy was tuned into her sibling's sense of being shut out. 'You'll like him. He loves computers…anything technical and other worldly.'

Kealan held out the fistful of long hair, clearly disappointed. 'They're a bit dull really. I mean,' he added hastily, lest Lucy take offence. 'They don't seem very magical.'

'Ah,' Mother nodded and switched the light off.

'Ooo….' The hairs shimmered invitingly in the dark.

Lucy wrapped the hairs round her hand and placed them on the mantelpiece with the other reagents. She turned to look at them all, biting her lower lip. 'That just leaves the dragon's claw!'

CHAPTER THIRTY-FIVE

The Greasy Spoon

During the night, a cold front crept quietly across the borders from England into Scotland. No one noticed, so it carried on going. By midnight, Edinburgh Castle lay under two inches of snow. By four in the morning, the snowfall had reached the highlands, where it fell on already frozen ground.

Lucy woke early to find the world smothered in white and Truffle snoring loudly on her pillow. 'I'm horribly scared,' she had admitted privately to Oliver as she sat on the bottom of her brother's bed wrapped in a duvet, the previous night. 'Really scared. How can I possibly get a dragon to give me a talon?'

'You'll find a way, sis,' Oliver held her hand and tried to smile convincingly. 'Just you wait and see! And Douglas will be there to protect you! I don't think I'd be brave enough to face a dragon!'

Lucy sat up in bed and buried her head in Truffle's warm coat for comfort. 'You and Tantrum stay here and look after Mum and Oliver, and take a look to see if anything is happening at the Old Grange,' she gave the cat's head a kiss. 'You can't help me look for dragons; it's too dangerous, I don't want either of you to get hurt.' Shivering, she dressed quickly in warm dark clothes. Packing her librarian robes, she hurried down to the kitchen. By the time Mother got up, her daughter was a world away.

As Lucy opened the front door of the Bear's cottage in the Fifth Dimension, bringing down a shower of snow, she found Douglas sitting next to the fire waiting for her.

'Hh-h-hi.' He smiled weakly. 'I t-t-thought you might want some h-h-help.'

'Douglas,' Lucy began, 'it's going to be dangerous. You've already saved my life once - '

'I k-k-know,' her friend said, talking rapidly 'I know all about the danger and difficulty, but U-u-uncle Barnaby said you'd need help and that friends a-are worth their weight in gold. In that case,' he added, smiling wanly, 'I'm worth a lot of gold.' Throwing off his blanket, he rummaged in a stuffed leather saddlebag.

'Uncle Barnaby asked me to give you this. He said it was a gift from the Grand Master himself.' He held out an old faded and stained leather-bound book.

'Lullabies and Fairy Stories by Winter Firstfoot? 325th Edition. First published, the Year of the Hairy Tailed Dormouse?' Lucy read doubtfully, before opening the pages of the book. 'Children's Rhymes?' she was baffled. She opened a page. 'Music?'

'Well,' Douglas was also confused. 'He said that magic and music were sometimes one and the same thing.

Lucy leafed through the pages. 'Dragon Lullabies?!' Lucy tried a few notes, then a bar or two, before breaking into song. 'Does music calm dragons?' In the sky over the Bear's cottage there was sudden chaos, as a half dozen dragons veered towards the cottage.

'I don't know, but I think you should study it.'

Lucy sang a few more bars. Pilots who had just got

their mounts under control, suddenly found them going into freefall again. There were several mid-air collisions and a distant crack of ice on the loch as an Imperial crushed a galleon. Oblivious to the chaos she had caused, Lucy added the book to her bag.

'I've got a bundle of old maps from Mrs Bracegirdle too,' Douglas held up a rucksack. 'She thinks we'll find clues here to where the dragon is. Dragon roosts or eyries get marked so the travellers can avoid them.'

Lucy frowned. 'We can't stay here, Uncle Barnaby said it might be being watched.'

'The Greasy Spoon.'

'What?'

'The Greasy Spoon. It's my Aunt's inn. Mum works there and she's got a small room in the attic. Even if the Black R-r-ra - ' He couldn't get the word out. He changed tack. 'Even if the White Sorcerer's enemies are looking for us, they'd never think of looking there. It's pretty ... well, it's in the Gutters down on the Artisan's Circle, and that's a very poor part of the city. We could hide there easily.' Douglas laid his last card on the table. 'Uncle, err, Uncle Barnaby said it was a great idea.'

Joined by Bucksturdie, they crossed the ice-covered loch on whale-bone skates strapped on by thongs of leather, and entered unnoticed into the city along with creaking farmers' carts. Water-drakes supplied with tuns of water were hosing down the steps and streets, and those too sleepy to move fast enough. Rotten fruit and rubbish swirled down the guttering on its way back to the loch.

Lucy stopped to watch one of the small dragons as it swelled out to twice its size with water, before turning its long snout towards the road and blasting the water out. Douglas took several steps backwards.

Up in the shopping district, artisans and merchants were opening shutters and setting out their wares. So far there were few customers; it was early yet, and a pale moon still hung in the brightening morning light. But as Lucy and Douglas wended round carts and crates they came across one shop that was already doing a roaring trade. Outside, a crowd of unusually subdued dwarves were collected in a queue of sorts. As the apprentices drew closer, Lucy saw that many of them were bruised and bandaged.

Narrowing her eyes, she read the shop sign with disbelief. 'Crack ... Crackjaw Brothers Tooth Emporium? Tooth Emporium? What's a tooth emporium?'

'That's just a fancy name for shop,' Douglas explained, misunderstanding her question.

Curious, and blissfully unaware of the glowering dwarves around her, Lucy pressed her nose to the window. Teeth were displayed in numbered trays. She turned questioningly towards Douglas, who was hanging back with good reason. Hungover dwarves were notoriously bad-tempered and quick to take offence, and Douglas was making poor progress in Wand-Sergeant Major Pounder's martial arts classes.

'Well, gnomes,' Douglas began reluctantly, in a hushed tone, 'you know they can travel between worlds? Like Truffle and Tantrum?' Lucy nodded. 'One of the things they do is to collect teeth. It's one of the few inter-dimensional trades licensed by the Guild. Mother says it's a, ... a civic service. They leave a coin,' he added hastily. 'It's a fair exchange.'

'But where do they get the teeth from?' Lucy was still baffled, although a bell was beginning to ring.

'From children in the Otherworld.' It was Douglas's turn to look baffled. 'Who else? The Postgnomes go on rounds every night all over the country, collecting teeth from under pillows. Then they're sorted and graded and auctioned at the Tooth Market.'

'Tooth Market?' echoed Lucy.

'Yeah. Traders like the Crackjaw Brothers go early every morning and buy loads to sell to the dwarves.'

'Dwarves? Why?'

'Err,' Douglas mumbled, edging Lucy away from the waiting queue towards a wagon, 'they're, err, always, err, getting into fights. Especially over festivals, or when they have one drink too many or someone insults their honour. The 'Way of the Warrior' and all that. They take fighting seriously, see, so they're always getting teeth knocked out or knocking someone else's out. They come here for new ones.'

'But,' Lucy protested, 'isn't it tooth fairies?'

'Pardon? Tooth fairies?'

'We've always thought it was tooth fairies,' Lucy explained. 'We leave our teeth under the pillow for the tooth fairy.'

'Fairy? Huh!' a contemptuous voice snapped in Lucy's ear. It belonged to a gnome unloading parcels from the wagon.

'It's a little gnome fact,' she continued haughtily, 'that it's gnomes who do all the hard work. Tooth fairies indeed! What do they do but fly around looking pretty? Totally overrated, if you ask me.'

Turning a corner, trying not to step in steaming piles of horse dung, Lucy saw a large inn and stable block, and a chandler's shop bordering a small courtyard. She squinted up at the creaking sign.

The Greasy Spoon
Proprietors: Master & Mistress J Boggins

Clouds of wispy smoke wafted out from every door and un-shuttered window and boiled from the three rickety chimneys. Piles of knives, coshes and dwarf-picks lay discarded outside the front door under the lopsided sign:

No Weponarry Alloud Xcept Eating Knives.

Without waiting, Douglas deftly stepped over discarded bottles and broken ale horns and shouldered the heavy door open with a grunt. Lucy quickly followed close behind. They walked into a wall of noise. Despite the early hour, the inn was thick with smoke and the babble of a dozen different tongues. 'Time's up' was not a cry heard in the Fifth Dimension: any publican foolish enough to utter those two words would indeed find that his or her time was up – permanently!

Candlelight and whale-oil lamps revealed a low room strewn with benches and tables packed to bursting. Crusts of bread floating on congealing gravy lay discarded on wooden trenchers. Pewter tankards and their owners lay tumbled and fallen in the rushes, where dogs and a few boars were rooting for discarded scraps. The low beams were blackened with soot, and the stench would have knocked a skunk off its feet.

'C'mon,' Douglas shouted, elbowing his way through the press, past dwarves playing chess, groups of gnomes dicing with bone and wood pieces, and through the back towards the heat and noise escaping out of the kitchens. Deftly avoiding the steady stream of gnomes and goblins carrying trays stacked with beer and bowls, Douglas stepped through the saloon doors.

A fire pit in the centre of the room smoked and spat as grease dripped down from meats turning on the spit. Lucy ducked to avoid the strings of sausages and smoked meats that swung by the dozens from the ceiling. Sideboards were stacked with baskets of bread, firkins of butter, wrinkled fruits and cheese. The food might be basic, but it looked good.

' 'Scuse me, dearie.' Lucy jumped as a gnome hustled past.

'Watch out, dearie, comin' through, comin' through.' An elderly gnome wove past her with a stack of dirty crockery, tipping it loudly into a sink.

Lucy blinked, trying to clear her fogged-up contact lens, while Douglas stood on tiptoe, trying to locate his mum in the milling throng.

'Table ten, comin' up. Richt ye go, dearie, cannae stand there. Oot the wae now.'

Moving out of the troll's way, Lucy recognised Mrs Archibald. The red-faced cook was pumping steaming water into two huge porcelain sinks. Turning back to the open range, she dipped a wooden spoon into the bubbling pot and tasted the brew. She added a handful of salt. Turning back to the sink, she suddenly noticed the visitors.

'Douglas, love!' She hugged the boy affectionately, wiping her hands down on a red apron tucked round neatly patched skirts before offering a shy handshake to his companion. 'And how are you, Lucy?' Hazel eyes flickered over the girl before turning anxiously back to her son. 'It's right lovely to see you, but why are you here? Is everything alright?' she asked, looking from one to the other. 'Is there any news?'

'Yeah, Mum, everything's alright. But no, there is no news. We just need somewhere safe. Can we go use our room?'

Lucy followed her friend up a rickety staircase, across a landing, up another narrower staircase and into a cold dark room.

'This is the highest room in the inn,' Douglas said proudly. 'Isn't it grand?' He pulled back threadbare tapestries and threw open the shutters. It was plain but clean. Heavy blankets covered the bed in one corner with a low cot at its foot. Otherwise it was sparsely furnished, with only an ash-filled fireplace, a small stack of peat, and several chests, a single candlestick and a couple of stools.

'That's where I sleep when Mum's working late,' Douglas told her, pointing to the cot as he lifted the stools to the table. 'Right, let's get started.' He carefully laid out the rolled maps in waxed cloth that Mrs Bracegirdle had given him. With a sigh of relief, Lucy carefully unpacked the heavy texts.

The candle had nearly burnt down. Open books and maps were scattered. Douglas was perusing Lullabies and Fairy Stories. 'There are some recent entries,' he turned a few more pages. 'New rhymes that they have added in...the ink isn't so fa....ded. Here! Read this, Lucy, read it!'

> 'Hush thee, hush thee, do not fret thee,
> The Black Raven will not get thee.
> Moon weeps its silver tears
> To still your heartfelt fears
> Gold laughter warms the day
> To banish dragons far away
> Hush thee, hush thee, do not fret thee,
> The Black Raven will not get thee!'

'We must be on the right track! Moon weeps with silver tears ... gold laughter... dragons...the rhyme!' Lucy was suddenly wide awake. 'But it still doesn't make any sense – why would a dragon sit on a horde of gold? It would be so uncomfortable!' She squirmed. 'Anyway,' she pointed out with infallible logic. 'What would a dragon do with it? They can't spend it!'

'But,' Douglas protested, 'you told me you yourself had been to...you had seen a dragon called Smaug who stole gold from the dwarves.'

Lucy sighed. Trying to explain what movies were had been a spectacular failure. She tried again. 'The Hobbit: it's a story, and a film is a kind of book with actors. We use technology in the same way you use magic. We don't have dragons in our world so nobody really knows what they are like.' *But we all remember don't we? All over the world... Chinese dragons... Celtic dragons...St George and the dragon...*

Although the shutters had long since been closed to shut out the chill December night, the single candle flickered and danced as draughts caught the wick. Lucy pushed her stool closer to the small fire and shivered, wishing Truffle were with her, but hunting dragons was no place for cats or gnomes, both could get eaten! Douglas rolled out a map and weighted it.

'Mrs Bracegirdle, that is,' Douglas was saying, 'um, she said we should concentrate on this area.' He pointed a finger towards a rocky coastline to the north of the Sorcerers Glen, called Wreckers Cove. 'She said that this map's three hundred and fifty years old and it came from the wreckage of the Old Grange; not long after the Raven was captured and killed by your people.'

Taking the candle, Lucy peered forward to examine the cracked wax parchment, showing little icons for castles and villages. 'But Wreckers Cove, it's just to the north of here. Not far away at all. How could a dragon be there and no one has found it?'

'But it must be close by, mustn't it?' Douglas persisted. 'If it was seen in the Sorcerers Loch? And you said that it wasn't the first time, that there have been other sightings of your 'monster'?

'Not very many, but I suppose it's a good place to begin.'

The candle burnt out. As they huddled together, Lucy softly practiced some dragon songs by the light of the dying fire. Before long, she was joined by the resonant bass of Douglas's snoring. Bucksturdie slipped out into the night to forage for herself. Then Lucy curled up beside the boy in some blankets and went to sleep in front of the glowing ashes. Shortly afterwards, Mrs Archibald crept quietly into the room and pulled a heavy blanket over the pair. In the bright new morning, they told her of their plans.

'No, Douglas, I forbid it,' she cried in alarm. 'That place is haunted. Fishing boats and galleons have disappeared, never to be seen again.' The argument swung back and forth all morning until the children's tearful pleading forced Douglas's mother to give way. She only relented when her brother climbed the rickety attic stairs to find out what kept his sister.

'Jean, Jean, hush,' Douglas's uncle calmed her. ''Tis a good thing these children are doing. Remember, it was the Sorcerers Trust that gave us a grant to take this inn on; we'd have nothing if it weren't for the White Sorcerer. We owe him and the Guild both. I'll tell you what, lad,'

he offered, turning to his nephew, 'how about I take you?'
He turned back to his sister. 'Business is good, Jean. I can
afford to lose a day or two, and you and Jane will keep
the inn right well, I know it. How else could they get
there, anyhow? It'll take no time at all on a broom.'

The snow had only just stopped as Uncle Jamie took to
the sky on an old rickety broom that had seen better days,
with Lucy and Douglas clinging to him tightly. Mrs
Archibald waved until they dwindled to a distant speck of
ash against the heavy-bellied snow-laden sky.

CHAPTER THIRTY-SIX[1]

Dragon's Horde

The ancient castle loomed black and forbidding on the edge of the Cape Wrath cliffs overlooking Wreckers Cove, its walls falling away into the encroaching sea far below. Once a mighty fortress, said by many to be impregnable, the Guild's avenging armies had reduced Carrack Castle to blackened rubble and the history books, before banishing the Raven to the mortal world. Now only wheeling gulls and puffins lived here amongst the broken towers, while the crumbled halls, the cellars and prisons peeled open to the unforgiving sky. A rusting and broken portcullis hung from smashed guard towers. Even the gorse looked wind blasted. Douglas and Lucy had been exploring the ruins for an hour or more, but there was no

---

[1] Dragon drawing by Natalie Maclean, pupil at Sir E. Scott School, Tarbet, Isle of Lewis.

trace of gold or silver or dragon scales or anything to suggest anyone had visited this castle since it fell.

The waves pounded the craggy shoreline below, where the outer baillie had fallen into the sea. There were no beaches here; the sea pounded the cliffs night and day. Black reefs broke their power out to sea, but still the waves smashed against the basalt rock. How many ships had met their end here on the treacherous tides and reefs? It seemed a haunted place, a good place to hide secrets.

Lucy looked eastwards towards a scatter of crofts several leagues away, where Douglas's uncle had landed to talk to the few families who risked their lives to fish here, to see if they knew anything of the sea dragon. Douglas was exploring the tumbled outer baillie when Bucksturdie yipped. Running forward to investigate what the vixen had found, Douglas stumbled upon a huge shaft torn out of the rock.

'Lucy! Lucy! 'What do you think? Could we get down here?'

They had ripped away the briars and ferns and found steps. Worn and loose, but a hidden entrance to whatever lay below the castle? Lucy hesitated in front of the ragged shaft, seeking the calm of Gaia. She could sense no immediate threat. If there were a dragon, it was sleeping. Tentatively, she started down the worn, bramble-choked steps. Bucksturdie raced round and round, yipping anxiously, but refused to follow Douglas down into the frozen earth. It became darker and darker as they left the opening far behind. The steps seemed to be getting very steep.

'Ahh!' Lucy slipped, hands and feet flailing in all directions. One minute she was there, the next Douglas heard a shriek that rapidly faded into silence.

'Lucy, wha - ?' Then Douglas, too, lost his footing and found himself rattling down the steps, his breath coming in bumps and gasps. Then, just as suddenly, the chimney spat him out.

'Ooouuufffh!'

Something cracked and splintered as Lucy landed, softening her fall. She reluctantly felt about her, trying to identify what it was. Broken ragged edges split the skin of her fingers. In the next second Douglas landed on her with a squeal. Doubly winded, Lucy lay there gasping and wheezing, trying futilely to pull a jaggy-edged something from under her bottom.

They could barely hear the frantic yips and barks echoing and booming down the chimney as Bucksturdie leapt anxiously around the cliff-top entrance. Douglas, not surprisingly, was the first to get to his feet, having had a reasonably comfortable landing. 'Where are we?' he whispered, groping in the dark. 'I can hear the tide.'

'We must have fallen all the way down the cliff to the sea.' Shivering from the damp and cold, Lucy cast around to find the torch that had fallen out of her pocket.

'I've got it,' said Douglas, switching it on and turning to face her. In its reflective glow Lucy saw Douglas's face turn mushroom-pale. His mouth opened and shut as he gazed behind her. He tried to speak, but nothing came out but a pathetic squeak.

'What?' Lucy turned around then leapt into Douglas's

arms. The pair didn't dare to move a muscle. Nothing happened. Douglas shook, partly with fright and partly with the effort of hanging onto Lucy. She cautiously opened an eye. The huge gaping jaws hadn't moved. Yellowed teeth were cracked with age. Empty eye sockets the size of wells gazed vacantly.

'It's just a skull,' Lucy said, clambering off Douglas and feeling ever so foolish.

'Oh,' said Douglas sarcastically, mustering what dignity he could, 'that's all right then, is it? But what kind of skull is it? It's the size of a cottage!' He stepped backwards into an enormous bone with a crack. 'Ouch!' He rubbed his smarting head angrily.

Douglas swung the torch to where its feeble light barely described massive bones, which rose like the fluted columns of a cathedral into the dripping darkness above.

'Newt & Toad!' Douglas said reverentially. 'We're in a rib cage, look!' .

Douglas was right. Spinal vertebrae locked sixteen pairs of ribs that curved down to the floor like the bars of a giant birdcage. Only...these were...*dragon bones?* Lucy didn't know whether she should be relieved or disappointed. 'It's a dragon.'

'Phew!' Douglas sounded a lot brighter. 'It will be a lot easier to get a talon if it's dead!'

Lucy nodded; secretly that part had been worrying her. 'But where is the other one?'

'Other one?'

Well...this dragon didn't die yesterday. It's been dead a long time. So where is the one the Bear fought, and that

Jamie Harper saw?'

Oh!' Douglas was instantly deflated. 'Well, maybe it doesn't live here? There is no sign of another dragon – it looks like a graveyard.'

'Maybe that's what both alive and yet asleep means? One is dead and one's alive?' Lucy was unsure whether to be happy or disappointed. She inspected the great talons, cracked and dulled with age, that lay beside the rib cage. They were huge. Brittle fragments of scaled webbing still clung between the toe bones. Lucy pursed her lips in thought. It was clear that a JCB would be needed to lift one of these talons, let alone she or Douglas. Would a slither do? The rhyme had made no mention of quantity...

'Douglas, do you have a knife?'

It made no impression at all. The boy put his full weight behind the blade and managed a few slithers. Then the blade snapped with a crack.

'Is that enough?' Douglas asked anxiously.

Lucy pulled a face. 'It must be!' The young girl began to walk around the ridged skull examining its strange shape, the curving serrated teeth. 'What's that?' A metal collar hung from gigantic vertebra at the base of the skull. Despite the damp there was no sign of rust, although the smooth metal was heavily scored, gouged violently. A black aura hung about it, darker than the cave. Lucy frowned, her head suddenly aching. Looking with her inner eye she could see strange runes running through the dull metal. Curious, she reached out only to fall back with a cry as her wrist snapped back.

'Lucy? Lucy, what's wrong?' Douglas scrambled over

the bones. Lucy swayed, retching as the boy held her.

'It's making me ill,' she was breathing heavily. 'That thing...it killed the dragon!'

'Come on,' Douglas anxiously pulled her away, setting off a small avalanche of bones. The pair tumbled down and down and down. Something clinked and chinked as they fell head over heels.

'Ouff! Douglas grunted as he came to a sudden halt, but he barely noticed. 'What's that?' Amongst the brittle bones something gleamed in the dark. Douglas dived into the pile scrabbling. 'Here! And here!'

Metal lit up the darkness like stars, twinkling wherever Lucy pointed.

'Coins!' Douglas shouted unnecessarily. 'Newt & Toad! There must be a fortune here, enough to care for my family for life!' But Lucy was looking at the shattered prow of a ship looming above them out of the sea of bones which had stopped their headlong fall. She reached out to touch the oak; it was moist and soft, almost spongey to the touch. A broken mast and shattered spars hung festooned with mouldering rope. A rusting anchor poked through its dark hull. Everywhere rotting wood, cannon...pewter plates, helmets, a ship's bell, longbows, and...skeletons ...skulls...a lot of them...cracked and broken. She shook her head in disbelief ~ it was Pirates of the Caribbean, only it was true! 'Where has this come from?'

Only the keel appeared to have survived intact the storm that had driven the *Almirante di Florencia* onto the rocks of Wreckers Cove all those centuries ago, when lanterns had falsely beckoned her in to safety, only to smash her on the reefs and drive her into these caverns, bringing chests of gold. Enough gold to rule England and depose its protestant heretic Queen, Elizabeth. Or enough gold to build an Elizabethan grange in the Sorcerers Glen, to pay for ships to venture to the New World where the land and its wealth were unlimited. What Douglas and Lucy had stumbled on truly was a horde of treasure and the source of the Black Raven's great wealth in America: the remnants of the paymaster's chest of the Spanish Armada. The year: 1588.

As Douglas was stuffing his rucksack, pockets and even his boots with coins, Lucy walked round the battered galleon. Stranded by storm tides, the wreckage was widely spread over the floor of the cavern. The pebbles beneath her feet began to get very slick and slippery.

'Euk!!' she wrinkled her nose. 'What a stink!' Then the slippery shingle gave way. Barely keeping her balance, Lucy toppled down, cobbles rattling her ankle bones. Arms flailing, she was brought to a stop unexpectedly by something soft – and wet – raising an involuntary cry of disgust as globules and gubbins stuck to her. The shredded carcass looked like the remains of a killer whale. Looking at the blood splattered on her T-shirt, Lucy felt her heart skip a beat as she saw what she was standing on: it looked horribly like the hindquarters of a Highland cow! And that skull underneath...that was human. Realisation was reluctantly dawning. 'Oh no! Douglas?' she shouted. 'There's a carcass, it's fresh. Sort of.' She felt sick.

'A carcass?' Douglas croaked from above 'Fresh? Sort of?'

'And a skeleton...err, bits of a skeleton and it's got a shred of clothing...It's a lair, Douglas,' Lucy was suddenly certain. 'This is a larder, not a dragon graveyard.'

For some reason, Douglas did not share her excitement. 'A larder?' he squeaked, 'the second dragon lives here?' There was a breathless moment of silence as Douglas played the torch about them, as if a dragon might be lurking quietly in a corner, but its searching light was thankfully swallowed up by the darkness, not an open mouth. If there were another dragon, it clearly wasn't at home. Then a mournful call shivered through the air. They froze, staring at each other. It sounded close by.

'You've got the talon! I've got some coins. M-maybe it's time to g-go?' Douglas said hopefully.

Frantically scrabbling up the hill of bones they returned to the chimney they had fallen down. It was quite beyond their reach.

'If you climb on my shoulders could you grab onto anything?' Douglas suggested making a stirrup with his linked hands.

'No,' Lucy jumped down breathlessly in a shower of dirt. 'We can't get back that way, we'd need ropes...I can't get a grip on anything!'

Their predicament was beginning to dawn on the two adventurers. No one save Bucksturdie knew where they were. What if they were trapped; by the tide or the dragon? Suddenly swash and buckle seemed a lot less romantic and exciting to Lucy. Dark was falling swiftly

and it was very cold. Lucy had a sense that the veil
between worlds was weak here. 'I think we're between
worlds here. I think the dragon can exist in both. It's
hidden somewh-'

The ground shook. Pebbles tumbled into sudden silence
as the tide went out and did not return. The ground shook
again. A cold wind ghosted through the tunnel, buffeting
them. The basalt pipes sang. Yellow haar flooded the
cavern. The ground shook again.

'Hide,' Lucy whispered urgently, 'inside the wreck.'

'B-b-but, Lucy,' Douglas warbled, 'the – the – d – d -'
He was so scared he couldn't get the word out. 'The-the-
d-d-d-r-r-agon's coming...'

'Hide!' Lucy nearly screamed, shaking him. 'Hide! Or
we'll both die!'

As if waking from a dream, Douglas dropped his sack.
Spilling coins as he went, he struggled up the shifting
mound, collapsed breathless behind a rotting chest in the
hull. Relieved that he was at least hidden from sight, Lucy
turned to confront the master of the dragon horde.

CHAPTER THIRTY-SEVEN[2]

Imprisoned

Lucy felt the wall of rage rolling ahead of the onrushing sea dragon building like thunder, its desire to smash and destroy...anything that would alleviate its pain. The pressure in the cavern rose unbearably. Phosphorescent light flickered in the darkness. Chunks of rock fell into the sea as the sea dragon slammed into the cavern, huge talons scrapping and sparking the riven bedrock. The cliff shuddered as a great tail lashed from side to side. Intent on killing, the sea dragon entered its lair in a rush of seawater and foam, bringing with it darkness deeper than

---

[2] Dragon drawing by Hamish Scott, pupil at Sir E. Scott School, Tarbet, Isle of Lewis.

the night ~ the marks of *binding...obedience...servitude...*
The temperature plummeted.

Shuddering, Lucy fell to her knees retching... *Chaos!*
The mark of the maelstrom...a burning cold collar of sky
iron...the great creature was bound...into servitude...to
obedience by the maelstrom. Against all the tenets of the
Guild, the Raven had harnessed a noble dragon: one of
the last with magic of its own. No wonder it was enraged!
Freezing seawater cascaded about her as the great maw
opened. Lethal venom dripped from poison sacs, dissolv-
ing rock and pebbles. On shaking legs, Lucy stood
defiantly, seconds from death. *I am not your enemy...*

The language of the Elders stopped the dragon's
headlong attack. Ancient reptilian eyes considered her;
deeply intelligent eyes flecked with gold ~ terrible pain sat
behind them. Pain and power ~ a deadly combination. *It
was you who sang the song of the sea...of my kindred...*

*Noble one...*Lucy affirmed bowing her head. *I wish
only to serve...*

To serve...? I am bound! Rage thrummed through the
air. *Bound to serve...to protect... She died!* The dragon
roared its grief. Douglas cowered down in the wreck,
burying his head. *The cold magic killed her...*

Killed her...? Ice shivered up Lucy's spine as realisation
dawned. *The other dragon was... your mate?*

The great head drooped and the leviathan shuddered.

It's killing you, too! Lucy felt her rage rise and with it
sudden realisation. *But I can free you...*

Free me...?

I am born of both worlds...it is within my gift... Lucy

brought down a clenched fist. *Fire to kill ice..! Creation to defeat chaos..!* There was a flash of light and a crack. The immense collar fractured, falling away and the great head whipped down to where Lucy stood. Douglas whimpered.

Be at peace, noble one. Return to the deeps where you belong...

The sea dragon was used to awe, to fear and anger in mankind's world where he hunted; but most of all, to jealousy. Mankind tolerated nothing greater than himself. Dragonkind were long extinct in this world of men.

None has answered my calls...they are gone...I am alone...

Lucy groaned, feeling the creature's desperate longing for its own kind, the emptiness the Raven had condemned it to...

In this world...but the way is still open...return to your own world...to your kindred...go in peace, noble one... return to the Fifth Dimension...you may find your kindred in the ocean deeps...

The great tail disappeared in a rattle of pebbles.

'Luc-ow!' Unable to believe they were still alive, Douglas tried to stand on wobbly legs and fell over several times before he succeeded, and gingerly rubbed his aching backside. Something had been horribly uncomfortable, but his mind had barely registered. Now he turned to look at what he had been sitting on. In the light of the torch the crescent was tarnished, almost black. And beside it, undoubtedly the object of his discomfort, was a heavy disk with rays. *The sun?* The boy stooped to lift them with shaking hands. His sack had disappeared beneath the sea dragon's talons and he had no wish to linger here. He stuffed them hastily into his jerkin and clambered down, just in time to catch Lucy as she fainted.

The thinning haar churned. A final call rattled around the bay, bouncing off the cliffs...an ear splitting challenge that promised retribution and a debt unpaid as two worlds divided. Far to the south in Thistleburr, an echo of the uncanny cry carried on the wind. Wide-eyed shoppers paused to stare at each other, goose bumps making them shiver. Cameras were swung towards to the open sea.

'There! There!' The BBC helicopter combing the rocky shoreline to the north carried the only TV crew close enough. 'It's the Sorcerers Loch Monster. You've seen it here, live on BBC News 24, the first authentic footage...it is a muckle beast!'

Spinal crests arced, then with a smash of its tail the sea dragon dived into the greenstone depths, and was gone from the mortal world of men. The inter-dimensional barriers merged and a doorway between two worlds slammed shut with a clap of thunder.

Clutching on to each other on the icy cobbles of the sea cavern, Lucy and Douglas were both shaking uncontrollably with cold, fear and exhaustion. The deepening sky was still light, but it was pitch dark in the cavern. Drenched through, Lucy was unbearably cold. Douglas had already swapped jerkins with her and wasn't in a much better state. Then they heard the hoarse calling of men's voices booming through the thinning fog. '

'Douglas...Douglas...Douglas' the faint shout echoed off the cliffs. 'Lucy...Lucy...Lucy!'

'It's Uncle J-jamie! H-here, here!' Douglas shouted. Excited yips answered the boy's call, as Bucksturdie greeted her friend's voice with delight.

'Douglas?'

They could hear the splash of oars...rough voices praying...

'It's the f-f-fishermen!' Douglas cried joyfully as a glimmer of flaming pitch brands lit the sea to gold 'They've come to rescue us!'

~Claw of dragon swimming deep, both awake and yet asleep~

No more, Lucy thought. *God speed, noble one...I hope you find your kindred...* Eyes drooping with fatigue, Lucy placed the shards of talon next to the small blue vial. She took out the rumpled rhyme and scored through another line. That left tears of the moon and laughter of the sun still to find for another day. Yawning she headed up to the attic to bed. School tomorrow.

CHAPTER THIRTY-EIGHT

Aztec Artefacts

As Lucy and Oliver came crashing through the front door and into the kitchen after school, Mother was looking very pleased with herself.

'Is there news?' Lucy was suddenly hopeful.

'Ah no, Lucy,' Mother said, knowing instantly what her daughter meant, 'no word. I fear we have to wait until he returns to our world. The SDS are hoping to track an unauthorised jump.'

Lucy turned away to fight back the tears that stung her eyes. She was dreadfully tired and strung out after their adventure with the sea dragon.

'But I do have good news,' Mother encouraged her daughter, drawing her and Oliver into a hug. 'I think we should all pop round to Mr McGill's directly after supper.'

'The antiques collector?'

Mother nodded. 'Make sure you bring the coins, gold and silver.'

'Why?'

But Mother smiled and wouldn't say another word.

Supper had been demolished in record time. Now the Pemberton family and Kealan trooped through the large panelled hall of Archerfield House, past the brass and walnut grandfather clock and antiques, and into a cosy wood-panelled study that smelt of beeswax, leather and books. Around the room, display cases held countless collections of coins, armour and artefacts. Rising from behind a glass desk, a bemused Mr McGill welcomed his guests. Planting a kiss on Mother's cheek, he airily waved the children to a burgundy leather sofa covered in cushions.

'Please sit down. Make yourselves comfortable. Michael,' he instructed, turning to the young butler hovering nearby, 'please bring the children some ... Coke? Oliver? A Mountain Dew? And Janet. A wee dram, perhaps, or a coffee? Coffee. And some biscuits and cakes.'

'Indeed, sir.' McCuthbert inclined his head and departed.

'Wow,' Oliver breathed. 'Is that a...?

Mr McGill smiled. 'Ah, a young man with an eye for quality I see. Yes, it's a Retina 5K. Would you like to play with it?

Lucy looked at the large screen which looked like a slice of apple. 'Where is the comput-'

'Fusion drive, 3.5GHz Quad-Core Intel Core i5!' Oliver announced reverentially, as if that meant anything to anyone else.

Lucy rolled her eyes.

'Yes, 14.7 million pixels and-'

Mother coughed.

'Ah, right, yes!' Mr McGill took a seat, only slightly embarassed. 'To business first!'

'Well!' The antique dealer smiled. 'What have you brought to show me? And why all the secrecy?'

Lucy opened her rucksack and took out two wrapped packages. Taking the smaller and laying it on the desk, Mr McGill opened up the soft blue folds. His grey eyes widened, and he whistled softly. Lifting the coins out, he studied them one-by-one through an eyepiece. Breathless, the children sat on the edge of the sofa and watched his every move. He seemed to take forever before finally laying the looking glass down.

Impatient, Lucy could not hold back her questions any longer. 'What are they?' she burst out, knowing that somehow they were tied to her grandfather.

'Yeah,' Kealan agreed, 'what are they, Mr McGill? We looked on the web. We think they're doubloons.'

'Can Lucy keep them?' You could count on Oliver to get down to basics. 'Is it a treasure trove or maybe salvage?'

'Whoa!' Mr McGill held up a hand to calm the barrage of questions. 'One at a time,' he laughed, 'and then I have a few questions of my own.'

'Well,' he said thoughtfully, laying the coins out on the glass-topped table, 'you're right. It's Spanish gold, or more accurately Aztec and Inca gold, plundered by the Spanish Conquistadors when they conquered the New World in the sixteenth century. The Spanish melted artefacts and jewellery down into ingots and eventually into coins like these. This,' he explained, holding up a large-rough edged coin, 'is, as you rightly guessed, a gold doubloon. And these,' he continued, indicating the smaller rough-cut triangular coins, 'are what are called 'pieces of eight', in other words a doubloon cut into eight pieces to pay for smaller transactions ... the stuff of treasure ships and pirates.'

Everyone in the room sat up, wide-eyed, and exchanged grins.

The antique dealer opened the second bundle, lifting the gold disc with pointed rays and the black crescent. 'Ahh,' he breathed, 'now these *are* rare. *Very* rare. *Very* valuable. You see?' Mr McGill held up the two pieces in turn. 'The Aztecs and Incas believed that gold represented the laughter of the sun, and silver the tears of the moon. It's rare to- What?' His entire audience had suddenly sat forward and were staring at him.

'-tooo find original artefacts like these... Museums and private collectors would pay a small fortune for these two pieces. Well, now.' He paused and looked at his guests. 'Are you going to tell me where you found them?'

'Um,' Lucy managed, 'err –' In their excitement they hadn't thought about explanations. She glanced at Mother.

'Wreckers Cove, Brian,' Mother said bluntly. 'Guarded by a collared sea dragon. The Guardian thinks it was hidden by a cloaked inter-dimensional pocket.' The children looked aghast. 'The sea dragon has been set free.'

'Ah!' Mr McGill nodded. 'So GI6 were correct that the Black Raven had Spanish treasure? '

'You know?' Oliver asked disbelievingly, eyebrows taking off into his fringe. He'd always thought the millionaire was a bit of an old fogey. 'About the dragon? About Lu - ... about the Fifth Dimension?'

'Children,' Mother announced as she stood, with a

theatrical bow, 'meet the Master of the Ptarmigan Lodge from the City of the Seven Lodges.'

Mr McGill beamed at them all.

'The whereabouts of the sea dragon called the Sorcerers Loch Monster, and the source of the Raven's great wealth, have been among the great unsolved mysteries of the last four centuries. You freed the sea dragon? That was well done, Lucy. Very well done!'

~Laughter of sun shining bright,
Tears of moon in cold moonlight~

That night Lucy walked round the loch to Osprey Cottage and placed the golden sun and the silver moon next to the claw shard, along with the small vial, and scored off the last two unsolved lines of the rhyme. They had all the reagents, but they still didn't have their grandfather back, although GI6 believed, with only days to go, that he was now back in Thistleburr. The Old Grange had been kept under surveillance and no one had come near. They had only days to find him, and then somehow to spirit him to the Necromancer's Ring, before the Raven returned to claim his brother. Truffle had said she had a cunning plan the moment they had news the Bear was back in Thistleburr, but was still out on the prowl by the time an exhausted Lucy fell into bed in the Nook & Cranny.

Oliver too had something to celebrate.

'Well, young man,' Mr McGill's eyes briefly caught Mother's over the boy's head. The millionaire had been looking for just such an opportunity to give Oliver a better computer, given the work the boy was doing for his grandfather and the Guild. 'I find myself with this MacBook Pro and I wonder if you might put it to good use…?'

CHAPTER THIRTY-NINE

The Cunning Plan

'Mistress! Mistress, wake up!' a voice mewed in the dark. *Pppuuuuuuuuuuprrrrrrrurrrr.* Whiskers tickled her cheek. Paws treadled her chest.

Groggily, Lucy struggled awake. The air was frigid and her hot water bottle had long since cooled. It was pitch black. Sensing movement, she turned to put on her bedside light and blinked. Seven strange cats were occupying her bedroom. Seven rather overweight, strange cats. In various reclining poses they were grooming away as if they didn't have a care in the world. They ignored her completely. Tantrum and Truffle were sitting on the bed, staring at her intently.

'Truffle?' croaked Lucy, sitting up carefully, feeling brittle from lack of sleep and jangling nerves.

Stretching gracefully, the cat nimbly leapt from the bed, fluidly transmogrifying in mid-leap into her familiar, better gnome self. Unfortunately, her gnome persona had none of the surefootedness that felines take for granted. As the gnome tripped on a bootlace, Lucy noticed that thankfully, Truffle had found a new pair of tights from somewhere – even if they were bright pink.

'Oh yes. Bottoms up, why don't we?' Tantrum muttered bitterly into his beard, as the mortified gnome bounced upright and hastily pulled her tunic back down. Cheeks flaming hotter than a barbecue, Truffle tried to regain the initiative.

'Ahem. Squad,' the plump gnome squeaked. 'Ahem. Ssquuad Aaattennna … shun!' In the wink of an eye and a blur of fur, the Thistleburr Gnome Intelligence Brigade (TGIB) came to attention. Well, most of them did, but outlying areas couldn't quite make it due to an excess of good living. There was a lot of puffing and blowing, as the gnomes sucked in deep breaths and held their trembling tummies in, and tried to look like they meant business. Fur, Lucy realised, covered a multitude of sins. The ragged line shuffled nervously under Lucy's poker-faced stare as she put on her dressing gown and got out of bed. 'Volunteer Rrrrrescue Squad ready for inspection, Ma'am.' Truffle attempted a salute.

Well, Lucy thought, no one could say that they hadn't made considerable effort with their appearance. Someone had been busy with a sewing machine, and dark green face paint and purple lipstick had been liberally applied to every visible square inch of skin. It looked as if half of Mother's favourite rhododendron bush and a fair chunk of the Wychs Wood was now stuck into webbing to serve as camouflage. Lucy suspected that if she checked out her makeup kit from Hallowe'en, she might find it empty

'Um,' she ventured, noting the inventive use of pudding bowls as helmets and the variety of pots and pans and wooden spoons that served as weaponry. 'Very, um, very fierce,' she said. Seven sets of sharp white teeth flashed in a sea of green. 'Um, is this your cunning plan? What are you going to do?'

'The Guild says your grandfather is here in Thistleburr;

they detected a flicker of an illegal jump today, but it was shielded and they could not pinpoint it. We're going to search every loft and garage and garden shed for him. We can get into tight squeezes where you couldn't.'

'Mmnnn...' Lucy nodded with a straight face. 'Well, try and not get stuck anywhere,' she suggested. 'I don't want to have to come searching to rescue you!' Within moments, the feline brigade were gone into the snowy night, and the kitchen cat flap settled.

The body lay there in the dark cellar as cold as ice, green-veined like marble. The spirit of the man remained inside his body but hovered between living and surrendering to death's cold embrace. With every laboured breath, he prepared the way for another to claim his life. Somewhere deep down, deep in his subconscious, a tiny spark rebelled; was horrified at what he was becoming. But he was so weary, and the battle had ravaged him, stripped him bare. He could feel his spirit slowly slipping away as paralysis tightened its grip like a tourniquet. He had fought at every turn, for every cell, for every drop of blood. Now the White Sorcerer just wanted to sleep. He was unaware of his grand-daughter's grey cat that leapt nimbly down through a broken window, and whose gnome-self pressed a potion of *healing* and *strength* between his frozen lips. The White Sorcerer had finally been found.

CHAPTER FORTY

One Day to go

Invited by the Black Raven, winter arrived and, liking what it found, unpacked its bags and settled in for the duration. Blizzards blasted the Highlands, blocking roads and cutting off remote villages and farms. The Sorcerers Loch froze over for the first time in living memory. And then the snow stopped, and the land lay silent and exhausted. The temperature plummeted to a record low.

Warwick DeSnowe's limousine left Downing Street and headed through the rush-hour traffic towards the City Airport; one more arms deal signed and sealed. It was finally time to put his global strategy into motion towards his ultimate goal of war across two worlds. As Chesterton manoeuvred around other smaller cars with the deft hand of a taxi driver, or of someone who had driven tanks and basically didn't care too much if someone got in the way, the Black Raven smiled to himself, although no emotion showed on his pale glistening face. *Finally, dear brother mine*, he thought, *we'll be together. We will act as one. But perhaps not in the way our dearly beloved father – or you – intended.* Even now the bile of jealousy rose hot and sour in his throat. He snarled and thrust the disquieting memories from his mind.

He looked at his Excalibur Quatuor watch. Just two days to go and then he could shed this weak and broken body for his brother's and none would know. The north should be paralysed by blizzards that would mask his activities from prying human eyes, and beneath that convenient mantle, the spell of pure and perverted Maelstrom Magic should already be spreading unseen through the far reaches of the glen, damping the power and reach of the Guild. A test of what would be unleashed once he was strong again.

His all-weather, Dark Nebulae military helicopter, on standby at Edinburgh airport, should be able to fly when all other air traffic was grounded, and by dawn he would be back in the Sorcerers Glen. The weak Deputy Headmaster had outlived his usefulness; he would feed on him before taking his brother's body. Countdown, and his revenge, had finally begun.

Far to the north, a muted celebration was taking place at the Pembertons; Oliver and Lucy's grandfather had been found, and much closer to home than anyone would have guessed.

'Weasel-face?' Lucy gasped. 'We should have guessed! He was going to do something horrible to Fergus. We should have guessed!'

Mother nodded. It had been difficult to believe the Deputy Head would have kidnapped a school child for goodness knows what foul purpose, or left four children to die in an abandoned mine. Nothing surprised her now.

'We found him,' Truffle could not keep quiet. 'We found him!'

'Yes you did,' Lucy scooped up the black and white cat to kiss and cuddle her. 'You found him when no one else could!'

It was a triumph for Truffle's nascent GIB. Who, after all, pays attention to a foot-high, brightly dressed gnome in the middle of the dandelion patch? Or, more accurately at this time of year, buried in a snow drift? And cats are well suited to covert surveillance: they are the ultimate hunter, easily finding evidence of an Imperial Black round the back of the cottages in Drystane Road; the tracks in the snow were so large that no humans would be able to identify the pattern of the indentations in the field unless they looked from the air. Moran never knew he was being followed, nor noticed the broken window in his basement.

Rehearsing time and time again what Lucy, Truffle and Tantrum – helped by Douglas – were going to do, lasted into the wee hours of the morning, when Mother finally sent everyone off to bed.

The temperature dropped another five degrees overnight and the snow fell thickly again, challenging the gritters and snow ploughs. Not quite enough to close the last day at school, although children from outlying farms didn't make it through the five-foot drifts. Throughout the day on Monday, Lucy, Oliver and Kealan kept a secret watch on Moran. Oliver even created a mock fight in the playground to give the Deputy Headmaster an opportunity to bully them. As long as he stayed in the school, Weasel-face couldn't be seeing what was happening at his rented cottage on the outskirts of Thistleburr.

Mrs McGregor from number six peered through her lace

curtains at the men in hard hats and bright orange vests who had spilled out of the back of the Highland Gas van

'Gas leak, Ma'am,' the handsome young man said, politely tipping his hat. 'Won't take a moment to fix, but we'll have to check your piping and number ten's as a precaution. May I come in?'

Once inside the basement of number eight next door, the comatose body of the White Sorcerer was cast in a cocoon of *healing, strength* and *life,* and he was removed to the Nook & Cranny. The down-draft from the Imperial's wings removed any trace of their presence.

Lucy and Oliver raced home, breathless, eager but anxious to see their grandfather for the first time since Hallowe'en. The family stood there silently.

'He looks dead,' Lucy said, tears spilling over. 'How can I possibly save him?'

'Hush,' Mother comforted her daughter, as Oliver took her hand in his. 'You're not alone, Lucy dear. Tonight you, Tantrum and Truffle are to meet Douglas at Thistlestone Palace, where Uncle Barnaby will be teaching you everything you need to know to save your grandfather.'

And everything you need to know to survive. 'You won't be alone tomorrow!'

Later that evening, Lucy and Douglas plus two cats were met at Thirlestane by the Vice-Chancellor, Mrs Brace-girdle and some unexpected guests. Passing through battle-ready soldiers gathered in the hall, the pair were led up to the library to discover black armoured dragon lords gathered about maps on a table.

'My dears,' Mrs Bracegirdle swept forwards. 'May I introduce you to the Guardian of Dragon Isle, Lord Commander Somerled, and Strike Commander Maldock of the III FirstBorn.'

Lucy and Douglas tried their best not to gawp in astonishment and to close their open mouths. The Guardian's mouth briefly twitched in amusement.

'The winter solstice falls tomorrow. It is certain that the Raven will return to execute his plan, and our task is to prevent him. You, young Lucy, must draw upon the power of the Sentinels, what you call the Necromancer's Ring, to save your grandfather from Sea Dragon's Bane. It is your task, difficult and dangerous though it is, but you are not on your own. Your cottage in Thistleburr has been guarded by three cloaked Imperials since the White Sorcerer was moved there.'

Lucy's mouth dropped open again.

'Likewise, there are three AirWings of frost dragons already deployed to the mountains and out on the moors of your mortal world, now concealed beneath a blanket of snow. Frost dragons can survive these plunging temperatures and their flight crew have the very best spelled winter armour and are trained for winter warfare. A rapid reaction force of Imperials is on standby on Dragon Isle to deploy to your world the moment you set out from your cottage. You, young man,' the Guardian turned to Douglas, 'are about to experience your first flight on an Imperial. You will fly with me and will join Lucy and the gnomes at the edge of the moorland.'

Douglas's mouth opened. 'What? An Imperial?' He forgot to be scared and punched the air. 'In Lucy's world?'

The Guradian nodded. 'In times of great peril, rules must be cast aside, else they shackle us. When the Raven finds his prize gone, he may guess where the White Sorcerer has been taken and he will most certainly attempt to reclaim him. This may be his only chance.'

'We still do not perfectly understand what he has planned,' Rumspell admitted with a heavy sigh, 'but we *do* believe he thinks himself safe, that he has not been discovered, and that may buy you enough time to complete your task,' he looked at Lucy and Douglas.

'Either way, he will not be alone,' Maldock said grimly. 'We know we have been betrayed, but we have yet to find out by whom; who knows how many across the SDS are pledged to the Raven? The discovery that their master is thwarted may force those in the SDS who wish the return of the Raven banners to reveal themselves, and we will be ready for them. There may be fighting. Do not be afraid. We will protect you.'

Rumspell nodded. 'Now, I have to borrow young Lucy here to discuss the spell she must cast tomorrow. Douglas, you, Tantrum and Truffle and your small friends are expected by Wand-Sergeant Major Pounder in the broom arena, where he will teach you the basics of winter survival techniques and equipment.'

In the library, the Vice-Chancellor sat Lucy down to discuss what needed to be done to save her grandfather.

'Our greatest spell-masters and battlemages have been working together this last moon to create a spell that binds everything needed to thwart such a baleful curse as Sea Dragon's Bane; but a spell that they believe is possible for you to safely conjure, given your lack of training and experience.'

'What does it all mean?' Lucy asked, trying to make sense of the words.

'These first four lines tell us that the cauldron itself is crucial to your success. Given the fell nature of Sea Dragon's Bane, we must use a cauldron of sky metal; cast from what you would call a meteor. Only it will withstand the maelstrom. Your mother has one such, which has been held by her family for countless generations. That is the same iron which forms the molten core of the One Earth and the eye of the EarthWyrm herself. *Tempered in Sea* is your sea dragon and *fashioned through toil* your gold and silver mined by the Inca and Aztec.

The *stone* here referred to is the central cromlech of the Necromancer's Ring, which is imbued with great power, without which, given your age, you would fail. Now these lines here...*blood and bone*... tell us that only one of the same blood line has any chance of succeeding. That is why it must be you, and you alone, who cast the counter-spell.'

'And the *cup?*' Lucy asked. 'Does that have to be special too?'

'Yes,' Rumspell nodded. 'It must not contaminate the spell. Grandmother Bracegirdle chose this one for you.'

Lucy picked up the offered horn cup. 'It's heavy! What

is it?'

'It's the hollowed tip of a noble dragon claw. Noble dragons have magic of their own and were the greatest that ever walked the One Earth.' Now, he gave her a small parchment. 'Can you memorise the spell?'

Lucy nodded. 'I'm good at remembering things. I'll do it before I go to sleep.'

'Good! Good! Now – one final thing. You must use a wand. I would like you to take this. Go on! Take it,' Rumspell nodded encouragement as Lucy dubiously accepted the wand, not entirely sure if Uncle Barnaby was being serious, but he continued gravely.

'The ancient power of the Sentinels that you will draw upon *must* be funnelled and focused...but not through you... you would need to be a BattleMage to conjure this spell without a wand or staff, and even then the risks are high. It's wychwood...so it knows what to do.

'Now, we shall collect your friends and see you safely home to bed. Tomorrow is the shortest day of the year, but it shall also be the longest day you have ever known!'

Meanwhile, Catastrophe was currently up a chestnut tree swishing his tail with boredom and bad temper. His stitches hurt and his ribs still ached, following the blow from a mucklegrub cudgel. That was nothing, however, to the aching emptiness he felt since his soul mate had been kidnapped. Dispirited and morose, the wildcat had fought with every cat and dog in the glen, and none of them would come out to play anymore. Too many painful visits to the vet tended to have that effect.

With the boredom threshold of a three-year-old, Catastrophe had turned to tormenting the local wildlife, but frankly there was hardly anything worth bothering about. The odd badger put up a good fight, and once he had come across an exceptionally bad tempered grey tabby that gave him a run for his money, but all in all, Thistleburr didn't hold a candle to the Fifth Dimension.

And then a familiar cat had arrived. A cat yet not a cat. Like all animals, Catastrophe could see straight through morphogenetic fields, and his brain told him on their first meeting long ago that this plump black-and-white and actually very attractive female was in fact, disappointingly, also the short, podgy gnome that often accompanied Lucy. Then Truffle had explained that this puny man walking up Drystane Drive was responsible for his soulmate's sudden and inexplicable disappearance. Recognising an uncompromising animal hater when he saw one, Catastrophe hissed and drew back into the foliage to study his prey.

Tomorrow he was going to take his revenge. As he carefully groomed himself, Catastrophe considered his opening move. The *Drop Out Of A Tree From A Great Height* made an unforgettable entrance, perhaps followed up by the *Full Claw Rake & Disembowel* routine finished off by the *Sharp Exit*; that normally worked a treat. But this was personal. Tomorrow night he was going to give this human *The Full Treatment*.

The wildcat paused momentarily, instantly motionless as he heard an unusual sound in the air above Thistleburr. As the Dark Nebulae helicopter flew softly overhead on its way to the North Lodge, Catastrophe, the White Sorcerer's huge wildcat and friend, bristled and spat his defiance.

CHAPTER FORTY-ONE

The Winter Solstice

The winter solstice arrived: the shortest day of the year. Only council snow-ploughs, 4x4's and tractors could still travel the roads. Those foolish enough to try had been stuck overnight without heating or food, and ten people suffering from hypothermia were being air-lifted by Sea King rescue helicopters to local hospitals. Only half a dozen local farmers made it through the snow drifts with geese and turkey for Christmas dinners and fresh cut Christmas trees. Bad tempered queues of desperate parents formed, each determined to snap up what little there was for their families. Those snowed in were turning to shopping on-line for presents and food, in the probably vain hope that somehow the post would get through where they had failed. But neither food nor Christmas trees were on the Pembertons' minds.

As the temperature continued to drop, they gathered together after lunch in a small circle in the lounge, looking at the collection of reagents and tools required for the Sea Dragon's Bane counter-spell. Outside the back door, a sledge from Osprey Cottage was being prepared by Tantrum and Truffle. Inside, Oliver was admiring the ironstone cauldron that Mother had recovered from the loft.

'This was my first cauldron,' she told the family as she presented the three-legged cauldron for her daughter to inspect. 'My mother gave it to me. It's a family heirloom which has been handed down from generation to generation.'

'Why must it be a cauldron?' Oliver asked Mother as he examined the intricate Celtic knotwork and animals that decorated its sides and rim. 'Why can't you just cook up a spell in any old bucket or pan?'

Mother smiled. 'A good question, Oliver, dear, but the answer is very simple indeed: a cauldron is magical – it has to be. A cauldron is a tool that sorcerers use where ingredients are transformed into something else by spells and theurgies.' She smiled. 'If you tried to brew up a potion or spell in an ordinary pan, the magic would blow the bottom out of it in no time at all. The Fire Brigade would have to put out yet another chip pan fire! Kealan, dear,' Mother added, putting out an arm to waylay the tall boy running through the house with Napoleon, 'don't do that. We don't want you taking off-'

Crash! As the broom obligingly rose, Kealan caught his head on the door lintel and fell off backwards in a tangle of arms, legs and bristles, setting Midge off barking.

'Ow!' Kealan cracked his head a second time standing up, before reluctantly returning the broom to a disapproving Truffle, who took it round the back to strap on the sledge.

Lucy and her brother were looking at the now faded and torn rhyme, going through the check-list one more time before packing them up in one of Charlie's mountain rucksacks.

'Claw of dragon,' Oliver said.

'Yup.'

'Goblin's, err,' Kealan wrinkled his nose in disapproval, 'gob...here.' 'Troll toenail? Yeuch!'

'Yes.'

'Hedgewitch's broom...'

'Strapped to the sledge,' Truffle kicked snow off her boots.

'Kelpie's tail?'

'Here!'

'Laughter of sun...'

'Into the rucksack, Oliver dear.'

'Tears of moon.'

'Yes!'

'Now...' Oliver turned to a second list. 'We still need a wand?'

'Here,' Lucy pulled the wand from a crumpled bag.

'Yeah, right!' Kealan said sceptically. 'Pull the other one.'

'No, really,' Lucy said. 'It really is a wand; an old and powerful one. Uncle Barnaby gave it to me.'

'But...but it's all warped and knobbly and it's still got an old leaf sticking out of it!' Kealan was horrified. 'I thought it would be...more...magical looking!'

'Are you sure, Sis?' Oliver was no more convinced than his friend.

'Now remember, dears' Mother reminded them gently. 'You can't judge everything or everyone merely by appearances!'

'Drinking horn?' Oliver continued.

'Here.' Lucy lifted the burnished, hollowed talon tip banded in silver, now attached to a narrow leather baldric, a belt worn from shoulder to hip. 'I'll wear this,' she decided, handing it to Tantrum.

'And last but not least,' Oliver crumpled his list and threw it in the fire. 'The cauldron.'

'We'll take this, mistress,' Tantrum and five gnomes struggled off with the cauldron to pack it on the sledge.

They didn't talk any more as the sun dropped behind the woods and the glen plunged into darkness. Fear of the coming night and the task before her was lying heavily on Lucy.

CHAPTER FORTY-TWO

Arctic Vortex

As the blood-red sun sank in the Fifth Dimension, the temperature plummeted. On the Black Isle, braziers were lit the full length of the battlement and parapet walls to ward off the numbing cold. Winter had the land gripped in an iron fist, and the old and vulnerable were dying in droves. Mountain passes were buried beneath strides of snow and the loch had frozen, cracking galleons like eggshells. All but the frost dragons of the IX Winter Knights regiment had been grounded in stable and roost; it was death for dragon and pilot to fly without very powerful spells.

On Dragon Isle, the SDS's Rapid Reaction Force watched and waited, whilst two full air wings of cloaked and densely warded Imperials took off for an inter-dimensional jump. One wing, led by the Guardian himself, was to deploy along the length of the road from Thistleburr to the open moor and the second, led by Strike Commander Maldock deployed about the Necromancer's Ring. For the first time in centuries the SDS were going to do battle in the mortal's world.

Douglas sat between ranks of white armoured Bone-Cracker commandoes on the Guardian's own mount, Strike to Kill, in the smallest, lightest body-armour that could be found, buckled on top of white padded leather jerkin, leggings and thick boots. They had explained about the rapid climb, the momentary passage through the jump gate and what Drop Dead meant. He was petrified.

Tick.

The Pembertons were anxiously watching the weather forecast on BBC News 24.

'There is an amber warning in force covering most of the country and a rare red warning for the Highlands and Western Islands has been issued by the Met Office, as the Artic vortex will see temperatures falling to -39 degrees in some parts of the north.'

Mother changed channels to STV, trying to hide her growing fear for her daughter.

'The snow ploughs and gritters of the Highlands and Islands are out in force,' a spokeswoman for the Highlands Council said: 'Heavy snow tomorrow is likely to lead to widespread accumulations of eight inches with twelve to fifteen inches over higher ground. Roads are closed and all flights grounded. This area includes Ben Nevis and the mountains around Glencoe and the Sorcerers Glen. In the east, it includes Ben Alder south to Loch Lomond and the Trossachs...'

'You're going to have to wrap up really well, Lucy dear,' Mother was fretting. It was cold enough to kill.

By darkfall the snow was blowing horizontally, burying Thistleburr's familiar landscape beneath huge drifts. Head down, the thin, sharp-faced man almost tripped over a garden gnome buried in the snow. *Good grief*, Moran thought, as he retrieved his shopping bags and unlocked his front door, *the wretched gnomes were multiplying.* His landlady had obviously totally lost the plot; there must be at least a dozen of the ghastly things in the garden, all dressed up as if they felt the cold! *Well,* he smiled smugly, knocking snow off his boots, *maybe it was time to change accommodation. After all, he would soon be going up in the world. His patron and master had promised him that.*

Half an hour later, muffled up against the pervasive chill spreading throughout the glen, he struggled through the snow towards the Guddlers Arms for his usual pint or two or three, and perhaps a dram of whisky to celebrate. By the time he got back home 'the package' should have been collected and £500,000 transferred into an offshore bank account hidden from the grasping hands of the Inland Revenue. At least the snow had stopped, and a clear moon was on the rise. It didn't occur to him to check his basement.

Tick...

Ordinary folk and families in the Fifth Dimension crowded together with their animals around stoked fires in round houses and halls, to ward off the advancing cold. Wordsmiths and gleemen recounted stories and sagas, to cheer those gathered together for nigh on a half moon.

'The Earth Song,' the children cried, wanting to hear their favourite story. 'Tell us about the Earth Children!' The Earth Children ~ those few born of the worlds of magic and men in times of dire need. The most famous across both worlds was the tale of King Arthur and his knights of the round table, with his magical sword, born just before Avalon faded forever into the mists of the Fifth Dimension. And so the bards obligingly plucked the strings of their harps and began the first verses of the ancient lay of the Earth Child that took many bells to tell.

Under the halls of the moon
When dark claims all
Beneath its thrall
When harvests fail
And strong hearts quail
When rivers flood
With mankind's blood
And ocean songs are heard no more.
When woodland falls
And trembling One Earth calls
When stars fall down
And low lands drown
When magic fails
Then out of tales
A Child born to the One Earth will come.
Born of Earth and Wind, Fire and Water
Earth's own son or Earth's own daughter

Tick.

Finally! The Black Raven's eyes flared green in the darkness of the Wychs Wood, as he climbed into his helicopter for the short trip across Thistleburr to where his brother lay waiting. Finally the time had come to return to his rightful world, and not a moment too soon. Somehow, the Black Raven did not understand as yet, his sea dragon was gone; had managed to break the collar that bound it to his will. Even worse, footage captured by the BBC had gone viral on the internet, and the world's media had turned the spotlight on the Sorcerers Glen, which until now had been an obscure rural backwater in the Scottish Highlands. But the dropping temperatures and poor satellite reception were driving them away, particularly since a young journalist had died when camping out overnight next to the loch, as there was not a free bed to be had in Thistleburr.

But his sea dragon's disappearance had far more serious repercussions: Nemesis Armaments biotechnology weapons labs had been trying unsuccessfully for years to synthesise sea dragon venom, but now the need was urgent. The Raven had no idea how much elixir he needed to be able to switch aspect at will between his brother's body and his own, but there was little left. That would have to wait, for by early tomorrow morning the reclusive billionaire, Warwick DeSnowe, would re-join his family in London for a press conference before flying back to the United States and their mansion in the Appalachian Mountains for Christmas.

By the end of January, when he returned secretly to the Sorcerers Glen, the White Sorcerer would 'escape' his imprisonment and return to the Fifth Dimension, where he would resume his place at the heart of the Guild and the SDS, learning their strengths and weaknesses, their strategies. At the same time, technology would show the billionaire to still be in the United States, thereby concealing his deception. And all the while, his Raven Brotherhood would spread their wings ever wider.

Tick.

The snow-shrouded glen lay in shades of silver and deepest black. Befuddled by drink, the gloating Deputy Headmaster foolishly attempted his usual shortcut through the Wychs Wood heading home. The snow lay thickly, disguising bogs and briars and burns. With several pints too many, and a dram or two to celebrate, it was not long before Moran stumbled through the icy crust of the Adder burn, before getting trapped by brambles. Crouched on the branch of a conifer, lying in wait, Catastrophe watched with interest as a car on the far loch-side road hit black ice, pirouetting into a ditch. That was the third crash in half an hour. Why humans didn't use brooms was quite beyond him. His head whipped round as branches snapped and curses rang out nearby.

Catastrophe gathered his powerful hindquarters, his fierce eyes gleaming pinpricks in the dark, his thick black banded tail switching from side to side. A flailing figure stumbled into view. Moran started with fright as a ptarmigan took off in a flurry of feathers at his feet, crying out its alarm. Losing his balance, the Deputy Headmaster fell heavily. Cursing, he climbed slowly to his feet. Snow and pine needles showered down onto his bald head and down his neck as he stooped to gather up his fallen hat.

Then something hissed and spat from the depths of the spruce. Frozen to the spot, his heart banging painfully in his chest, Moran looked up just as a vengeful ball of stinking frozen fur landed on him.

Tick

It was piercingly cold out on Rannach Moor. Hoarfrost lay thickly on everything, growing visibly like living coral. Eight feet of snow had long since devoured familiar landmarks. All the creatures of the Scottish moorlands had long since fled the unnatural silence and the penetrating chill by retreating into the sheltered heart of the Wychs Wood, where a power older than man stood impervious to the Raven's magic. Across the Highlands and Islands, the electricity power grid and telephone lines were brought down by the weight of ice. Where they could, locals congregated for warmth and companionship around the blazing fires in the Guddlers Arms or The Foosty Bannock.

Across the other side of Goose Green above the post office, Mrs McFeeley sat in her favourite comfy chair with Haggis curled on her lap and knitted by the light of the fire. The tomcat had bad-temperedly refused to go out for his nocturnal spree of fighting and bin raking and had bitten Mr McFeeley to make the point; there was a seriously scary wildcat out there. Relegated to the kitchen, minus a bowl of milk and a tin of tuna, George dutifully washed the dishes and prepared for an early night. Heavy snows were making postal deliveries almost impossible, but with Christmas only days away and the phone lines down, he had to try. He carefully laid out the home-knitted thermal underwear (last year's thoughtful Christmas present from Mrs McFeeley), placed heavy socks and Wellington boots by the back door, filled up his hot water bottle and prepared a medicinal hot toddy for his throbbing fingers.

Further up the darkened Glen, Kealan, Mother and Oliver helped Lucy and the gnomes into the layers of white survival gear provided by Wand-Sergeant Major Pounder, insisting on another mug of hot chocolate or soup before they set out. Oliver and Kealan, with the help of Tantrum and Truffle, carefully strapped the Bear onto the sledge, wrapping him first in thermal sleeping bags. Lucy had practised the counter-spell until she was word perfect, and Mother had insisted that her daughter also repeat the final verse of Lay of the Earth Child, learnt as a very young child.

'This is not just a nursery rhyme,' Mother held her daughter's anxious gaze. 'It draws on the power of the One Earth. Like wychwood its power will nurture and protect you. You can call upon the One Earth in times of danger.'

Hiding her fears, Mother waved her daughter, Tantrum and Truffle and seven assorted gnomes goodbye. Even though the SDS would guard every step of her daughter's way, she was still deeply afraid for Lucy. Kealan and Oliver helped pull the sledge as far as the moor, where Douglas was waiting hidden beneath a cloaked Imperial's wing. With clumsy hugs and bright cheerful words, Kealan and Oliver wished Lucy and the gnomes luck and returned with heavy hearts and footsteps to the Nook & Cranny. Douglas took their place.

Tick.

CHAPTER FORTY-THREE

Countdown

Staggering up the deserted white street, the Deputy Headmaster stumbled over a hidden kerb and collapsed against a parked car, setting off its alarm. He was leaving the moment the roads were cleared and he could get a flight from Inverness airport. He was clutching a handkerchief to his face and head, and drops of hot blood sprayed darkly between his trembling fingers onto the snow. Sipping a wee sherry, old Mrs McGregor at number six peeped out to see if the snow had stopped, just as her neighbour reeled through his gate and fell over. The Deputy Headmaster was audibly cursing as he fumbled for his fallen keys, and his torn jacket was hanging wide open despite the cold. Swearing as his tattered scarf snagged round the gatepost, he fell a second time, coughing and retching into the snow.

The wretched man was drunk again! Mrs McGregor thought, as she stroked her cat. *And he'd obviously got into a fight. What an appalling example to set the children!* As she turned up the TV, she made a mental note to contact the head of Thistleburr school's governing body. *The man should be sacked!*

As her curtains fell back into place, the darkened door of number eight swung open and hands hauled the profusely bleeding Mr Moran inside. Because she was rather hard of hearing, Mrs McGregor never heard the short and fearful exchange that took place in Moran's basement, nor the inhuman scream of rage. Nor did she hear his fearful muffled cries as the Deputy Headmaster was bound onto the same bench that his previous, but now inexplicably departed, captive had occupied.

The attack was furious – the feeding frenzied.

Tick.

Rannach Moor was a vast featureless wasteland, brow-beaten by the winter into submission; an endless sea of white undulations caused by drifting snows and the dozens of burial cairns from a bygone age. Should anyone be counting, there were at least five score too many scattered across the bogs and rolling crannogs now; but observers were more likely to notice the cars and jeeps stranded and abandoned by foolish motorists over the past week, blocking the roads. Mountain rescue Sea King helicopters had been busy airlifting those with hyper-thermia to nearby Fort William hospital.

The gnomes' hot breath smoked in the freezing air as they wrestled with the laden sledge. A flurry of thick snow eddied around them and icicles hung from red noses and beards. Time and time again, small shovels dug the heavy sledge free from drifts four times their height; only the freezing crust made it possible for them to make headway. In front of the gnomes, the brittle harnesses creaked as Douglas and Lucy took up the strain once more. About them, unseen shadows on the snow began to move.

Tick.

'Dread Lord.' Strike Commander Calin bowed his head as the Raven lifted his blood spattered face from feeding. 'Our hope for deception has gone. The witching hour fast approaches. The Sentinels? It may yet be we can kill those who rescued him, and retake him. They cannot know what you intended. If he is dead, we find another to take his place. Your orders, Dread Lord? The ShadowBlades await your command.'

'None can save my brother, despite the power of the Sentinels.' Yet doubt crept into the Raven's mind. 'I must discover who has taken him. This stupid mortal has got drunk and spoken carelessly,' he snarled. *Who had dared thwart him?* 'I will destroy whoever is there and reclaim my brother! If I cannot, they must all die and another can take his place.'

Six cloaked Imperials lifted into the night and turned towards the Necromancer's Ring; the downdraft from their wings raising a blizzard in their wake. Thunder rumbled. Moments later, the house in Drystane Drive blew up. Fire engines failed to reach the house, but there was nothing they could do anyway other than hose down the smouldering rubble and hope that no one had been home. Mrs McGregor from number six had been blown clear across the bedroom, but the cast iron bedstead and horse-hair mattress had saved her and her little cat. She told the police about the gas leak.

Tick.

The outer perimeter of twenty cloaked SDS Imperials of

the III FirstBorn Regiment had sat motionless as the sledge bearing the White Sorcerer passed unawares between them. The Imperials were suffering badly in the bitter cold despite the talon sheaths, extra brimstone and their heavy winter harness; whether they or their Bonecracker Commandos could fight in this cold or not remained to be seen. Only the frost dragons scattered across the moors were at ease, motionless beneath two strides of fresh snow. It was not just the dead who would try to claim the White Sorcerer tonight.

Tick.

As the sledge bearing the Bear drew closer, Lucy could feel the pull of the magical tides that ebbed and flowed around the Necromancer's Ring growing stronger with every torturous footstep.

'Nearly there,' squeaked Truffle. 'Push, push.' Her nose was running and her face bright red and blotched with cold, despite the protective face mask. Thankfully the craggy crown of the Necromancer's Ring loomed on a hillock ahead of them. Rope taut over his right shoulder, Douglas paused to gather his breath and raised his head. Blinking, he squinted through frosted lashes into the night. Shadows on the snow were pooling, clotting together! 'Lucy!' he husked. 'The dead are rising! Go! Run!'

Seeing that Truffle and Tantrum were already taking the weight of the sledge, Lucy plunged into the waist-deep snow of the outer ditch. Grabbing the heavy cauldron by its handle, she caught the rucksack thrown by Douglas and struggled with her burdens towards the outer Sentinels of the Necromancer's Ring. Behind her the sledge lurched and bounced as the gnomes and Douglas tried to break into a run, the freezing air flaying their raw throats. Already, wraiths wreathed in ragged darkness swooped down from the sky, tearing at hair and clothes, and skeletal fingers, and skulls with gaping mouths punched up through the icy bogs, tugging and tripping and trying to pull them down before they could reach the sanctuary of the standing stones. The dead were rising!

Lucy was jerked off her feet. Wraiths had snatched at the precious rucksack; without it, the Bear was lost. Hanging on, Lucy screamed. Then a snowy mound in front of her exploded outwards and there was a blur followed by a crunch as bones shattered. Then the frost dragon sprang into the air, snapping right and left, and the wraiths veered away. Trembling from head to toe with shock, Lucy scrambled forwards into the Ring.

Out on the moors, there was a flash followed by a dull thump. Fearful heads turned towards the Glen. The Raven had discovered his prize already taken!

'Come on, pull!' Douglas screamed. 'Pull!'

It began snowing heavily.

Tick.

Over confidence that the SDS would not risk a fight in the mortal world made Commander Calin careless. The lead Imperial of the ShadowBlades triggered a camouflage nexus, and blue coruscating flame lit it up.

'Weapons free, weapons free,' Strike Commander Maldock urged his Imperial forwards at a run. Huge wings powering up, it half ran, half flew over the bogs, purple flame raising a cloud of fog. The ground shook as twenty Imperials converged on the embattled Shadow-Blades. From the high rocky cromlech he was stationed on, with a view across the moor, the Guardian calmly ordered his airwing:

'Down! Down! Down! De-cloak! Let them see us!'

'Sea Dragon Tower, Scramble the rapid reaction force! Scramble... scramble... scramble!'

On Dragon Isle, dragon pads bearing a dozen Imperials, each with a payload of two-score sabretooths of the Heavy Brigade, launched on downward slopes: shooting out of tunnels in the cliff face, they turned east. The Guardian gave the Imperials their head. They had rare permission to jump at four-thousand strides. Speed was of the essence, and the snow storm obscured mankind's satellites and any risk of detection.

Thump! Thump! Boom!

Douglas turned. Light flared in the dark beyond the stones. Thump! Thump! An Imperial flamed, blinding purple lighting the night. Starbursts bracketed the sky overhead. Imperial Blacks collided with a bone jarring shock.

'Alpha Strike pattern. Strike, strike, strike.' The Guardian entered the fray himself. 'Light Frost Brigade, defend the Sentinels.'

Imperials uncloaked and six of the III FirstBorn faced

down the shock attack Imperials of the ShadowBlades.

'Dread Lord,' Strike Commander Calin turned to the Raven as his Imperial was bracketed by a cluster of bombs. Shrapnel rattled off armour, raining death amongst his troopers. 'We will hold them. The Shadow-Blade Regiment awaits your return to the Fifth Dimension!' He saluted.

Reeking of malice and madness, the Black Raven shrugged his fraying body and flowed out across the snow faster than any man could move; one shadow amongst many, closing in on the Necromancer's Ring.

CHAPTER FORTY-FOUR

The Sanctuary of the Sentinels

The moment Lucy crossed the outer stone circle, the world outside became blurred and the air thickened. Sounds of battle dulled. Redolent with magic, two worlds were merged within the cromlech and the power of it made her dizzy. She scrambled for the two stones at the very centre of the circle which glowed with more than captured moonlight. Their capstone lay broken and ruined to one side, partially buried by the drifts. That is where the Bear must be laid.

Come on, come on, come on! Throwing down the cauldron, Lucy unlatched her rucksack and tumbled its precious contents into it. Douglas found her there; between the Sentinels, checking through the reagents with numb, shaking hands. The *silver moon* crescent and the *golden sun* disk, *troll toenail* and *dragon claw, kelpies tail*. Lucy struggled to get the stopper out of the vial of *goblin gob* and it was frozen anyway, so she threw that in and the vial broke. Hesitating, pulling a face, Lucy took the small knife and jabbed at her thumb, but couldn't bring herself to do it. They hadn't practised this part of the spell! Frowning fiercely, she laid her hand palm up on the stone and tried again. Her hand was so numb she didn't feel a thing! She let two beads of *blood* drop into the cauldron and swiftly put her gloves back on. Thanking Grandma Bracegirdle for teaching her, Lucy quickly drew the signs of Merimack's cauldron combustion in the air and fired the spell. The ground obligingly burst into comforting fire about the base of the cauldron. Immediately, Douglas shovelled in mounds of freshly fallen snow that hissed and steamed and fogged the air.

'Quick,' Truffle implored, as wraiths snatched at the sledge in growing numbers, dragging them almost to a halt. 'Quick, into the centre. The stones will guard us for a time!' Douglas leapt up to help as the sledge slewed to a halt in a shower of frozen crystals. Tearing at the brittle bindings he helped the gnomes lift the inert White Sorcerer onto the central stone slab at the heart of the cromlech. Unlashing the broom, Douglas gave Napoleon to Lucy. Then the boy, Bucksturdie, and the gnomes with their pans and pots, formed a protective circle around the body, in turn encircled by the Sentinels.

It was nearly the witching hour and the dead were clamouring to be let in. Where was the Raven? Time was running out. Wound tight with nerves, Douglas hopped from foot to foot. The night was filled with ragged fluttering shapes and, despite the frost dragons circling the stones attacking the wraiths with tooth and claw, their number was growing with every heartbeat. Lucy looked down at her grandfather to remind herself what was at stake, and touched the back of her hand to his frosted cheek; it was hard to believe life still beat inside. Reaching instinctively for the One Earth, Lucy swiftly embraced Gaia and gathered the four primordial elements to her need: *Earth, Wind, Fire and Water,* and for good luck also *Ice and Stone.* Tentatively, she raised the unlikely knobbly wand to cast the spell to banish death and protect those of her blood, then hesitated, suddenly very afraid, uncertain; just a thirteen-year-old girl out of her depth. Then Lucy felt a small spark of magic leap beside her, lending her its strength. Douglas had taken her other hand. Teeth chattering from cold and tension, she conjured the potion Rumspell had given her,

> *Wrought from iron that fell from sky*
> *The liquid metal of the Earthwyrm's eye*
> *Tempered in Sea and fashioned through toil*
> *Nurtured within the Earthwyrm's coil*
> *This is the cup and this is the stone*
> *This is my blood and this is my bone*
> *This life is mine and mine alone*
> *Now hearken all and listen well*
> *Heed my power and obey my spell*

There was a sound like pebbles rattling on the shore line. Liquid swirled in the cauldron but nothing remarkable happened. No luminescent green as in Hocus Pocus. No special effects! No wall of light rolling out from the cromlech. Hesitantly, Lucy dipped the horn cup into the dark brew. Lifting it with both hands, she reluctantly sipped, prepared for it to taste foul, worried she would gag and spit it out. Thankfully it didn't taste of any of the raw ingredients, it was like tea. She took a mouthful and then a second, feeling the warmth trickle into her stiff clumsy body. No one had thought to say how much she needed to drink to protect herself! She took another for luck, before carefully lifting the horn to the Bear's lips.

The potion spilled down his cheeks, freezing instantly! Had any gone in? 'Can you hold his head?' she asked Douglas, trying not to panic. She scooped more potion from the cauldron and tried again, first prising the rigid lips apart; she emptied the horn.

'Lucy! Lucy! Hurry! They're in!' It was true. More wraiths were darting into the circle, swooping down over the embattled gnomes. The ground was boiling now, as bony fingers clawed upwards, tilting the sledge in a seething sea of dirt and ice. Tantrum, Truffle and friends were busy about the prone body of the Bear with pots, pans and rolling pins; splinters of bone rattled off the frozen ground like hail. Douglas ducked and fell backwards into the snow as a wraith snagged his jacket and tried to lift him. Others streamed around him, tugging, pulling and he was off the ground!

'Bucksturdie!' the boy screamed, struggling and kicking. 'Bucksturdie!' Then the vixen was there snapping and crunching, mauling and breaking ~ a whirlwind of russet and white. Shrieking with rage, the wraiths let go of their prize and Douglas fell face down in the heaving snow, with Bucksturdie snuffling and dancing about him, trying to pull her friend to his feet as bony fingers grasped at his legs.

'Lucy! Fly!' Douglas rasped, wiping bloodied snow from cracked lips as he struggled to his feet, stamping on a skull and kicking another from the sledge which was sinking into the bog. 'Fly, before it's too late!'

Throwing the drinking horn to the ground, straddling Napoleon, Lucy was trying to take off but the weight of the dead dragged at her. She stumbled as the ground gave way beneath her feet and a bony hand grabbed an ankle. Bucksturdie attacked. Skulls shrieked, their jaws gaping darkness, but they let go of the broom. As Napoleon picked up speed, the young girl thumped into wraiths, the impact almost knocking her off. Lucy screamed as the experienced broom bucked upwards, trying to break through the rattle of bones into clear air. Frantically grasping the icy shaft hand-over-hand as Napoleon levelled, Lucy crouched low over the broom as they rose above the Sentinels.

Thump... thump... thump...ragged wraiths clotted about Lucy. Had they gone round once? Lucy couldn't tell; this was nothing like the calm atmosphere of the training arena at Thistlestone.

Below her, all nine gnomes were straddling the Bear, standing on him, trying to weigh the body down and to keep the grasping dead from carrying him away before Lucy could work her magic. Tantrum swung his pan with a meaty thump. Tail frizzed like a squirrel with fright, Truffle had turned back into her cat self and her claws were a blur. Lucy had almost completed the third circuit when a blizzard of swirling ravens hit the stone circle. She screamed, blood pouring down from shallow cuts on her head as wings and beaks attacked, but the power of the spell was strong within her and she instinctively held up a hand to ward them away. White light blossomed in the darkness and radiated explosively outwards from the Ring, briefly turning night into day. With screams and wails, the wraiths and banshees vanished in puffs of smoke. Black feathers wafted down to the ground. Dismounting, shaking with tension, Lucy turned to her grandfather to complete the spell, and Douglas and the gnomes suddenly found themselves in the calm at the centre of the storm.

Taking a deep breath, Lucy knelt in the snow. Worryingly, she didn't feel any different. Shouldn't she be feeling…she had no idea how she should be feeling! Had the potion worked for the Bear? He didn't look any different either! Green veins still laced the pale skin. Kneeling beside her, Douglas took her hand and nodded his encouragement, his raised brows frosted. 'It probably takes time to work! Look! Something's happening.'

It was true. The frost on the Bear's skin was melting and shallow breaths clouded the air above his lips! Lucy reached out to touch his cheek, to *bond* with her grandfather, to lend him her strength. There was an electric crack. Head ringing, spitting snow, Douglas sucked in a choking breath as he struggled to his feet. His friend was hunched rigidly over the prone body and her skin was rippling! Douglas was stunned. Maybe Lucy hadn't drunk enough potion! The venom shouldn't be hurting her! But it wasn't the venom. Programmed as predators and sensing an intrusion, the nanoparticles in the Bear collectively surged in their millions towards Lucy, greedy for another victim for their intended master; a younger victim, decidedly more malleable than their first – a delicacy indeed.

CHAPTER FORTY-FIVE

A Conspiracy Uncovered

The unkindness of ravens was decimated. Bloodied feathers blackened the stone circle. Drawing himself into a single raven, diminished, wings smoking, one eye partially blinded, the Raven felt the power and purity of Lucy's spell and knew it meant the ruin of his plans. *How? He was weak! So weak! A child had denied him?* How? Who? His brother was there, still in the Ring, still alive, and somehow so was she. It was intolerable that his brother should survive. All about him the air thumped and shivered, as the dead tried and failed to breach the sanctuary of the Sentinels. The Raven, too, circled, searching for a weakness. This had been *his* domain for centuries; a gateway between worlds that was now barred to him. The power here was his to command and no other! He tried to gather himself but had no strength to breach the ward. The witching hour was fast approaching.

Tick.

Lucy stiffened as she felt the predatory nanobots flowing through her, seeking to change her to their parasitic purpose; but their cargo of venom could no longer harm her. But Lucy couldn't find the Bear in the empty, splintered, no-man's-land of his soul, laid bare by his own battle for life. The vein of gold disappeared into the dark seams of his mind. And the baleful power of, and damage done by the Sea Dragon's Bane, could not so easily be undone. Lucy's heart rate began to slow and beat in time with the Bear's. Her blood was his blood. Her breath faltered as her stricken lungs, like his, gasped for air. She felt the strength of her grandfather's rigid, unused muscles paralysing her body and dragging her down to his lifeless depths. The antidote was wearing off. Lucy fought down her rising panic. The nanobots still held her in their inexorable grip and she couldn't speak, couldn't cry for help. Then Tantrum and Truffle were there, lending her physical strength, and Douglas too.

'Here, drink this!' The boy frantically forced more of the brew between Lucy's rigid lips as the gnomes held her up. Fire trickled through her cold body barely warming her leaden limbs. 'Lucy! Fight, fight back!'

Then Douglas began chanting loudly, his voice growing stronger as the gnomes joined in one by one, and hearing them, Lucy joined in the last verse of the Lay of the Earth Child.

> *I am the wind that blows across the sea*
> *I am a wave of the deep*
> *I am the roar of the ocean...*

Tick.

Boom...boom...boom...boom...

Blanketed by the snowstorm, the battle out on the moors was fierce. Battle spell and counter-spell sent fountains of dirt and ice high into the air. SDS Imperials flamed, fire sweeping along battledragon backs, spelling death to all save the Dragon Lords. Strike Commander Calin knew it was a fight to the death; betrayal had no other outcome. His six ShadowBlade Imperials were vastly outnumbered, as wings of Imperials from Dragon Isle, supported by the University Faculty Guard, dropped out the snow-laden sky, dropping thousands of commandoes and a score of battlemages whose sole target was the Raven ~ kill or capture.

Without outlawed dragon collars, Calin's Imperials refused to attack their own kindred, and it came down to a fight between Dragon Lords, battlemages and BoneCrackers. He had no frost dragons, and the troops he dropped in support of his master's assault on the Sentinels were unprepared when the Light Winter Brigade exploded from the moorland all about them. The young Strike Commander's regimental base was far to the north in the Howling Glen, too far to call for aid; the Raven Brotherhood had imagined their conspiracy secret, still less that the SDS would risk a fight here in the mortal's world. Blood pouring from wounds, Strike Commander Calin cursed as an Imperial turned flaming from the sky, its tail smashing into troopers from a second Imperial.

Fierce fighting broke out behind his pilot's chair as Mountain Rangers abseiled down from the Guardian's mount onto his battledragon. It was over. The young warlock recklessly spurred his Imperial towards the Sentinels.

Tick.

Eleven voices were braided together, their chant rising in power and ending in a shout of defiance, lending their strength to Lucy.

> *I am the wind that blows across the sea*
> *I am a wave of the deep*
> *I am the roar of the ocean*
> *I am the stag of seven battles*
> *I am the hawk on the cliff*
> *I am a ray of sunlight*
> *I am the greenest of plants*
> *I am a wild boar*
> *I am a salmon in the river*
> *I am a lake on the plain*
> *I am the word of knowledge*
> *I am the point of a spear*
> *I am the lure beyond the ends of the earth*
> *I am that which rules the elements*
> *I am earth, wind, fire and water*
> *Earth's own son, Earth's own daughter*
> *I am life!*

With each shouted word, Lucy felt the blazing heat of creation deep within the One Earth well up inside her, giving her the strength she needed to reach her grandfather. This time she plunged in like a kingfisher, a flash of colour in the dark. This time the speed of her attack and the power of the spell surged beyond the damage wrought by the nanites to where the corrosive venom had wrought its mischief. Fire ~ she must conjure fire to melt the ice of the maelstrom! Then, faintly, Lucy saw a white spark bloom in the dark landscape. The Bear! With a cry of joy she surged towards it.

Tick.

The ground shook. There was a massive impact on the moor. A wave of ice and snow and shattered stone blasted the cromlech as an Imperial's hind-leg talons gouged out the frozen earth in an effort to get airborne again. Another standing stone fractured and fell into the outer ditch. The hedgewitch wards were broken. Blackness flowed over the snow into the Necromancer's Ring, bringing a deeper chill.

Clambering to her feet, protected by the central cromlech, Lucy turned to face the figure coalescing between the tumbled Sentinels. It was a man...of sorts. Blackness crawled about the figure so that its silhouette shifted and warped as if the warlock had not the energy to tame it. Green flickered and leaked from his eyes and mouth. Lucy stared, gripped by the horror of it. *So many masks for one person to hide behind...* The American billionaire, the dreaded Warlock, the countless nameless people he had robbed of their lives to maintain his own. So many faces... But beneath them all, only one man who could barely bind the illusion of his borrowed body. A warlock wraith seeking a new host body to disguise his return to the Fifth Dimension. And they had denied him! The Raven had *failed* to take her grandfather. But elation turned to fear.

'So, man-child,' the cold thin voice hissed about the standing stones. 'You survived our last encounter? You will not survive this, I promise you. I have strength enough to kill him and consume you.'

Lucy stood petrified as the smoking figure advanced, bringing certain death with it. Out of sight, Douglas had picked himself up from where he had been thrown along with the tangle of gnomes. Signalling Truffle and Tantrum to move behind him, Douglas crept sideways behind a fallen stone. Bucksturdie bellied forward beside him, instinctively knowing his intent.

Truffle? Douglas whispered. '*My shoulders... get on my shoulders.*'

Lucy finally managed to raise her hand, hoping the potion's magic would protect her again, but its power was spent and she had none of her own. Laughing, the Raven opened his smoking maw and reached out. Darting in, Bucksturdie struck first.

'Ah!!' the Raven screamed. Bucksturdie struck again then yelped as green tendrils struck her, hurling her backwards into a stone. The Raven's concentration wavered for an infinitesimal fraction of a second, but it was all Truffle needed. There was a resounding and very un-magical metallic thump. The Black Raven folded like a deck chair. Lucy stared then looked down at her hands in amazement.

Midnight passed into morning. At Lucy's feet, an empty black cloak settled on the ice. Dark motes dispersed from human form into a pool of darkness. An enraged wail shrieked round the Ring and faded into the tumultuous night. Where the black Raven had stood, a cast-iron pan lay embedded in the ice.

As SDS flares lit up the scene and BoneCrackers rappelled into the Necromancer's Ring, Lucy gawped at Douglas, standing with a grinning gnome balanced on his shoulders.

'Bucksturdie!' The boy cried, reaching down and gathering the limp fox into his arms, as Truffle tumbled into the snow jumping with delight.

'I executed Night Folding!' Truffle demonstrated by assuming a martial-arts stance and then chopping a hand down. 'Hai-ya! Alright,' she glared at Tantrum. 'I may have hit him with a pan and not my hand, but -'

Wand-Sergeant Major Pounder of the SDS would have been proud.

CHAPTER FORTY-SIX

Happy Christmas

'Lucy! Lucy!' Oliver hugged his sister as she dismounted the Imperial, relieved to see her safe. 'You look awful!' he said worriedly as Mother hugged her daughter and nodded to the BoneCracker commandos who had helped Lucy down the icy wing to the ground, along with the cauldron. No trace of what happened out on the moors would be left behind. Speculation as to the craters pitting the peat bogs and crannogs where Imperials fell, or the smashed outer circle of the Necromancer's Ring would no doubt occupy many long nights to come, as would the strange lightning, if it had been seen at all. Oliver tried to wipe the gusting snow from his glasses, awestruck again by the immense size of the departing Imperial already fading from view. 'Is that blood?' he stuck them on his nose again. 'You're hurt!'

'No. It's not mine,' Lucy turned anxiously to where Truffle, Tantrum and the other gnomes were gently bearing a bundle wrapped in a blanket into the cottage. 'It's Douglas's fox ~ she's been badly injured! We need Megan, mum. Bucksturdie's been badly hurt! I promised Douglas we would save her! She attacked the Raven! She saved us! And Tantrum and Truffle!'

'I'll ring her right away,' Mother bustled indoors. It was just one a.m. 'I think she is on call tonight so she'll be here in no time at all. Bring Bucksturdie in by the fire to keep her warm, and then you can tell us everything, Lucy dear!'

High up in the stratosphere, a Yellowstone battledragon guarded by five uncloaked Imperials emerged out a jump gate and dropped down towards the Sorcerers Glen. The pilot glanced at the arm mounted glyph display to check her coordinates.

'Search and Rescue One. Search and Rescue One,' her helmet crackled, 'you are cleared for immediate landing. All vectors are clear. An emergency medical team is on stand-by.'

'Acknowledged. The White Sorcerer is on board. We have the White Sorcerer.'

The pilot could barely see the crested skull spines of her Yellowstone, eighteen strides in front, let alone the landing lights on Dragon Isle. Maintaining her approach vector, she touched an icon. The storm imager visor built into her helmet snapped into place over her right eye, and the world turned into a red, three-dimensional grid.

The contours of Dragon Isle jumped into sharp relief, with the Shard peaks to the north and the Sea Dragon Tower to her left; the pilot locked onto the homing beacon on pad one. The tactical grid decreased as her altitude scrolled rapidly down. With a subtle touch to the reins, the Yellowstone spread its powerful wings and put down. The White Sorcerer was home.

The polar vortex suddenly broke its icy grip on Scotland as the maelstrom magic behind its summoning collapsed, while the Raven Brotherhood scattered. Council gritters and snow ploughs worked round the clock to open roads. Electricity board engineers were trying to connect power lines before Christmas. Farmers began bringing in fresh provisions for the local shops. All of a sudden, everyone was out Christmas shopping like mad, and Mr McFeeley and Haggis were run off their feet trying to deliver Christmas cards and presents in time. The Chocolate Cauldron had hour-long queues for their festive treats ~ chocolate trees full of surprises inside, white chocolate snowmen and polar bears, boxes of whisky truffles and tree decorations. But the star attraction every year, which drew people from surrounding towns and villages, was their 'wicked' famous festive window as Oliver put it: milk chocolate mountains covered in white chocolate snow, with a chocolate sledge loaded with boxes of chocolates pulled by twelve reindeer and a rotund Santa half-way down a chimney with a sack of goodies. Everyone was out and about celebrating the festive season; everyone except Lucy, that is. Lucy slept and slept...and slept.

And then on Christmas Eve, the sun rose in a clear sky, and the glen sparkled in its pristine white mantle. The ice on the loch began to melt as Mr McFeeley slogged round the lochside to the Nook & Cranny with parcels from Amazon. Lucy woke to hear Mother's voice welcoming the postman in for a coffee and mince pies. Faint song from the Salvation Army band carried on a westerly breeze from the village. Christmas Eve in a few days' time! She opened bleary eyes.

Bright dappled light played across the quilt and danced on the far wall, reflecting the snow outside. She lay contentedly in bed. The mouth-watering smell of fresh baked bread wafted up from the kitchen, and her tummy rumbled. Moments later, Lucy heard quiet footsteps on the circular stairs.

'Mum!' Lucy sat up for a hug and kiss, as mother put down a tray of porridge and buttered toast on the bed.

'I'm starving!' Lucy admitted, as she lifted the spoon then put it down, suddenly remembering the night before ~ how could she ever forget! 'The Bear! How is he? Is h-'

Mother's sparkling smile reassured her daughter. 'He is in safe hands on Dragon Isle and doing very well indeed. Thanks to you and~'

There was the patter of paws on the stairs and Truffle leapt on the bed. She was licking creamy milk from her whiskers, and smelt of tuna. 'And Truffle and Tantrum!' Mother added with a smile. 'Uncle Barnaby sent a bat last night. The healers are very pleased with his progress. And~'

'But when will he be home?' Lucy interrupted, nearly knocking her bowl in excitement.

Mother sighed and reached out a hand to comfort her daughter. 'I don't know. He has been very ill. Lucy, love, don't cry. He's alive and getting better. We just have to be patient.'

'But he might be home for Christmas?' she asked hopefully.

'Christmas is tomorrow, Lucy, dear. You've been asleep nearly four days.'

'Four days?' Lucy echoed. 'I've been asleep *four* days!'

'Using magic when you are not accustomed to it can do that, it's perfectly normal. Your body needed time to heal itself, although Oliver and Kealan have wanted to wake you up. I told them you would wake when you were ready.'

'What happened to the Black Raven? Is he dead?' Lucy glanced at Truffle, who had transmogrified into a gnome in a bright red Santa Claws outfit, with cream on her chin instead of a beard. 'Truffle hit him really hard.'

Mother shook her head. 'He survived to return to London. The newspapers say the family are returning home to have Christmas in New York.'

'Then he'll be back? He won't have given up will he?'

'Yes, he will be back. But next time we will be better prepared for him. His plan was foiled, but it is only a question of time before he attempts to seize power again, and as every day passes, technology takes quantum leaps and bounds. But,' Mother concluded on a positive note, 'who can say what the SDS and the Guild ~ and Truffle's gnomes will be able to do in a month from now, let alone a year?'

'And those people who fought for him?' Lucy smiled with fond exasperation at Truffle, who was eating her untouched breakfast. 'What happened to them?'

Mother sighed. 'Most of them died, some escaped. Sadly, they were led by the youngest battlemage ever to hold the rank of Strike Commander of a regiment, let alone the elite ShadowBlades; the eldest son of one of the great noble houses ~ Darrim Calin. His family have disowned him. He and his personal guard who were with the Raven fought to the death. Unfortunately, apart from them, we don't know who else was involved in the conspiracy. Whoever they are they have gone to ground. We do know that the Raven Brotherhood has returned; those who supported the Raven before he was banished, she added seeing Lucy's confusion. 'Uncle Barnaby fears that there are many scholars in its ranks. Suspicion and fear is rife. No one knows who to trust.'

The front door banged and the babble of voices talking ten to the dozen filled the cottage.

'Mum?' Oliver shouted. 'Lucy?'

'We're up here, dears,' Mother replied, smiling. 'I'll leave you to catch up with each other.'

Footsteps thudded up the stars. Mother winced. The small cottage was struggling to cope now that the children were growing up, literally and figuratively!!

Kealan bounded into the room grinning, carrying a bag. Oliver followed more cautiously. He had only just had his plaster removed; the ghastly episode in the mine had stressed the break. After new x-rays, he had had to have a plaster put on again.

'Here, we bought these for you with our pocket money. An early Christmas present,' Kealan emptied his pockets of sweetie bags from The Chocolate Cauldron. 'I queued for forty minutes to get these.' He sorted through the jumble. 'This is from Johnnie Cochrane; these are from Morag...Oh!' Kealan suddenly remembered. 'Moran...'

'The Deputy Headmaster,' Oliver put in. 'Everyone is talking about it. He~'

'He's dead,' Kealan finished his news, glaring at his friend. 'His cottage had a gas leak and blew up, damaging a few others too!'

'Dead?' Lucy echoed.

'The Raven won't have been happy to find the Bear gone!' Oliver suggested.

They looked in horror at each other.

'And the BBC weather forecasters are saying that there was an unusual electrical storm at the height of the vortex. The International Space Station filmed lightning in the snow clouds, almost like a volcano!'

Lucy nodded. 'That will have been the battle between the Raven and the SDS.'

'Wicked!' Oliver said wistfully. 'Real battle magic! I wish I'd seen it!'

'No, you don't,' Lucy said. 'It was seriously scary!'

'Listen,' Kealan looked at his watch. 'I've got to go and help dad with the Christmas shopping, and we are going to choose a tree this afternoon. See you Boxing day as usual?'

'I'll get up now,' Lucy said.

'Mum says you have to rest,' Oliver said, departing downstairs to see his friend out, 'so you are to stay in. Once the mince tarts are cooled we're going out to deliver them as presents. But we've waited for you to decorate the tree; we'll do it this evening once GrandMa has arrived. Mr McGill's driver, McCuthbert, will be bringing her round from the train station. Anyway, you have another visitor coming this afternoon.'

'Who?' Lucy was baffled. 'Who's coming this afternoon?'

But Oliver just grinned infuriatingly and left.

In fact Lucy had two visitors that afternoon. The first was heralded by a throaty roar coming closer and closer, followed by a loud firm knock on the door.

'Up you go,' she heard mother say. 'Oliver and I are away on out. But you'll be coming round to us for Christmas lunch with your special guest as we agreed? Wonderful!'

Lucy didn't recognise the tread on the stairs, but she did recognise the face poking around the door.

'Megan!' And then Lucy realised why the young vet was visiting. 'Bucksturdie? She's not dead is s-'

'Oh no! No!' Megan shook her head. 'But she is very ill. I did what I could for her, and then drove her straight down to the Royal Dick Vet just outside Edinburgh. They have a Wildlife Emergency Clinic with state of the art, specialist wildlife facilities and a dedicated wildlife ward. She's in the best of hands.'

'How badly is she hurt?' Lucy dreaded having to tell Douglas. He must be so desperately anxious about her.

'I don't know how she came by them, but she...' Megan frowned. 'Bucksturdie, has bad burns like she was electrocuted, and they have had to amputate a leg, it was badly smashed. But that's not a problem,' Megan continued brightly. 'Animals can do very well with tripaws. And they know she is not wild, that she has been brought up by Douglas, that they are bonded. They understood. When she is well, we can drive down, if you like, to collect her?'

Lucy nodded, delighted, wondering if Douglas could cope with cars.

'Um...err...' the vet looked a bit uncertain. 'Um, did your mum mention I'm coming round tomorrow for Christmas lunch...?'

'Are you?' Lucy grinned. 'That's wonderful! You've helped us so much! You and Gargoyle! We couldn't have saved the Bear without the...gob...'

'Err, thank you. Um, Gargoyle's coming too...but he's had a bath and I've bought him new biker leathers...' she hastily added. 'For Christmas!'

Megan had barely left when there was another knock on the door, far more tentative. Now dressed and up, Lucy opened it.

'Lucy!'

'Douglas!'

They stared at each other then both moved at the same time to hug, cracking their heads together.

'Ouch!'

'Argh! my dose!'

'Come in!' Lucy was astounded and delighted to welcome her friend to the Nook & Cranny. The Guild were breaking several of their own rules ~ but Douglas had earned it.

'Lucy,' her friend swallowed, his hands were shaking, dreading the worst. Tears spilled down his cheeks. 'Buck-sturdie, I-'

'She's alive,' Lucy said quickly to reassure her friend,

distressed by his tears. 'She's in the best possible place where they can treat her burns. They had to amputate her leg, but they are the best surgeons in the country. T~'

'A surgeon would operate on a fox?'

'Oh, yes! It's a hospital just for animals!'

'Just for animals?'

'Yes! Look I can show you,' Lucy took Douglas's hand and led him up to Oliver's bedroom for a crash course in computers and the internet. Not that Lucy was the best person to explain such things, but she had got the hang of Google, and Douglas was thrilled to bits. Totally absorbed, they didn't hear Mother and Oliver return, until a voice behind them made the pair jump.

'Err, hi, I'm Lucy's brother,' Oliver stared at his sister's friend, who had fought a real battle beside her. 'Um, thanks for looking after her. We...mum and I, we bought you a present.' He held out a small bag.

'The Chocolate Cauldron,' Douglas slowly read out the unfamiliar word. 'Chocolate? What's that? Where is the cauldron?'

'Lucy can explain,' Oliver grinned. 'You'll have fun finding out. Anyway, thanks, she needs someone to look out for her.'

'Douglas, dear,' Mother stuck her head round the door. 'It's getting late. The Lord Rumspell has sent Justin here to take you home.'

As Douglas was leaving, a car drew up. McCuthbert got out and went to help an elderly lady out of the car and safely along the salt-scattered path to the Nook & Cranny. Fitted with a snow plough, the Edinburgh train had made it through the drifts on Rannach Moor!

'Grandma!' Lucy and Douglas hugged her gently, careful of the Zimmer frame. The old lady was becoming very frail. 'It's lovely to see you.'

'Is that young man of yours coming tomorrow?' Grandma asked hopefully, as she settled down beside the range in the kitchen with Truffle on her lap. 'The one I met at Hallowe'en?'

'He was Megan's young man, Gran,' Lucy replied. 'And he isn't coming, but a good friend of his is, and I think you'll like him just as much!'

'Perhaps he can teach me some Gaelic?'

'Maybe, Gran,' Lucy doubted it. And gobbledegook was notoriously hard to learn.

Out in the garden, under a dark sky scattered with stardust, Oliver and Lucy put the finishing touches to their snowman. Lucy retrieved a washed and carefully patched white wizard's hat from her bedroom and placed it on the snowman's head. Then Oliver put in a pipe that Lucy had brought from Osprey Cottage. With his arm around his sister, Oliver and Lucy stood there quietly for a moment.

'Sis, don't cry, he'll be home soon. You just wait and see! Promise! Come on, let's have a snowball fight!'

Overhead, a hawk hurtled down towards the welcoming lights of the Nook & Cranny. In the kitchen, peeling Brussels sprouts with Grandma, Mother removed a small cylinder from the leg of the large osprey. It gently pecked at her hand before flapping onto the back of its favourite chair, where it tried to provoke Tantrum into a fight. Smiling, Mother popped the crumpled piece of paper into the range, stoked it up and made her final preparations for a Christmas culinary feast. She handed Grandma a wee sherry.

The grandmother clock in the small hall struck midnight. The advent candle smoked and sputtered and went out.

'Happy Christmas, Happy Christmas,' everyone called out, laughing and hugging each other. But Mother noticed that the wide smile on Lucy's face didn't reach her eyes.

'Children!' Mother's eyes sparkled. 'Traditionally, we share presents after breakfast on Christmas Day, but this evening – this morning – I have a special present for you all, but especially Lucy.' She opened the hall door latch.

Smoke rings drifted through the open door; large red ones with an inner circle of white. Shooting around the lounge, they shot up the chimneystack. Everyone held his or her breath. Somewhere nearby in the woods a cock pheasant called, and across the village the sound of the Watchnight service drifted over the snowbound glen. The floorboards creaked.

A tall, broad shouldered bear of a man entered the lounge, carrying a sack over one shoulder, snowmelt running from his boots, a huge wildcat at his heels. He was not dressed in red and white; he was not plump. In fact, his sweatshirt seemed two sizes too large, and the baggy jeans were tightly belted to keep them up ~ he had lost so much weight. But he did have white hair and a beard pearled with melting snow. He didn't have a rosy complexion: his face was gaunt, and the his eye sockets were sunken and bruised. But slate-grey eyes twinkled as the visitor drew on a long-stemmed pipe carved like a dragon. With a squeal of delight, Lucy leapt forward.

The Bear had come home.

Scottish Glossary

Aye	Aye means 'yes'
Brae	A hill or slope
Burgh	A town which has been granted a charter by the monarchy
Cannae	(rhymes with granny) Cannae means 'cannot'
Ceilidh	(pronounced kal-ee) dancing, music, singing and story telling
Chitter	To chitter is to shiver with cold
Claymore	Two handed broadsword (used by William Wallace)
Creel	A wickerwork trap for catching lobsters or a large basket
Croft	A small enclosed plot of land with a house
Cromlech	A circle of prehistoric standing stones
Cullen Skink	A thick, Scottish fish soup, normally made from smoked haddock and potatoes
Dook	To dip or bathe. Dookin' for apples is a traditional Hallowe'en game involving trying to pick floating apples out of a basin of water.
Dreich	(pronounced dreeCH) Dreary or dismal
First Foot	First person to enter a house at Hogmanay (New Year's Eve) in Scotland
Foosty	Mouldy, dusty
Gaelic	(pronounced gal-lik) A Celtic language spoken in the Highlands and Islands of Scotland
Glen	A glen is a valley with a river or a stream running through it
Gillie	(pronounced gill-ee) A guide for people who

	hunt or fish
Gloaming	Dusk or twilight.
Guddle	Untidy or messy. To guddle is to catch a fish with one's bare hands
Haar	Cold mist or fog
Kelpie	In Scottish folklore, a kelpie is a wicked water spirit that takes the form of a horse
Kilt	A knee-length, pleated skirt, worn as part of a man's highland dress
Kirk	A church
Laddie	Boy or young man
Laird	Local lord
Lassie	Girl or young lady
Lochan	A small loch
Loch	A loch is a lake
Midden	Dunghill or rubbish heap
Midge	A tiny biting insect which occurs in dancing swarms
Muckle	Very large (or just large)
Peely-wally	(Pronounced peel-ee-wal-lee) Pale and fragile
Richt	(Pronounced riCHt) Richt means 'right'
Stramash	(pronounced stra-mash) A disorderly commotion

11642203R00254

Printed in Great Britain
by Amazon.co.uk, Ltd.,
Marston Gate.